CATFISH CALLING

(FLORIDA MAN 3)

MIKE BARON

Paperback Edition

Published in the United States by Wolfpack Publishing, Las Vegas

Wolfpack Publishing
5130 S. Fort Apache Road 215-380
Las Vegas, NV 89148

wolfpackpublishing.com

Paperback ISBN 978-1-64734-566-2
eBook ISBN 978-1-64734-554-9

CATFISH CALLING

(FLORIDA MAN 3)

1 | CATFISH CALLIN'

Gary Duba put on his Razorbacks hat, slathered Deet on his neck and arms, picked up a bucket of garbage and walked to the end of his pier where he sat in a folding chair. A nine-iron leaned against the seat along with a bucket of golf balls. He used a garden trowel to ladle slop into the murky water as mosquitoes swarmed. The garbage reeked of garlic. Catfish loved garlic. He gazed across the placid waters at the faint light emanating from Kensington Gardens, the swank gated community in which he'd lived, off and on. Now he was back in the trailer in the swamp. Easy come, easy go. Gary was ready for his next get rich quick scheme. Leotis would give it to him.

The seven-hundred-pound catfish bumped into the dock and spoke in a rich bass.

"Good evening, Gary. How can I assist you tonight?"

"Leotis, we're shipping water and circling the drain. We're sinking, Leotis. Toss me a safety line."

"How low can you go?"

"The sky's the limit. I'm down to two credit cards and we done spent all the money Krystal made from her last bout, and she ain't got another fight for six weeks."

"Why so long between bouts?"

"They're skeered of her. Sure, it's all staged 'cept when it ain't. Now every manjack in the Stunning Ladies of Wrestling is gunning to see who can dethrone the Queen of the Glades. The IRS is breathing down my neck and Cardmember Service is crawling up my ass."

"Well, Gary, I've suggested looking into crypto currency and commodities trading..."

"Come on, man. Do I look like a financial wizard to you? I had one good idea. House suspenders. And I just can't seem to get them off the ground. Look. I'm a meat and potatoes kind of guy. I can sell door to door; I can hustle my ass off. But commodities and crypto-currency, you may as well be talking French."

"Gary, you have that certain *je nes se quai* and *ne plus ultra* that proves irresistible to the average Floridian. You would make an excellent door to door salesman, were it not for the unfortunate habit of residents of these here parts to shoot first and ask questions later."

"I could make a fortune selling reefer and blow, that's fersure. But I learned my lesson after they killed El Cheapo. I ain't no drug dealer. Sure, I like to get high in the evening and maybe snort a little blow when I see Krystal in that maid's outfit, but a man in my position can't afford to be busted for dealing."

"Are you still doing the show?"

"We hadda stop on account of the virus. I got three shows in the can. Don't know when we'll regroup, if ever. I got some ideas though. How to open packages. You buy a charging cord or a thumb drive or something, and it comes in a solid plexiglass container. I went to Walmart the other day to get some tin snips, and it come in a solid plexiglass container. I hadda buy a hacksaw and two clamps to get the tin snips. Damn near cut my thumb off."

Gary held up his thumb, covered with a dirty bandage.

"Gary, do me a solid and squeeze a little blood out for me."

"Howzat gonna help?"

"Gary, Mekong catfish have highly sensitive membranes. A mere whiff of your essence and I can see your entire history back to the dawn of time, when the first primordial clump of cells swam toward the light."

"Oh yeah? Ya think I'm Scots/Irish? That's what the old man always said."

"Squeeze me off a drop, why don'tcha."

Gary pulled off the filthy bandage, held his thumb out and worked the wound open. It was fresh yesterday. Three drops of blood fell into the water. Leotis inhaled.

"Mmm mmm mmm," he said. "My my my. Yes indeed. Mostly Scots/Irish with a smattering of Mongol."

"Are you shittin' me?"

"Gary, I never joke about matters of the heart. Your future reveals itself through the blood."

"What, now you're a fortune teller? You and Delilah oughtta go into business together. Fish and Witch. Open a fishwich restaurant. Hand out fortune cookies."

"You joke, but the fact is, I can see your future through your blood. Not all the way to the end. No sir. But if you was to bleed out on me rightchere, right now, I could. No, what I see is the next six months. They hold many surprises. There are risks, certainly. But there are rewards also. You need to go door to door."

"Selling what?"

"Buying old comic books."

"Comics?"

"Indeed. While most are trash, every era has its rarities, and they can be worth big bucks. *Action Comics #1* sold for over two million. The first appearance of *Spider-Man* brought three hundred thou, rated nine point four. More recently, certain *Star Wars* comics have brought ten thou. Of course, condition is everything. Every week, someone advertises online or in local shoppers to sell their comic collection. Some are seniors who have scrupulously saved every issue of *Superman* since 1959. Some are aging hippies who must part with their *Fabulous Furry Freak Brothers* or *Moondogs.* A sharp dealer can generate a couple thou a week."

"Lemme think about that, Leotis. I know a little bit about the collectors' market 'cuz I been collecting baseball cards since I was ten."

"The world of comic resellers is rife with scoundrels and hustlers. Don't kid yourself that because it's the lowest form of entertainment it doesn't attract cutthroats and sharks."

"Nobody gets the best of Gary Duba. Nobody."

"Give me a day or two and I'll come up with some other ideas. But that's not why you called me here tonight."

"It ain't?"

"Gary, you will be visited by three harbingers in the coming weeks, each with a powerful but cryptic message. These are the harbingers of destiny."

"Lay it on me."

"A bat, a rabbit, and a turtle."

"You're shittin' me."

"All native species, not invasive like me."

"I never minded your invasiveness."

"I appreciate that, Gary. I feel you're the only human I can talk to. That's all I can tell you tonight. I might have more tomorrow."

"Thanks, Leotis!"

"You might bring me a cat. I wouldn't turn my nose up at a cat."

"Whatchoo want with a cat? I never figured you for a cat person."

Leotis rolled on his side and gave him the fisheye.

"Well jeez, man, the only cats around here are pets up the street at the trailer park. I can't very well go kuipin' people's pets."

Bubbles popped in the muck. "I wouldn't turn my nose up at pig lips." Leotis swam away singing "B-B-Bad to the Bone."

2 | WHAT'S YOUR PROBLEM?

Gary rinsed the bucket out in the swamp and headed back to the trailer, raised three feet above the ground on cinder blocks. The trailer was only six months old. Larry and Regan, the Duke and Duchess of Ducats, had bought it and lived there for a month before decamping. They moved to Brentwood in Los Angeles where Regan made the rounds of aspiring actresses until, miraculously, she was cast as *Captain Megastar* in the first film treatment of the venerable Marvel superhero. The first *Captain Megastar* had been a Viking warrior chosen by an alien race to defend them against another alien race, who were even worse. In the original comic, they'd plucked Paul McTavish out of 6th century Scotland in the midst of battle.

McTavish was clan leader and a fierce warrior. In the nineties, Marvel rebooted McTavish as an African Prince of Botswana's Jimbobway Tribe. Only now his name was Ndugu Chanticleer, played by Gordon Walker in *Avengers: Pre-Assembled.* Regan Sparkle's resume included commercials for

Downy and Avis Rent A Car. The industry was dumbstruck that a woman with so little acting experience would suddenly shoot to the head of the line, but industry insiders understood her appeal. She was internationally famous for breaking up the royal family, and her mother was black. That made her a black actress. A star was born.

The AC on top of the trailer thrummed. A loon cried in the swamp. Up the street at the trailer park, a car horn blasted. Honk honk honk honk honk honk. Yelling. Cursing. The car abruptly stopped. Gary tossed the bucket to the ground and went up three steps to his veranda. He went inside, shutting the cheap aluminum door behind him. Krystal, wearing pedal pushers, with her hair in curlers, sat on the sofa watching *What's Your Problem* on the sixty-three-inch flat screen, which they'd salvaged from the Kensington Gardens house, which had been destroyed by a thousand pound feral hog.

Problem's host was a big, buff man with a bad wig and the bombastic manner of a used car salesman. "Greetings, and welcome to tonight's edition of *What's Your Problem*, the show where ordinary people can vent about the little things that get them down and win up to a hundred thousand dollars! As always, I'm your humble host, Randy Glockenspiel. Tonight, we welcome back our reigning champion, Ramona Faber, from Scranton, Pennsylvania!"

A petite woman in a blue dress strode out waving.

"And let's give a big *Problem* welcome to new contestant, computer programmer Brad Hu from Omaha, Nebraska!"

Hu wore thick black glasses, black hair cut short, and

a dark blue suit. Smiling and waving, he took the podium across from Ramona.

"The winner of the coin toss will air their grievance first."

Glockenspiel stood between the two contestants. "Ready?"

"Go for it, Randy!" Ramona said.

"Ready," Hu said.

Glockenspiel spun the silver dollar in the air.

"Heads!" both contestants blurted out.

Glockenspiel retrieved the coin. "Let's try that again. Ramona, you go first."

"Heads!" Ramona barked.

"It's tails. All right, Brad, what's your problem?"

"I have a big problem with the passive tense. Every day we are told a decision was made. Yes, a decision was made. But who made the decision? The passive tense should be avoided at all costs."

"You stink!" Krystal wailed, pointing to the hall. "Take a shower!"

"Wait a minute! I want to hear what Ramona's problem is!"

Krystal grabbed the remote and switched to news.

"Take. A. Shower."

"I will, babe, but I gotta tell you, Leotis was on fire tonight! He gave me a shitload of advice!"

"Gary, baby, there is no giant catfish. You should see a shrink."

"Leotis is real, little girl! Come out with me and I'll show ya!"

"I ain't setting foot outside this house 'til morning. You

brought sixteen skeeters in the house."

She grabbed a copy of *Tidbits*, "The Neatest Little Paper Ever Read", and swatted. *Thwap. Thwap Thwap.* Three with one blow. When she was done, she showed him the splotches.

"You see that blood? That's *my* blood, you dumb sonuvabitch, 'cuz you let them skeeters in the house."

Gary snatched the paper out of her hand. "TIDBITS ADMIRES JAMES BOND" said the headline. He took it into the master bathroom and tucked it into the magazine rack on top of *Shooting Times, Salt Water Sportsman*, and *Guns & Ammo.* He took a shower, dabbed his bites with Bug Stop, splashed himself with Axe, pulled on clean shorts and a Dolphins sleeveless sweatshirt. The temperature in the living room was sixty-five.

Gary turned the dial up. "It's fucking freezing in here!"

Krystal thumped the sofa. "Sit your ass down."

Gary sat. Krystal rotated to face him. They smooched.

"Mmm," she said. "Now you don't smell like pig slop."

Gary rocked forward, threw her over his shoulder, marched to the bedroom and threw her down on the bed.

Krystal wriggled out of her Daisy Dukes. "You're a monster!"

"Rawwwr!" Gary growled, pouncing.

They writhed, they wriggled. Krystal screamed in Gary's ear.

"Owwww!"

Krystal squirmed out from under, pulling up the covers. "There's a bat in here!"

"Where?"

Krystal pointed to a corner of the ceiling where the bat clung to a hook. The Royals had taken their hanging fern with them.

Gary gaped. "It's the harbinger!"

"Get it out of here!"

"Leotis said I would be visited with three harbingers! This is the first!"

"You're fucking out of your mind! You're sick! There's no talking catfish! Get rid of that bat! What if it's rabid?"

Gary pulled on his pants and got down on his knees. "Tell me, oh harbinger! What should I do?"

The bat was an inscrutable black blob.

Krystal threw back the sheets and put on her shorts and top. "Gary, you're sick. You need help. If you won't do it, I will." She stomped out of the room slamming the door behind her.

"Tell me, harbinger, what is the path? How can I make some quick bucks? Something other than roofing or exterminating?"

Krystal stormed back in wearing Gary's Rumble Wear hoodie with the hood up, clutching a rolled-up newspaper. The bat flew around like a butterfly, no direction, no rhythm. Krystal followed taking wild swings. It landed on the drapes. Krystal leaped off the bed and whacked it with the rolled-up newspaper. The bat fell to the ground. Krystal crouched and whomped.

"Die, bat! Die!"

She stopped, panting. The bat lay unmoving.

"Thanks a lot, babe! That bat was the key to our future!"

"We ain't got no future less we get the IRS off our backs."

"What? What?"

"Didn't you see the letter? We owe them seven hundred and fifty thousand dollars. If we don't pay up, they'll garnish our wages."

"I can barely scrape together lunch money! Where we gonna get seven fifty thou?"

"I'll call Aldo. Maybe he can get me a bout on the mud wrestling circuit."

"No! I forbid it! I won't have my wife rolling around in slop like a pig!"

"You got a better idea, smart guy? You're talking to an imaginary catfish!" She threw the paper down in disgust. It fell open to the classifieds.

COMIC COLLECTION FOR SALE

Four Long Boxes, 60's through 80's

Bagged and boarded

3 | FUBAR

Gary was up until two researching old comic books on nostomania.com. He ordered the *Comic Book Price Guide* off Amazon. Ten minutes later, there was a thump on the door. He opened the door to see the blue van driving away. He picked up his *Comic Book Price Guide* and went to work. Gary had six hundred dollars in cash. Fortunately, the Duke and Duchess had paid cash for the trailer and had the utilities moved to their name. They used a *nom de plume.* The Clampetts. They'd left stuff behind including a hideous painting of a big square head sitting in a desert that looked like a therapy painting.

A bleary-eyed Gary clutching a cardboard coffee waited outside Eleven Spicer Boulevard in the Wokenoki Trailer Park at eight the next morning. Eleven was a white Cappaert with neat green shutters perched on a domino of lawn. A Big Wheels lay on its side in front. Gary was the first one there. He waited until the blinds rose in the living room before dialing the number from the shopper.

"Hello," a man's voice slurred.

"Yes sir. I saw your ad in *Tidbits* about the comics. I'd like to take a look."

"Well let me see. Why don'tcha come by in about an hour."

"I'm here now."

A hairy man with a paunch wearing boxer shorts peered out the living room window. "It's Sunday morning."

"It's a keenly competitive business. I'm ready to pay cash on the barrel head."

"All right. All right. Give me five minutes."

He came out wearing Bermuda shorts and a Banlon tennis shirt stretched over a taut belly, tiny sailfish stitched on the breast.

"Harf Bosley."

"Gary Duba."

They shook hands. Gary grabbed his *Comic Book Price Guide* and followed Bosley around to the back where there was a swing set taking up most of the yard next to a prefab plastic storage shed. Bosley twirled the combo, unsnapped the lock and opened the door. A whiff of old newsprint drifted out.

"Yeah, I hate to sell 'em, but the boy needs braces. Been collecting since the eighties. Haven't bought a comic in years. They were just taking up space. You can bring 'em out here and take a look, but don't take 'em out of the plastic bag."

Gary gripped the first long box and brought it into the light. A man came around the trailer with balled fists. "Hey!"

Bosley and Gary looked.

"Hey! I called you yesterday and you said you'd let me have the first look! Remember?"

Bosley shifted his feet. "Yeah, well, sorry about that. This guy just showed up. He hasn't actually looked at any of the comics."

The newcomer advanced. He was tall with a face like an Easter Island statue and wore a dickey. "Yeah, well back off, okay! I got first dibs."

Gary got in his face. "Fuck off. I was here first."

The man eyeballed Gary, blinked, and took a step back.

"I'll tell you what," Bosley said. "Gary was here first, so he can look at the first box. What's your name?"

"The Main Man."

"Okay, Main, you get to choose the next box. That's fair."

"Look here, Main Man," Gary said. "Howzabout we have a shin kicking contest, and whoever wins gets first dibs."

Bosley pointed to Gary's box. "Why don't you open this one over here, and you open the next one over there."

Sullenly, Main Man grabbed a box and set it down ten feet away.

Gary squatted and pulled off the lid. It was chock full of comics, each in a plastic bag with a backer board. He flipped through them. *Avengers, Batman, Flash, Aliens, Star Wars. Star Wars #1*! Gary examined it with a practiced eye. He'd learned all about grading collecting sports cards. The comic was in near mint condition, with almost imperceptible fade at the staple. Sitting Indian style, he looked it up in his *Price*

Guide. A near mint was worth up to a thousand dollars. He closed the book.

"I'll take this one."

"I'm selling them by the box."

"How much for the box?"

Main Man perked up like a prairie dog. "What is it?"

"None of your beeswax."

"Two fifty," Bosley said.

"Two hundred and fifty dollars?"

"Yup."

Gary rippled through the remaining box. *Doom 2099.* A handful of Valiants with variant covers including *X-O Manowar #1.* Gary reached for his wallet. Up popped Main Man.

"I'll give you two seventy-five."

"You don't even know what's in here."

"Look. Do you want to make money or not?"

Bosley crossed his arms. "Man's got a point."

"First you say we can look through individual boxes, now you want to sell to the highest bidder."

Wheels on gravel. Car doors slamming. Five people rounded the back of the trailer, each trying to outpace the other.

"ARE YOU THE SELLER?"

"WHERE ARE THE COMICS?"

"Just show me the silver and bronze age boxes."

"I'll give you a thousand bucks right now for the whole lot."

Main Man wheeled. "Fuck off! I was here first!"

"Technically," Gary said, "I was here first."

Bosley waved his arms. "Everybody cool it! We'll take turns! Don't remove the comics from their mylar sleeves!"

"TWO THOU FOR THE LOT!"

One thou turned on his competitor with a snarl. "You're not even a comic guy. You're just a speculator."

A small boy rolled around the other end on a Big Wheels. "Daddy, Mommy says the neighbors are complaining."

One thou shoved two thou. They tussled. Everybody started fighting. A human ferret crept into the shed and tried to open a box. Bosley grabbed him by the nape of his shirt and hurled him to the dirt like a rag. A man with a thyroid condition threw his arm around Bosley's neck. Bosley grabbed the arm and tried to throw the man, but his assailant weighed over three hundred pounds.

"Too much monkey business," Gary muttered, going around the far end of the trailer. "Too much monkey business." He got in his truck, carefully backed up to avoid hitting a windowless Ford Econoline, circled around the jumble of cars. More cars poured through the gate, surrounding Bosley's trailer until it looked like a police raid on a meth lab.

Gary carefully turned onto Weldon Way and headed for the swamp. The Wokenoki Trailer Park disappeared around a bend in his rear view. A half mile from home, a dozen feral hogs blocked the road, snorting and rooting at something. Gary laid on the horn.

"GET THE FUCK OUTTA HERE!" he shouted. The hogs looked up with mean little piggy eyes. They snorted, they shuffled toward the truck. They surrounded the truck, snuffling and honking. Gary put the truck in gear and drove slowly forward, not wishing to crush any lest he have to clean hog blood off his undercarriage. As soon as he was free, he accelerated, leaving the swine behind. He wheeled into his yard and got out.

The hogs followed, snorting and gnashing. The lead hog, with tusks like an Indonesian mask, grabbed his pant leg as he reached the stairs and dragged him to the ground.

"HELP!" Gary yelled.

4 | HEAVEN RAINS GOOD FORTUNE

Krystal banged open the screen door and stared. "Oh my God."

"GET THE GUN!" Gary yelled, kicking a hog in the snout while another sunk its fangs into his leg.

Krystal banged back out with a shotgun. She fired a shot in the air. The hogs looked up. Gary got to his feet and raced for the truck, throwing himself inside, opening the glove compartment and grabbing his .357. From the shotgun seat, he blasted away, killing one hog with a shot between the eyes, hitting two others who ran squealing into the brush.

Leaving the shotgun on the deck, Krystal leaped to the ground and ran to Gary who was sitting up, looking at the rip in his leg. His sock was soaked.

"Honey, let's hope thet hog wasn't rabid."

"I sure hope not. Help me up."

In the bathroom, Krystal washed the wound and poured shine on it. Gary grunted and closed his eyes. She dressed the wound. "What about tetanus?"

"Ah got my tetanus booster last year when that poodle bit me. 'Spose we should haul that dead hog into the state crime lab and see if it had rabies." Placing a hand on the counter, Gary got to his feet and took a few tentative steps.

"That ain't so bad. Least I can walk. Come on. Help me put that hog in the truck."

"How'd it go with the comics people?"

"I hightailed it outta there when it turned into a riot."

Outside, two seagulls and a turkey vulture disputed the dead hog. Gary waved his arms.

"Go on! Get outta here!"

They put on plastic gloves from the glove compartment and tossed the hog in the back of the truck.

"Where we gone take it? State crime lab or the county coroner?"

Krystal pulled out her Fonebone. "Omma Winnow it." She wrote rabies testing Florida.

"Says here the Department of Agriculture. I'll see where the nearest officc is at."

Gary turned the corner. A gull and two turkey vultures were tearing at the spot he'd encountered the hogs. Gary pulled over and shut off the engine.

"Something funny's going on. You stay here."

Grabbing his pistol, he got out of the truck. The birds took flight leaving a crushed plastic storage bin, scraps of plastic and a residue of white powder. Gary hunkered, ignoring the pain in his calf, dipped a finger in the white powder and brought it to his tongue.

"Is it blow?" Krystal said.

"I wish these cartels would leave us alone. This ain't exactly Grand Central Station. Shee-it."

"What?"

Across a ditch filled with empty fast-food wrappers, used condoms, and crumpled aluminum cans lay the jungle wall. Several feet in Gary glimpsed something white. Thrashing through the undergrowth, he found a parachute trailing off into the trees. Keeping an eye out for snakes, Gary bashed his way to a corpse wearing camo trousers, lace-up boots, and a Sergio Mendes and Brasil '66 sweatshirt, bamboo stem poking up through the thorax. The corpse wore a parachute harness, a backpack, a helmet, and a KelTec nine in a shoulder holster. Krystal came up behind him wearing a zippered hoodie to protect her arms from the saw grass.

"Holy shit."

"I guess I must be some kind of shit magnet the way stuff keeps piling up."

"Depends on your attitude. If he got any more on him, we could lay it off for a few bucks."

"Yeah, but if we keep that shit in the house, I'm afraid one of is gonna break down."

Krystal put her fists on her hips. "Not me. I got a fight comin' up."

"Not me, I got to think about my followers."

They stared at the corpse. With a sigh, Krystal crouched, unzipped the backpack and peeked inside. She pulled out several accordion folders.

"Just papers."

"Dayum. Them hogs got it all. No wonder they were all het up."

"Maybe it's better this way. Remember what happened last time we had blow?"

"Bring that backpack."

"We still gotta get that hog tested for rabies."

"That hog was higher than John Belushi."

A search of the corpse produced a wallet and a passport. Immanuel Elvarez, Caracas, Venezuela, a Lieutenant Colonel in the National Bolivarians. Gary passed Krystal the passport. She jammed it in a pocket and consulted her Fonebone.

"Oh great. The Venezuelan special forces. They work for President Elfuncio Quetzacoatl."

"What we got here is a conspiracy to bolster the Venezuela gummint by selling this shit to Americans!"

They stared at one another. Krystal hummed a little ditty. Both were thinking the same thing. They didn't need that kind of publicity.

"What about the body?"

"Swamp."

They stared at the dead body.

Gary pulled out his folding knife, cut loose the parachute harness and removed the backpack. He pulled the man up by his armpits. Krystal shrugged into the backpack and picked the sky diver up by the ankles.

A half hour later, they rolled the corpse off the side of

the swamp buggy into the pea soup water and headed back to the pier. They returned to the house tired but exhilarated.

They went inside. "Dibs on the shower," Krystal said. "Howzat leg?"

"Throbs a little bit. I spose I ought to go get something for the infection."

"I got probiotics in the fridge."

Outside two vehicles entered the yard and stopped. Krystal and Gary stepped out of the air-conditioned trailer and looked down on a black Cadillac Escalade and a History Channel van.

"Hot diggity!" Gary said. "We're back in business!" He headed down the steps.

A man in a dark suit, sunglasses, and earpiece ran around the front of the Lincoln and opened the rear door. The Duke and Duchess of Ducats stepped out.

5 | TALK TO THE NETWORK

Prince Larry was six one with curly red hair and a GI Joe beard. He wore an olive safari jacket, khaki cargo pants, and lace-up boots. Regan was ravishing with long black hair, wearing a Venum hoodie with the top down, artfully torn Dolce and Gabbana jeans and Alexander McQueen sneakers. A no-nonsense woman in a black crew neck, *pince nez* dangling from a gold chain, got out of the van with a cameraman and a sound technician.

"What are you doing here?" Gary, Krystal, Larry and Megan said.

"I came for my Claude Balls."

"Say what?"

"My Claude Balls painting. It's hanging in the living room. Do you mind?"

Gary gestured for the Duke to lead the way. He followed the Duke and Duchess up three steps into the trailer where the Duke put a knee on the sofa to reach the framed painting of a giant, square orange head sitting in a desert. The Duke turned, proudly displaying the painting.

"The man was a genius."

"We figgered it was from some cartoon show."

"Claude Balls was a visionary. He toured with Lord Buckley. He knew Jack Kerouac."

"I was gonna take that into Billy Bob's, see what I could get for it."

"This is our home," The Duke said.

"Wait a minute," Gary said. "Y'all moved to Hollywood. You just abandoned the trailer and we still own the land."

Regan touched Gary on the arm. "I'm sorry, we should have told you. But we didn't know we were going to have our own reality show at the time. We'll try not to intrude. We just need to film here for a day or two."

Her nose wrinkled in disgust. "What is that awful smell?"

Pince Nez advanced. "I'm Karen Sullivan. Who are you?"

"We're the Dubas."

"That's Gary and Krystal," Regan said.

"Well you have to sign release forms if you want to be in the show."

"Wait a minute. We got our own reality show. You have to sign release forms if you want to be in ours."

"Where's your manager?" Karen sang. "I'd like to speak to the manager!"

Krystal called Major Sutton.

"Whassup, girl?"

"Gary got bit by a feral hog and now those damn royals

are here making a stink."

"What royals?"

"The Duke and Duchess of Ducats!"

"Hang on. I'm fifteen minutes away."

"The manager is on the way."

"Now look here, you two," Lawrence said in a toff accent. "Do you eckshually know who we are?"

"You're from that Harry Potter book!"

"Eckshually, no. We are literally the Duke and Duchess of Ducats. See here old chap. Haven't you heard of the British Royal family?"

"We don't get the Discovery Network," Krystal said.

"Look here, you ignorant doxy..." Prince Larry said. Gary punched him in the mouth. The Prince staggered, but he didn't go down. He stood up straight, holding his fists like a proper English pugilist.

"All right then, you stinking git. Let's see what you've got!"

Karen the manager signaled her crew to start filming. Krystal pulled out her Fonebone. Gary put his head down and took the Prince to the ground. He'd wrestled for the Turpentine Gators. They rolled in the dirt. Princess Regan turned red and put a hand to her mouth.

"Larry, get up! You're making a fool of yourself!"

They rolled over and over in the mud. Prince Larry used his bulk to get on top and rain down blows.

"Take that, you ignorant peasant!"

Gary grabbed Larry's hair, dragged him down and rolled

so that he was on top. They tussled.

"Oh my God!" said the Duchess of Ducats. "He smells terrible!"

"It's them feral hogs. See in the back of the truck? We're gonna butcher it. You want to stay for ribs?"

The Duchess looked in the back of the truck and fainted. The manager rushed to her side. "Get up, Duchess! Get up!" She whirled on the cameraman. "Don't film this you idiot! Film them!"

The cameraman whirled. Krystal caught the whole thing, turned back to the combatants who were now on their feet, gasping and circling. The Duke juked and jabbed Gary in the jaw. Gary rubbed his chin. "Nice shot!"

Gary faked a looping right, went low, and took the Duke down on his ass. They were rolling in the dirt when Major Sutton arrived in his new Edison and spun to a stop. Major leaped out. He was a stocky black man with a head like a bullet, wearing suit pants and vest over a white shirt, and a bowler.

He waved his arms. "Wait a minute. WAID A MINUTE!"

The combatants continued to tussle.

"Whomp that sucker!" Krystal cheered.

Major turned on her. "Are you nuts? Don't you know who that is?"

"Some asshole."

"Get a bucket...never mind!"

Major strode toward the trailer, took the steps in two leaps and went inside, returning minutes later with a plastic bucket filled with water. SPLOOSH! He doused the combatants. Gary laughed and waved his limbs in the air. Lawrence leaped to his feet.

"Bloody hell! You've ruined my jacket!'

"Come on up to the house, Prince. We'll find you something to wear."

The prince stalked toward the trailer. Major Sutton walked over to Karen.

"Major Sutton. I produce the *Gary Duba Show*."

"Karen Sullivan. I produce the *Royal Ducats*. Do you mean to tell me this idiot has a show?"

"We have over three million followers on YouTube and a weekly show on Rustix."

"But why?"

"You don't know about the Dubas?"

"I have no idea."

"Gary's the guy who caught Plastic Surgeon to the Stars and serial killer Dr. Vanderlay Mukerjee. You must have heard about that."

"No, I'm sorry. I only follow the trades. We're gearing up for a June premier on the *History Channel*. The world is intensely interested in the Royal Ducats. And in case you've been hiding under a rock, Regan just landed the lead role in *Captain Megastar*. Sean Sheen is her co-star."

"What's *Captain Megastar*?"

"She's a very popular Marvel superhero. She's the first Baha'i superhero."

"Are you planning to use this video on your show?"

"I hardly think so. The Duke of Ducats wrestling with a commoner like a pig in the mud!"

"Do you mind if we use it?"

"You can't use that footage! Absolutely not and in no way!"

"I don't see how you can interfere with video shot on my clients' own property."

"We'll sue!"

"Well let's not go running off half-cocked. Maybe we can make a deal. How would you feel about having Gary and Krystal appear on the Royal Ducats?"

"These rednecks are antithetical to everything we stand for."

"Yet here you are on their property, filming."

"Believe me, if we'd known they were still here, we never would have come."

The trailer door banged open. Prince Larry stood on the deck wearing a HONK IF YOU EAT ASS Tee-shirt and striped bell bottoms. "How do I look?"

Regan put her hand to her face and turned away. "This is the most embarrassing day of my life."

Karen cupped her chin. "Let me talk to the network."

6 | THE NIGHTLY RITUAL

Gary showered, ate a tube of Necco wafers, and sat in front of his computer in his air-conditioned home office wearing a clean Lynyrd Skynyrd Tee-shirt. "Folks, we got a real treat for y'all tonight. Yasterday, after I got done wrassling that pig, who should drop by but the Royal Couple, the Duke and Duchess of Ducats! The Duke called Krystal a ho, at least I think that's what he meant, so I popped him one in the kisser! Next thing you know...well hell. Take a look for yourselves."

The fight played out to a cartoon soundtrack. Krystal came in and rubbed his shoulders. "He's a big 'un, isn't he?"

"I got to hand it to him. He had some moves, that's for sure, but my Turpentine Gators wrestling training was just too much for him."

They watched Gary pull a reversal.

"Love thet," Krystal cooed, running her hand along his jaw.

The video moved right along. At the end, the Duke came out and posed in his HONK IF YOU EAT ASS Tee-shirt. America's last image was of the Duke smiling broadly at the head of the stairs and saluting an unseen army.

Gary's comment board marched like fire ants.

WHOMP THAT SUCKER – Pin Okio

KICK HIS ASS – The Ever Lovin' Booger Eater

DUKE IS KINDA CUTE – Lena the Hyena

"The Duke axed me to play polo. I told him I ain't getting up on no thousand pound creature with the brainpower of a snail. No sir. But if he's a mind, I could borrow Floyd's Fat Boy and we could go riding. But listen. Here's the big news. We've agreed to appear on each other's shows. Me and Krystal are gonna be on the *Royal Ducats*, premiering in June on the Discovery Channel, and Larry and Regan are gonna come spend the weekend with us for the *Gary Duba Show*! Omma take him gator hunting!

"Jolene in Cassadaga! Whassup?"

"You ever need an oracle, Gary," a husky voice said, rife with suggestion. "You come see ol' Jolene in Cassadaga. I'll give you a palm reading you'll never forget."

"Why thank you kindly, Jolene, but Krystal might take exception to that."

Krystal grabbed the mic. "I might come to Cassadaga and kick your ass."

"That's no joke, folks! They don't call her the Black Dildo, excuse me, Steely Danielle for nothing! She's in training for the Javelina in six weeks. Y'all hear about Javelina? She's from Juarez. Now we ain't got javelina in Florida, but we got feral hogs. Yesterday I found myself drug down by six of them suckers, and sure as shit they would have had me for dinner had not my dear sweet Krystal come by and scared 'em off with a shotgun.

"Well look here. Speak of the devil. We got Delilah on the line and she's Krystal's trainer. What up, girl?"

"Jolene's a whore and a liar."

"Well let's talk about the fight. What can you tell us about Javelina?"

"Her real name is Marcela Aguilar, and like her fierce namesake, she's as ferocious as an eagle."

"Now wait a minute. Who's Javelina?"

"Marcela Aguilar."

"Why don't she call herself the Eagle?"

"They already got an eagle. She fought for four years on the Lucha Libre circuit before joining the Stunning Women of Wrestling. She's five eight and weighs one hundred and twenty-five pounds."

"Well, she ain't no Javelina! Tha's false advertising! We oughtta sue her ass! We oughtta call it off!"

"You can't call it off. The contracts are signed. Also on the bill are Lena the Hyena versus Howler Monkey, Bandicoot versus Stick Bug, and Sweet Charlotte versus Baby Jane. It's the women's pro event of the summer! It's already sold out. Chunky Thighs will perform before the show."

"I love Chunky Thighs!" Krystal squealed.

"Delilah, what you got to say to my three million listeners?"

"Ya'll come down and see your girl Steely Danielle whup Javelina's ass! And also tomorrow's a full moon. You going out be sure you pack a gun."

"Folks, we've given you a lot to think about. Maybe too much. I think omma call it a night. So goodnight to all my friends in Florida and across the universe, this here's Gary Duba signing off."

His phone rang.

"Why'd you cut me off like that?" Delilah demanded. "I wasn't finished!"

"Well go on then."

"I know you're worried about money, and they's six weeks 'til the match. So I cut up a chicken, and it told me you should invest in old comics. Lotta people selling their collections these days, and there's good money to be had, if you know what to look for."

"Woman, you a day late and a dollar short! I was at a comic sale this morning and nearly got my hair parted with a meat cleaver! You're s'posed to tell me what'll happen. Not what happened. That's why they call you the oracle. If you was telling people what already happened, they'd call you the anucle."

"I need that girl to start training Monday. You be here Monday morning, hear? Fifty thou ain't nothing to sneeze at."

Krystal yelled over Gary's shoulder. "I'll be there!"

Gary leaned back and stretched. His chair squeaked. "And that's a wrap!"

"C'mon, hon. Let's watch *What's Your Problem.*"

"Again? It was just on last night!"

"It's on every night."

"No, you go ahead. I gotta talk to Leotis."

"Don't give me that shit. I don't know what you're doing out there, but you sure as shit ain't talking to no giant catfish!"

"Well hell, girl. Why don'tcha come along and see for yourself?"

"You oughtta see a shrink!"

"If I'm lying, I'm frying. Come on out. He's a wise old fish. You'd be surprised at what all he knows."

"Well let me get a joint first. Soon's I start training, I won't even be able to have a drink."

They shared a fat doobie on the deck.

"All right. Show me the damn fish."

Gary turned off his phone, pulled a hog leg out of the back of his truck. "This here's for Leotis. I don't like to come empty handed."

"You're crazier 'n a snake on crack."

"You just pray we don't run into any of those."

They walked to the end of the pier. Krystal sat on the old wood bench. Gary got down on his haunches, stuck two fingers in his mouth and emitted an ear-piercing whistle. "Leotis! I got a nice hog leg for ya!" He tossed the leg into the soup. Nada.

"Leotis! Come say hi to Krystal! You may know her as the Black Dildo!"

Zipco.

"Leotis! Who you like? The Heat or the 76rs?"

A loon crooned. A pelican plopped. Far across the bay, the faint sound of traffic.

Krystal stood. "You are so full of shit."

She stalked off the pier back into the house. Gary remained where he was.

"Is she gone?" Leotis rumbled from under the pier.

7 | RECRUDESCENT BILIOUS ENZYMES

"Why you wanna do me like that, Leotis? I been nothing but good to you."

"I'm sorry, Gary, but my words are for you and you alone. The world isn't ready for a talking catfish. It may never be ready. I chose you because yours is the first pier I bumped into. No offense. One minute, I was swimming down the Stoeng Basak, a mere hatchling, barely an inch in length. The next thing I knew, I was fully grown, seven hundred and twelve pounds, and found myself a stranger in a strange land. What happened next beggars all description. I'm saving it for my book. But here I am."

"You need dream therapy, Leotis. I can hook you up."

"You fed me when I was hungry."

"I was just throwing slop in the swamp."

"There are many fakers in Florida, those who claim to have the power but have none. Charlatans and liars. Like that woman Jolene."

"Wait a minute. You heard my podcast?"

"I hear many things. Down here. In the swamp."

"You ever watch *What's Your Problem*?"

"It's one of my favorite shows."

"What about Delilah?"

"Delilah's the real deal."

"*Garrrrr*-eee!" Krystal yelled from the deck.

"Gotta go. You like that hog leg, I got plenty more where that came from."

Krystal stood on the deck wearing a Wynona Earp Tee-shirt and short shorts, arms crossed gripping her Fonebone. "That video of you and the Duke blew up. Everybody's calling. Everybody wants the rights. Everybody wants to talk."

"Who wants to talk?"

"Everybody. Bobby Bilbo wants you on his show Friday night."

"Who's Bobby Bilbo?"

Krystal did a double take with bared fangs and popping eyes. "DUH! The Good Night Show?"

Gary shrugged. "Can they do it here?"

"They want to fly us into Burbank."

"Man, I had a belly full of Burbank. I offered those suckers the chance of a lifetime and they whiffed!"

"That was more you than house suspenders. Forget it, honey. We can parlay this into a real opportunity. Now's your chance to get your house suspenders in front of the world!"

Gary put one hand to his head and the other in a Doc Strange situation. "You know what? I'll dress like a house and I'll wear suspenders! I'll get shoulder pads that look like roofs and wear a chimney hat!"

"*Vogue* wants to interview you."

"Who?"

"It's like *Guns & Ammo* for wine drinkers. *The Scene* wants you on their show in New York. They want to fly you up Thursday afternoon so you can do the show Friday."

"That's tomorrow!"

"No shit, Sherlock. They have seventeen million viewers."

"Who's the *Scene*?"

"Happy Sapperstein, Joyce Baywatch, Gwendolyn Nuplazid, and Tammy Tellmetrue. They ask softball questions, and you can pitch the house suspenders, but they really want to dish about the Royal Couple."

"I hardly know them!"

"You're going."

"How can I do *The Scene*, which is in New York, Friday morning, and then do the *Good Night Show*, which is in Burbank, Friday evening?"

"Hmmm. Let's ask Major."

"Where's my phone?"

"In your pocket."

He turned it on. It played "*Margaritaville*". He turned it off. They went to bed. Gary dreamed he was a contestant on *What's Your Problem?* Randy Glockenspiel was dressed like Ronald McDonald.

"Gary Duba! What's your problem?"

"Number one. Individual fruit labels. Number two. People

who fall asleep at red lights. Number three. People leaving their dog shit in little plastic bags by the side of the road. Number four. Pop up ads. Number five. Problem shoppers. Number six. Leaf blowers. Number seven. Pop-up ads."

"You mentioned pop-up ads."

"Well, here they are again. Number eight. Fitted sheets. Number nine. The Pillow guy. Number ten. The Allstate Guy. Number eleven. My hose kinks. Number twelve. The word foodie. Number thirteen. Doug from Liberty Mutual."

"What about the emu?"

"Fuck the emu."

"Gary," groaned a familiar voice.

Glockenspiel was gone. Gary lay in bed staring up at the ceiling, Krystal softly snoring. A coyote yipped. A loon looned. Up the street at the Wokenoki Trailer Park, a car horn borked with maddening regularity.

"Gary."

Gary pinched himself. He was awake.

"Gary, come out here please."

"Izzat you, Leotis?"

"No, Gary. Come out here please."

Moving slowly, so as not to wake Krystal, Gary got up, pulled on his pants and padded out onto the deck. He could tell by the faint glow in the east that dawn was near. A bronze bull stood in the yard. The most famous bull in the world. Charging bull, also known as Wall Street Bull. It looked up, massive horns aimed at the sky.

"Who the fuck are you?"

"I'm Tallywhacker."

"You look different."

"I've reinvented myself. The flesh you see is real. I retain my bionic abilities."

"How'd you do that?"

"Recrudescent bilious enzymes."

"Whadja do about the alien multiple personalities?"

"I'm seeing a therapist. She's a genius. It was her idea to set the alien multiple personalities against each other to determine the square root of infinity. Whoever wins gets to plunder Earth. Amazingly, I now wake without headaches. I can finally think for myself. I have decided to dissolve the Church of Necroeconomics, disperse its wealth among the faithful, and seek a life of penance and penury. I'm writing a book. I wonder if I could hang out here for a while."

"Well sure, but you gotta act like a bull. Like, if someone comes out here to interview me, you can't suddenly butt in and start talking crypto currency."

"That would be no problem. But that's not why I'm here. I came to warn you."

"Warn me about what?"

"That catfish lies."

"'Bout what?"

"Everything. That catfish would rather climb a tree and tell a lie than stand on the ground and tell the truth."

"How do you even know about that?"

"I listen through your phone."

"That there's an invasion of privacy!"

“I’m only looking out for your best interests.”

“Well do me a favor! Don’t go snooping in my private business!”

Tallywhacker sank to his knees and wept. “Gary, please forgive me!”

“All right. All right. Get up. You’re embarrassing yourself.”

“Gary.” It was Krystal.

Gary lay in his bed looking up at the ceiling. A coyote yipped. A loon looned. Up the street at the Wokenoki Trailer Park, a car horn honked with maddening regularity.

“What?”

“You were talking in your sleep.”

“Did you hear anybody else?”

Krystal looked at him funny. “Did you take that psilocybin I was saving for when I beat Javelina?”

“Was it in the Necco wafers?”

8 | LICENSED AND BONDED

When Krystal woke the next morning, Gary was in the living room watching *The Scene.*

"Let's go, Gary. The studio wants you at the airport by noon."

"I ain't going."

"What do you mean you're not going?"

Gary pointed at the TV. "Me and them harpies got nothing in common. I don't understand what they're saying half the time. Plus, they'll make me wear a mask on the plane, and all I got's the Stars 'n' Bars, and you know how that went last time."

"We'll get you another mask."

"I ain't going, and that's final. They're not my type of people."

"What about Bobby Bilbo?"

"Rhymes with dildo. 'Nuff said."

"Well, are you jes' gonna hunker down here until whatever it is blows over?"

"That's about the size of it!"

Major called. "The Royals have agreed to a crossover. They would like you and Krystal to be their guests at their Brentwood estate for a week, beginning November 15. They will then return to Florida to be your guests On December 15."

"Can't do it. That's Krystal's fight with Javelina. Tell the royal couple they got front row seats."

"Actually, they will stay at the Breakers. We are negotiating the terms of the agreement, including subjects they would like to cover and events in which they are willing to partake. They would like you to prepare a list of twelve activities."

Gary counted his fingers. "Making shine, hunting gators, hog butchering, fishing, getting rid of palmetto bugs...might bring Floyd in on that one...hunting anaconda, house suspenders, paintball..."

"Write 'em down, Gary."

"Yeah, well I'm thinking me and the Prince oughta have another go, and we would televise it and raise money for charity."

"It's a thought, fersure."

"Save the manatees."

"You owe the IRS seven hundred and fifty thousand dollars. If we don't pay, they're gonna garnish our wages!"

"What wages?"

"Any advertising revenue you get offa YouTube, and whatever Krystal wins in the ring."

Gary phoned Habib.

“I have five minutes before I’m in court.”

“Habib, the IRS is threatening to garnish our wages.”

“What wages?”

“Well, like any advertising revenue offa YouTube, and whatever Krystal gets when she fights.”

“Let’s meet tomorrow. Bring any correspondence you may have. Gotta go. They’re bringing in my client.”

“Okay.”

“How’d you and Krystal like to be my guest at Wacky World on Saturday?”

“Y’know, I ain’t never been to Wacky World. That’s where they got the crazy rides, right?”

“Yes. One of my clients is a senior executive and fixed me up with season passes.”

“Thanks, Habib. Krystal starts training Monday. This’ll remind her what she’s fighting for.”

“Who’s she fighting?”

“Javelina.”

“Gotta go. See you Saturday.”

“Hey Krystal!”

“What?” she called from the spare bedroom, where she was stretching.

“Get out your party dress! We’re going to Wacky World!”

“Seriously?”

“Habib’s got tickets! We’re going Saturday!”

“Hell no. That place scares the crap out of me! Ever since I was a little girl and my mother left me alone in the living room watching *Funky Monkey Fan Club*. That monkey scared the shit outta me! But he got nothing on Rapid Rabbit. *BRRRRR*. Just the thought of a man-sized rabbit!"

"Where you get this shit?"

"You ever see *Donnie Darko*?"

A car pulled up in the yard. Gary went out on the deck. A man who looked like a Russian nesting doll, wearing a cheap black suit and a patently false toupee, got out of a rented Ford.

"H'ep you?" Gary said.

The man looked around defiantly. "Where is she?" he said in a nasal accent.

"Aw, don't tell me. You one of Krystal's exes?"

"Don't lie to me. I know she's here."

Gary turned to the house. "KRYSTALLLL!"

Krystal came out wearing gym shorts and a Boris and Natasha Tee-shirt. "What?"

"Is this one of your exes?"

"Never seen him before in my life." She went back in letting the screen door bang.

"You got the wrong house, bud."

"I don't think so. I believe you're covering for her. Just produce her and I'll be on my way."

"I don't care if you're James Bond! Whatever you want, it ain't here!"

"I'm a licensed and bonded bounty hunter." He whipped out a foolscap. "I have a warrant and order to appear for one Alice C. Wentworth, wanted for mail fraud, check kiting, shoplifting, assault, grand larceny, distribution of controlled substances, and public menacing."

"She ain't here!"

"The agency warned me that she would have accomplices. What is your name?"

"Fuck you, cadwallader! What's your name?"

"I am Theosophis J. Ronstein, a licensed and bonded agent of the court!"

"Yeah, well I'm Gary Duba!"

The little man glared. "Is that supposed to mean something?"

"You're not from around here, are ya?"

"I'm Rhode Island bred and raised, and I find nothing attractive about the so-called Sunshine State, whose name is disputed, by the way, by Arizona."

"I'm the guy who caught Plastic Surgeon to the Stars and serial killer Dr. Vanderlay Mukerjee."

"And I'm the King of Sheba!"

"You got internet?"

Ronstein looked around. "I very much doubt you can get internet out here."

"Show's how much you know. Take out your phone and do an oogle search. Gary Duba."

The little man glared. He reached for his phone. He poked. He frowned. His eyes widened. "I had no idea."

"Now do you believe you're in the wrong place?"

Ronstein squinted and looked around. "You may very well be an accomplice. You have a rap sheet a mile long."

"I put all that behind me. I am now a public personality. I

got a show on Rustix! Follow me on Twitter @kangoftheever-glades, on Facebook as Gary Duba, Kang of the Everglades, on Twitter as GaryDuba, and on Tik Tok as gatorhunterint-ernational. My website is GaryDubaShow.com."

"My source is unimpeachable. How 'bout I just have a little look around."

"How 'bout you get your ass outta here or I'll call the hogs on you."

"Hogs? What hogs?"

Gary inserted two fingers in his mouth and emitted a piercing whistle. Ronstein crossed his arms and looked around with distaste. The jungle rustled. They heard snort-ing. Six snouts poked from the undergrowth. With a shrill squeak, Ronstein ran for the car. Sensing fear, the hogs attacked. He booted one in the snout, slammed the door, and threw it in reverse.

9 | FIREWORKS

Saturday was unusually bright and balmy for October. Gary and Krystal drove to Habib's place in Pamplemousse, a gated community with a club house, a par three golf course, and a swimming pool. Of course, Habib had his own swimming pool too. Aubrey wore a purple velour jump suit with gold stripes and a wide-brimmed straw hat. She was five ten in her bare feet with more curves than a Ferrari. Krystal wore cargo pants from Farm and Fleet, a Green Bay ball cap, and a My Little Brony hoodie. Gary wore jeans and a Glad Machine shirt. Habib wore a Western sports jacket and a Stetson. They transferred to Habib's car for the two-hour drive to Orlando.

Wacky World was doing big business. Where else could people go? Habib joined a long line of vehicles outside one of Wacky World's six parking garages. When they reached the gate, a fiberglass statue of Regis Gator slid out a ticket on its tongue. The gate rose. Habib drove up two levels and found a spot big enough to hold his Lexus GX. They eyed the happy throngs waiting in line at the main gate. Surly families. Japanese tourists.

"Follow me." Habib led the way past the masses to a gate marked VIP ENTRANCE. The ticket taker, a neat young man wearing a LaCoste shirt with Regis Gator on the breast, smiled and lowered the rope.

"Welcome to Wacky World! Let me get you complimentary goody bags and a map. There's no need to wait in line. Simply show these VIP passes and they'll take you right in."

"What's the scariest ride you got?" Gary said.

"That would be the Rapid Rabbit Express, the world's biggest roller coaster."

"Do they hand out barf bags?" Krystal said.

The young man smiled brightly. "We prefer motion discomfort receptacles. Millie here will be your docent."

A smiling Latina girl with long black hair, wearing a Greta the Garter Snake outfit greeted them holding a tablet. "Hello! I'm Millie. It is my honor to take you on a tour of Wacky World. Is this your first time?"

"Yup," Habib said.

"Ours too."

"Well, as you know, Wacky World is the brainchild and gift to humanity of legendary creator Carl Wackheim, who arrived in this country a penniless orphan, but by dint of pluck and ingenuity, created the greatest entertainment empire the earth has ever seen. Working out of his garage in Tallahassee, Mr. Wackheim created one of the first sound animations, Egregious Regis starring his first great creation, Regis the Gator! The six-minute musical features Regis at the wheel of a steam locomotive bringing a load of oranges to market. Please follow me."

Millie led them down a spotless cobblestone trail toward a public square featuring a fifteen-foot Regis the Gator holding a brass fire hose spewing water. Little Lottie, a homing pigeon wearing a leather aviator's cap, sold lemonade. Lilypads, ferns, and fish thrived in the pond. Lizards and turtles sunned on artfully placed rocks and lawns.

Gary stared at the turtles.

"Millie, is it true that when ol' Carl died, they had his body frozen until a cure could be found? And that it's in a cryogenic chamber beneath the Enchanted Castle?"

Millie laughed gaily. "We get that all the time. It's just an urban legend, like thousand-pound feral hogs."

Millie pointed to an elaborate, fairy-tale wrought iron grate behind which rose a castle. "Yonder lies the Enchanted Castle, home of Philomena the Fair, Fiona the Foul, and Dunnigan's Dungeon. Would you like to take the Dungeon Ride?"

"It's too nice a day," Habib said. "Lead on."

They passed Spaceland with its No Grav Dome. They passed the Big Rock Candy Mountain, with Goth Sloth, Punk Skunk, Grunge Sponge, Upchuck Duck and Bluegrass Ass. Ahead lay multiple Alp-like steel peaks. The Rapid Rabbit Express.

Millie smiled brightly. "This is our most popular ride! I recommend you take it before lunch."

Habib looked around. "How 'bout it?"

"No way," Krystal said. "That rabbit gives me the creeps."

"This could be a way for you to work out your fear of the rabbit," Auburn said in a whiskey-tinged voice. "Once you conquer the Express, nothing will ever be able to touch you."

"That's right," Habib said. "You have that bout with Javelina coming up. Don't tell me you're not just a little bit concerned. I looked her up! She ran down and ate a coyote when she was fourteen."

"By the way," Millie said, "if y'all see Governor Chickenlooper, feel free to wave, but don't bother him. He's on a fact-finding mission."

"The governor is here?" Habib said. "I know the governor."

"You feel free to say hello. Are you taking Rapid Rabbit's Wild Ride?"

Habib looked around, hands out.

"I guess we are!" Krystal said. "Gimme that barf bag."

As they passed through the turnstile to the roller coaster, Millie got Krystal a heavy white bag with a picture of Rapid Rabbit, "Rabbit Rarebit" printed in red letters.

There were five cars. Each car held a dozen. The two couples sat side by side in the first row, strapped in with a steel beam in their laps. Behind them was a party celebrating a Quinceanera filling two rows.

"Oh my God," Krystal said. "I can't believe I'm doing this."

"Driving that train, high on cocaine," Gary sang.

Krystal elbowed him in the ribs. "Shut up."

"Trouble ahead, trouble behind..."

"Shut up!"

The car ascended an alpine peak. At the top Regis Gator beckoned. "Come on! You're almost there!" he said.

The car reached the apex and hung there. It lurched forward. The girls screaming behind them were heard in Jacksonville. The car plunged into the abyss, and for an instant, Krystal experienced the full force of vertigo, her stomach in free-fall, landscape kaleidoscoping. The car bottomed out, piling on the gees. Krystal belched. She put a hand to her mouth.

Gary gripped her hand. "You all right, honey?"

"Whose idea was this?"

Habib and Auburn traded high fives.

"Wheeeeeeeeee," Auburn piped.

The tracks bent to starboard and the car began its second ascent. Halfway up the climb, Krystal bent over her Rarebit bag and barfed. Utilizing her years of training, she confined her barf to the bag, which she rolled tightly over and sealed with the attached prongs.

"You feel better, honey?"

"I want the fuck off. How do we get off?"

"I think we got to ride the whole nine yards. We'll be off soon enough. Can't get any worse'n that."

"You always say that, and then what happens? A goat drops from the sky!"

The car reached the apex and hovered there. With a lurch

it started forward.

"Oh!" Krystal exclaimed, the vomit bag flying.

The car began its ascent. A party of dignitaries stood just outside the gate. Men and women in smart tropical suits, security in sunglasses and ear tags. As the car gained momentum, Gary watched Krystal's barf bag arc through the sky, striking Governor Chickenlooper in the head.

10 | RAPPIN' RABBIT

Ten police waited for the Rapid Rabbit to pull into the station. Security had whisked the governor away. Habib started talking before the car screeched to a halt.

"Total accident, very sorry. Any of you boys ever ride this thing?"

The governor's personal assistant Anthony Viola stepped forward in a blue Brunelo Cuccinelli suit, Berluti Scrippo loafers, and sunglasses, long black hair slicked back.

"Tony," Habib said. "That was an accident."

Viola exhaled. "The governor is upset."

"I know the governor. Tell him what happened."

"I will. Don't worry about it. He'll calm down. Hey, how are ya?"

"Tony, this is Auburn, and this is Gary and Krystal Duba. You know who Gary is."

Viola's face scrunched. "Did you shoot that hog? The big one?"

"Gary's the guy who caught Plastic Surgeon to the Stars and serial killer Dr. Vanderlay Mukerjee."

"Of course. The flower of Florida manhood."

Gary gaped. "You calling me a flower?"

"I meant fruit."

"You calling me a fruit?"

"Gary, this is the governor's right-hand man."

They shook hands. Viola saw Krystal's white face, the tissue in her hand.

"Are you all right?"

"She'll be fine. She just needs to get something in her stomach."

"And wine," Krystal said.

"She's fighting Javelina at the Roxy in November," Gary said. "You and the governor could be our guests."

"I'm afraid he has a very busy schedule."

"The Duke and Duchess of Ducats are coming."

"Really?"

"You bet. We worked out a deal. We're gonna appear on their show, and they're gonna appear on our show."

"Hmmm. I will certainly bring this to the governor's attention. I think such an event could be mutually beneficial."

Viola motioned Habib over.

"What?"

Viola winked. "Bullseye."

They walked toward the main square. "Gubnah Chad Chickenlooper," Habib said in a cornpone voice. "They call him Hanging Chad."

"Why do they call him Hanging Chad?"

Habib poked his phone and showed Gary a picture of the governor hanging from a windowsill, pants down around his ankles, a naked woman with long blonde hair leaning out above him.

"Somebody got a tip he was seeing his mistress. He's a deacon of his church, you know."

Auburn and Krystal freshened up before making their way to the Princess Cafe, designed for six-year-olds with all the Wacky characters lined up in a hall of kings. Regis Gator, Hannity the Manatee, Funky Monkey, Goth Sloth and Punk Skunk. They got a table on the veranda overlooking Town Square, Wackheimer's recreation of a turn of the century gas lit New England town. Wacky World greeters, dressed as the iconic characters, approached groups of tourists. They danced, they juggled, they told jokes.

Their waitron was the French Fop from *Cutie and the Feast.* "Allo! I am Gaston! Can I get you anysing to drink?"

"Do you have a nice California Cabernet?" Krystal said.

"Alas, zis is a family-oriented restaurant and we serve no alcoholic beverages before five pm."

"We're a family," Gary said. "How is that family friendly? Do you know how many weary parents stumble in here and just want to get plastered?"

"Alas, it is not my decision. If it were up to me, I would bring ze finest French champagne. Would you like to hear today's specials?"

Gary picked up the oversize laminated menu featuring all

the Wacky characters. "Give us a few."

Krystal had the Florida Roll. Gary had a burger. Habib had camel fajitas. Auburn had sushi. Habib picked up the bill. By the time they were finished, it was three p.m. As they crossed the grand plaza on their way to the parking garage, a six-foot Rapid Rabbit popped out of a manhole. Elbows on the ground, it looked around. It sprang from the hole—some kind of catapult—and landed on roller blades. It zeroed in on the quartet. A freestyle beat blasted from the PA system.

"I'm Rapid Rabbit, the people's choice. I'm in the habit of giving voice. To disillusioned institutions and illusory solutions in situations that require Rapid Rabbit to inspire."

Krystal clutched Gary's arm. "Don't look. Keep going."

Rapid Rabbit skated along. "Waidaminit! Waidaminit! See that fool? He ain't cool. All he does is vape and drool. It takes a toll to be that droll, be be that troll up on a knoll."

Krystal caught a whiff. "He's drunk."

Rapid Rabbit chased after them. "Come on, lady, don't be that way. I may be shady, but I'll have my say! Dump that clown and come with Rabbit! Drop that loser like a bad habit!"

Gary got in Rapid's face. "Wha'd you say?"

"Hey hey, ho ho! Peckerwood has got to go!"

The rabbit stank of gin. Gary punched the rabbit in the snoot. The stiff cloth bore the brunt of the blow. The rabbit lunged, taking Gary to the ground, but its thick gloves prevented it from doing any damage. Gary pulled its ears, twisting, slithered to the side and sprang to his feet. The rabbit got up. They circled. Visitors deployed their cameras. Funky Monkey danced around the fringes carrying a huge butterfly net. Every now and then he would rush forward and swipe at one of the combatants.

Gary and the rabbit traded punches. Krystal jumped on the rabbit's back, tried to apply a rear naked choke, but the rabbit's stiff costume prevented her from linking up. A Keystone Cops Model T rolled up, bell clanging. Out jumped two Keystone cops blowing whistles. They separated the combatants. One cop with a black walrus mustache backed Rapid Rabbit up with his nightstick.

"Rodell, you're drunk. That's three strikes and out. Turn in your suit and get out. Your last check will be mailed to you."

Rapid Rabbit slugged the cop in the kisser. The other cop piled on. The two Keystones and Rapid rolled on the cobblestones as visitors rushed to the scene. The whoop of a real patrol car cleared the way for a Chrysler bearing WWPD on the doors. Two cops wearing blue uniforms and shorts rushed the combatants, grabbed the rabbit by his arms and hauled him to their vehicle.

Regis Gator appeared in spats, carrying a diamond-headed cane. Using an in-suit amplifier, he addressed the crowd.

"Folks, every now and then we like to shake things up a bit with some performance art. I want to thank our guests for being good sports and participating, and to assure you that this was all planned and that no one was hurt."

Goth Sloth approached Gary and Krystal. "Are you all

right? Are either of you injured?"

"I been hit harder by a mosquito!"

"I'm fine."

"I would like to apologize on behalf of Wacky World. The person in the Rapid Rabbit costume was let go last week. He apparently sneaked into the facility, donned the costume and put on this disgraceful display as retaliation. He will be charged, I assure you."

"No problem."

"Would you be willing to sign a hold harmless disclaimer? We would be pleased to give you both lifetime passes. The only things you would have to pay for are food and drink."

"Talk to my lawyer."

Habib stepped up. "Let me see the documents. We'll get back to you."

Goth Sloth handed over a manila envelope.

It wasn't until they reached Habib's car that Gary smacked himself in the head.

"Holy shit! The Rabbit! He was supposed to tell me something!"

11 | BACKPACK

Back home, Gary had Krystal set him up with a Zoom call to Irving Pincus, the computer expert who'd shot Hogzilla. The twenty-three-year-old Pincus, from a strict Orthodox family, had short black hair and a curly black beard as he sat in his apartment in front of framed posters of *Les Mis* and *La Bohème*. He wore a Punisher Tee-shirt.

"Pincus! You a comics fan?"

"Yes, but I was forced to sell my collection. What can I do for you, Mr. Duba?"

"Pincus, I need you to track down the Rabid Rabbit that got shit-canned by Wacky yesterday."

"Do you mean Rapid Rabbit, Mr. Duba?"

"Rabid, Rapid, whatever. And you can call me Gary."

Pincus poked and stroked. "All right. I'm in Wacky's personnel file. Rodell Grosz was let go this afternoon for public drunkenness and brawling. He lives at 4556 Wayzata Court in Union Park. Do you want his contact info?"

"Gimme."

"Rapid@domo.com. I'm looking at him now."

"Really? How do you do that, Pincus?"

"I've accessed his home computer."

"Can I see?"

"Are you sure you want to see? It's pretty vulgar."

"I can handle it."

Gary's screen flickered. A swarthy man with pock-marked skin and greasy hair moaned as he spanked his monkey.

"Mr. Grosz is watching *Anal Antics XXX*."

"Holy shit, Pincus! That's enough!"

"What do you want with this man?"

"Leotis told me I would be visited by three harbingers: a bat, a rabbit, and a turtle. I think Grosz has something to tell me."

"Who is Leotis?"

Krystal spoke over Gary's shoulder. "Every night Gary gets shit-faced and talks to an imaginary catfish."

"Leotis is real!"

"Is there anything else, Mr. Duba?"

"Pincus, how'd you like to come on my show? I'll introduce you to the Duke and Duchess of Ducats."

"I really can't, Mr. Duba. My dog Elisha's sick. I have to stay with him." Pincus turned away, hand to eye.

"What's wrong with him?"

"He's got cancer. It's currently confined to one tumor. I just can't afford to have him treated."

"What's it cost?"

"About a thousand dollars. If I don't do anything, he won't live another two months. He's not that old. He's only eight. He's all I've got."

"I thought you had an older sister."

"She and I don't talk."

"I'll pay for it."

"You don't have any money."

"I will soon! Just hang in there."

A dog whimpered in pain. "I have to go now."

"Real sorry to hear it, Pincus. What do I owe ya?"

"You don't have any money, Mr. Duba."

"No, but I'm always working on something. Thanks, Pincus.

Gary wrote the address down in his notepad. "You coming babe?"

"I told you, I got to get my rest! You're driving me to Delilah's tomorrow, remember? You'd better be back here in the morning!"

"I just want to talk to the guy."

Gary hit the road in his F-150, one hundred and fifty miles from Turpentine to Orlando through the center of the state. He stopped at a Friendly's Supermarket and picked up a six pack of Gator Beer. Gary slipped a George Strait CD into the dash and drove with his elbow out the window, right wrist draped over the wheel until he ran into a cloudburst east of St. Pete's and had to button up. It was just past eleven when he pulled up in front of a run-down bungalow at 4556 Wayzata Court. A piece of shit Saturn was parked in the driveway with an EAT MORE POSSUM bumper sticker. Pale light glowed through yellowed Venetian blinds from the living room window. Taking the six-pack, he knocked on the door.

"Who the fuck—!" issued from within.

The door opened to the limit of the chain. Grosz was five eleven wearing a grimy wife beater and boxer shorts, Popeye chin covered with stubble, suspicious.

"Fuck you want?"

"Hey, take it easy! Don't you remember me? We traded blows at Wacky World."

"You! You motherfucker! You're the reason I got shit canned!"

Gary held up the beer. "Chill, dude! I ain't here to fight. And you called my old lady a slut! What kind of man would I be if I just stood there and took it?"

"Whatchoo want?"

"I just want to talk to you for a minute. See? I brought beer."

"Got any blow?"

"Well it just so happens I got a gram in the truck. Here. Take the beer."

Grosz unlatched the door and took the six pack. Gary retrieved the bindle and entered the house which smelled of old socks and reefer. The Rabbit's computer sat on a door resting on cinder blocks. A grubby rug lay on the scratched hardwood floor. A cast-off cloth sofa backed against the wall beneath a *Men in Black* poster. The lamp shade on the end table was stained yellow. The Rabbit snapped off a can and passed the rest to Gary. The Rabbit grabbed a chipped porcelain tray off the end table and handed it to Gary, who placed it on a steel steamer trunk that served as a coffee table and laid out a couple lines.

Outside, a couple screamed at each other in Spanish.

"Those fuckers!" the Rabbit said, got up, opened the door and shouted, "*Chinga tu madre!*"

He sat on the sofa raising a cloud of dust, reached for the chipped plate and hoovered a line through a cut-up straw. "I like a man who brings gifts. What can I do for you?"

"You're supposed to tell me something."

The Rabbit chugged a can of Gator Beer, crumpled it and tossed it into the darkened kitchen where it clattered across the linoleum. "I already told you to go fuck yourself."

"No, man, I'm in touch with my spirit animal and he told me that I would be visited by three harbingers: a bat, a rabbit, and a turtle. You're the rabbit. You're supposed to tell me something. Something important. Something I can take to the bank."

"Buy a homing pigeon. You can sell it over and over again."

"That ain't it."

"How the fuck do you know?"

"You sure curse a lot."

"I just lost my fucking job so fuck you."

"Awright, how's this. You tell me something, and if I make any money off it, I'll give you a cut."

The Rabbit leaned back and regarded Gary through slitted eyes. "What's your story?"

"I'm the guy who apprehended Plastic Surgeon to the Stars and serial killer Dr. Vanderlay Mukerjee."

"So what?"

"I invented house suspenders."

"You think I got some kinda info or something that's gonna make you rich?"

"So says the catfish."

"What catfish?"

"Leotis."

The Rabbit broke into a sunny grin. "You're all right. You're a crazy motherfucker. Gimme another line. I might have something for ya."

Gary laid out another line. The Rabbit hoovered, snucked, and howled. "Awright, awright. I got it. Pickle flavored toothpaste."

Gary grimaced. "That ain't it."

"Waidaminit, waidaminit...cold lightbulbs."

"Huh?"

"Yeah. For fridges. That way, when you open the door, the lightbulbs don't thaw the food."

"Nah."

"Okay, waidaminit...mannn, I need to smoke some skunk. Let's get high."

"I can't. I gotta drive."

"Awright, awright. Hang." Rabbit got off the sofa, went into his bedroom and rummaged around, returning with a frayed green denim backpack which he set on the table. He pulled out a flashlight, a pack, of tissues, some rubbers, a pen knife, a pack of cigarettes, and a baggie filled with ditch weed.

"Here we go. Here we go."

Gary jolted forward, eyes blazing.

"Whu?"

Gary pointed at the table. "Backpack!"

12 | MIRABILE DICTU

Gary hit the road, high as a kite. Used to driving under the influence, he entered a fugue state, eyes at the limits of the headlamps as he cruised through the moist Florida night, insects splattering the windshield. June bugs hit like shrapnel.

Gary tuned into the Ferd Ludlow Show.

"...we'll be right back after this short commercial break."

"Hi! Slick Niveleski here, with a true story about how you can save thousands of dollars on life insurance. Ray, a real person, is forty-five years old with a minor heart condition..."

Gary twisted the dial.

"Have you been injured in an automobile accident and the insurance company refused to pay you what you deserve? Contact the law offices of Habib Rodriguez. I specialize in personal injury claims. I've been dealing with insurance companies all my life and they don't scare me. We don't collect unless you collect. Sonia Real is a real customer."

"My name is Sonia Real, and I was broadsided by an

eighteen-wheeler that ran a red light. The insurance company refused to pay me what I deserved so I called Habib Rodriguez and he got me eight hundred and fifty thousand dollars."

"I'm Habib Rodriguez. I can't promise to get you eight hundred and fifty thousand dollars, but we will never know unless you call me today. My number is..."

Gary switched back to Ferd Ludlow.

"We are witnessing an unprecedented invasion of unidentified flying objects. The media won't report this. They are in cahoots with the government to suppress all information regarding this influx of alien invaders. Yes, you heard me. Earth is under assault by alien invaders. They are snatching our cattle, and even human beings, seized late at night, beamed into their craft via anti-gravity, where they are experimented upon and anally probed. Listen to this account from Luke Spacey of Pembroke Pines. Luke? Thank you for hanging on. Please tell our listeners what happened."

"I was walking my dog Herman around the block. It was past midnight. Some nights I don't sleep so I walk Herman. It's a real quiet block. All of a sudden Herman starts going crazy, barking like a maniac, and I hear this weird humming noise and the air smelled of fried potatoes. A yellow beam came down and surrounded me. I could see my shadow, and then I started to drift upward. I let go of the leash and Herman took off barking. I was transported upward inside an alien craft. It was a saucer, Ferd. The aliens who examined me were tiny gray persons with big heads and eyes. They gave me some kind of gas..."

It was around one when he turned onto Weldon Way, the dirt road that dead ended at his trailer. Weldon Way was three miles long. The first mile was okay. A pack of feral hogs huddled in the middle of the second mile, grunting, lunging, snorting. Gary laid on the horn. They looked at him, their tiny pig eyes red in the headlights. They were eating something.

"Get out the way, you pigs!" he yelled through his open window. He shook his fist. They ignored him. Gary advanced slowly and it wasn't until he was a foot away that they grudgingly parted. The tires rolled over something with a thump. Gary didn't want to know. He kept driving. He turned off the music and let the sounds of the swamp flow. Crickets. Frogs. Loons. He turned a corner, and a scrum of turkey vultures occupied the middle of the road poking and pecking.

Gary laid on the horn. The turkey vultures didn't even look. Gary advanced slowly until he was a foot away. A turkey vulture hopped onto the hood of his truck and looked him in the eye. Another flew in the passenger side window and went for his face, opening a gash above his right eye, claws slashing at his arms. Gary grabbed it by the neck and flailed around the cabin, smashing its body into the seat, dash, roof, and floor until he broke its neck. He sat there panting, covered with gore, blood, and feathers.

Gary grabbed the magnum from the glove compartment and stepped out of the truck. A dead hog lay in the middle of the road, ribs gleaming white in the moonlight where the vultures had stripped the flesh. "I take it all back! You guys are doing a great job!"

As he approached his lot, a row of pink flamingos filed across the road, right to left. Gary counted twenty-two before the last flamingo disappeared into the brush.

Gary parked and went in the house. Krystal's gym bag, a suitcase, and a six-pack of Tab lay on the living room sofa. Since learning Coca-Cola had decided to terminate the beloved diet cola, she'd been stocking up. A four-foot stack of cases lay in the larder off the kitchen. Gary smelled himself. He took a shower, washing off blood and feathers. When he came out, Krystal stood arms crossed in the entrance to the bedroom.

"What happened to you?"

"I got in a death struggle with a turkey vulture. It was him or me. I won! I talked to the Rabbit and he gave me the key. Where's that backpack we took off the dead parachutist?"

"Geez, I forgot all about that. I think I put it in the attic." It wasn't a real attic, just a space between roof trusses to house electrical and conduits. The Duke had cut his own hole in the ceiling of the larder. Gary stood on cases of Tab, lifted the hatch and shined a flashlight. A raccoon hissed at him. Gary climbed down, filled his super soaker with water, climbed back up and let the raccoon have it between the eyes. The masked intruder scurried to a far corner and disappeared through a gap. The Duke and Duchess had left all sorts of junk. He'd go through it later. The Kelly green backpack lay within arm's reach. Gary grabbed it and took it into the living room.

"Come to bed, Gary. It's two-thirty. You got to drive me to Delilah's in a couple hours."

"I'm wide awake, babe! Don't worry about me."

He set the backpack on the living room table and opened the top. It was jammed with documents in manila folders. He pulled one out. The document bore the letterhead of the National Bolivian Armed Forces in Spanish. He kept digging. Documents. Lists of names. Finally, he came to the last envelope. It was stiff, sealed with transparent tape. Using his pocketknife to slit the tape, Gary removed a rectangle of white cardboard sealed in a mylar sleeve. He turned it over.

Detective Comics #27. Slabbed and graded nine point eight.

13 | INVASIVE

"We're rich!" Gary crowed. "Thank you, Lord! Thank you, Rabbit! Thank you, Leotis!"

Krystal came out of the bedroom with a pained expression. "What the hell, Gary! Go to bed! We have to drive to Delilah's in a few hours!"

Gary held up the comic. "Do you know what this is?"

"A comic."

"Do you have any idea what this comic is?"

Krystal squinted. "*Detective Comics.*"

"This is the world's single most valuable comic! It's worth over a million dollars!"

"No shit. Who'd pay that kind of money for a comic?"

"Nicholas Cage!"

"Nick Cage doesn't know where his next meal is coming from. Where'd you get that?"

"It was in the backpack we got from that dead guy."

"Why would a Venezuelan Special Forces op parachute

into the middle of a swamp with a comic book?"

Gary shrugged. "Maybe Quetzacoatl's selling his private collection to raise money for widows and orphans."

"Let's go. Nobody's getting any sleep around here."

Gary carefully repacked the backpack including all the documents and shoved it back in the crawl space. He carried Krystal's bags to the truck, and they booked. Krystal's trainer Delilah lived in the Big Cypress Indian Reservation. The sky lightened in the east as they turned from State Highway eighty onto Old County Eight Thirty-Three, a lonely path through endless everglades. Krystal found Country WKIS on the radio, Humph Greenwald singing "*My Dawg Done Left and He Took My Truck*."

"Aw hell no, little lady! It's too early in the morning for that shit!" Gary switched to BIG 105.9.

"Here's Blue Oyster Cult's latest, and it hits close to home," said the deejay.

"Should you settle down in the Sunshine State, you should know of its tangled fate. How the conquistador came to Florida, long before it had a name. The medicine man of the Seminole knelt by the sacred flame..."

Krystal switched to Ferd Ludlow.

"Muriel Spurlock of Lehigh Acres, you're on!"

"Ferd, I'd like to change the subject if I may. Florida is being overrun by invasive species. If we don't do something to stop them, it's only a matter of time before they take over our homes. You've seen the pictures of alligators trying to get into houses, climbing up trellises, banging on the front screen door."

"I got to correct you right there, Muriel. Alligators are indigenous. They were here before the white man."

"That may be so, Ferd, but they're being egged on by Burmese pythons. There's a reason they're called Burmese pythons. They come from Burma, Ferd."

"I grant you that. The state recognizes the threat which is why they sponsor the annual python cull. But in my opinion, they are ignoring potentially greater threats such as the proliferation of the South American iguana."

"I don't see how you can say that. Pythons eat people and pets. The iguana eat leaves. If properly trained, they could replace leaf blowers and we would all benefit."

"What about the hippos?"

"What hippos?"

"The hippos that escaped from drug kingpin El Nariz's zoo and are now propagating in the Everglades."

"That's ridiculous. Are you serious?"

Gary braked for a hippo crossing the road. Krystal switched to WLRN in Miami.

"...Professor Anderson Aardvark, on Florida's most endangered animals. Professor?"

"Thank you, Alice. There is no question but that the Florida panther, a North American cougar, leads the list. Only one hundred and sixty of these beautiful animals exist in the wild. Their habitat is under constant attack. Although the panther is fiercely territorial, there is not a single incident of a panther ever attacking a human being. Shooting or otherwise harming a panther is a violation of the Endangered Species Act. Florida considers it a third-degree felony with a maximum of five years in prison and a $5,000 fine. The federal punishment is a maximum one year in jail with a $100,000 fine. Personally, I wish it were higher."

"How many people have been charged under the Endangered Species Act?"

"Well, Alice..."

Gary turned the dial to New Country 103. The Grateful Dead's "Uncle John's Band" warbled over the speakers.

"That ain't country," Gary said, weaving all over the road.

"Careful there, Gar. You want me to drive?"

"Hell no. I got this."

"Let me see your eyes."

Gary turned toward her. His eyes looked like laser dots.

"Aw hell no. Stop the truck. I'm driving."

"Okay, but I get to choose the music."

Gary pulled over. There was only a foot of shoulder before it dropped off into endless cattails, mangroves, cypress, pond apple, and sawgrass. Gary stumbled getting out of the truck and caught himself on the door. Krystal slid across into the driver's seat as Gary pulled himself up and shut the door. They wheeled south, tires rumbling on the crumbling blacktop, thumping over potholes.

A man staggered out of the bush, wearing dress pants soaked to the knee, white shirt torn, stubble on his face and fell to his knees. Krystal pulled up next to him and stopped. Gary got out.

"What's going on?"

"I was abducted by aliens!" he said in a British accent. "They probed me anally! They're coming! Take me to the police!"

Gary jumped back in and shut the door. "Drive!"

Krystal tromped on the accelerator. The old truck surged forward with a chirp of the wheels. Gary twisted around and looked through the back light. The fugitive disappeared on the other side of the road.

Gary wiped sweat off his brow. "Close one!"

Krystal stopped for a troop of pink flamingos crossing the road.

Gary appealed to an uncaring god. "What's with all these flamingos?!"

"What do you mean?"

"Last night as I was coming home, I ran into the same thing. A line of flamingos crossing the road."

"Maybe they want something."

"But what? They haven't made any demands."

"They're blocking traffic. They must want something."

"But they're moving! See? There goes the last flamingo."

They pulled up in front of Delilah's geodesic dome around ten, her Jeep pickup poking out from behind. Delilah sat out front on a stool, legs spread wearing an ankle-length red, black and green dashiki, head wrapped in a black turban, shucking oysters with a knife. A couple of chickens poked for bugs at her feet. A thin Creole with prominent cheekbones, she spat a wad of chewing tobacco as Gary and Krystal got out.

"'Bout time you got here."

"We woulda been here sooner but we were held up by hippos, aliens, and flamingos."

"Did those flamingos block the road again?"

"Yeah. They been giving you trouble?"

Delilah inserted her bone-handled filet knife in an oyster shell. "Nothin' I can't handle. Thank you, goodbye."

"Delilah, I'm falling down. I need to sleep."

Delilah sighed, leaned back, and crossed her long legs. "Ain't that just like a man. You can crash in the house while we get to work. Stay outta my loft."

Gary walked out back, pissed in the swamp, went inside, filled a glass from the cistern, drank it, checked the fridge and flopped on a wicker divan in the living room. He fell asleep almost instantly and dreamed he was riding a huge feral hog at the head of a stampede. Feral hogs, all headed for a cliff. Gary gripped the stiff bristle and whooped, waving his CAT hat. The hogs piled over the cliff. It was a long way down to where the surf rolled in. Halfway down the scene switched to giant holographic sharks and rogue military forces. Gary rolled to the side and came up with a Ruger mini 14 in his hands. He blasted the sharks. He was struck in the gut.

He woke. Delilah's black cat Pork Chop sat on his belly. Gary was parched. He refilled his glass and drained it. The grandfather clock beneath the spiral staircase said it was four o'clock. No sign of Krystal or Delilah.

He went outside just as a man in a safari jacket and pith helmet, a camera around his neck walked up smiling, with a gap between his front teeth that would accommodate an AMTRAK train.

"Ah, Mr. Duba! Garrison Gland. You remember me. I'm a producer for the History Channel. Congratulations on your show! I'm riveted. Can't wait for the next episode."

"What are you looking for out here?"

"The giant Sumatran corpse flower."

"Why ain't you in Sumatra?"

Garrison looked around to make sure no one eavesdropped. "I have it on good authority that the *Amorphophallus titanum* is making significant inroads in the Everglades."

"What's it look like?"

"It's hard to miss. It's ten feet tall and smells like a rotting corpse."

"Ain't seen it. But I'll keep a look out."

Garrison squinted, nose wrinkling. He sniffed. "The game's afoot!" He ran into the jungle.

14 | WHOOPS

Krystal and Delilah returned at five, Krystal drenched to the skin in shorts, halter top and waffle stompers, her red hair done up in a ponytail, Delilah cool in a red and yellow jumpsuit on her mountain bike. Gary lounged in a lawn chair, smoking a doobie.

Krystal stripped off her clothes and stood naked beneath a fifty-gallon barrel strapped to a cypress tree and pulled the cord. She lathered up in warm rainwater. Delilah had rigged funnels all through the branches and the barrel was never empty. Gary watched her towel off and wondered if there was time for a quickie. They could do it in the truck.

He was famished. "Hey what you got to eat around here? All I found was some turkey bacon and a box of baking soda."

"You know how to shoot?" Delilah said.

"Duh!"

"Wait a minute."

Delilah went in the house and returned with a mini Ruger

14 and a box of ammo. “Here, big shot. Go get us something to eat. Get one of them hogs.”

“You ain’t got none left?”

“We done et all the hog. Come on. Shouldn’t be that hard. They’re all over the place.”

“Will you eat flamingo?”

She stared at him.

“What about fish?”

“Sick of fish. If I eat any more fish, omma turn into a fish.” Delilah thrust the rifle at him. “Go on. Git. Make yourself useful.”

Gary heaved himself to his feet, put on socks and work boots, fetched his fishing vest from the toolbox in back of the truck: sunglasses, sunscreen, pocket knife, first aid kit. He stuffed a pocket with .223 ammo, pulled his Gators cap low over his forehead and set off into the brush. He had ninety minutes of light left. Gary headed west toward the lowering sun on a marshy peninsula. His feet squished where he stepped. Pea-soup colored swamp water filled inlets like jigsaw puzzle parts. Hearing some movement in the brush Gary froze, brought the rifle to his shoulder and listened.

Some kind of fracas. Creeping forward, stepping on marsh grass, he hunkered down behind a hedge. Bubbles, splashing, and weird high-pitched squeal. Gary carefully parted the grass and beheld a scrum of nutria, the rat-like invader from South America, battling with a horde of iguana. They went it at tooth and nail. An iguana seized a nutria by the throat and shook it violently. Two nutria ganged up on an iguana, thrusting it beneath the surface.

Gary had owned a restaurant that served iguana. The Lizard Lounge. It opened and closed on the same day. Iguana were tasty, but these were scrawny, and Krystal was in training, so she needed extra protein. One shot and the rest would skedaddle.

Gary rose, circumnavigated the battle counterclockwise heading toward a dense stand of cypress. A covey of wood storks took flight, flapping above the trees toward the sea. He thought about taking a shot, but his chances were slim and he didn't know how they tasted. With hog, you knew what you were getting. Ribs. Hams. Bacon. Gary preferred it to the store-bought stuff.

"Here, sooey sooey," he muttered under his breath. Something gleamed at the base of a mangrove. A Dixie beer can. Gary stomped it flat on a rock and slipped it into his vest. He paused at water's edge to look across to another dense glade, thirty feet away, surrounded by saw grass and cattails. The cattails swayed like a Marlins crowd doing the wave. Something big was moving over there.

"Lord, send me a big fat hog," Gary said under his breath, stalking the edge of the inlet. He was hungry enough to eat nutria. Some genius decided the way to thin invasive species was to eat them. Thus, the explosion of nutria and iguana-themed restaurants. Lizard On A Stick. More Than Rats. Rodents of Distinction. I Wanna Iguana. Monty's Python.

Gary loved to barbecue. But he just wasn't cut out to manage a restaurant. When his first customer complained, the Dominican cook beaned him with a cast iron pan and Gary went to jail. What was wrong with that old witchee woman that she didn't have any vittles? Delilah knew how to hunt. He'd seen hogs she'd bagged. She tried to get him to eat some rattlesnake once but he wasn't that drunk. The problem was power. It went out every time there was a hurricane or even a heavy rainstorm and if it didn't come back on with twenty-four hours, everything in her freezer went bad. She had a power generator, but she didn't like to run it because it made too much noise. She needed freeze-dried survivalist fare.

He'd been meaning to ask her about Leotis' prophecy. Delilah was a fortune teller and an oracle. She'd read his palm and told him he was gonna have his own show and damned if she wasn't right. She had a standing invitation to appear.

"Don't need the aggravation," was her standard response.

A feral growl emanated from a copse of cypress. A snort.

"That there's a hog," Gary whispered to himself, creeping forward like Elmer Fudd hunting wabbits. Fudd always got the short end of the stick. Gary admired Fudd. Fudd was a woodsman who knew how to dress. And Bugs Bunny was an irritating prick. Just a smart ass. He reminded Gary of every smart ass he'd fought in high school. Gary had to fight his way through high school because the smart asses were always disrespecting him. He was in and out of the principal's office more often than the janitor. They gave him so much detention, he had his own bench with a plaque.

Bugs Bunny reminded Gary of Rodell Grosz. Grosz

was a smart ass who dressed like a rabbit. He wondered if Grosz had stolen the costume. Couldn't wear it in public or Wacky would land on him with hobnailed boots. Wacky was litigious. Everybody knew that. They offered rewards to snitches for little girls selling Little Lottie Lemonade in the suburbs. They paid the police to arrest trick or treaters wearing homemade costumes. Don't mess with the gator.

Some kind of ruckus erupted ten feet in front of him. All he saw was movement among the saw grass, two animals locked in combat. Two feral hogs going at it! Gary sank to one knee and sighted along an alley between the cypress. A flash of movement. Back again. Had to time this just right. Sensing the beast about to move, Gary led it and squeezed the trigger.

A yowl raised his hackles as he stomped through the brush to a small clearing where a wounded hog, rear leg torn off, squealed and scrambled into the water. A Florida panther with a tracking collar lay on the ground.

14 | BLOOD OATH

The light was fading as Gary returned, panther draped over his shoulders like a mink stole. Delilah sat out front husking corn. Gary plopped the panther at her feet. She stared at it. She looked up.

"A year in prison and a hundred thousand dollar fine."

"I thought it was a hog!"

"Does it look like a hog?"

"I thought it was two hogs fighting."

"Does it look like two hogs fighting?"

"I figger if we eat it, there'll be no evidence."

Delilah pointed at the collar. "What about that?"

Gary pulled his pocketknife and attempted to saw through the collar. It was like cutting through a tire. "Dang thing won't come off!" He went to his truck and retrieved a pair of tin snips.

Krystal came out in sweatpants and a Florida Gators shirt as Gary knelt by the dead panther, cut the collar, put it on the butcher stump and smashed it with a rock. He threw the remains into the swamp.

"Is that what's for dinner?"

Gary looked up. "Sure, why not?"

"I ain't eating no cat! You ever had cat?"

"Once at a Chinese restaurant but I can't be certain."

Delilah handed Gary a filleting knife. "You killed it you clean it."

Gary hoisted the panther onto a cypress stump stained with dried blood and went to work. He chopped off the tail and tossed it in the bushes. Gary marinated the lean and stringy meat in olive oil and Dr. Bob's All-Purpose marinade in a roasting pan, shook out the Weber, shredded the *Clarendon County Crier* in the bottom and filled the rest with charcoal. Krystal wiped the bird shit off the picnic table and set out a salad bowl filled with purslane, betony, spiderwort, swamp cabbage and saw palmetto.

Gary lit the grill. "Got any shine?"

Delilah heaved herself out of her chair, went in the house and returned with a clay jug and two Mason jars. Krystal looked over.

"Where's mine?"

Delilah wagged her finger.

Gary and Delilah sat next to each other in cheap plastic lounges, sipping shine and listening to the bugs, loons, and macaques. Gary got some reefer from the truck and rolled a doobie. Krystal held her hand out.

"Come on! Reefer ain't gonna interfere with my training."

Delilah gave an imperceptible nod.

Gary put the corn and the panther on the grill. They sat in a mellow haze watching smoke wind up into the trees.

Garrison Gland entered the clearing. "What is that divine smell?"

Delilah exhaled a smoke ring. "Who are you?"

"I'm Garrison Gland. I'm with the History Channel! I've been exploring this section of the swamp looking for the elusive giant Sumatran corpse flower. It's so near, I can smell it!"

"That ain't what's cookin'."

"Yes, I can see that. I hate to impose, but if you permit me to join you, I can give you invaluable publicity for Steely Danielle's next bout!"

"Venue's sold out," Delilah said.

"Is that a bottle tree?"

"Yeah. Want me to read your future? Get the fuck outta here or omma kick your ass. No. I'm not even gonna sully my shoe. I'll have my girl Krystal here kick your ass, and we'll film it and post it!"

Gary put up his hand. "Now hold on, hold on. Garrison's all right. The History Channel does *Swamp People*! That's my favorite show next to *What's Your Problem?* What are you working on, Gar?"

Garrison stared at the grill. "I'm developing a series on invasive species. It's called...what is that?"

"What's what?"

Garrison pointed at the grill. "What are you grilling here? What animal is this?"

"That's an axis deer," Delilah said. "It's an invasive species."

"Axis deer? I don't think so. I know deer and that's no deer."

Garrison glanced to the side, did a double take. He walked into the brush, picked up the panther tail and held it out accusingly. "Did you do this?"

"Do what?" Gary said. "What's that?"

"You know damn well what it is. Did you kill a Florida panther?"

Gary's jaw dropped. "Who? Me? I ain't even seen one! I would never kill a Florida panther! I got too much respect for 'em."

Garrison held his phone to his eye and dropped to one knee to get the grill, Gary, Krystal, and Delilah in the shot. Gary shot out of his seat, tripped on a mangrove root and fell on his face. Garrison turned to run. Delilah snapped her fingers and pointed at the fleeing photographer.

"Get him!"

Krystal sprang from her seat and ran into the jungle whooping. Garrison's pith helmet looked like a flying saucer fleeing through the trees. He tripped and sprawled. Krystal landed on his back with a blood-curdling shriek, ripped off the helmet and put him in a choke hold. She got off, waited for him to revive, pulled him to his feet with a wrist lock and marched him back into the camp. When they got back, Delilah had changed into a turban and ground length leopard pattern dashiki. She looked up from her seat with disdain.

"Sit your cracker ass down."

Garrison sat in the folding lawn chair Gary placed for him. Delilah pointed at her kohled black eyes.

"I am a shaman of the Calusa. I'm the seventh daughter of the seventh son. We have the right to kill the leopard on our sacred hunting grounds. DO YOU DISPUTE ME?"

Garrison eeped and fell over backward.

"I'm a witchee woman and an oracle. The panther has been terrorizing my people for a hundred years. The panther has killed our livestock and our children. We have prayed to our sacred gods and asked for guidance. In the middle of the hurricane, our gods spoke to me, and told me that the only way to rid ourselves of its curse was to bring in the one man who could kill it. The man who caught the biggest python in Florida history. The man who killed the biggest feral hog in Florida history. The man who caught Serial Killer to the Stars and plastic surgeon Doctor Vanderlay Mukerjee!"

"Delilah," Gary said. "Psst."

She turned on him furious. "What?"

"It's Plastic Surgeon to the Stars and serial killer."

"Whatever. And you have performed your duty nobly. Now, one final step remains to excise the curse. And that is to partake of the flesh of this demon panther. It is a sacred ritual. You have arrived at the right time. We are willing to let you participate in the ceremony, but you must make a blood oath to never speak of it to anyone."

Garrison gaped. "Seriously?"

Delilah drew a twelve-inch blade from a sheath strapped to her calf. "Very few white men are chosen to participate. In fact, you're the second. Only this man, Gary Duba, has proven worthy. We know Duba's character. We do not know yours. But by taking the ancient oath, and consuming the flesh of the panther, you will become one of us. You will become a Calusa. What say you?"

16 | GARRISON TAKES A POWDER

Garrison stared at the blade. "What does the blood oath entail?"

Delilah drew the blade across her left palm leaving a red streak. She flipped the blade, caught it by the handle and offered it butt first. Gary and Krystal hunched forward in their chairs, hands on knees.

"Did, uh, did these fine people take the blood oath?"

"Laws, yes."

"And, uh, you know, could we at least disinfect the blade first?"

Gary picked up the shine and poured it over the gleaming blade. Garrison looked around nervously. He took the blade. Eyes squeezed shut, he drew the blade across his left palm, opened his eyes, and fainted. When he woke, he was lying on one of the cheap plastic chaise lounges, Delilah standing over him. Her smile turned down at the corners.

Garrison blinked uncertainly. "What happened?"

"You fainted."

He looked at his hand and blanched. His palm was full of blood.

Mosquitoes buzzed in the twilight. An orange glow shone through the trees to the west.

Delilah extended her left hand. Garrison had no choice. If he didn't comply, these hillbillies would kill him and eat him. She pulled him to his feet.

"Do you solemnly swear, by Razzmatazz, Guilfoyle, and Rihuli, that you will heed the diktats of the sacred council, never betray your brothers and sisters of the Calusa Tribe, and observe the sacred protocols?"

"What are the protocols?"

Delilah counted them off on her fingers. "No eggplant. When the light turns green, you go. Shower daily. Never spit in a man's face unless his beard is on fire. Thou shalt not put ketchup on your hot dog. Bacon must be fried to a crisp. No white after Labor Day..."

Garrison fumbled in his safari jacket and pulled out a pen and pad. "Would you start again, please?"

"Eight. No kimchee. Nine. No mayonnaise. It might be simpler to just give you the book."

"What book?" Krystal said.

"THE BOOK! Go get it."

Krystal went inside and turned on the lights. Two bookshelves met at one of the six corners. With no internet, Krystal had looked at all the titles. She pulled what she wanted and presented it to Garrison.

"*Random Acts of Badness* by Donnie Bonaduce?"

"It is our alpha and omega."

Gary placed seared panther steaks on a platter. They weren't so much steaks. More like strips. They sat at the picnic table and passed the shine. Gary dropped two panther strips on Garrison's paper plate. Delilah put her hands together and bowed her head.

"Great panther who lives in the sky, look after your people the Calusa, and imbue us with your strength and courage."

"And thank you," Gary added. "Thank you for ending the abomination that was *The Curse of Oak Island*."

"Excuse me," Garrison said. "Didn't you just tell me the panther had been terrorizing the tribe?"

"That was before we killed it. Look here. Do you intend to take this seriously, or do I have to put a curse on you?"

Garrison blanched. "Believe me, I'm taking this very seriously. I think there might be potential in exploring the Calusa for the History Channel. We would like to hear more about your history and customs."

Delilah slammed her Bowie knife into the table so hard it quivered. "Not one word," she hissed.

Garrison shrank. "Of course. Of course not."

Delilah pointed at his plate. "Try the panther."

Gingerly, Garrison sawed off a portion and put it in his mouth. He chewed gamely. He chewed and he chewed. He looked like a snake swallowing an apple. "Delicious," he croaked.

Delilah shoved a Mason jar across the table. "Try the shine."

Garrison looked around fearfully, picked it up and sipped. He hacked, sputtering. "Delicious," he croaked.

"Say, Garrison!" Gary said, "I might be able to help ya with your invasive species. I bagged the largest python in Florida history, you know."

"Yes, I've been thinking of devoting a segment to you."

"I got my own show. I already got the royals booked."

"What royals?"

"The Duke and Duchess of Ducats."

"Seriously?"

"Oh, hell yeah! We got our trailer from them. He used to be my renter 'til they went all Hollywood. Now the Duchess gonna play *Captain Megastar*."

"Really, I'd prefer to concentrate on invasive species."

Gary dropped a panther chop on Garrison's plate. "You wanna talk invasive? Used to have an iguana restaurant. The Lizard Lounge. We served nothing but invasive species. Nutria, cassowary, you name it."

Garrison stared at his plate. "What's a cassowary?"

"Giant wingless bird from Australia! My gal Krystal fought Cassowary last year, only it was a bush woman who took the name, but she was a bitch on wheels; ain't that right, girl?"

"Sure was," Krystal said with her mouth full. "I can still smell her pomade."

"Now she's fighting Javelina."

Delilah looked up. "You don't like the panther?"

Garrison looked down. He hiccoughed. His gorge rose.

He ran from the picnic table into the woods and upchucked.

Delilah waved her knife. “The interloper has rejected the food of the gods! He must become the food of the gods!”

She pointed her knife at the jungle. “What are you waiting for?”

Gary looked up. “You’re kidding, right?”

Delilah smiled. “I think he’ll keep his mouth shut.”

“I was gonna tell him about the giant Mekong catfish.”

“Shut up about the stupid catfish!” Krystal snapped.

Delilah looked at her. “What catfish?”

“This fool thinks he talks to a giant catfish every night.”

“Leotis ain’t been wrong yet!”

“You talk to a giant catfish?”

“Yeah. And he told me I would be visited by three harbingers: a bat, a rabbit, and a turtle. I already done checked the first two off my list. What do you got to say to that, little lady?”

Krystal looked away in disgust. “You moron.”

Gary appealed to Delilah. “Well how ‘bout it, witchee woman? Let’s do a seance and find out who’s telling the truth!”

“All right. Let’s go to the table.”

Krystal and Gary followed Delilah inside where she sat at the round maple table, inlaid with mother of pearl, bones and shark teeth in a pentagram. They pulled up rickety wood chairs. It was dark now. Delilah turned off the lights and lit five candles at the corners of the pentagram.

Delilah retrieved the panther head and set it in the center of the table, buzzing with flies.

"Seriously?" Krystal said.

"Join hands."

As they held each other's hands, Delilah spoke to the buzzing skull in a low voice and strange tongue. She lifted her head, eyes shut, and ululated at the darkened skylights.

She bowed her head and muttered. Her head snapped up, eyes fixed on Gary.

"Two of the harbingers have already contacted you. Tell me about them."

"Well you know about that danged rabbit. His name's Rodell Grosz. He told me to look in the backpack and that's where I found the comic."

"What backpack?"

Gary told her about the parachutist.

Delilah turned the color of milk chocolate. "Was his name Immanuel Elvarez?"

"Yeah. Why?"

"It is foretold in the ancient prophecies. *He* is the harbinger. You can expect a visit from the Bolivarians."

17 | ENORMITY

Too stoned and drunk to drive, Gary slept on a futon on the floor while Krystal slept on the sofa. He woke to a rooster standing on his chest crowing in his face. Gary swept it away.

Krystal sat up on the sofa. "What was that?"

Gary pointed at the rooster. "How'd that get in here?"

Krystal pointed up. One of the skylights was propped open.

"So, this fucking rooster flies up on the roof to come down here and scream in my face?!"

Delilah appeared over the rail of her loft clutching a quilt. "Oh, that's just Rufus. Don't mind him."

"I wouldn't mind if he didn't stand on my chest and scream in my face!"

"Girl, I'll whip up some scrambled eggs and sausage and then we hit the trail!"

Gary hung around for breakfast, got in his truck and booked. The events of last night seemed like a hallucination.

He was in enough trouble without being charged with the Endangered Species Act. He didn't think Garrison would spill the beans, but you never knew. Delilah could always pull that First Peoples' card. Made Gary think about the casino and trying his luck. There was the Seminole Brighton, the Seminole Hard Rock, and the Miccosukee down in Miami. Gary knew his way around a deck of cards. He played Texas Hold 'em and five card stud. He'd won hundreds of dollars off Floyd and some others over the years, but he was no card shark.

He'd ask Leotis.

Gary wound through dense vegetation for twenty minutes before the road straightened out between saw grass, cattails, and low mangrove on either side, flat as a cookie sheet, ending hundreds of yards away in splurge of green furze. The sky was blue with heavy clouds gathering in the east. It was hurricane season. Muriel was gathering her skirts down near the Bahamas. Gary had to put on the house suspenders. He'd do it as soon as he got home. He'd call Floyd. An egret erupted from the gorse.

Gary twisted the knob until he found Hank Williams Jr. singing "*A Country Boy Can Survive*". Hank really hit those bass notes. The whole truck shook. The ground rumbled. The road disappeared beneath the front tires and the truck dove headfirst into a sinkhole. Gary slid toward the center of the earth, watching in amazement as rocks, sand, bones, and loam crumbled with him. The truck stopped twenty feet down, front bumper jammed in the sediment. He turned off the engine. He barely had room to climb out through the window.

He stood on the cab. No way was he going to scramble out of this thing. He'd have to rig a grappling hook and use rope from the toolbox. Sinkholes were common. Four years ago, one opened up at the intersection of 4th and Wooster in Turpentine and it took the city two weeks to fill it in and pave it over.

It was dark in the hole. Gary slithered back into the truck and retrieved his magnum and a flashlight from the glove compartment. He crawled out and shined it on the earthen wall. He plucked a shark tooth from the mud. It was four inches long. He put it in his pocket. People paid big money for shark teeth. He searched the walls more carefully, pocketing four teeth.

When he worked his way round to the back, something gleamed white in the flashlight beam. Gary inspected more closely. A massive jawbone.

"Lord O' Mighty," Gary said, "I found a dinosaur."

He cleared densely packed sand and loam from the sides with his hands, revealing a foot and a half of fearsome bone. The head had to be five feet. Who knew how long it lay concealed beneath the surface? A single tooth was six inches long. He rocked it back and forth with both hands until it popped loose. He stuck it in his hip pocket.

Gary took pictures with his phone. Nobody used the road but Delilah and the occasional wanderer like Garrison Gland. Gary had to get out of there, return to civilization, and conceal his find. It lay on Seminole tribal land! He might have to cut Delilah in on the deal! But first he had to get out. The truck bed was filled with sand and rubble. Gary laboriously cleared it away with his hands until he could unlock the metal toolbox. Inside he kept fifty feet of good hemp, a spade, crowbar, pick, hammer, screwdrivers, clamps, duct tape, WD40, vise grips, Gorilla Glue and two boxes of ammo.

Now he needed a grappling hook. He tied one end of the rope around the crowbar, which ended in a big hook. He stood on the cab, but when he tried to whirl the crowbar to get up some speed, it kept hitting the walls or banged into the truck.

He underhanded the crowbar which arced over the edge and fell back in. He arced it to the side. If only he could get it far enough to hit the ditch, it would latch onto some mangrove roots. An hour later, he burrowed back into the cab, found a half full bottle of water and glugged. If someone didn't come along soon, he would be stuck there for hours. He leaned on the horn until the battery started to wane. There was a rancid pack of beef jerky in the glove compartment.

He returned to hurling the crowbar until finally, it held firm. Wearing leather gloves, Gary pulled himself up and out, emerging from the sinkhole like a mole man, covered with sweat and grime. Sitting on the ground cross-legged with a pack of Oreos in his lap was the victim of the alien abduction, a short man with a big nose and thick glasses, still wearing suit pants and a filthy white shirt. Gary collapsed in the dirt. Mosquitoes zeroed in. The man nibbled an Oreo.

"Didn't you hear me honking my horn?"

"Aren't you the man who passed me when I was begging for help by the side of the road?"

A wave of shame washed over Gary. "Yeah, you got me. All I can say, I had enough of this alien shit. I don't want to hear about it. You been hanging out here since we passed you yesterday?"

"Living off berries and saw palmetto trunks."

"Where'dja get those cookies?"

"Found 'em. Like they fell from an airplane or something. They're all broken up. Want some?"

Gary held out his hand. The man passed the Oreos.

"Gary Duba."

"Bruce. Dave Bruce."

"Tell me about the aliens."

"They're eight feet tall with four arms and tusks."

"You're describing Green Martians."

"Is that what they are? Have you been abducted?"

"No, numb nuts. You're describing the Martians from *John Carter of Mars.* I had all the comics."

Bruce deflated, tented his hands and looked down. "I wasn't abducted. I was just practicing."

"For what?"

"The Ferd Ludlow Show."

Gary laughed. "What's the big deal?"

"Ferd told me I couldn't come back unless I came up with some new material."

"Are you telling me the Ferd Ludlow Show is faked?"

"It's all lies."

Gary's head swam. "I can't..."

"What happened to you?"

"Sinkhole."

Bruce went to the hole and looked down. "Cor, that is wedged in there. Gonna take a construction crane to get it out."

"I ain't got jack shit."

"Come on. I'll give you a ride."

18 | SUCH SWEET SORROW

As they rolled down the gravel road in Bruce's Nissan Leaf, Bruce punched the CD player, the Taylor Swift warbling "You Belong To Me".

"Now that's country," Bruce declared.

"That ain't country."

"Excuse me, how is that not country? Number four on Hot Country Songs!"

"She's about as country as *crepes suzettes*! All she sings about are her ex-boyfriends!"

"That's country!"

"None of her ex-boyfriends are country! What does a Brit even know about country? Now Carrie Underwood, she's country. Miranda Lambert! Country!"

"Miranda Lambert?"

"Country."

"I piss on Miranda Lambert!"

"Fuck you!"

The car slid to a halt. "Get out."

"What?"

"You heard me! I offer you a ride into town and this is how you repay me?"

Feeling a storm surge in his gut, Gary threw the door open and got out. The Leaf sprayed gravel as it fishtailed down the road. Gary pulled out his phone. He might as well have been on the moon. He fingered his gun. No telling what might come out of the swamp. He would have told Garrison about the hippos if he'd hung around.

His finances looked like the aftermath of a tidal wave, wreckage and debris as far as the eye could see. The IRS was on his ass for seven hundred and fifty thou. They'd shut off the cable. The only reason the electricity was still on was because the Royal Couple had paid a year in advance. Onward he trudged, lonely and put-upon. He watched an alligator cross the road. For a split second, its head disappeared into the grass on the left while its tail remained hidden in the grass on the right. All that showed was a four-legged green cylinder.

Whooping, Gary sprinted and leaped, clearing it by two feet. Onward he trudged. The Ford was totaled. They had no health insurance. It was six weeks until Javelina. Then he remembered the *Detective Comic*! But where to sell? He needed top dollar. Billy Bob was out. The comic shops were out. Those poor bastards were lucky to stay in business. That left eBay, certain auction sites, and nostomania.com. eBay was rife with Chads and Karens waiting, nay, eager to renege on a deal, demand their money back, bitch about the quality and delivery time, and call you a scumbag.

He could borrow Rodell's rabbit suit and hold up a liquor store.

Then he remembered the joint in his pocket. He pulled it out. It was laced with acid. Floyd gave it to him.

Hands on hips, Gary surveyed the lush landscape, nothing but swamp, saw grass, mangrove and cyprus far as the eye could see. A crane stood on white leg like a piece of origami. Dragonflies buzzed the swamp. Gary lit the doobie. Smoke hung in the air as mosquitoes circled. He grabbed his hat and swung it nunchuk style.

"Yeah! Hai!" He morphed into a low karate stance and struck the air. "Strike first! Strike hard!"

He got dizzy and spiraled down to the road, sitting on a thorn and rising like a Trident missile.

"Whoop!" he whooped. He trucked down the road R. Crumb style, feet in front, leaning back. He fell on his ass. Godzilla rose above the trees to east, towering eight hundred feet above the tree line.

Gary plucked two pussy willows from the marshes and held them up in a cross. "NOT TODAY, GODZILLA!"

He was sweating like a pig. He had an urge to throw himself in the swamp. With his luck, water moccasins, gators, python and leeches would latch onto his body.

The world's worst ear worm played in his head. It had no beat. The melody was ugly, like bad stripper music. It crawled around smashing into things like an armored caterpillar. He tried to summon other, better ear worms but nothing would come. He slapped himself. Woah. Fucking Godzilla. Couldn't take a hint. Gary gathered rocks and hurled them at the monster, taunting him from beyond the fringe.

"GET OUTTA HERE! WE DON'T NEED YOUR KIND!"

Godzilla looked hurt. Turning away, Godzilla wiped a tear from its eye. Godzilla thrunched off into the swamp leaving silo-sized footprints.

Now Gary felt bad. He hadn't meant to hurt Godzilla's feelings. On he walked, reading signs and portents in the gravel, the saw grass, the ripples. It seemed as if he'd been walking all his life. Clouds began to gather.

"Fucking Muriel, man," he muttered. "What did I ever do to her?"

The turgid clouds rolled toward him in slo-mo. He came to a squiggle in the road. The Army Corps of Engineers who'd built the road during World War II, had done their best to lay a straight line, but sinkholes or Indian mounds forced some deviation. Here, the road circled a coral mound rising six feet above the water, topped with a dense crown of cypress and coconut palms. Gary followed the rutted gravel clockwise. He had just reached nine when he heard soft bellowing. Snap! Karate stance!

"Gary," lowed at him from a dense stand of cypress and pond apple.

"Is that you, Godzilla?" Although he was alone, Gary spoke softly, fearful of offending the ancient spirits.

The grass parted, tips of white horns appeared, followed

by Tallywhacker, bold and black as a steer can be. "Gary, it's your friend Tallywhacker. They're after me, Gary."

"Who's after you?"

"The aliens. The ones I told you about. I've said too much! They're planning to obliterate the Earth."

"Why?"

"The broadcasts! They warned you about the broadcasts! You promised to stop showing episodes of *The Curse of Oak Island*! But it's still happening! And *What's Your Problem?* It's driving them mad!"

"I'm only one man, Tallywhacker. I can only do so much."

"You have three million followers, man! Get on the horn! Warn them! Send them into the streets! Arm them with pitchforks and torches and have them march on NBC, ABC, CBS and all the rest!"

Tallywhacker hunched. He looked fearful. "It's too late for me, my friend. They're coming. Save yourself! Hide!"

The air hummed. The hairs on the back of Gary's neck stood up. His eardrums throbbed. He bolted into the thicket on top of the cone and lay among the weeds, enduring mosquito bites, saw grass cuts, and army ants crawling up his crotch.

The humming grew. The lowering clouds parted. A glowing saucer descended, hovering over the cowering bull as a giant iris opened in its belly emitting a golden glow. The tube of light surrounded the great bull who rose slowly into the air until its hooves disappeared and the iris snapped shut. The saucer tilted and spun into the sky with a cartoon whoosh, leaving a cartoon after image.

19 | THAT AIN'T COUNTRY

The clouds parted. It was a beautiful day with the sun beating down as Gary resumed his trek. Ahead, shimmering in the heat like a mirage, lay David Bruce's Leaf, hood open. David Bruce leaned against the back of his car, watching Gary through dark sunglasses.

"Did you see it?" Gary said.

"See what?"

"The saucer! It came out of the clouds and snatched up Tallywhacker!"

"Who's Tallywhacker?"

"A robot bull. He was invaded by alien multiple personalities. Then he took over the Church of Necroeconomics. Then he ran for governor. Therapy can't help everyone. I fear he was eating locoweed. Now he's a victim of alien abduction."

"You think that's funny?"

"That's the God's honest truth."

"You think because I 'fessed up and told you the truth,

you're gonna hold that over my head?"

"Dude, I don't even know you!"

"Let me see your eyes."

Bruce peered at Gary's pinpoint pupils.

"You're tripping."

"I smoked a little reefer soaked in acid. Want some?" Gary reached in his pocket and took out the two-inch doobie. They lit up. Bruce looked around.

"Christ we're vulnerable here."

"Let's get moving."

"And abandon my car?"

"Outta juice?"

"Obviously."

"Can't be more than ten miles to Highway Eighty."

"Yeah okay."

Bruce rummaged around in the Leaf's back seat and handed Gary a bottled water. Gary drained it. They walked side by side in silence.

Bruce put his fingers to his face and flung them away. "Swooosh!"

"This is snake country."

"Snake country. Don't talk to me about snake country."

"What do you know about snake country?"

"I know we're surrounded by water moccasins and Burmese pythons!"

"I caught the largest python in Florida history."

"Bullshit."

"It's a fact, Jack. You can look it up. Gary Duba. Largest

python in Florida History. I won a hundred grand."

"What happened to the money?"

"I spent it."

"Bullshit."

"It's true. I cut its head off with a samurai sword, then I hadda duct tape it back on to claim the reward. What do you do for a living?"

"I'm an insurance adjuster."

"Bullshit!"

"Why would you doubt me?"

"'Cuz you don't got the good sense God gave a green apple!"

"Least my truck isn't down a hole!"

They marched.

"Sorry I bad-mouthed Taylor Swift."

"She's not for every taste."

"Me, I like the classics. Old Hank, Merle, Tammy, Loretta, and Roger McGuinn."

"Who?"

"Roger McGuinn! The Byrds! Hey Mr. Tambourine Man!"

"That's Dylan."

"Yeah, but the Byrds hit it out of the park and that's the version that's remembered."

"I never even heard of the Byrds."

"You're joshing."

"Fuck if I am."

Gary stopped. "Just go on then. Go on. I don't want to have a thing to do with you."

"Fine."

Gary crossed his arms and watched as Bruce dwindled in the distance. When the fake abductee was a half mile ahead, Gary resumed his march.

Twenty minutes later he reached Eighty. Bruce stood on the north side, thumbing west. Gary stood on the south side thumbing east. Bruce crossed the road, stood a hundred feet to the west and stuck out his thumb.

"Hey! I was here first!"

"Sod off! I can go any way I want!"

Gary grimly marched up the highway, shoved Bruce into the road and continued on until he was further east. He stuck out his thumb. Bruce rushed him, butted him in the gut and put Gary on his back. They wrestled in the drainage ditch, scraping their skin on discarded cans and bottles. A snake slithered away in disgust. Gary grabbed an empty beer bottle and bounced it off Bruce's skull. Bruce reached for Gary's testicles. A Hendry County cruiser pulled to the shoulder with a whoop and a huge man wearing a Smoky hat got out.

Gary and Bruce stopped fighting. The Smoky looked down on them like King Kong. A badge on his chest said Stallings. "What's going on?"

"Nothing, officer. Just a friendly dispute."

"Let's see some identification."

Bruce produced his wallet. He forked over his license and a business card. "For all your insurance needs."

Gary produced his driver's license. Stallings turned toward his cruiser. "You boys stay right here."

"Shit," Bruce said. "I gotta pick up my bird at six."

"What bird?"

"This bird I've been seeing since my wife ran off."

"She ran off?"

"Cunt run off with a liquor wholesaler."

"Now that's country!"

They bopped fists. A produce truck full of Mexicans passed heading east. A boy in a Renk seed cap stuck out his tongue and drew his finger across his throat.

The sun beat down. Mosquitoes buzzed. Stallings trudged down the shoulder to them.

"Mr. Duba, we have a complaint that you killed a Florida panther."

"That's bullshit, officer! I know who made that complaint. Did you actually meet that motherfucker? He makes Randy Quaid look rational!"

"Mr. Duba, I'm aware of your contributions to the community and I think I speak for all law enforcement in thanking you for apprehending Plastic Surgeon to the Stars and serial killer Dr. Vanderlay Mukerjee. I'm inclined to give you the benefit of the doubt. What the hell are you two doing out here anyway?"

"My truck sank, and his Leaf croaked."

"All right. I'm going to give you a ride into town. God, you stink. You're covered with garbage, stale beer, blood and Christ knows what else. First let me spread some newspaper over the back seat. Then I'll call you boys over. I'll give you a ride into Turpentine and you can call whomever to come get you. Now, Mr. Duba, we are required by law to inform any possible violations of the Endangered Species Act to the Department of Natural Resources, so you can expect a call from them one of these days. You were previously charged with killing a whooping crane."

"I was aimin' at the gator! I was trying to save its life!"

"All I'm saying, where there's smoke, there's fire. You boys wait here."

The trooper returned to his ride, opened the shotgun door, took out a copy of the *Miami Herald*, spread it around the rear seat and motioned them over.

Bruce got in the left side. Gary got in the right. Bruce pointed. "There's something stuck to your bum."

Gary pulled an eight and a half by eleven pale blue sheet from the seat of his jeans.

MULLET CONTEST
PALMETTO BUG EATING CONTEST
MONSTER TRUCKS
OVER $50,000 IN PRIZES
HENDRY COUNTY FAIR
THIS WEEKEND

20 | FORTUNE FAVORS THE BRAVE

It was five o'clock by the time Stallings dropped Gary off on Weldon Way, three miles from his home. Gary set out. He was hungry, thirsty, and covered with filth. As he approached the Wokenoki Trailer Park, a feral hog poked its snout out of the bushes.

"Don't even start," Gary snarled. The hog withdrew.

A rental Ford sat in Gary's yard, a middle-aged man with a Stalin mustache, wearing neatly creased khakis and a matching button-down shirt sat in a chair on the deck. He rose as Gary approached.

"Mr. Duba?"

"Yeah."

The man stepped down into the yard and offered his hand. "Onyx Lorenzoni, Venezuelan Cultural Affairs Commissioner. We love your show. You have many followers in Venezuela. The President is a big fan!"

They shook. "We'd love to have him on the show, Onyx!

What's his name?"

"Elfuncio Quetzacoatl. He is an enthusiastic outdoors man and hunter. He greatly admires your achievements. The python, the massive puerco..."

Gary went up the steps. "Can you hang while I take a shower? I smell like a drainage dish."

Lorenzoni grinned and grimaced. "Of course."

"Can I getcha a beer or something?"

"But of course."

Gary went inside, grabbed a bottled Dixie, gave it to the commissioner and took a shower. He put on fresh blue jeans and a Yosemite Sam shirt, grabbed a beer and went back out.

"What's up?"

Lorenzoni gazed at the dense undergrowth. "Have you seen any skydivers or parachutists around here?"

"No. Why would I?"

"From time to time the Venezuelan special forces conduct clandestine training exercises around here and we are missing a man. Several days ago, we tracked him to this peninsula but then his transmitter went silent. His name is Immanuel Elvarez. He is a highly decorated soldier with a wife and two small children in Caracas. They are very concerned. El Presidente himself sent me here to search for him."

Lorenzoni showed Gary a picture on his phone. "Have you seen him?"

"Nope, sorry. We don't get a lot of skydivers around here. This here's private property, you know."

"Yes. I understand. The wind blew him off target. Is it

possible he landed somewhere on the property and has not yet been discovered?"

"Do you mean like he pancaked?"

"Yes, that is what I mean."

"Well, I dunno. If he came down in the swamp, the gators may have got him. Or the hogs. Out here by the swamp, fresh meat don't last long."

"Would it be possible to search the property? To provide closure for his family."

Gary racked his brain. Had they left anything behind? The parachute? A boot? He felt bad about Elvarez's family, if there was a family. Lorenzoni might just be throwing smoke. He knew what the Venezuelan wanted. He wanted the comic and the blow. But why would they send a single agent in a night jump carrying, maybe, a couple keys of blow and an old comic?

"Sure. Look out for water moccasins, gators, feral hogs, and pythons."

"I have a pistola in the car."

"Don't shoot no whooping cranes or panthers."

"I'll be careful. Will you be here when I get back?"

"Most likely. Stop by and tell me what you found."

Gary watched Lorenzoni open the trunk of his rental, remove a holster and strap it to his belt. He put on a wide-brimmed hat, slipped into a backpack, and headed into the brush. Gary called Floyd.

"Floyd, my truck's stuck twenty feet down a sinkhole in Big Cypress. Gonna need a construction crane to get 'er out."

"What do you want me to do about it?"

"Thought you might know someone."

"Ax Habib. Chris Tottenham is one of his clients."

"Who dat?"

"Big developer. He's in hot water for destroying habitat reserved for the lower keys marsh rabbit."

"Marsh rabbit?"

"That's right."

"Can you come over and give me a lift into town?"

"I'm on a job here, hoss. I'll call you when I'm done."

Gary had to get the comic out of the house. He had to bring in some bucks to salvage his truck and his reputation. He called Habib. Brenda answered.

"Habib's in court, Gary. I'll tell him you called."

He called Pincus.

"Pincus, can you help me sell *Detective Comics #27*? It's worth a cool mil! I'll give you fifteen per cent."

"Let me look that up and get back to you, Mr. Duba."

Lorenzoni had been gone forty-five minutes. Gary decided to look for him. He took his magnum in case he encountered feral hogs or another panther. He owned five acres, left to him by his father, encompassing swamp inlets and dense sub-tropical growth including saw grass, mangrove, cypress, plum apple trees, and cattails.

He doused himself with Off, put on his Dolphins cap and waffle stompers, and headed into the brush, following a narrow game trail pioneered by feral hogs. He came to the spot where they found the body. It had rained since then, and the hogs held an orgy. The site was unrecognizable. A flicker of movement in the swamp to his left. Picking his way carefully among the saw grass, Gary came to the brackish water where an eighteen-foot python was swallowing Lorenzoni, with a water moccasin attached to his calf. Lorenzoni was a goner, up to his waist headfirst. Soon his pockets would disappear. Gary pulled his knife, waded into the water, and cut off the Venezuelan's holster, cut the pockets and pulled out his wallet and keys.

The python didn't notice.

Gary slapped the holster on his belt, returned to the clearing and unlocked the rental. Lorenzoni's passport was in the glove compartment. In the trunk were five kilos of cocaine and a copy of *Zap Comix #0*.

Gary stashed the comic in the house, cleaned the vehicle of any personal items, drove five miles on rutted hunting trails to a place where the swamp lay over a sink hole, put the vehicle in neutral, and pushed it into the water. Glub.

By the time he got home, his clothes were soaked.

21 | PENNIES FROM HEAVEN

Pincus called. "Gary, if you can overnight your comic to nostomania.com in Madison, Wisconsin, they can guarantee eight hundred thousand dollars. Do not use the Post Office. Use Fed Ex and make sure you insure it."

"Thanks, Pincus! I won't forget!"

"You don't have to pay me, Mr. Duba."

"I will soon's as I get some cash."

Gary showered, changed, retrieved the sacred comic from the attic and stopped. How was he going to get to FedEx? He called Floyd.

"What?"

"You still gassing?"

"Belmont Holistic Pest Control. All-natural ingredients that have no harmful effect on the environment."

"Listen. I need a ride to FedEx. Can you help me out?"

"Man, I'm beat. I've been wearing a hazmat suit all day."

"What happened to the all-natural ingredients?"

"Some of those ingredients are highly toxic! Arsenic's one of your basic elements! You can look it up."

"Come on, man. Do this for me and I'll give you a nice Taurus G3. It's clean." Gary drew the pistol and sniffed. Clean.

"What size?"

Gary stared down the muzzle. "Looks like a nine."

"Shit. Those only cost three hundred bucks."

"It's clean. No registration."

"Where'dja get it?"

"I'll tell ya when I see ya."

Gary heard Floyd thinking over the phone.

"Okay. I'll be there in a half hour."

"Great. You can buy me dinner."

Gary went in the bathroom and admired his pompadour. He stood a good chance of winning the mullet contest. Of course, there were a lot of mullets in Hendry, and some were formidable. Gary brushed his hair back, added a touch of Krystal's seibella oil, and brushed it to a lustrous glow. He turned sideways, hands on hips, admiring the way the back perked up like a NASCAR spoiler. He drew his palms back across his shaved sides. Yassir. He was the human equivalent of a Dodge Challenger.

However, it was the palmetto bug eating contest that intrigued him. He'd eaten bugs before. He'd won twenty bucks in high school eating a palmetto bug. It wasn't so bad. Of course, he was plastered and flying. He'd starve himself the day before. He'd bring his own sauce.

He filled a backpack. Binoculars, clean Tee-shirt, clean socks, knife, leather gloves.

A car horn sounded. Floyd was waiting in his shiny red Viper. Gary flew down the steps clutching his backpack. Gary put his hand on the car sill and leaped into the passenger seat, smashing his nuts on the belt buckle.

"Ouch! Fuck!"

"Careful! I just picked it up last week!"

"Bug biz be good!"

"Bug biz be boomin'. Let me see the Taurus."

Gary opened the backpack between his feet and pulled out the Taurus in pancake holster. Floyd pulled it out and cleared the chamber. The discarded cartridge struck Gary on the temple.

"Ow!"

Floyd dropped the magazine, jammed it back in, took a two-handed grip and swept the perimeter.

"Wha'd I say? It's a clean piece."

"Okay."

"I got some blow for ya too. I'm afraid to give it all to you at once 'cuz you know how you get."

"How much?"

"I'll give you a key."

"Holy shit. I know a dude who'll buy that."

"Will he buy five?"

"Let's go."

Floyd put the Viper in gear, revved, popped the clutch, and executed a stationary one eighty, spraying gravel and mud everywhere. They roared down Weldon Way sending turkey buzzards flapping. The Viper rumbled over roadkill like a Tommy Lee solo. They swooshed by the Wokenoki Trailer Park. They hit the highway and headed into town. The Fed Ex was on the west side in a strip mall with a liquor store, a shoe store, a coin-op laundry and a free-standing Chipotle.

"What's so important you got to overnight it?"

"I'll show ya when you stop."

Floyd pulled into the lot, parking at an angle across two spaces. Gary unwound a legal binder and withdrew a stiff plastic rectangle. Floyd gazed at the image of the primitive Batman swooping across the rooftops.

"I don't get it."

"Dude! That's the first appearance of the bat guy! It's worth a cool mil!"

"It's worth a mil and I'm buying you dinner?"

"Who bought your van?"

"Whaddaya gonna do with it?"

"Sending it to some dude in Wisconsin who can get eight hundred thou for it."

"I thought you said it was worth a mil."

"I need money now."

"I getcha."

Gary went inside, had them package it in a big box, insured it for a hundred thou.

"Sorry," said the young man with dishwater hair, a pale yellow shirt and a green tie. "That's as high as we can go."

"Fuck it. I need cash in hand. Let 'er rip!"

Gary used Lorenzoni's money. When he came out, Floyd was in the liquor store. He came out toting a cardboard box loaded with beer and bourbon. It barely fit in the Viper's trunk.

"Hey, let's go to that Qdoba."

They ordered beef burritos and sat outside in the paved courtyard.

Floyd sawed up his burrito. "How come you're suckin' air?"

"Man, the IRS is on my ass for seven hundred and fifty thou! I don't know where they get that, but Habib says I gotta pay up. The show was on hiatus 'cuz of the crud, but we're getting back together. The Duke and Duchess of Ducats are gonna be on."

"Fuck happened to your truck?"

"Sinkhole. Gonna need a crane to get 'er out. I discovered a new dinosaur."

"Huh?"

Gary reached in his pants pocket and pulled out the tooth. Floyd whistled, picked it up, held it like a dagger. "Holy shit! What do you think it is?"

"It's a Dubasaurus, brother. I'm thinking of selling it to the Florida Museum of Natural History. It would have its own wing. The Duba wing."

"Well how do you know it ain't a giant shark or somethin'? Like a megalodion?"

"Have you ever seen a tooth like that?"

"Just on that one gal."

"How am I gonna get my truck out of that hole? I have to

guard the Dubasaurus. There's gonna be a rush of speculators and fast food franchises."

"You should talk to Habib. He repped Philmont Greister when that building collapsed."

"Who's Philmont Greister?"

"Developer." Floyd grimaced and tilted his hand. "Where'dja get the piece?"

"Okay. Remember I told you some dude pancaked in the trees?"

"Yeah. What's up with that?"

"Fuck if I know. He was carrying that comic in a back-pack. I think he had some blow, too, but the hogs ate it and then they got all crazy."

"Venezuelan?"

"Yeah. But that ain't where I got the gun. I get home today, and some greaser's waiting for me on my front porch. Looks like one of those South American hit squads. Says he's a Venezuelan official and he's looking for his buddy. Never mind what these assholes are doing skydiving on my land. Asks if he can look around. Sure. Half hour later, I find him half et by a python, headfirst. That's where I got the gun."

Floyd stared dumbfounded.

21 | PEACE SIGNS

It wasn't until Floyd dropped him off back at the swamp that Gary realized he had to see Habib. Gary borrowed the Duke's Raleigh ten speed and rode to the Law Offices of Habib Rodriguez. A billboard surmounted the building.

HABIB RODRIGUEZ. WE'LL GET THE JOB DONE ONE WAY OR ANOTHER. YOU DON'T PAY A DIME UNLESS WE COLLECT. YOUR FIRST CONSULTATION IS FREE.

Gary brought the bike in with him. Two other clients waited patiently on the vacuum-formed hard plastic chairs, leafing through dog-eared copies of *The American Lawyer, Justice Weekly, Guns & Ammo,* and *Road & Track.* A woman of uncertain age wearing fishnet stockings, too much mascara, lipstick and a blonde wig spoke at her cell phone.

"You tell that motherfucker he'd better have that piece of shit out of my driveway by the time I get back or I'll have it towed! I will ream his ass with a piledriver. I will poke out both his eyes with a corkscrew! And be sure your little sister eats her breakfast."

The other was a black man with gray hair, wearing a worsted jacket and holding a cane between his knees. Habib's receptionist Brenda smiled when Gary entered.

"Put it behind my chair," she said.

Gary leaned the bike against the wall beneath a framed painting of alligators playing poker and took a seat. Habib came out of his office and looked to the man with the cane.

"Mr. Alphonze, come on in. Gary, I'll be with you shortly."

The woman set down her phone. "How come he gets to see you? I was here first."

"Mr. Alphonze has an appointment. You are a walk-in."

"What about this motherfucker over here? Is he a walk-in too?"

"Mr. Duba works for me."

"Listen. I got T-boned by a semi! My case is worth a million dollars. You want to see any of it, you'd better stop fuckin' around and treat me like a serious client."

"I intend to, ma'am."

Alphonze and Habib went into his office. The woman muttered and poked at her phone. Gary pulled out his phone and looked up *Zap #0.* He found a quote for a hundred and thirty thousand. Not too shabby. He picked up a copy of *People.* Actress Mona Tiefenbacher promised an epic gender reveal party for her baby. Survivor super star Hans Ludicrous described a harrowing six hours spent at the transportation department trying to renew his license.

Alphonze and Habib came out. Habib motioned Gary into his office.

"I ain't got all day!" the woman snarled.

Habib pointed to the door. "Try Anthony Legume. He's right down the street."

The woman rose, kicked over the magazine table and marched out, slamming the door behind her. Gary took a seat in Habib's office.

"Habib, my truck's down a sinkhole on the Big Cypress. I'll need a construction crane to get it out. You think maybe you could get Chris Tottenham to give me a hand?"

"Well Tottenham owes me a lot of money, but I was thinking of asking him to upgrade my beach cottage."

"Come on, man. You must have something you want me to do."

"In fact, there is a matter. I was thinking of calling you. I have a client who suspects his wife is cheating on him."

"Not another peep job!"

Habib spread his hands. "You want my help or not?"

"Who is it?"

"What I am about to tell you must be held in strict confidence."

"I ain't no snitch."

"The client's name is Waldo Wipperfurth."

"The news guy?"

"That's right. I will send you pictures of his wife, Rose Wipperfurth. Waldo thinks she's seeing a tennis pro named Harold Stanton, who works at the Cosgrove Country Club in Palm Beach."

"How soon you need it?"

"The sooner the better. I can give you Rose's and Stanton's home addresses. You'll have to follow them."

Habib reached in a drawer and removed a black box the size of a matchbox, with a magnet on one side. "This is a tracking device. I will send you the download for your phone. You will go to the club and attach this to her car. That way, you can follow her. I am also providing you with a drone. You know how to use it."

"How'm I gonna do that without a vehicle?"

Habib drummed his fingers on the table. "How did you get here?"

"Ten speed bike."

"I don't suppose..."

"No."

Habib sighed. "Can you drive a stick?"

Gary just stared at him with his mouth open.

"Okay. You can borrow Lonnie's Volkswagen."

"Who's Lonnie?"

"My boy. He's clerking for Justice Marion Starr in D.C. and doesn't use a car anymore. He says they're part of the death culture. It's at my place in Turpentine. I'll drop you off."

"Awright. Is it an old-fashioned Nazi bug, or is it one of those new-fangled blobby bugs?"

"It's a 1974 Volkswagen Beetle. I hope it starts."

"Yeah, okay. How soon do you think Tottenham can get my truck out?"

"I'll talk to him."

"Cuz down in the hole, I discovered a dinosaur." Gary reached in his pocket and tossed the tooth on Habib's desk. Habib picked it up.

"What the fuck?"

"Big, ain't it? I'm thinkin' whole new dino. Dubasaurus. Omma sell it to the Florida Museum of Natural History. They always got money for this sorta thing. Omma do a reveal party on my show when we dig the sucker out."

"Where did you find this?'"

"In the sinkhole."

"It it's on Seminole tribal land, it would rightfully belong to the Seminole."

"I found the fucking thing! How is it not mine?"

Habib sighed. "This is why you're always in hot water. You go running off half-cocked about something without knowing the facts. Even if you found this on your own property the state would likely declare it an important zoological discovery. They might compensate you for your time and efforts."

"Well, what's that worth?"

"Right now? Nothing. All you did was grab this tooth, and the state's not likely to look kindly on that. You're supposed to leave fossils intact."

"Now I'm pissed. I might just get my truck and to hell with the Dubasaurus! I risk my life to find this thing and this is how they treat me."

Habib looked at his watch. He went to the door. "Brenda,

are we through?"

Brenda looked around the empty office. "Yes, Alphonze was your last appointment."

Habib turned to Gary. "Let's go."

They got in Habib's Denali and drove east on Eighty.

"You have a better shot of picking her up at the club. She's there most afternoons taking tennis lessons."

Habib lived in Pamplemousse, a gated community. He turned on the light in his three-car garage and peeled a tarp off a lime green VW bug with yellow peace signs on the doors. He grabbed a carbon fiber case off his workbench and put it in the passenger seat. "Here is the drone. You've already downloaded the app. It's all charged up. I'm texting you pictures and data. Get in and start 'er up."

"Are you shitting me?"

"What?"

Gary pointed to the peace signs.

"You want my help or not?"

23 | WHO COULD POSSIBLY

Gary parked the bug of peace in an upscale shopping center featuring Abercrombie & Fitch, American Eagle, Banana Republic, J. Crew, Dillard's, Blue Martini and P.F. Chang's and walked the mile to the Cosgrove Country Club. He wore a yellow knit Lacoste shirt sporting an alligator, neatly creased Dockers, and Vans and looked like a caddy. He'd caddied for Tag Mooselung to get the goods on Chief Justice Wither Weatherspoon, who'd been screwing the gardener in the laundry room of his estate.

No one questioned Gary as he circumnavigated the low-slung clubhouse in his Master's Tournament cap. He spotted Rose's Lexus in the parking lot. Gary ambled over. When no one was looking, he stooped as if to tie his shoes and stuck the tracking device underneath the chassis. Standing outside the pro shop, he mingled with two caddies who were waiting for their clients.

"Howdy, boys. This is my first time at this club. How

ya doing?"

A Cuban caddie with crew cut and hairline mustache wore a knit green shirt, Eusebio stitched on the breast in red. "It's all right. Depends on who you get. Last week, guy tipped me a hundred bucks."

The other caddy, a fresh-faced black youngster in khakis and a Cosgrove Tee, said, "Marv Albertson. How ya doin'?"

They shook. Gary introduced himself as Greg Dobbs, his caddie persona. "Where the tennis courts? I'm supposed to meet my guy there."

"Who's your guy?"

"Tag Mooselung."

They directed Gary to the tennis courts, the hurricane fencing overgrown with ivy. Gary spotted Rose as she slipped her racket into a vinyl case. An attractivc brunette thirty-something in a pleated tennis skirt and knit Cosgrove shirt, she smacky-faced Harold Stanton and they headed for the clubhouse. Gary was out front when the two emerged. They walked to Rose's Lexus where they hugged and parted. Stanton returned to the clubhouse. Rose drove. It took Gary fifteen minutes to return to the parking garage, the banlon wicking sweat away. He climbed to the second level where he'd parked. Someone had left a hand-scrawled message under his wiper.

"Fuck you, hippy!"

He got in the car and turned on the tracking app. Rose headed north to Pahokee. Gary rolled down the ramps. Problem. No attendant. Everything automatic. Credit card only.

He'd already received two threatening letters from the bank. The tab was only three dollars. Gary had three dollars but no way to give it to the damned machine. A Mercedes pulled up behind him. Gary slid out through the narrow gap allowed by the gate, walked back. A middle-aged man with a comb over raised his eyebrows.

"Sir, my tab is three dollars. I have it." He held up the bucks. "It only takes credit cards. I don't have it. If I give you the three dollars, will you use your credit card? Otherwise, I'm doomed to spend the rest of my life in here breaking into vehicles and foraging for food."

"And you are?"

"Gary Duba. I'm the man who apprehended Plastic Surgeon to the Stars…"

"...and serial killer Dr. Vanderlay Mukerjee!" the man finished with enthusiasm. He put his vehicle in park, walked up to the machine and inserted his card. "It's on me."

"Thank you, sir! What's your name? I'll give you a shout out."

The man handed Gary his card. Vernon Oswald. Real Estate.

The gate lifted. Gary pushed the aging bug as he zipped north on Eighty-Eight, the flat four thrashing like a cement mixer. A car with Massachusetts plates passed him, staying even for several seconds while a woman in the passenger seat snapped a picture, gave him the peace sign, and drove on.

Rose entered Fillbach Gardens, a gated community. Gary pulled over on the shoulder a hundred yards down and watched as vehicles entered and left. A uniformed guard occupied the gatehouse. Gary pulled the bug up a rutted mud path where the dense vegetation shielded it from traffic. He stripped off the yellow Lacoste shirt and put on a Belmont Pest Control shirt. Putting the drone in his backpack he bushwhacked through the saw grass until he saw billiard-smooth greensward through a hurricane fence through the trees. A clean demarcation. The jungle stopped. The grass started. Beyond lay lavish, five thousand square foot haciendas with stucco walls and red tile roofs, grounds decorated in royal palms, jasmine, and jacaranda.

Gary walked up to the fence. The jungle poked through. Gardeners and chemicals drew the line. He heard a lawn mower in the distance. He was behind a big house with the shutters drawn and no water in the pool. Putting on his leather gloves, Gary took a running start and boosted himself up and over the wall, landing in a crouch.

The app showed that Rose's Lexus was parked at 319 Brassia Orchid Drive. Hunkered behind a hedge, Gary studied a map of Fillbach Gardens. Like most such communities, it was laid out in loops with dead end courts radiating inside and out. Three nineteen Brassia Orchid lay at the back of the development, opposite the gate. It was ninety degrees out. The only human activity Gary saw was a Latino gardener on his knees with a trowel in front of the house across the street. Gary crawled through the gardens. He sought the confluence of two transfer boxes, which provided him one hundred and eighty degrees of cover.

He pulled out the four-prop drone and the control harness. Up went the drone, circling over the house, hovering a foot above a royal palm that lined the street, looking down on the front door. Arched door, stucco pots containing succulents, red flagstone path, a burbling fountain. Around the side, the open garage revealed a mud splattered Rav4. Rose's silver Lexus was behind it. Gary zoomed around back and looked in through an upstairs window. Rose and a man passed the narrow gap dropping their clothes. Even from fifty feet away Gary could hear the bed springs squeaking. He gave it five minutes, but the man didn't appear.

His best bet was to hang by the garage and see if the man revealed himself. Gary pulled a bottled water from the bag and chugged. Had he really seen a saucer grab Tallywhacker, or had he been tripping?

Where was the turtle?

What should he have for dinner?

Maybe Habib would let him keep the Beetle until he could get new wheels. Every cent he made from the show went to his creditors. Krystal had better win that fight. At least the money would be under her own name and the IRS couldn't touch it.

A door opened. Gary focused like a laser on the image in his hands as he raised the drone above the foliage, where it wouldn't be noticed, and zoomed in. Two figures emerged inside the garage. Rose stepped into the sunlight, holding hands and smiling.

Garrison Gland stepped into the sunlight.

24 | BIZARRE BAZAAR

With a hug and a kiss, Rose got in her car, backed up and headed out. Gary waited until Garrison went back in the house and shut the door. He pulled his Belmont Holistic Pet Services cap down and knocked on the door. Garrison opened it, his smile congealing into a rictus grin.

"Gary!"

"You fucking rat! You turned me in! You violated your sacred oath!"

Garrison turned white. He held his hands up and backed away, left palm showing a scar. "I had to! I was bound by my oath as naturalist and producer for the History Channel!"

Gary leveled the finger of doom and spoke in the voice of Mephisto, a late-night shlock horror host who showed shitty movies. "You have betrayed the sacred oath. Now Delilah's gonna curse you. Your balls are gonna shrivel to the size of marbles. You're gonna break out in warts and pimples. Your navel will disappear and reappear on the back of your neck. Every time you step outside, every mosquito, alligator, python, iguana, monitor lizard and red fire ant is gonna crawl up your ass. There won't be enough left to fill a thimble. Piles! Scabbies! Rosacea!"

Garrison looked like printer paper. As Gary advanced, Garrison retreated, cringing, through the kitchen into a dining room that had been turned into an office. A computer sat on the dining room table along with notebooks, books, and a sealed terrarium holding palmetto bugs.

"What the fuck is this?" Gary demanded.

"I'm doing a show on cockroach milk. It's the next big thing."

"You ain't from around here, are ya?"

"New Jersey, originally."

"Cuz no native Floridian calls 'em cockroaches. They're palmetto bugs, get it?"

"I see."

Gary hunkered down next to the glass. He was eyeball to eyeball with a two inch brown beetle. "How do you milk 'em?"

"You extract fluid from their bellies and crystallize it."

"Well hell! It must take you a week to get up to a glass of milk!"

"We're just studying it, but if we can learn to synthesize it, it could feed millions."

Gary jabbed his finger at his open mouth and made a gagging noise. He looked at the next terrarium. "What's with the frogs?"

"Not frogs, toads. Highly venomous. Licking a toad is equivalent to ingesting thirty milligrams of lysergic acid diethylamide."

"You mean like acid?"

"Exactly."

"Well who the fuck goes around licking toads?"

"You'd be surprised."

"You sell many of these?"

"I don't sell them. They're for research."

"Are they legal?"

"Yes. Toad licking is not illegal."

Over the credenza were dozens of photos, including one with Garrison and the governor.

"You know the governor?"

"I interviewed him for an episode. The cane toad."

"What about the cane toad?"

"'Toxic, Dog-Killing Toads Are Invading Florida. Here's How To Get Rid Of Them.' They secrete a milky white substance called bufotoxin. A dog or cat can get it just by sniffing. They'll be dead in fifteen minutes. Signs of poisoning include drooling, loss of coordination, head shaking and convulsions. If these signs appear, run water through the side of the mouth for ten minutes. But don't flush it down the throat. You have to angle the hose just so."

"What the fuck?! How'd they get here?"

"Nobody knows. They come from South America and have been found as far north as Texas. We think exotic pet purveyors or reptile stores may have brought a few in and they either escaped, or their owners turned them loose."

"Can I have a couple?"

"I can't. They're test subjects."

A long, curving white tusk occupied a corner, mounted in a brass stand.

"What the fuck is that?"

Garrison mumbled something.

"It's an elephant tusk, ain't it?"

"It's perfectly legal! My father gave it to me! He was a big game hunter!"

"Your father was a big game hunter?"

Garrison begged. "Please, I'm sorry I ever said anything! It's just that as a trained naturalist I felt obligated…"

"You were on tribal land observing a sacred tribal ritual! Didn't you get the memo, Jack? Tribal land, tribal laws! Does the History Channel know that you're hoarding ivory?"

"I inherited it! It's perfectly legal!"

Glimpsing a shaggy mane in the next room, Gary marched into the library. A lion's head hung over the fireplace.

"What's that?"

"My father killed it! He was a big game hunter! I only keep it as a remembrance!"

Gary pulled out his phone and snapped a picture. He went back into the dining room and took a picture of the elephant tusk.

"Wait. Stop. You can't do this. What can I do to make it right?"

"Stop seeing Rose Wipperfurth."

"Huh?"

"You heard me."

"What does any of this have to do with Rose?"

"She's a married woman."

Garrison gawked. "Are you for real?"

"I need a thousand bucks."

"What?"

"Call it a loser's fee. Give me the thou, stop seeing Rose, and I was never here."

"I don't have that kind of cash around."

"Let's go to the bank. And one more thing. You should have me on your show."

"What?!"

"You want to talk invasive species? I caught the largest python in state history. Maybe you heard about it. They gave me a prize."

"That was you?"

"You bet your ass. I cut its head off with a samurai sword. Then I had to duct tape it back on to collect. And I'm the guy who shot the hippo on the Shangri-La golf course."

"That was you?"

"Yeah. Those hippos escaped from El Nariz's zoo. He was a big time Colombian cartel player who mysteriously disappeared last year. Someone opened all the cages. Now the hippos are breeding in the swamp. They're the most lethal animal in Africa. Soon, they'll be the most lethal animal in Florida."

"So, let me get this straight. You want me to stop seeing

Rose, a thousand bucks in cash, and to appear on my show as an expert on invasive species."

"Pretty much. What's the name of your show?"

"Bizarre Bazaar."

"Book me."

"I'll have to consult my producer. What's the angle?"

Gary pulled out the tooth. "Found this in a sinkhole. It was attached to a dinosaur skeleton."

Garrison turned it over in his hands. "Who else knows about this?"

"Me, you, my attorney, and a man who eats shit sandwiches and howls at the moon."

"Could you show me this fossil?"

"Maybe."

"Don't you have your own show?"

"Currently on hiatus."

"Why?"

"I think it was the episode where we cooked the possum."

25 | A CHANCE ENCOUNTER

Flush with cash, Gary headed home in the peace bug. He turned on the radio.

"Come to the Hendry County Fair this weekend! Governor Chickenlooper will be judging the Mullet Contest! Sign up for the palmetto bug eating contest! First prize is ten thousand dollars! Ride the Wild Mouse! Take part in the jambalaya eating contest! Vote for the best hog! Dance to the music of Nature's Toothbrush and the Independent Fact Checkers! Gates open at ten Saturday and the event will be going strong all through the night until we finally ring the bell at ten pm Sunday!"

Gary pounced the wheel. "Hot damn! I'm ready!"

He pulled into the yard at five pm, startling a pack of feral hogs who ran under the trailer. Gary went in the house, grabbed a flashlight and a BB pistol, went outside, shined the light on the hogs.

"Go on! Get out of here!"

They looked at him, gauging the possibility of taking him down. Gary pulled the slide and pinged them with BBs. Honking and snorting, they left. He went inside, took a shower, and admired his mullet in the mirror. He'd had the mullet since high school. Business in front, party in back. He brushed it, added a little hair spray, turned to admire himself in the mirror. His laptop sat on the dining room table. Nostomania: "I have found a buyer for the *Detective Comic*. He is offering eight hundred and sixty-three thousand dollars and seventy-five cents. If this is amenable, I will proceed with the sale. My cut is fifteen per cent."

Gary wrote back, "Do it!"

Nosto wrote back, "How do you want me to send you the money? Do you have a Paypal or Venmo account?"

"My Paypal account is Latergator@gmail.com."

He forwarded his video footage to Habib, along with Garrison's name and address. Habib called.

"Excellent. Exactly what we need."

"Habib, my truck's a goner. I don't even know if I can collect on the insurance. I think I may have missed a payment. Can I borrow the Love Bug for a while?"

"Go ahead. Lonnie's not using it."

"I know Gland. He showed up last year at Delilah's place while we were training. He showed up again over the weekend. He has a show on the History Channel. *Bizarre Bazaar*. Wants to do a show on the Dubasaur."

"Wait a minute. You know this guy? And he's the guy shtupping my client's wife?"

"Correctomundo."

"Well, this should be enough to break the prenup. Do what you gotta."

Hogs squealed. Gary ran out on the porch where a dozen feral hogs milled about blocking a dark blue sedan that contained two visitors. Gary grabbed his pump action from the closet, went out the back door and lay in the tall grass. The car eased through the scrum, stopped next to the Love Bug. Two men got out, swarthy with black mustaches, wearing fancy boots. The taller had ostrich skin boots. The shorter had alligator boots. Their bulky leather jackets failed to conceal the pistol bulge. Gary watched as they mounted the steps and knocked politely on the door.

An iguana stared at Gary from the branch of a cypress tree.

"I wish these fucking Venezuelans would leave me alone," he muttered.

"But what if they brought more comics?" the iguana said.

The Venezuelans circumnavigated the porch. The Venezuelans kicked in the door. The Venezuelans ransacked the trailer. It was one thing to skydive and peacefully die or get eaten by a python. It was quite another to bust in a man's door and ransack his home. Fifteen minutes later, they came out carrying Gary's computer and his Duvante Culpepper Dolphins jersey. Gary waited until they reached the car. He popped up and fired a blast over their heads. The dude dropped the computer as they whirled toward him, reaching for their guns. Gary came out of the woods leveling the shotgun between them.

“Don’t try it. Use your left hands to remove your guns. No tricks or I go for the knees, and this baby holds eight rounds. I took out the plug.”

Unnerved, the intruders carefully pulled their guns and dropped them on the ground.

“Now kick ‘em Kick ‘em good and hard.”

They kicked the guns away.

“Fuck you doing with my computer?”

Ostrich boots smiled with dazzling teeth. “We’re just opportunistic criminals. We thought this place was deserted. We’re sorry. We’ll go now.”

“You damned Venezuelans think I’m stupid?”

“What makes you think we’re Venezuelan?”

“You mean aside from the accent, swarthy complexions, and shoe brush mustache? Just a hunch.”

Ostrich boots did the talking. “Could it be because we are not the first? Could it be because you have already disposed of our countrymen who came to you with an honest proposal?”

“Honest proposal my ass! The first guy went splat in the mangroves. The second guy got et by a python. Ain’t you dudes never been in a jungle?”

Alligator boots said, “I find that hurtful. You’re just stereotyping. Have you even met any Venezuelans?”

“The second dude right before he got et.”

“He was eaten by a python, you say?”

“They were working on it when I left him.” Gary put a hand on his belt buckle. “The snake had him down to here. I should have grabbed his boots when I had the chance.

They was nice boots. Probably wouldn't fit. What size shoe you boys wear?"

Ostrich boots held his hands up in a placating manner. "Momento! Momento! This is all very much a misunderstanding! We are merely looking for our friends!"

"What were their names?"

"Immanuel Elvarez and Onyx Lorenzoni!" ostrich boots declared. "I am the Assistant Undersecretary of State to the Minister of Cultural Affairs! My companion is Secretary of Humus!"

"All right, take outcher passports and toss 'em over here. I like to know who I'm dealing with."

Ostrich scowled. "We don't got to show you our passports! Who do you think you are? Policia?"

"I'm the guy who bagged the biggest python in Florida history! That's right. I cut its head off with a samurai sword and stuck it back on with duct tape."

Gator boots looked confused. "Why did you have to tape the head back on?"

"Well, gollee! So they could measure it! How else they gonna know it's the biggest python in state history?"

"Well does that mean it was the longest, or that it weighed the most?" Gator boots said.

"The longest."

"How long was it?" Ostrich said.

"Twenny-two feet."

Ostrich threw his arm at the trees. "Look there!"

Gary whirled. The boots charged. Gary whirled back and

let them have it in the abdomen. They were running so close together, they both took a belly full.

The boots fell to the ground gasping and squinting.

"I am murdered!" Ostrich cried.

"Oh, for fuck's sake. It's just rock salt. Ya think I'd kill somebody over a pair of boots?"

The Venezuelan special forces examined their jackets and shirts. Gator lifted his shirt to expose a spattering of red dots across his gut like measles.

"Did you bring me any comics?"

The boots exchanged a furtive glance. They got to their feet.

"We have no comics. Why do you mention comics?"

"You can pick your passports up at the Hendry County Sheriff's Office in the morning. And don't come back here. I'm calling my kin right now and inside an hour this place is gonna be crawling with angry armed rednecks. This here's the swamp, bwah!"

Gary gestured with the shotgun. They cringed.

"Get outta here. Go on, git!"

Gary picked up the passports, waited until they were out of sight before going inside and surveying the damage. Everything was tossed around, a couple of glasses broken, and one of them took a dump and didn't flush. It took him an hour to clean up, put everything back in its place. He thought about booby-trapping the place but decided not. Floyd might stop by and blow his head off. He thought about talking to Leotis, but he was just too tired.

26 | HOMELESS COUPLE FOUND LIVING IN WALMART ATTIC

The next morning, Gary phoned Pincus. "Pincus, can you get me the goods on two Venezuelans who trashed my house last night?"

"What's this about, Mr. Duba?"

"These Venezuelans won't leave me alone! This last batch didn't even bring me any comics! Their names are Ignacio Fermino and Thiago Barbosa. And see what you can find out about Elfuncio Quetzacoatl. He's the president."

"Mr. Duba, I have Zoom meetings all day."

"Tomorrow's soon enough. You a comic fan?"

"Yes."

"I'll give ya the first *Spawn.* It's in near mint condition."

"I'll get back to you, Mr. Duba."

The sale went through. Nosto deposited eight hundred thousand dollars in Gary's Paypal acct. Within fifteen minutes, the IRS filed a lien and Paypal froze the account. That left *Zap #0* to last him until Saturday. He sat on his front porch with his magnum on the table and the shotgun leaning against the balcony in case any more Venezuelans showed up. He called Nosto.

"Nosto."

"Yeah, this is Gary Duba, you sold my *Detective Comic #27*."

"Mr. Duba! That was a great find. Do you have something else for me?"

"I have a bagged and boarded *Zap #0* in near mint."

"Hang on a sec. Let me look that up."

"Whoozis?"

"Tommy Jasmin."

"Izzat all you do? Sell comics?"

"No, I'm a rocket scientist. This is just a hobby."

"Har."

"Okay. Going price is a hundred thou. You want to do what we did before?"

"Yeah, except this time, don't use Paypal. Send me a check."

"Are you sure you want me to send you a check of that amount in the mail?"

"I'm sure."

"It will take a few days for those funds to clear my business account, so you might not see it until next week."

"That's fine."

Gary plucked a palmetto bug from the kitchen counter and popped it in his mouth. It tasted brackish and acidic. It scraped a little. "Alexa!" he said. "Can you eat palmetto bugs?"

There was no answer. There was no Alexa. He hopped in the Love Bug and headed into town. Gary got all his computer equipment at Walmart. The Walmart anchored a mall on the west side of town. Gary parked the Love Bug apart from the crowd next to a lamp post and hot footed into the store. He grabbed a cart and loaded up on pork rinds, mini pies, chips, curls, dogs, Red Bulls and a Burt Reynolds four-pack: *The Longest Yard*, *Sharky's Machine*, *Stick*, *Smoky and the Bandit*, and *Gator*. He hit electronics. A woman clerk with black hair tied in a ponytail approached.

"Can I help you?"

"Looking for Alexa, or one of those smart boxes that answers questions."

"You want the Amazon Dot. It does everything but take out the trash."

Gary wheeled his cart toward the fourteen checkout lanes. Only two were open, with twelve shoppers backed up at each lane, blocking the aisle. Gary went to the self-checkout area. There were six machines, everyone taken, with five people standing in line.

Gary pulled out his phone and played video slots. He was on a roll when the person behind him said, "Excuse me. You're next."

Gary rolled up on the machine and scanned Burt. The screen flashed and read, "Please rescan." He scanned it and scanned it. No dice. The one clerk on duty was in deep conversation with an elderly woman purchasing several cases of cat food and enough cloth to drape a hotel. Gary put the item back in his cart and scanned his pork rinds, mini pies, Red Bulls et al. The screen beeped and printed in red letters, UNIDENTIFIED ITEM IN LOADING ZONE. CALL ATTENDANT."

Gary looked around. The clerk and the old lady huddled over a graph chart. Other people checked out and moved on. The next station opened up. No one was waiting. Gary hustled on over. It took Burt. It took everything. The tab came to seventy-nine dollars and sixteen cents. Gary fed it one of the hundred-dollar bills Garrison had given him. It hoovered the bill like John Belushi. The screen indicated his change. No change came out. Gary looked around. The clerk and the old woman were examining pie charts. Deep in conversation. No help there.

"Come on, come on, gimme my goddamn money," Gary muttered. The machine said "processing". Five minutes passed. Gary punched the screen.

A siren wailed and the screen flashed, WARNING. WARNING. MACHINE IS UNDER ASSAULT. The clerk looked up. She pulled a whistle on a lanyard out of her bosom and blew. Red lights flashed, the metal gate to the self-scan area slammed shut, and two beefy men wearing Ajax Security uniforms zeroed in from the entrance. Gary had a fat joint in his pocket! He couldn't afford another bust! Leaping the closed gate with one hand, he ran toward the rear of the store as red lights flashed and the PA system blared, "INTRUDER! INTRUDER!"

Several clerks joined the chase. Startled shoppers backed away. He ran through the electronics department through a swinging rubber door into the warehouse. Burly shelf stockers gathered at the back entrance. A red, wheeled staircase led to an open panel in the ceiling. Gary scrambled up the ladder into the voluminous attic, criss-crossed with steel girders, three-foot ventilation pipes, catwalks and cables. It was warm in the attic, air filled with the thrum of fans.

Hubbub from below. Gary raced down a catwalk into darkness, startling a family of rhesus macaques who scrambled up the grid work and hurled feces. A flashlight pierced the darkness as the first security guard reached the top of the ladder.

“I think he’s over there.”

“No, you hear those damn monkeys. He’s over there!”

The chase was on! Four bored and eager clerks joined the Ajax guards, heading in four directions. Gary high-tailed it toward the darkest corner of the vast space. A flash of light momentarily revealed a green pop tent under the eaves, with a camp stove set up. A bearded man with a neck tat wearing a new Dolphins jersey with the price tag still attached stuck his head out.

“Get the fuck outta here. You’ll blow my cover!” the man hissed, bulbous nose lined with veins, gin blossoms blooming.

Gary stopped, stooped, and looked. Behind the bindlestiff crouched a bug-eyed woman with a shock of dirty hair. The tent reeked of chemicals and body odor. Gary got down for a better look.

"What the fuck?!"

"Listen, motherfucker," neck tat croaked. "Don't mess this up for us. Me and Giselda have been living here for two years! It's a sweet gig, see? Don't fuck it up."

Gary glimpsed a mini-fridge, stacked boxes of cereal, bags of almonds, cans of soup. Behind the tent, a packing box bulged with trash. "Are you cooking meth?"

The bindlestiff cackled, teeth like a vandalized graveyard. "We sure are! Want some?"

"How do I get outta here?"

The man pointed down an unlit corridor. "End of that catwalk, there's a ventilation grate. I took the screws out. All you gotta do is lift it off. Wait a minute." The man ducked into his tent, came out with a long, coiled nylon rope. "Use this!"

Gary grabbed the rope. "Thanks, pal!"

"Good luck!"

Behind him, the searchers spread out, calling to one another. Gary came to the end of the catwalk. Pale light shone through the grate's louvers. Gary uncoiled the rope, tied one end firmly to the catwalk rail and pulled the grate out with a screech.

"Down there!" a pursuer called.

"All units converge on northwest corner!" ordered a cop wannabe.

Gary threw the rope out the open grate and looked out. Thirty feet to the loading zone. Gripping the rope in both hands, he Batmanned down the side of the building. Hands bleeding, Gary hit the tarmac! Gary sprinted counterclockwise around the building, weaving among the Suburbans and Subarus for cover until he reached the peace bug, now surrounded with parked cars.

Gary leaped in, started the engine, and drove toward the highway, as fast as the Beetle could go.

27

Gary headed east. He phoned Pincus on the run.

"Pincus! I'm coming over."

"I'm in the middle of a project, Mr. Duba."

"Yeah, well that's what I want to talk to you about. You got an Alexa, or one of those chatty Cathy things?"

"I have an Amazon Blue Dot."

"That's what I was trying to buy when they chased me out of the store! I'll be there in twenty."

Pincus rented a modest bungalow in Pahokee with a fat grass lawn and a date palm in the front yard. Pincus' Rogue perched on the cracked concrete of his single car garage. Gary parked on the street and knocked. Pincus answered the door wearing a bathrobe and fuzzy slippers.

"Sorry the house is a mess."

"Like I give a shit."

The small living room looked out on the front lawn. A flat screen TV perched on a Goodwill table. A DVD player, game console, and stacks of DVDs sat on the lower shelves. A thrift store sofa lay against the opposite wall beneath a thrift store landscape to which someone had added a three-legged Martian invader looming over the trees. An old border collie mix lay on a blanket on the sofa, tongue lolling.

"That's Elisha."

The old dog thumped its tail.

"Would you like some coffee?"

"Man, I gotta settle my nerves. Got any vodka?"

"Sorry, Mr. Duba. I don't drink."

Gary looked around. The room smelled of Febreze. "Where's the doo-hickey?"

Pincus pointed to the hockey puck perched on the edge of the table.

"What do I say to it?"

"Just a sec, I'll turn it on. Then you just ask it whatever you want."

Pincus flipped a switch.

"Hey Blue Dot. Can a man eat cockroaches?"

A soothing female answered, "Yes, you can eat cockroaches. Contrary to popular belief, cockroaches can actually be very clean and tasty insects, especially if they are fed on fresh fruits and vegetables. They can be eaten toasted, fried, sauteed, or boiled. Madagascar Hissing Cockroaches have a taste and texture like greasy chicken."

"Mmm! Where can I get some of those hissing cockroaches?"

"Madagascar."

Gary flipped the switch.

"She's just itching to get involved in our conversations, maybe offer dating advice. No thank you."

"How's Krystal?"

"She's training for Javelina. You're coming, ain't you?"

"I'm not really a wrestling fan, Mr. Duba."

"Oh, come on. I'll leave two tickets for ya. Bring a date."

"I'm not really seeing anyone at the moment."

"You ever get your cherry popped?"

Pincus turned red.

Gary slapped him on the back. "Don'tchoo worry. Omma he'p you get that done. Look at you. What woman wouldn't want you? You're the dude who popped Hogzilla! Why you don't have women throwing themselves atchoo, I don't know. Krystal's got two girlfriends, Jen and Barb. They're hot! Hang on..."

Gary pulled out his phone, scrolled through his pictures until he found one of Jen and Barb leering from the staircase in his former home. Jen had pulled her shirt down to expose a breast. Barb cocked a leg over the banister. They were both shit-faced.

"Come on. Tell me you wouldn't like to pork 'em both."

"Mr. Duba...I haven't had good luck with women."

"You just ain't met the right woman. Don'tchoo worry about it. I'll fix you up. Time I'm done telling them about you, they'll be frantic to get in your pants."

Pincus stared at the picture.

"I'll send it to you if you like. Pick one. That's Jen higher up. Hell. Maybe you can have both."

"What are you doing here, Mr. Duba?"

"I need to find out about those fucking Venezuelans. Why do they keep coming to my house? Why do they keep bringing me comics?"

"I don't understand."

Gary flopped down on the sofa smacking it into the wall. He told Pincus about the flattened sky diver and the dude in the rental. "I shoulda checked their rental. They were probably hiding comics in the trunk. I need to know about Ignacio Fermino, Thiago Barbosa, and Elfuncio Quetzacoatl."

"Quetzacoatl is President of Venzuela. He seized power six years ago in a military coup."

"Whatever. They keep bringing me comics and coke. I don't want it around. Krystal's got a nose like Rudoph the Reindeer, and she's got a fight coming up."

"I have a Zoom meeting in fifteen minutes with a client. It will take about a half hour. If you want to hang around, I'll look into it then."

"Sounds good. I'll check my email and shit."

Gary went out the back door to the blotchy lawn, sat in a lawn chair and looked at his phone. Major Dutton wrote, "WHERE'S THE SHOW? Millions of viewers are clamoring."

Gary wrote, "I got a humdinger, Major! I'm entering the Best Mullet and the Palmetto Bug Eating Contest at the Hendry County Fair this weekend! Come on by and we'll do it live!"

Next was a letter:

"Dear Gary: When you stopped in at our mission last December, I neglected to thank you for your offer. We are deeply appreciative of any Samaritan who wishes to help the less fortunate. Had the iguana been a little fresher, we would have accepted with alacrity. Nor was I aware that you were behind the apprehension of Plastic Surgeon to the Stars and serial killer Dr. Vanderlay Mukerjee. I must admit, I cheered your subsequent dealings with the charlatans at the Church of Necroeconomics, and I credit you, at least partly, with leading to their collapse. They were a stench and an abomination to all who believe in Christ.

"In any case, I would like to invite you to worship with us sometime. We have a chapel at the mission, and you are welcome anytime. I hope to see you again. Yours in Christ, Sister Agatha Papparazzi, the Nuns of Gavarone, West Palm Beach."

Next:

I've invited you to fill Dear Friend. Please carefully read this and you will find it interesting.

In my banking department we discovered an abandoned sum of 50,000,000.00$ [Fifty Million Dollars Only) in an account that belongs to one of our Foreign customers who unfortunately lost his life with

his entire family on his way to the Airport of Heathrow.

Since we got information about his death, we have been expecting his next of kin or relatives to come over and claim his funds because we cannot release it unless somebody applies for it as Next of kin or relation/Business Partner to the deceased as indicated in our banking guidelines.

We want you to come in as the Next Of Kin, all needed cooperation to make the claims will be given to you by us. If you are interested kindly let us have the below information and I will give you more details.

Kindly send your personal details to this very email:

1. Full Name

2: Your private telephone and Fax numbers.

3. Occupations and Nationality.

4. Date of Birth

5, Present Location

6. Home Address

We are offering 40% of the total sum to you as our partner. We will discuss much in details when I receive your response. Thanks and good luck to us.

Best regards, Mr. Paul Bradley.

Gary threw his hands in the air. "My troubles are over!"

Next:

Dear Sir / Madam,

We, LLC "VGL ", are proud to introduce the list product of our End Seller JP54, Jet A1, D2, D6 Etc in our fairness and line of work of Trust. We can guarantee that we never compromised on our quality standards and services which we also have a bound relationship with our Russia End Seller who deals in fairness of Trust on delivering and

we has made its grasp on the overseas Trade market and getting excellent feedback.
We have a very reasonable price for our client and are negotiable.
We look forward working with you on short and long time bases.
GENERAL DIRECTOR:
Mr. Kruk Alexander Vladimirovich
LLC " VGL "

Kruk Alexander Vladimirovich

Gary got up and boogied, bent over, snapping his fingers. "I'm on a roll! I can hardly wait to see what happens next!"

He tapped the news app.

Homeless Couple Found Living In Walmart Attic With Hot Plate, Meth Lab, And 42" LED TV

"Being homeless has to be very difficult, especially in the colder times of the year. But not for this Turpentine couple who had been "living in the lap of luxury" above a Turpentine Walmart store. The 'homeless' man, 48-year-old Nard Wilberforce, admitted to police that he and his girlfriend 54-year-old Anastasia Guacamole, had been living above the store for over two years. What they did to the attic, baffled police and store employees."

"I don't mean to laugh, but these people really got one over on Walmart," said Lieutenant Orville Wang. "We recovered two pounds of meth they had produced on a hot plate, food, drinks, mini refrigerator, a big screen TV, surround sound system, bedroom set, hangers, clothes… I mean, if Walmart sells it, they had it. These people were living good. They even managed to splice into the satellite TV wire and ordered NFL Sunday ticket!"

Gary felt terrible. If it weren't for him, they would still be living in the lap of luxury. Gary knew he'd been neglecting his viewers. It was too bad the cops had busted the Walmart couple. They would have been perfect for his show. He was still waiting to hear from Rufus Pinkerton, who'd been arrested in Miami and claimed that the syringe found in his rectum wasn't his. But Rufus had not returned his calls from the Dade County Jail.

Pincus came out blinking like a mole, wearing baggy jeans that hung on his skinny legs like drapes and a button-down short-sleeved sports shirt with a pocket protector and a weird little ruler.

"Mr. Duba, President Quetzacoatl is an avid comic book collector. He has a complete run of *Capitan Venezuela, Memin Pinguin*, *El Hombre Nuclear*, and *Venezuela Comics*. He put them on display at the Venezuelan Institute of Art under the eye of armed guards, but nobody wants to steal them because they're not worth anything. It is alleged that during the recent coup he confiscated several private comic collections and is selling them in the United States to raise money."

"Aha! But why me?"

"You live in an electronic blank spot. It's one of the least scrutinized pieces of real estate in the state."

"Maybe you can help me draft a letter to this Quetzacoatl thanking him for the comics, but asking him to stop sending thugs."

"I'm going to have to charge you for that, Mr. Duba."

Gary pulled out his wallet and peeled off a thousand dollars. "That's for your dog."

28 | LETTER TO QUETZACOATL

Dear President Quetzacoatl: What's going on? Have we met? 'Cuz you keep sending your flunkies to look for this El Nariz dude, who I never met. Then that second dude got eaten by a python, but at least he brought me that comic book. I figure you don't mind my taking the comic book, 'cuz he was trespassing and besides which, he got et. So he won't miss it. Then those next two dudes, they didn't bring me nothing. They just ransacked my house. I woulda been within my rights to shoot them, but I'm trying to maintain good relations here between Florida and Venezuela.

You know what we really need? Ocelots. What with all the damn invasive species tearing up the state, including but not limited to python, iguana, and hippo, some of those ocelots would be welcome. Our own Florida panther is endangered, and we need flesh blood. If the ocelots would mate with the panthers, it would create a new breed which we could call pantalot, and would bring in badly needed tourist dollars.

I was happy to learn you are a comic fan. I only wish I had all the comics I collected as a kid, but my mother threw them out. Bet you heard that before. In any case, peace between our great nations and all that shit, and please use a regular airport from now on.

Yours sincerely, Gary Duba.

29 | A VALUABLE DISCOVERY

On Thursday, Gary drove back to the Big Cypress to retrieve his truck. Tottenham was already there, the massive flatbed carrying the construction crane filling the road, as a worker backed the crawler crane down the ramp. The truck was pointed south. It had been unable to turn around. Gary wondered how they would get the construction crane to the sinkhole. Gary backed up and left the Love Bug on a hummock just off the road.

A man in carpenter's pants, blue work shirt and yellow hardhat stood in the road, back to Gary, signaling to the crane operator. Gary watched as the crane inched down the ramp until it was off the truck.

"Chris Tottenham?" he said.

The hard hat turned, a broad, middle-aged face with a bulldozer chin. "Are you Gary?"

"Yes, sir. Thanks for doing this."

"My pleasure. Any friend of Habib's is a friend of mine.

We took a look at the truck and we got a man down there running straps under the chassis. It's pretty tight in that hole, and I gotta warn you in advance, your truck may not be operable. Looks like a total writet-off. Hopefully. And it's old. Can't be worth much."

"Don't matter. I got no insurance. I've half a mind to just leave it there and fill the hole in on top of it."

Tottenham and Gary backed up to give the crawler room as it turned west and rumbled into the swamp, water rising over the bottom of the track. Tottenham and Gary swung on board. They rode the rumbling beast a hundred and fifty feet south, leaving enormous ruts, until it was able to crawl back onto the raised road and confront the sinkhole.

Tottenham and Gary walked on the tread to the front and leaped off. They edged around the sinkhole to the south side and looked down, where a man in a hard hat had just finished linking enormous nylon straps together above the truck. He gave a thumb's up. An aluminum ladder lay in the bed, top end poking out.

"Come on up, Ron," Tottenham said.

The worker climbed up and joined them. Two sets of straps cradled the truck, one just behind the front axle, and the other under the bed. Tottenham led them twenty feet south and gave the signal to the crane operator. With a whir, the cables tightened. The cables quivered and with a horrendous screeching noise, the truck rose several inches, lurched upward, and was free. It looked like a child's toy that had been run over.

“Where do you want us to take it?” Tottenham said.

“Aw hell just take it to the junkyard, but lemme go through it first. I mighta left a few things.”

Ron stood at the edge of the sinkhole, hands on hips. “What the hell is that?”

Tottenham and Gary joined him. “What?” Tottenham said.

Ron pointed at a massive white jawbone jutting from the sediment, teeth like battlements. “That.”

“That’s the Dubasaur. I found it. It’s mine. And I can prove it.” Gary pulled the tooth from his pocket. “Lookie here. I dug this out last week when I was stuck.”

Tottenham held out his hand. “May I?”

Gary handed him the tooth. Tottenham felt it, turned it, looked at it. “We’re required by state law to report any prehistoric remains. You mind if I borrow this?”

“Hell yes, I mind! That’s my tooth! Why don’tcha jump down there and get your own tooth?”

“I just pulled your piece of shit truck out of a sinkhole, and this is how you repay me?”

“No, numbnutz! I repaid you by getting video of some whore leaving Garrison Gland’s house so her husband could blow up the prenup!”

“That has nothing to do with me.”

“Don’t it? The only reason you helped me is the same reason I shot that video! We both owe Habib Rodriguez money!”

The crawler crane swiveled and churned through the swamp toward the back of the flatbed, the crushed truck snugged tight.

"I've half a mind to just drop your piece of shit truck in the swamp!"

"Go ahead! I don't give a shit."

Grumbling, Tottenham stalked around the sinkhole. Gary followed, past the huge flatbed to where he'd left the Love Bug. He wouldn't put it past Tottenham to crush his ride like an insect. He got in, turned around and drove north until he came to a turn-off broad enough for the truck to pass. He tried to phone Krystal, but it was no go. A half hour later, the truck rumbled past, Tottenham flipping him the finger from the shotgun seat, his squashed truck snugged tight behind the crane. Gary returned to the sinkhole, uncoiled the rope he'd brought, tied it to the Love Bug's front bumper, and crawled down to where the massive jawbone stuck out of the sides.

"Gawddamn," Gary muttered to himself. He had to secure it before Tottenham ratted him out. He climbed out, got in the Love Bug, edged around the sinkhole, and headed south to Delilah's. He arrived around noon. No one home. Gary grabbed a bottled water, a spade and a pick from Delilah's Jeep and returned to the sinkhole. It was ninety-five degrees, and the mosquitoes were thick as a veil. The sandy soil gave easily, revealing the contours of a monstrous skull. Gary was no expert, but he'd seen *Jurassic Park.* This was like no skull in Jurassic Park. It was bigger. It was a monster.

He stopped every fifteen minutes to rest and drink. He used the spade to scrape soil from around the sides. An hour later, he came to the base of the skull. It was six feet long. Gary knew from Jurassic Park that the T Rex's skull was only five feet. The whole skeleton had to be huge.

Gary forged ahead, likening himself to the brave soldiers in *Stalag 13*, or Sylvester Stallone in *Daylight.* He came to the back of the skull. He used the spade to lever the skull away from the packed side. He wrestled the exposed jaw to work it loose. The moist earth slipped and sloped. Grabbing two eight-inch tusks, he grunted and strained, working it side to side while pulling it toward him. It broke loose and he fell on his ass.

Gary slithered out. "Oww!" He put a hand to his head. He was bleeding. The skull was too big for the Love Bug. He might be able to get it into Delilah's old Jeep pickup. It looked like a World War II truck, like something you'd see in a movie. Gary climbed out and returned to Delilah's. Krystal was taking a shower. Delilah was smoking a pipe and skinning catfish.

Krystal squealed, ran naked and leaped on Gary, who staggered, but stood. He laughed and kissed her. Maybe he could slip in a quickie after he got the skull.

"Delilah, I need to borrow your truck."

"What for?"

"I found a fossil in the sinkhole. Might be valuable."

Delilah pulled the pipe and spat. "Whatever you found belongs to the Seminole Nation. Pull up a chair. I'm cookin' catfish."

Gary blanched.

30 | CASH COW

After dinner, Delilah phoned her brother Bob who met them at the sinkhole with Arly and Mo, two tribal members. Their Dodge Ram sat on the north side of the hole. They'd brought ropes and tackle and with three people pulling on either side, they raised the monstrous skull and put it in the back of the Ram where Bob lashed it to the bed with bungee cords. It looked like a giant bird skull. Arly yanked off a six-inch tooth.

"Put that back!" Delilah snapped. "That belongs to the Seminole Nation!"

"I'm Seminole! I deserve something for volunteering and coming out here on short notice. It's only a back tooth."

Delilah held out her hand. "Hand it over unless you want your pecker to fall off."

"Why would my pecker fall off?"

Delilah's hand formed a claw and she started chanting in tongues.

Arly turned white and handed her the tooth. "All right! All right!"

"Come on back to my place and I'll give you some catfish."

Mumbling, Arly set the tooth back in its socket.

"Nothing a little super glue won't fix," Gary said.

The three Indians went back to Delilah's place where they sat around a fire passing a jug of shine. Delilah cooked more catfish. She looked over at Gary.

"What's the matter, Gary? All of a sudden you don't like my cooking?"

"Sorry, Delilah. I had a couple palmetto bugs for breakfast and I'm feeling a tad sick."

"I ain't even gonna ask."

"Hooo-WEE!" Arly exclaimed, heaving himself to his feet. "Ah gotta drain the lizard."

"Y'all gettin' shit-faced," Delilah observed. "Best you stay here tonight. I got a tent."

Krystal surveyed the guests. "They'll never be able to put it up. Look at them."

"You're right. They can just throw down on the ground. You boys got sleeping bags?"

"You bet," Bob said. He had the same Roman nose and high cheeks as his sister. "We're ready for anything."

"Ya'll coming to the fight?" Gary said.

"Wouldn't miss it," Bob said.

Arly fired three shots in the air. Everybody jumped.

"Hey shit for brains!" Delilah said. "Put that away before you hurt yourself."

Arly snapped on a flashlight. "Omma shoot me a gator!"

Delilah rolled her eyes. "Bob, talk to him."

Bob walked over to Arly and knocked him cold with one punch. He stooped, got Arly in a fireman's carry, and dumped him in the back of the truck. He returned to the fire.

"Sorry about that."

"Hey, ya'll oughtta drop by the Hendry County Fair this weekend and cheer me on. I'm in the mullet contest, and the palmetto bug eating contest."

Potato-faced Mo rolled a cigarette, licked the paper, and lit it. "A what?"

"Palmetto bug eating contest."

"Why would you even contemplate such a thing?"

"Ten thou, that's why. Ah'm in training right now."

Bob pulled out a pack of Lucky Strikes. "What kind of training?"

"Every day I eat some palmetto bugs. Each day it's a little more. I'm up to two."

"I'll pass. What's the other?"

Gary drew a hand back over his hair. "The mullet contest. The governor's one of the judges."

"Hanging Chad?" Bob said.

"That's the one."

"You got my vote."

"You gotta show up in person. Noon Saturday."

Bob blew a smoke ring. "What the hell. What else I got to do?"

"What will you do with the dinosaur skull?" Mo said.

Delilah puffed on her pipe. "I'll alert the tribal authorities. They're gonna want to put it in the museum."

"What museum?" Gary said.

"Ah-Tah-Thi-Ki in Big Cypress. Add that to your resume."

"Maybe I kin get cheap plastic skulls made and sell 'em."

"It's a thought."

Bob got two sleeping bags from the truck, threw one at Mo. "I'm zonked."

Gary waited until everyone had sacked out but him and Krystal. "Awright, little lady. Let's do it!"

Krystal looked around, nose wrinkling. "Where?"

"We can do it inside. Delilah don't care."

"No, I feel funny. Let's do it in the Jeep."

And that's how they did it, with Krystal straddling Gary in the shotgun seat. They wiped themselves off with Popeye's Chicken napkins.

"How's the training going, little lady?"

Krystal posed with her fist up like Rosie the Riveter. "I'm ready to go five rounds with Ronda Rousey. I'm tougher than a bull gator! I can run for miles. I been training with Samson every day."

Samson was Delilah's female black bear.

"Javelina won't know what hit her."

"Ah don't doubt it. I been watching her tapes and I notice that she drops her right after she jabs. You might think about taking her down."

"That's exactly what I intend to do. I'll take her down, pound her face and when she turns over, I'll take her back and choke her out."

"But wait a minute. Aren't you fixing to get together with her before the fight and figure out your moves?"

"Well yeah. I'm just speaking hypothetically."

"We ain't had one of these yet go as planned."

"That's true. We're even Facebook friends."

"You and Javelina?"

"Me and Marcela Aguilar. We both like piña coladas and getting caught in the rain. Her husband is a used car dealer in Juarez. She says he can get us a good deal on a new truck."

"Hey lookit here." Gary grabbed his wallet and fanned out crisp new hundreds.

"Where'd that come from?"

"Garrison Gland. Motherfucker snitched me out to the feds. That was before I caught him on video making out with a married woman."

"Dude who crashed our panther dinner?"

"That's the guy. Sheriff's deputy axed if I'd kilt a panther. So I go to Habib for a job and he sets me up taking a video of whatever sad ass motherfucker is sticking it to Mrs. Rose Wipperfurth. So I follow Rose and guess what? She's seeing Garrison, that's what. I threatened to tell the History Channel that he was having an affair with the wife of one of South Florida's more prominent news anchors and he gimme a thou to shut me up."

"That's only four hundred."

"Yeah, I already had that. I gave the rest to Pincus."

"Why?"

"For his dog. It's got cancer."

"You idiot! Why didn't you ask him for more?"

"I kinda like Garrison. He might put me on his show. Sides which, I win this palmetto bug thing, you beat Javelina, we'll be sitting pretty. 'Course we can't deposit any or the IRS will snap it up. We'll just cash it all out."

"Why ain't you on YouTube?"

"I'm out here. I got too much to do, babe."

"That's the cash cow, hon. We need to get that up and running again. The people need to see you."

"I got tales, that's for sure. We're for sure gonna do a show about the contest. You gonna be there?"

Krystal put her arms around Gary and squeezed him. "I wouldn't miss it."

31 | MEMORIES OF HAPPY TIMES

Friday night Gary walked to the end of the pier with a six pack of Frog Ale and a bucket full of slops. A quarter moon gleamed over the swamp. A loon sang. Frogs ribbeted. Gary heaved the slops into the water and waited. He'd finished two bottles when Leotis swam up.

"Mr. Duba," the catfish said bass profundo.

"Leotis."

"What did I tell you about the comics?"

"Well I am making a little money thanks to those Venezuelans."

"What Venezuelans?"

Gary told him about the Venezuelans. "How come you don't know about them? You're supposed to be my advisor."

"Well I'm sorry about the Venezuelans, but I'm only a giant Mekong catfish. I can only do so much."

"You ever meet Tallywhacker?"

"Well, I know of him, of course. Didn't he take over the

Church of Necroeconomics?"

"Then he quit and ran for governor. Got beat by a Democrat. He taught Western Lit for a while at Baylor, but he quit because it wasn't fulfilling. Now he got sucked up by a flying saucer. I'm going to miss him."

"I'm sorry to hear that, Gary. I knew he was your friend. But is it possible you just hallucinated the whole thing? Don't think your predilection for hallucinogens has escaped me."

"How do I know *you're* not a hallucination?"

"That's an excellent question, Gary. If you would be so kind as to dip your pecker in the water, I will prove it."

Gary thought about it. He lit a doobie. "I believe you, Leotis."

"Thank you."

"Want some blow?"

"No thanks."

"Leotis, is Taylor Swift country?"

"I don't believe she is."

"What about Neil Young?"

"Not in a million years."

They floated in companionable silence.

"You know who's country?" Leotis said.

"Who?"

"Charlie Pride. Now that's country. But his boy Carlton plays reggae."

"I did not know that."

"Not many people do."

"You ever eat palmetto bugs?"

"Contrary to popular belief, cockroaches can actually be very clean and tasty insects, especially if they are fed on fresh fruits and vegetables. They can be eaten toasted, fried, sauteed, or boiled. I can tell you from personal experience that the Madagascar Hissing Cockroach tastes just like chicken. I wouldn't mind if you brought me some."

"I'll see what I can do."

"Why do you ask?"

Gary told Leotis about the Hendry County Fair.

"Well best of luck to you, Gary. Who knows? If you win, this could open up new possibilities. I regret I won't be able to be there in your moment of triumph."

"Krystal's gonna live stream it. You got wifi?"

"Alas."

"The governor's judging the mullet contest."

"Hanging Chad?"

"You know of him?"

"Well I know of him, of course. What experience does he have that qualifies him to judge the mullet contest? Is he a hairdresser?"

"He's the governor. It's honorary."

"What are the criteria?"

"It's subjective, but certainly length, width, depth, and density. Also, sheen."

"Do you have any more slop?"

"You could stand to lose a few pounds."

"I beg your pardon?"

"Seriously. You didn't get that big on the slops I give you. What the hell did you eat to get that big?"

"That's very hurtful, Gary."

"Just saying."

"I'll have you know that I'm about average for my species. I did not ask to be caught in a sport fisherman's net in the South China Sea. I did not ask to be brought to America as a wee tyke of a mere twenty pounds. Do you know who it was that caught me, fed me, and ultimately abandoned me in the Gulf of Mexico? It was the movie star Leonardo DiCaprio. I've never mentioned this before because I don't want you to think I'm vain, or a star fucker. He was very kind to me, at first. I have thought about writing a book. *My Journey: From the Mekong Delta to the Everglades.*"

"Maybe you could get Leo to write the introduction."

"He no longer takes my calls."

"I might be able to help you out. I'm tight with the Duke and Duchess of Ducats now, and once you're rich and famous, you know everybody else. Pretty sure they've met Leo. I'll ax 'em."

"I'd like to meet them."

"I'll bring 'em down. You ever hear of Claude Balls?"

"Well I know of him, of course. He was among the *avant garde* in Paris in the Twenties. Him, Picasso and Hemingway. They hung together. Balls' art transcended genre. He painted. He wrote. He composed music. His most famous work, *Concerto for Bicycle Horn*, was performed by the Trans-Siberian

Orchestra. I wish I could have been there. He worked as a magician. One of his most famous tricks was to whip the tablecloth out from under a dinner setting without upsetting so much as a single glass."

"I hope his music is better than his paintings."

"Well, he painted in the surrealistic style. He was a founding member of the Dada movement. His book, *Fallow Fellow*, is considered a classic. *Jachère* in French. I read it in the original French."

"You speak Frog?"

"Well of course. I come from the Mekong Delta. Vietnam was a French protectorate. Many of the natives still speak French. I am writing a book, by the way."

"What's it called?"

"*Etiquette For Catfish*."

"Great! You want to be on my show? It's good publicity."

"I can't do that, Gary. No one can see or hear me but you."

"That reminds me. That was pretty rude the other night when I brought Krystal out to introduce you."

"I'm sorry, Gary. It has to be this way. You're the only one who can see or hear me."

"Are you telling me I'm crazy?"

"Not at all. It's just that when I see someone else on the pier, I disappear. I'm bashful. It took me years to overcome my fear of strangers. You're the only person with whom I've spoken since I was released into the Gulf."

"Why me, Leotis?"

Leotis looked to the stars and stuck out his lower jaw.

"There's just something about you."

"Did you talk to DiCaprio?"

"Well of course. I owe him everything."

"Maybe you could ask him to appear on my show."

Leotis sadly shook his head. "He no longer takes my calls."

32 | BEST MULLET

Gary arrived at the Hendry County Fairgrounds at ten am Saturday. The mullet competition was set for noon. He arrived early to get a look at the competition and sample the corn dogs. Gary parked the Love Bug in a field full of pickups, rodded and 'roided Japanese screamers, banged up family sedans and Harleys. The Harley riders threw down paint can lids for their kickstands so the bikes wouldn't tip over in the squishy ground.

Krystal would be there by noon, along with Delilah and the boys. Even at this early hour, people filled the midway, buying corn dogs, lizard on a stick, and trying their hand at the Power Pole, the milk bottle toss, and the palm reader. A dozen men, women, and children lined the fence at the Gator Rassle, watching the creatures sunning. A boy threw a Ding Dong into the water and three gators entered the water.

"Hey, you dumb shit!" the gator wrangler, a carny with a drinker's face said. "Don't you see the sign, dumb ass? Do not feed the gators!"

The boy ran away laughing. The gators were unimpressive. Gary saw bigger gators off his pier. He stopped in at the palmetto bug eating contest to register and signed a waiver absolving the carnival of all responsibility in "this unique and unorthodox contest".

"The consumption of insects is widely accepted throughout the world, and the insects presented as part of the contest were taken from an inventory of insects that are safely and domestically raised in a controlled environment as food for reptiles", read a sign on a pole.

Next, he registered at the Mullet Contest. The woman who signed him up told him, "My money's on you."

Gary wandered the fair grounds. 4H Club, Girl Scouts selling Thin Mints, Gatorferd Insurance, Cannabis Oils, Organic Vegetables, Cruelty Free Eggs, Sacred Feather Hats, Free Range Filets and Hand Carved Soapbox Derby Cars. Nuns of Gavarone.

Gary couldn't believe his eyes. There sat Sister Agatha Papparazzi along with a cute brunette novitiate beneath a striped awning, both wearing blue habits, their heads covered. Sister Agatha's face lit up as Gary approached.

"Gary Duba! Praise Jesus!" She extended her hands. Gary took them.

"How the hell are ya, Sister? I mean, how are you?"

"Very well, thank you. We've been following your exploits with interest. I was particularly intrigued by that giant hog you put down."

"Wasn't me, Sister! It was actually a Jew boy named Pincus. He's my tech support."

"In any case, I regret we were not properly grateful for your gift."

"No prob. It all worked out for the best. That was the beginning of the end for the Church of Necroeconomics. Say, we're having a barbecue this afternoon. You eat pork, don't ya? Love to have you."

"Let me check my schedule. How can I reach you?"

Gary gave her his phone number.

"May I bring Helen?"

The novitiate twinkled and dimpled.

Gary's phone rang. Krystal.

"We're here!"

It was a quarter to noon. "Meet me at the Mullet Contest! It's going down."

The mullets lined up to receive their positions, in the order they registered. A crowd gathered. Gary saw Krystal, Delilah and Bob weaving toward him. Gary jumped up and waved. Setting down her backpack, Krystal flew into his arms, running her hands through his elaborately coiffed and fixed mullet.

"Don't muss the hair!"

She stepped back, grinning. "You think I ain't got a brush for that? Lookie here." She reached into her feedbag and pulled out a brush. She pointed to a bench. "Sit."

Minutes later, Gary took his seat in a folding chair arrayed in four rows of five. There were nineteen entries so one chair remained open. Fair goers were given chits of blue paper and asked to write their top three selections based on the chair's number.

Gary turned to the hairless man running the contest. "I thought the gubnah was judging."

The man said, "We've got two categories: Peoples' Choice, and Best Achievement. It's not just the governor. There are five judges including Latin singing sensation Sharika, Elvis impersonator George Grey, game show host Randy Glockenspiel, and the governor's hair stylist, Yolanda Kazoo.

Gary took his seat. He was number seven. Number six was a bald man cradling a ferret.

"What the fuck?" Gary said.

The man placed the ferret carefully on his skull. "Play dead, Norm." The ferret went limp, its long tail hanging down the back of his neck. The man grinned. "What do you think?"

"That ain't legal, pal. That's not your own hair."

"I read the rules. Nowhere does it say the mullet has to be your own hair."

"Dude! If that were the case, we'd have twenty-four people wearing rugs!"

"Look. I'm here. They let me in. Deal with it."

Delilah walked down the back of his row and crouched. "All right. Here come the voters. Smile. Turn your head fifteen degrees to the right. That's it. Keep your chin down."

The crowd oohed, ahhed, and clicked its way down the rows. A photog from the *Turpentine Gazette* arrived.

A vivacious blonde in Daisy Dukes took a picture. "You've got my vote, baby. You can have my phone number too."

Gary looked around. Krystal was buying an ice slush. Several judges told Gary they were voting for him. A little girl squealed at the ferret.

"That's not your hair!"

"Is too," the man said. The fact that he just sat there calmly with a ferret on his head impressed a lot of people. It lasted about a half hour. Next came Hanging Chad, Sharika, George Grey, Randy Glockenspiel, and Yolanda Kazoo.

Hanging Chad was movie-star handsome with a dimpled chin and wavy hair, wearing sunglasses, a white shirt, a rough knit blue cotton sports jacket, and tan cargo pants. He shook each contestant's hand. He came to the ferret.

"That's a ferret."

"Governor, a real pleasure."

"Is it tame?"

"It's sitting on my head, ain't it?"

"Aha!" Gary cried. "Disqualify him!"

The governor reached out to stroke the ferret. It bit his index finger.

The governor yanked his hand back and stared at the blood on his finger. The governor's personal assistant Anthony Viola spotted a sheriff's deputy and waved him over.

"What happened?"

"This guy's ferret bit the governor. He shouldn't be here. This is a contest for best mullet, not best ferret."

"Stand up, sir. You're under arrest."

"No!" the man wailed. "What will happen to Norm?"

Gary stood. "Hey look, it ain't exactly a felony. Just let

him go. Whaddaya say, Governor?"

Hanging Chad looked at Gary for the first time. He nodded his head. "Now that's a mullet. You're right. Just let him go."

The interloper stalked off clutching his ferret. The governor looked back.

"Do I know you?"

"Nope. We almost met at Wacky World."

The governor peered harder. Gary put his hands up.

"I had nothing to do with that! I was just along for the ride!"

The governor laughed. "Of course. Well, you've got my vote." As the governor went down the line, Viola whispered in his ear. The governor glanced at Gary and raised his eyebrows.

Fifteen minutes later, the certified mullet crew counted the votes. They tapped Gary, a squat guy who looked like he was wearing a raccoon hat, and a young ur-punk with a neck tat and a mullet that resembled a '59 Caddy tail fin. They handed the results to the governor.

"I'm pleased to announce the winners of the Hendry County State Fair Mullet Contest! Third is Carl Potts!"

The smiling ur-punk bounded up next to the governor.

"Second, John, Loveall!

Up went the fire hydrant. Krystal squealed and put Gary in a headlock. Delilah rose her palm for five.

"And the winner is the man who apprehended Plastic Surgeon to the Stars and serial killer Dr. Vanderlay Mukerjee, captured the largest python in Florida history, the inventor of house suspenders, Turpentine's favorite son, Gary Duba!"

Crowd goes wild.

33 | LIGHTNING STRIKES TWICE

Gary handed the five-hundred-dollar check to Krystal along with a certificate for a free style at Sasha's in Palm Beach.

"Let's get something to eat!" she said. "I'm starving."

"I'll tag along, but I can't eat. I got the palmetto in an hour."

"Oh baby, I wish you wouldn't do that. A man died from eating palmetto bugs."

"He was showing off. He was stuffing them in hand over fist. I ain't gonna do that. Omma judge my competitors and eat just enough to win. I guaran-dog-tee you ain't nobody can eat more palmetto bugs than me."

"Hanging Chad was staring at your ass," Delilah said.

"Maybe he recognized me. I accidentally dropped a puke bag on his head."

"I don't think he looked at your face."

They wandered the fairgrounds until they came to Nacho's Tacos. Krystal and Delilah got iguana tacos, everybody got soft drinks and they sat at one of the picnic benches near the infield where the Turpentine High Gators played baseball.

"Where's my skull?" Gary said.

Delilah held up a finger as she munched. She wiped her mouth. "It's at the museum. Nearly fell in that damn hole taking it there. Don't worry. You'll get full credit for the discovery. They're sending a team out to investigate. Meanwhile, they're laying steel planks over the hole so we can get into town and back."

"Who's responsible for that road?"

"The res. We'll fix it as soon as the paleontologists are finished. They promised next week. They got a crew coming in from the Florida Museum of Natural History."

Gary looked at his phone. "Welp, it's time."

The palmetto bug eating contest was held inside an enormous tent set up to accommodate two long tables laid end to end where the contestants would sit, plus seating for several hundred. The local ABC affiliate was on hand, and Garrison Gland, wearing jodhpurs tucked into cavalry boots, a safari jacket, and a Gators cap, accompanied by a cameraman.

Gary went over. "Garrison! What are you doing here?"

"I'm recording this for my program. What are you doing?"

"I'm a contestant, and we're recording this for my program."

"We can cross-promote. I'd like to interview you after the contest."

"If he's still alive," the cameraman said.

Hands clapped. Gary turned to see a thin old man with tufts of white hair over the ears speaking into a headset.

"Contestants to your seats please. Please sit in your assigned seats."

Mumbles, shuffling, chairs scraping as Gary took a seat at the end of one of the tables. Krystal set a quart bottle of Gator Ade in front of him. There were ten contestants, all men, and bottles of Louisiana Hot Sauce and Pick-A-Peppa every three seats.

The old man turned to the onlookers and clapped his hands. A signer dressed like a mime jived behind him. "Hello! And welcome to the Hendry County Fair Palmetto Bug Eating Contest! I'm Elias Duplex, professor of entomology at the University of Miami! I also have a degree in cooking from the *Ecole Ducasse* in France, which makes me uniquely suited to administer this contest! Did you know that insect protein is a valuable stipend throughout most of the world? It is only here, in the so-called enlightened West, that we shun what many consider to be an unclean animal.

"Cockroaches are not unclean..."

A young man in a knit shirt with a halo of frizzy hair rushed to the professor and whispered in his ear.

"I'm sorry. I meant to say, palmetto bugs are not unclean! The bugs we are serving have been raised in a safe and holistic environment, on a diet of fruit and vegetables. The contestants may eat to their heart's content, for we have an unlimited supply. We are serving the insects alive to ensure freshness. Each contestant will start with ten. You will see a wood cylinder in front of each contestant, one side painted green, one side painted red. If you are ready for more cockroaches, place the cylinder green side up. If you have had your fill, place the red side up. We ask that all contestants remain in their seats until the contest is over. This should not take long. Contestants! Are you ready?"

The signer frolicked like a kitten with a ball of twine.

The man next to Gary had the look of a gym rat with a tribal tat riding up his neck. He raised a fist. "Fuck an A Bob!"

Several seats away, another contestant, who resembled Bob's Big Boy, released a rebel yell. Dozens of people elbowed their way to the front line, phones held high. Some held plastic cups of beer. Some held flasks.

"Serve the first course!" Duplex commanded in the voice of a Roman senator. Giggling teenagers deposited bowls filled with palmetto bugs in front of the contestants, each bowl covered with plastic wrap to prevent their escape. Gary stuffed a roach in his mouth and crunched. He chewed quickly and thoroughly. He ran through his ten bugs like a machine gun. He slugged Gator Ade. He placed his marker green side up. His server made a chalk mark on the table.

Gary doused the bowl with Pick-A-Peppa and dug in. Crunch. Scratchy. Acrid. Gary needed that money. He was a machine. Finishing his second bowl before some finished their first, he turned the knob green side up. Contestant number seven, a two-hundred-and-eighty-pound sack of suet, abruptly pushed himself back from the table, staggered outside the tent and hurled. Contestant number three twitched and fell sideways. Two EMTs with appeared out of nowhere and spirited him away in a collapsible gurney.

"No reason to panic, folks," Duplex said over the PA. "We have an ambulance on standby. Once again, I must emphasize that these palmetto bugs are perfectly safe."

Gary was on his third bowl. Chewing proudly, he surveyed his competitors. The man in the Harley shirt looked green. A weasel faced man munched doggedly, hunched over his bowl to protect it from those who would steal his palmetto bugs. Someone screamed. A woman fainted. Calliope music sounded faintly in the distance. Gary looked up. He could just see the top of the Tilt-A-Whirl over the livestock building. No one else had the green side up.

Gary looked around with satisfaction. "Hey Elias! Are we done?"

Duplex walked down the row, pushing the red topped knobs on their side. He wheeled on the signer, two steps behind. "Who are you? Who sent you?"

The signer turned and ran.

"Who wants a bowl?"

The man next to Gary belched, spraying twigs of palmetto bug. Duplex picked up Gary's entry form. "Folks, we have a winner! Gary Duba, from right here in Turpentine! We have a winner! Gary has eaten thirty palmetto bugs! Gary wins the ten-thousand-dollar grand prize! Step up here, Gary."

To applause and yee-haws, Gary joined Duplex at the front of the tent looking out. A reporter thrust a mic in his face.

"What do they taste like?"

Gary held a bug from out to the reporter. "You tell me."

The reporter backed off. Garrison closed in with his cameraman.

"Bravo, sir! Bravo! How did you train?"

Duplex inserted himself between them. "Sorry to interrupt, but Governor Chickenlooper has to leave in a few minutes. Let the governor present the trophy and then you can talk."

Sheriff's deputies cleared a semi-circle around Gary. The governor approached holding a trophy with a gilt-plated palmetto bug atop a wood base, and a white envelope. Gary felt a seismic rumble in his gut. Anthony Viola assisted the governor with a headset.

Chickenlooper's voice boomed over the PA. "Congratulations again to Turpentine's favorite son, Gary Duba!"

Subterranean explosions pulsated. Matter and anti-matter mixed. The governor handed Gary the trophy and the envelope. "Inside is a cashier's check for ten thousand dollars. The festival promoters are concerned that if you hang around, you will bankrupt them!"

The crowd politely laughed. The governor offered his hand. "Congratulations."

Gary took his hand and vomited.

34 | KRAKOW!

Floyd called on the way home. "Sorry I missed it, man. I had an emergency job in Clewiston. Rats the size of bulldogs. I hadda club 'em to death."

"Didja get 'em all?"

"No. I had to lay down some peppermint, castor, and citronella."

"Yeah, we're heading for the swamp. Swing on by! I'm grilling ribs."

"Can I bring Ginger?"

"Sure. Grab some beer, willya?"

Gary and Krystal rode in the Love Bug. Delilah followed in her Jeep. As they passed the Wokenoki Trailer Park on Weldon Way, a Burmese python stretched across the narrow dirt road, both ends hidden in the brush. Gary down-shifted, coaxing the forty-year-old VW to heretofore unimagined ferocity. Krystal grabbed his arm.

"What are you doing?"

"Omma kill the sumbitch!"

"Why?"

BDOMP. The VW went airborne and came down on the left front tire. KRAKOW! The wheel collapsed into the fender. KAWHANGO. The Love Bug jittered across the road into the ditch. FWANG. The Love Bug came to rest on its side.

Gary lay there a sec, until he realized he was lying on Krystal. He raised himself up. "Krystal! Krystal baby! Are you all right?"

She opened her eyes, mouth twisted. "You fool! Why did you do that?"

"It just seemed like the right thing to do."

"Get me out of here, you moron. Now you've wrecked Habib's car."

Delilah stopped behind them, got out, opened the door and offered Gary a hand. "Didn't you see that python?"

"I saw it. I was gunning for it. I shoulda known better than to try it in this piece of shit."

Five Wokenoki residents wandered out clutching beers, smoking cigs. Gary waved his arm.

"We're fine! Thank you for coming."

A youth slow hoisted his middle finger. The crowd ambled back into the park. The VW was completely off the road, left tires in the air reminding Gary of a dead palmetto bug. Delilah lit a cigarette.

Delilah stood with hands on hips. "Broken bones?"

Krystal felt herself. Gary danced a little jig. "We're good."

"Get in the truck. Let's go."

Wokenoki disappeared behind them. The dirt road ran straight between jungle walls. A dark cylinder slithered across the road.

Gary reached over Krystal to nudge Delilah. "Look. There's one! Gun it! Show that sumbitch whatfor!"

"You gotta be kidding me," Delilah said. "Ain't you learned nothin'?"

"Come on, Delilah! This here's a goddamn Jeep! This ain't no piece of shit tin foil hat from Germany! This baby tips the scales at two tons and has two trans axles! Are you gonna let these damned pythons push us around? These interlopers? Who invited them? Nobody! They come here to live fat at the expense of the American taxpayer. Come on, Delilah! You ain't skeered, are ya?"

Delilah grimaced and grinned. "All right, baby. You asked for it."

Krystal rolled her eyes and cinched her seat belt tight.

Delilah accelerated to seventy.

BDOMP. The Jeep went airborne and came down on the left front tire. KRAKOW! The wheel collapsed into the fender. KAWHANGO. The Jeep jittered across the road into the ditch. FWANG. The Jeep came to rest on its side. The airbags deployed, pushing Delilah, Krystal, and Gary back into their seats like an overbearing aunt. Gary found his pocketknife and shivved the airbags. Whoosh. The interior smelled of ozone and talcum powder.

They crawled out of the Jeep. Delilah curled her fingers. "Why? Why did you force me to do that?"

“Why?!” Krystal cried.

“Any broken bones?”

Krystal and Gary checked their limbs.

“Nah,” Gary said. “We’re good.”

Delilah went over to Krystal. “You okay?”

Krystal clutched her left shoulder. “My shoulder hurts like hell.”

“See if you can move your arm. Real gentle.”

Krystal tentatively circled her arm, grimacing at the top. “Ouch.”

“Shit,” Delilah muttered. “May have to work some juju, if you’re gonna beat Javelina.”

“What about them pythons? They count as a sacrifice?”

“Maybe.”

“Y’know,” Gary said, “would it help if we ate a javelina? I mean, wouldn’t that like give her spiritual power over her opponent?”

Delilah walked down the road. “Let’s go.”

Gary had left his trophy in the crushed bug, but the check was snug in his pocket. He’d stuck his magnum in the back of his belt. No telling what would show up next.

“These damned snakes are rankling my ass,” Gary muttered. As they neared the final corner beyond which lay his trailer, Gary felt both anxious and excited. There was no telling what lay behind the next curve. It might be feral hogs, Venezuelans, python, Godzilla, or sheriff’s deputies. Gary would have vomited had he not already given all. In fact, he was getting hungry.

"Whatchoo got for a side dish, little lady?"

Krystal trudged toward the trailer, clutching her left shoulder. "I got beans and rice, but you'll have to cook it. I'm gonna lay off this arm for a few days. Gary, I swear, if your bullshit causes me to lose this bout, I will claw your balls off."

"Claude Balls!"

"What?"

"Remember when the Duke and Duchess came by to get their painting? It was a Claude Balls!"

"Who gives a shit?"

"Well, I was just thinking, what if they left more Claude Balls behind? Prints, books, anything? That might be worth some money."

Krystal's lip curled like Elvis. "Claude Balls my ass. You've got to get the show going! That's where the money is. You get enough followers you can sell ads! Hell, you can do ads! You're well known enoughl some insurance company might want you!"

"You really think so?"

"'Course I do! Aren't you the man who just won the Hendry County Fair Mullet and Palmetto Bug Eating Contest? Your life has been an incredible adventure! In fact, I think you should write your biography."

They approached the trailer. Gary kept an eye peeled for pythons, feral hogs and macaques. "That's a good idea. That's right! I'll write my story! I'll bet Major can sell it for big bucks."

"Now you're talking, big daddy."

"Who do you think should play me in the movie?"

"Matthew McConaughey or James Franco."

Delilah picked up her pace. "Is it unlocked? I need to use the bathroom."

"Those Venezuelan sumbitches broke the lock."

A furrow split Krystal's perfect forehead. "What Venezuelans?"

"It's a long story. After we found that one guy, there's been three more."

Delilah hot stepped into the trailer. Minutes later she popped back out. "There's a snake in your toilet."

35 | SISTER AGATHA

Floyd and Ginger arrived in Floyd's Viper. Floyd carried a cold case of Dixie into the trailer and stashed the bottles in the fridge. Gary put shredded newspaper in the Weber and laid down coal. Krystal put *Jerry Reed's Greatest Hits* on the boom box.

"Ja see that bug in the ditch?" Floyd said.

"I don't want to talk about it."

"And Delilah's Jeep?"

"I don't want to talk about it."

Pincus arrived in his Rogue with Elisha who leaped out barking and wagging. Gary waved from the deck.

"How the hell are ya, Pincus! Glad to see your dog's doing better."

"We just came from the vet. It's a miracle."

Pincus and Elisha came up on the deck. Pincus wore a striped sport shirt with a pocket protector, baggy blue jeans rolled up at the ankle and a kippah. Gary snatched the kippah and pocket protector and stuck them in his pocket. "I'll give 'em back when you leave."

Gary put his arm around Pincus and turned to Krystal. "Babe, we gotta fix Pincus up so he can lose his cherry."

Pincus turned crimson.

"Barb and Jen are on their way."

Gary dragged Pincus with him down the deck. "Not that Barb and Jen are easy, but they do like smart. Show 'em your drones. Here they are."

Barb and Jen pulled up in Jen's beige Corolla. Barb got out holding two bottles of wine. "Yeeee-HA!"

Elisha greeted them at the top of the steps. Barb crouched to pet and coo. "Who's this adorable dog?"

"That's Elisha," Gary said, steering Pincus toward them. "Belongs to Pincus here. Pincus is my tech support. Y'know how Punisher has Microchip? Well, I have Pincus! He's a genius! Ask him about bitcoin."

"Hi," Pincus said, sticking out his hand. Barb shook.

"So, you're a genius, huh?"

Pincus blushed. "No."

"Pincus here is the man who killed Hogzilla! You know that don'tcha? He actually pulled the trigger and drilled that giant hog through the eye. It was the first time he ever fired a gun. Ain't that right, Pincus?"

"Well I..."

Hands on hips, Barb looked at him with fresh eyes. "Is that so?"

"Hell yes, it's so!" Gary said.

"Let Pincus answer."

"I just got lucky. It was so big I couldn't miss. It was like shooting at a wall."

"You drilled it through the eye, Pincus! And then we served it to two hundred people. That hog weighed over a thousand pounds."

Barb regarded Pincus with admiration. "Oh my! Why weren't we invited?"

"It all happened kinda sudden like."

"We were on that boat with what's his name," Jen said.

"That's right. Torio."

"Torio!"

They laughed.

"'Say 'allo to my leetle boat!" Barb said in a fake Cuban accent.

"I swear to God. That's what he said."

"Then he wanted to show us his guns!"

"Oh, he was so awful that when he swung by the beach, Jen and I dove in the water and swam ashore."

"What about your phones?"

Jen dipped in her bag and pulled out her phone in a Zip-loc bag.

An old Ford that looked like a former police cruiser, with a black body and white doors, pulled into the yard.

"Holy shit! It's Sister Agatha!"

The sister and novitiate Helen got out of the car. Sister Agatha wore a blue nun's habit and wimple. Helen wore a knee-length pleated skirt, a sleeveless blouse, and an abbreviated white wimple.

Gary went down the steps to greet them. Elisha circled the nuns, barking until Helen crouched and cooed. Elisha sat and wagged his tail.

"Come on up, sisters. We're grilling ribs. How'd it go at the fair?"

Sister Agatha winked. "We cleaned up."

Floyd pulled out every chair and served beer. Sister Agatha asked if they had any Cheap Trick. Delilah manned the grill with a pair of tongs and a wire brush. Helen asked if she could help.

"No, thank you, but thank you for asking. I need to do this myself. This is my own secret recipe." She showed Helen a Mason jar filled with a thick brown liquid.

"What is it?"

"Barbecue sauce. I'm thinkin' of marketing it."

Helen pointed at Pincus. "Who's that?"

"That's Pincus. He shot Hogzilla. He's a genius."

Floyd wore a plaid shirt with the tails out and the sleeves cut off, baggy shorts that fell to mid-calf, and flip-flops. Ginger wore short shorts and a Belmont Holistic Pest Solutions shirt with the upside-down palmetto bug. They approached Gary and Sister Agatha at the rail, drinking.

Floyd clapped Gary on the back. "Ya won the mullet contest, the palmetto bug eating contest, and you spewed on the governor! That's a hat trick!"

"Never to be repeated," Gary said.

"How were the palmetto bugs?"

"Crunchy."

A fusillade of grunts filled the clearing. Nine feral hogs, ranging in size from thirty pounds to three hundred, entered the clearing, milling and squealing.

Gary squinted. "Oh, for Chrissake...sorry, Sister!"

Sister Agatha glared.

The hogs milled around Floyd's Viper.

"Aw no. Hell no! Get away from there!"

Sister Agatha put a hand on Floyd's wrist. "Have you ever minded hogs?"

"No, but how hard can it be?"

"You leave this to me." Sister Agatha went to her car, opened the trunk and pulled out a steel yardstick. The hogs regarded her with mean little eyes. She thwacked the yard-stick in her palm. She yelled like Tarzan. She rushed the hogs and laid about like Donnie Yen in *Rogue One*. Thwack! Thwack! Oink! Oink! The hogs milled about, confused, and angry. They were too stupid to run.

Krystal jerked Gary's arm. "Help her!"

"I might hit her!"

"Ask Pincus!"

Gary turned toward to Pincus, who was deep in conver-sation with Helen. Gary went in the house and grabbed his Louisville Slugger. "I'll do it myself."

He strode down the steps. Reinforcements rushed from the jungle. Now there were forty hogs milling around the yard, jostling Floyd's Viper, darting at Sister Agatha. Every time a hog tried to gore her, she whacked it across the snout with the steel ruler. The hogs spooked the birds which took to the sky, shrieking.

Gary lashed out with the bat, whacking them on the head. "Hang in there, Sister!"

Gary and Sister Agatha stood back-to-back, circling. Fresh hogs poured out like a kamikaze attack.

"Where are all these hogs coming from?" Sister Agatha said.

"This looks like a set-up!"

A black Lincoln pulled into the yard, two men in front, two in back, all wearing leather jackets and sunglasses. The driver got out. He had a thick brush mustache and a bulge under his arm. He looked at Gary and Sister Agatha whacking hogs, got back in and backed out of the clearing at fifty miles an hour.

36 | LEOTIS STRIKES OUT

Floyd confronted the hogs with a can of oven cleaner. He sprayed oven cleaner in their eyes and soon the whole tribe was on the run. Floyd chased them to the tree line.

"Go on! Get out! And don't come back!"

Floyd circled his Viper, stopped on the far side. "Aw no. Aw no. That fucking hog took a dump on my Viper!"

"Floyd, just wash it off with a hose."

They returned to the deck where Delilah was turning ribs. Krystal came over.

"Who was that in the car?"

"More fucking Venezuelans. Sorry, Sister! If it weren't for Sister Agatha here, we might all be dead."

"What do they want?"

"They want their comic back. But I already sold it. Sold the second one too."

"What second one?"

"Look, hon, suffice it to say these Venezuelans keep

coming at me and coming at me. They want to be my friend. They want to search the house. They're convinced I'm ripping off their coke and comics. Did I ask them to dive bomb the house? I hadda write a letter to the president. I thought that would be the end of it but I haven't heard back from him."

Jen and Barb brought out coleslaw, potato salad, paper plates, Red Solo cups, and plastic forks and set them on a folding table.

"Sister! That was awesome! You think you can keep these Venezuelans off my ass?"

"Gary, are you Catholic?"

"No, ma'am."

"Gary, you strike me as decent man. Have you considered converting to Catholicism?"

"Talk to Pincus. You'll have better luck."

People loaded their paper plates and sat or stood at the rail with the plates balanced. Gary saw Pincus with Helen, but only Helen had a plate.

"What's the problem, Pincus? Ain't you gonna eat?"

"It's not kosher, Mr. Duba."

"Well, what can ya eat?"

"Chicken. Beef, if it's kosher."

"What makes it kosher?"

"It has to be killed in a certain way and blessed by a rabbi."

"Hell yeah, we got that! Hang on."

Gary went in the house, found a frozen hamburger patty in the fridge, thawed it in the microwave, and threw it on the grill. He motioned Sister Agatha over.

"Sister, I'm passing this burger off as kosher so Pincus can eat it. Can you say a few words over it for extra added protection?"

Sister Agatha crossed herself. "God bless this burger."

"Great! I'll tell Pincus."

Pincus was deep in conversation with Helen around the corner, on the north side of the deck, Elisha seated between them, wagging his tail.

"Pincus! I found a kosher burger. Sister Agatha blessed it for extra added protection."

Helen looked up. "Gary, didn't Kierkegaard believe in individual existence—particularly religious existence—as a constant process of becoming? Didn't he believe in authenticity, commitment, responsibility, anxiety, and dread?"

"Huh?"

"Helen claims that Kierkegaard is the father of existentialism. I say Sartre. Who's correct?"

"Say what?"

Helen gestured with a rib. "Sartre's theory of existentialism presumes existence precedes essence. Only by existing and acting a certain way do we give meaning to our lives. I'm not saying he's wrong, all I'm saying is that Kierkegaard got there first."

"No way."

"Way."

"Aw right. Go get your burger. And when you're done, come see me. I want to introduce you to a friend of mine."

Gary returned to the front as Habib arrived with Auburn

in his Lexus. Hugs, high-fives.

"What happened to the Love Bug?" Habib said.

"We were attacked by a python."

"What about that Jeep?"

"Python."

"Dang, Gary. You and your animal magnetism."

Gary held his hands up curled. "Tell me about it!"

Jen, Barb, and Krystal boogied out to "*Bernadette*". Delilah brought out a jug of shine. Pincus and Helen appeared.

"Mr. Duba, you were going to introduce me to someone."

"That's right. If you folks we'll excuse us for a minute, I'd like to show Pincus something."

Gary grabbed a half dozen stripped ribs from the garbage and put them in a plastic sack.

"What is it?" Floyd said. "Show me."

Krystal poked him on the shoulder. "It's his imaginary catfish."

Tail wagging, Elisha followed Gary, Pincus and Helen around to the pier which extended twenty feet into the swamp. On one side, Gary's swamp buggy was cinched to two old tires fixed to pylons. At the end of the pier was Gary's chair, a bench, a plastic bin, the golf club, and the empty slop bucket beneath a cloud of flies. Gary pulled a bottle of Off! from his pants.

"Y'all might want to douse up."

Pincus held up his wrist, encircled by a yellow strap. "We're good, Mr. Duba."

Elisha jumped off the pier and went in the water. At

the end of the pier, Pincus pointed to the nine iron. "Do you play golf?"

"I'm trying to learn the game in case I gotta caddie again."

"When do you have time to caddie?"

"You never know. Last time out, I kilt a hippo. Now be quiet. Let me see if I can coax Leotis up to the pier."

"Who's Leotis?" Helen asked.

"Giant Mekong catfish. He's my mentor."

"I consider you a mentor, Mr. Duba."

"Thanks, Pincus.

He crouched at the end of the pier and tossed a rib into the green water. "Leotis! I got some folks I want you to meet."

Pincus circled his temple with a finger.

"A giant catfish?" Helen said softly. Pincus shrugged.

Gary tossed another rib. "Come on, Leotis! You can talk Kierkegaard." He half turned. "He's shy. He was brought to America by Leonardo DiCaprio. Hey, Leotis! You can talk about Claude Balls!"

They waited hopefully, music and conversation drifting from the trailer.

"Mr. Duba, what do you know about Claude Balls?"

"Contemporary of Lord Buckley and Jack Kerouac. The Duke and Duchess of Ducats came back for one of his ugly ass paintings. I could paint better."

Helen put a hand to her mouth. "The Duke and Duchess of Ducats?"

"That's right, little lady! They're gonna be on my show. I'm gonna be on theirs. In fact, I think it already happened."

An alligator surged from the swamp and seized Elisha. The border collie yelped in pain, ending in a drawn-out squeal. The four-foot gator struggled to pull Elisha into the drink as the dog fought back, paddling and digging in with its forepaws.

Pincus grabbed the nine iron, leaped off the pier, bringing the golf club down on the gator's head. THUNK. The gator's rear legs twitched and went still. With a foot on its back, Pincus pried its jaws open and gently pulled out the dog. Helen rushed down and crouched.

"Oh, the poor thing! Is he all right?"

Elisha had puncture wounds on his rear leg.

"Bring him up to the house," Gary said. "Delilah'll take care of him."

They turned to go. Gary flipped the bird at the swamp. "Thanks for nothing, Leotis."

37 | SANS CULOTTES

While Delilah treated and bandaged the dog, Gary got a text from Nostomania. "*Zap #0* sold for one thousand dollars, sending you cashier's check via UPS for that amount minus my fifteen per cent."

"Fat City!" he declared, stuffing the check in his biker wallet.

Floyd got drunk and tried to shoot an albatross. Habib and Auburn left to go to another party. Sister Agatha and Helen left, but not before Helen and Pincus exchanged phone numbers. Floyd, Ginger, Barb and Jen left around midnight.

Gary grabbed Krystal and dragged her into the bedroom. She fell face first onto the bed and started snoring. She sounded like a sucking drain. Gary grabbed some bedclothes for Delilah and threw them on the living room sofa.

"You good?"

Delilah gave him the thumbs up. "It was a good party. Tomorrow, back to the swamp."

"How ya gonna get there?"

"I guess I'll call an Uber. I'll call my insurance company in the morning."

"Whaddaya gonna tell 'em?"

"We was attacked by a python."

"That's right!"

Gary had been hoping for a poke from Krystal, but it just wasn't any fun when she was out cold. He lay on his back staring at the lazy turn of the ceiling fan.

"Gary," a voice rumbled through the open window.

Gary sat up. "Huh?"

"Gary, it's Leotis. Come and talk to me."

"Leotis!"

Krystal mumbled and turned. Gary got up, pulled his pants and shirt on, and padded out of the trailer down to the pier. Frogs and crickets filled the night. It sounded like ten thousand castanets. The pier squeaked as Gary walked out to the end, pulled the chair up and stared into the water. Leotis looked up, pale yellow in the moonlight.

"Where were ya earlier? I wanted you to meet someone!"

"Gary, I have a life of my own. I was busy."

"Doing what?"

"I was working on my autobiography as a matter of fact. It was your idea."

"How do you do that, being a catfish and all?"

"I have a perfect memory. Every word is ingrained on my soul. When the time is right, I will dictate to a transcriber."

"How you gonna do that?"

"I was hoping you could bring them swamp side. I would like to employ you as my agent. I will give you fifteen per cent."

"Fifteen per cent of what?"

"Book and any media sales that may result, such as film or television."

"Leotis, let me ax you sumpthin. If they was to make a film of your life, who would you choose to play your part?"

"Leonardo DiCaprio. I was hoping you could use your connections with the royal couple to bring it to his attention."

"You know him better than me."

"He no longer answers my calls."

"You gotta write it first."

"I'm almost done. It's over a hundred thousand words."

"That was fast."

"I write fast."

"You ever hear of Claude Balls?"

"You already asked me this. You're repeating yourself. I'm concerned. He was one of the great surrealists. He worked as a freelance mime in Paris until one day a group of American servicemen nearly beat him to death. After that he took up painting and sculpture. His most famous work is the Duck's Ass, part sculpture, part wig. It now sits on a bust of Jean-Paul Marat in the Louvre. Someone tried to steal it several years ago, so it is under armed guard."

"Geez, you gotta meet my pal Pincus. He's apeshit for that stuff."

"He was a vigorous defender of the sans-culottes and

seen as a radical voice. He published his views in pamphlets, placards and newspapers."

"What's a san culotte?"

"The lower classes of 18th century France. They were so poor they had no culottes."

"I been meaning to ax you about these harbingers. I got the bat and the rabbit, but I ain't seen hide nor hair of the turtle."

"Tell me about them."

Gary told Leotis about the *Detective Comic* and Rodell Grosz.

"One will bring you riches. One will cause you grief."

"I made a ton of money on that comic, but the IRS took it. I got nothing. And now I got these Venezuelans coming around, and the last bunch didn't even bring me a comic."

"I have to warn you about the Venezuelans."

"Little late, don'tcha think?"

"President Quetzacoatl is desperate to raise funds. Having emptied the treasury, he is now confiscating all the great comic collections and putting them up for auction. I was thinking of buying his mint condition *Twenty Thousand Leagues Under the Sea,* but where would I display it? He's also running cocaine."

"I'm sitting on five keys."

"Gary, this doesn't bode well for you. Those Venezuelans are thugs. They will demand recompense."

"Did I ax 'em to dive bomb my place?"

"It doesn't matter to the criminal mind. They will have

their pay one way or another. You might want to go into hiding until this blows over."

"Fuck that shit! We got a fight in two weeks! I ain't going nowhere. I'll have Pincus rig the place up with motion detectors. I'll perforate them sumbitches and dump 'em in the swamp! Will you eat Venezuelan?"

"I'll eat anything, Gary. You know that. But I am lactose intolerant."

"This is America! I ain't going nowhere. Let 'em come! I'll set traps! I'll dig holes and plant punji sticks! I'll get Claymores from *Cheaper Than Dirt*! It'll be like *Rambo: Last Blood*, only worse!"

"I don't think it's possible to do anything worse."

"If you was to come on my program, you'd be able to reach millions of new fans."

"Gary, I wonder if you'd listen to me read the start of my biography."

"What else I got to do?"

Leotis sang a few notes in falsetto like an opera singer warming up. "I never knew my mother. My first memory is of swimming up a tributary of the Mekong. Even as a tad, I could pick up radio broadcasts in the water coming from boats. Thus, I learned that I was an endangered species. You can imagine the effect this had on me at a tender age. The correct term is *Pangasianodon gigas*, which sounds better than it is. I dined on plankton and algae until one day an enterprising young fisherman scooped me up in a net and sold me to the film star, Leonard DiCaprio. It is here my story truly begins."

38 | NOTHING IMPORTANT

Sunday morning, Krystal rose, put on her sweats, and ran up Weldon Way, past the trailer park, all the way to the highway and back. Eight miles. She returned, showered, and by the time she came out, Delilah was packed and ready to go.

"I called an Uber. He'll be here any minute."

Krystal found Gary sawing logs on the bed, stooped and kissed him. "See you next weekend, stud muffin."

Gary mumbled and turned over. Krystal joined Delilah on the front deck with a cup of coffee. A flock of terns rose from the swamp as a Chrysler 500 squished up the road and stopped.

Delilah gestured with her mug. "There's our Uber."

A swarthy man with pock-marked skin and greasy hair got out. "Your Uber is here!"

Delilah grabbed her gym bag and backpack, Krystal her backpack and they tripped down the stairs. The driver peered at Krystal as she got in the car.

"Didn't I see you at Wacky World last week?"

"Who are you?"

"I *was* Rapid Rabbit. You and your boyfriend got me shit-canned!"

"You were drunk. You got yourself shit-canned. You don't want our business, say so."

Grosz turned the car around. "No, it's all right. Gotta make a living somehow. I may have been out of line. If so, I apologize."

"No prob."

They thumped over pythons. "Funny place to put speed bumps."

They cruised west on Eighty, passing a motor home pulling a Bronco with a motorcycle mounted sideways and an aluminum boat bungeed upside down on the roof.

"Preppers!" Grosz declared. "They disgust me."

"What's your name?"

"Rodell Grosz. I was just marking time at Wacky World. I'm about to release some sides that will stun the world."

"Sides of what?"

"Hip hop! The voice of a generation!"

Krystal examined his pock-marked neck and greasy hair. He had a pustule that looked like a nascent volcano. "What generation? The nineties?"

"I know what I'm doing. I've got mad skills. Subscribe to my YouTube channel. Mad Skills."

"You know, if you pop that zit on the back of your neck and film it, you'll get a lot of hits. You may need someone to hold the camera."

"You want to do it?"

"I'd rather gargle razor blades."

Grosz turned south on the long, lonely road to the res. "Okay. Here goes."

"Can't we just listen to the radio?"

"In a minute. I can't beat box myself, but I don't need a beat box.

"Huh huh huh, up above the bustle...

"Yo yo yo ain't lookin' for a tussle...

"Hey hey hey you really gotta hustle...

"Na na na lemme see some muscle...

"You do the crime, you got to do the time...

"How many ways can I milk that rhyme...

"Tarzan versus Conan, what could possibly go wrong?

"Tarzan versus Conan, who's got the biggest shlong?

"Man of steel and man of bronze...

"Which one has the biggest schwanz?"

"STOP THE CAR!" Krystal said.

"What?"

"Pull over and let us out or so help me God I'll strangle you."

Grosz veered to the side of the road and stopped on the swampy shoulder. Krystal and Delilah grabbed their bags and bailed.

"You sure you want me to just leave you lovely ladies like this in the middle of nowhere?"

"I would rather die of a water moccasin bite than have to

listen to any more of your crap."

Grosz cranked up the bird. "Yeah, well fuck you!"

Krystal flipped him back. "Fuck you and your neck zit!"

Grosz worked an awkward Y turn. There was a moment when he seemed as if his rear tire would slip into the swamp, but he found traction and peeled out, spraying gravel. Delilah and Krystal watched him recede into the distance.

Delilah shouldered her backpack. "Way to go, girl. Now what?"

"Who's up for a little road work?"

"Not me."

They headed south in the heat and humidity.

"Maybe someone will come along," Krystal said.

"Hunh unh. Not on this road."

But five minutes later a car did come along, a tiny, cheap Japanese pickup with picks and shovels rattling in the bed. The driver stopped and leaned out the window. He was a small man with a big nose and tiny eyes behind thick glasses.

"You ladies need a ride?"

"Wouldn't mind," Delilah said.

"Just throw your stuff in the bed and squeeze on in."

Krystal sat in the middle. "Thanks! I'm Krystal, and this is Delilah."

"Bruce. Dave Bruce. Weren't you in that truck that passed me several days ago?"

"You're the UFO guy!"

"That's right."

"I begged Gary to stop but he wouldn't listen! He's got a

thing about UFOs."

"Yeah. I ran into him later. In fact, I'm on my way to the sinkhole to look for signs of UFOs. They're everywhere."

"Huh. I lived here all my life and I ain't seen one."

Delilah stared out the window disgusted.

They arrived at the sinkhole, surrounded by rubble. Bruce got out of the truck and looked down. "What the hell?"

Delilah and Krystal joined him. "What?" Krystal said.

Bruce pointed to the hole in the wall. "What happened there? Did somebody find something?"

"Dinosaur skull. It's at the museum."

"You removed the skull? Is the rest still buried?"

"Dunno. I turned it over to the tribal elders and the Department of Natural Resources."

"But there are no dinosaurs in Florida! There never were! Nobody has ever found a dinosaur in Florida."

"There's always a first time."

"This has got to be a hoax!"

"Look here, Dave, if you'll just deliver us to my place, I'll pay you the fee I was going to pay the Uber."

"What Uber?"

"The guy with the monster zit on the back of his neck. We bailed when he wouldn't stop rapping."

"Rapping?"

Krystal vamped low. "Huh huh huh, up above the bustle...

"Yo yo yo ain't lookin' for a tussle...

"Hey hey hey you really gotta hustle...

"Na na na lemme see some muscle..."

Bruce held out his hand. "Stop! Get in the truck. Let's go."

He carefully skirted the sinkhole and they drove the eight miles to Delilah's place in the swamp. Delilah dug out her wallet and paid him twenty-five dollars.

"Do you mind if I take a look at the dinosaur skull?"

"It's at the museum, but I have photos." Delilah pulled out her Fonebone.

"I have never seen anything like this. I suspect it's alien."

"You think it might have come from one of those UFOs?"

"Yes. In my experience, they're capable of anything. I've been abducted twice and anally probed."

"They find anything?"

"Nothing important."

39 | A TRUE TALE OF ALIEN ABDUCTION

"Good evening and welcome to the Ferd Ludlow Show. Folks, I don't know what's going on, but we've had a plethora of UFO sightings in the past couple of days and we're eager to hear from a couple of callers who have gotten up close and personal. Our first caller is well known to this program. Welcome back, David the Bruce! What's up Dave?"

"Hello, Ferd. Last week I told you that I'd been abducted again by aliens. They took me up in their flying saucer high enough to see the curvature of the earth and the International Space Station. They probed me again. I don't know what they expect to find up there. I will say this for them. They have enough decency to use the blot out ray. The last thing I remember, I was strapped to an examining table. Then I woke up in the swamp and my ass hurt like hell.

"But that's not the reason I'm calling. Yesterday I picked up two ladies who'd been stranded on a remote road near the Big Cypress Indian Reservation. I was there to take a look at the sinkhole that swallowed a pickup truck. So I take a look and there's this big hole in the side about eight feet down. And one of the ladies says they dug a dinosaur skull outta the hole. And so, I says everybody knows there are no dinosaurs in Florida. The dinosaurs never came to Florida. So, she says well look at these photos and sure enough she's got this humongous skull sitting on a picnic table in the back! I sent you the pictures, Ferd."

"Yes, he did, folks, and they're astonishing. I will post them on my Instagram account shortly."

"It looked like a giant bird, only with teeth."

"You know, Dave, many scientists believe the birds are direct descendants of the dinosaurs, and somewhere along the way, ol' Ma Nature flipped a switch, and they became warm blooded."

"What happened to the teeth?"

"Well that's an interesting question, Dave. Perhaps one of our listeners can answer that. But please tell us more about the skull."

"So I'm looking at this thing, and it doesn't look like any dinosaur I've ever known. As a kid, I was fascinated by dinosaurs. I must have watched *The Valley of Gwangi* a hundred times. So what I'm thinking, we all know aliens have been visiting Earth since ancient times. Just watch *Ancient Aliens*. This skull is alien. I can't say for sure if it was intelligent, but certainly it's big enough to hold a big brain. Like the size of a basketball or something. I think that when scientists get around to tracking its DNA or whatever, they're gonna find that it is indeed of alien origin."

"What about the rest of the skeleton, Dave? Did you see it?"

"No. I didn't have time to get down in the hole and dig around, but I understand that the Seminole Nation has taken possession of the skull and they intend to get to the bottom of it. Whatever it is. But I mean, if the skull is five feet long, the whole thing must be enormous! Can you imagine the size of the saucer? This raises a whole bunch of questions. All this time, we assumed the aliens were little men with big heads and huge eyes. I've seen them myself. They're only four feet tall. What if the giant dinosaurs are actually the superior species, and they sent these tiny aliens to scout for them? And these giant aliens may still be out there."

"We'll be right back with Dave and his incredible story after this short commercial break."

"Have you been in an auto accident and the insurance company failed to give you what you deserve? The law offices of Habib Rodriguez specialize in insurance claims. You don't pay a dime unless we collect for you. Call the law offices of Habib Rodriguez today."

"Hi. I'm Quack Brannigan with a true story that could save you thousands of dollars on life insurance. I have a client Diane, whose husband, Ray, suffers from mild tachyardigram. I was able to save them forty-two million dollars on their life insurance by contrasting and comparing policies. If you think you can't afford life insurance, contact me, Quack Brannigan."

"Well, we're back. Ferd Ludlow here. Our last guest, Dave Bruce, bailed during the commercial break but we have a surprise caller who is no stranger to residents of central Florida. Gary Duba is the man who apprehended Plastic Surgeon to the Stars and serial killer Dr. Vanderlay Mukerjee, caught the biggest python in state history, and killed the biggest feral hog on record. Over a thousand pounds."

"Sorry to interrupt there, Ferd, but that wasn't me who killed Hogzilla. It was my pal Pincus. You need to track a feral hog, you call Pincus."

"Gary claims to have witnessed a UFO abduction. Go ahead."

"Y'all know about Tallywhacker, the animatronic bull who developed artificial intelligence, who was invaded by several aliens with multiple personality order."

"Are you saying his brain was a battleground?"

"It was Little Big Horn and the Battle of the Bulge all wrapped up into one. That poor bull didn't know whether to shit or go blind! Well, I guess he did, actually."

"Just so you know, we're on a ten second time lapse so we can bleep out the bad words. Go ahead, Gary."

"Sorry, Ferd. Anyhow, Tallywhacker took over the Church of Necroeconomics, ran for governor, and ran a taco stand in Little Cuba."

"Isn't that the same mechanical bull that destroyed the Miami Museum of Modern Art? What was that, eleven million in damages?"

"Well yeah, but they really jack the prices up. I mean,

who's gonna pay two mil for a blob of glass that looks like an ashtray? They tried to stick me with the bill, but it was ruled a *force majeure*."

"Why did they try to stick you with the bill?"

"Fuck if I know."

"Folks, if you hear a bleep in there, you know why. Tell us about the alien abduction."

"I was down in the Big Cypress getting Krystal ready for her fight with Javelina. Two weeks, folks! At the Roxy! Tickets still available. She trains with this witchee woman. Anyhoo, I was heading home on foot, on account I lost my truck in a sinkhole..."

"Wait a minute. Is this the same sinkhole where you found the dinosaur head?"

"That's right, Ferd. Dubasaurus. We only got the head, but we're going back for the rest."

"Tell us about the alien abduction."

"Yeah. I'm walking along this dirt road when all of a sudden clouds gather, there's thunder and lightning and Tallywhacker rises out of the swamp! I about shit a piston!"

"Folks, if you hear a bleep in there, you know why. Gary, were you on drugs?"

"I mighta had some reefer, but that don't make you see bulls! Anyhow, Tallywhacker is practically crying. 'I've got to go, Gary,'" Gary said in a wheezy falsetto. "'The elders are calling me home.' Then, out of the darkest, densest cloud I ever seen, this flying saucer descends, spinning like a top. It's huge, man. It was like thirty feet across. It hovers right over Tallywhacker, and he's crying! he's crying man, because he loves Florida, and he hates to go!"

Ferd Ludlow sniffed. "Folks, if this doesn't bring a tear to your eye, you have no heart."

"And this big iris opens on the saucer's belly. A glowing yellow tractor beam pulls Tallywhacker up into the saucer, the lens snaps shut, and SWOOSH! Off she goes. Five minutes later, the clouds are gone, and the sun is shining."

40 | SHOW BIZ

Tuesday morning, the incessant buzzing and whining of Gary's phone woke him from a dream in which he threw money from a hot air balloon to adoring crowds. He sat up and looked at his phone.

"What's up, Aldo?"

Aldo Moldanado was the Roxy's promoter, taking over from Downtown Brown. "Good morning, Gary. How goes the training?"

"She's pretty stoked, Aldo. She was in two auto accidents yesterday, but I think she'll be all right."

"Oh, I'm so sorry to hear that! We're almost sold out. Are you sure she'll be ready?"

"I'm sure. Krystal's no quitter. She just got bruised up a little."

"What happened?"

"We were attacked by two pythons. I mean, who could possibly have foreseen that?"

"How did that cause an accident?"

"They slithered out onto the road too fast for us to slow down. They wrecked one car, then another. Not to worry, Aldo! She'll be good to go."

"The reason I called, I'm thinking of adding some entertainment between rounds, maybe a comedian or a juggler."

"That's a good idea, Aldo. Who you got in mind?"

"That's why I called. I was hoping you might have some connections."

"Major Sutton does stand-up. He's my producer."

"Do you think he would do it for two hundred and fifty dollars?"

"Probably. I'll ax. Lemme send you some YouTubes. He cracks me up!"

"Nothing offensive or scatological."

"Aldo, this ain't ladies bingo night. Our audience loves offensive and scatological."

"Well let me see the videos. Do you know any jugglers?"

"No."

"Dancers?"

"It's too bad Tallywhacker got sucked up by the mothership. That bull could dance."

"I don't even know what you're talking about."

"No worries. Let me think. How about an ax thrower?"

"That's not a good fit."

"I know two girls who'll strip to 'Sweet Home Alabama'."

"No."

"They don't have to strip to *Sweet Home Alabama*. They

could strip to *Lift Every Voice and Sing.* That way you got the black crowd."

"What else?"

"I know a dude can pull wheelies in his wheelchair."

"What else?"

"Elvis Presley impersonators. I got two. A good ol' boy and a Frenchie."

"A French Elvis Presley impersonator?"

"That's right."

"What else."

"How 'bout a rapping rabbit?"

"A what?"

"Dude wears a giant bunny suit and freestyles. I saw him at Wacky World. Didn't make any sense to me, but hell, the audience is gonna be so drunk and stoned they'll laugh at a crippled cat."

"Can you send me video?"

"Lemme look into it. What about a palmetto bug eating contest?"

"That's not a good fit."

"We could catch rats and put little tags on 'em. Everybody gets a ticket when they come through the door, and then between fights, we let the rats loose and people hunt 'em down. If you catch a rat with the same number as your ticket, you win a prize."

"What prize?"

"A Nordic track, a free massage, a jar of kelp pickles."

"That's asking for trouble."

"All right. Suppose I get the rapping rabbit and I bring in a hip-hop skunk, and they go at it between rounds. A free-style rap-off."

"Can one of them be of Latin descent?"

"A rappin' Latin skunk?"

"Yes."

"Lemme look into it. Y'know, Major would do it if we could find a big enough suit. That way you got the black vote."

"How would they know?"

"Well the rabbit's white and the skunk is black. You'll know it from his voice. He sounds like Leotis."

"Who's Leotis?"

"A giant Mekong catfish. Too bad we can't bring him up there, 'cause he sings like Levi Stubbs."

"Who's Levi Stubbs?"

"Y'know, Aldo, I keep forgetting you grew up in a communist dictatorship and only listened to four-hour harangues on the radio. Levis Stubbs was lead singer for the Four Tops! *Baby, I Need Your Lovin', Bernadette, I Can't Help Myself*?"

"Doesn't ring a bell."

"It's just theoretical. You'd need a ten-thousand-gallon aquarium."

"All right. Send me clips of the rabbit and the skunk."

"Will you pay 'em each two fifty?"

"I guess I can do that. But no more!"

"Can they sell their CDs and downloads?"

"We'll work something out. There's a half hour break between the semi and the main event."

"Who's fighting in the semi?"

"Cobra versus Mongoose."

Happy that he'd lined up gigs for his friends, Gary nuked a Jimmy Dean sausage, cheese and egg muffin and drank reconstituted orange juice from the carton. He checked for Venezuelans, gathered some slops in a bucket and sat at the end of the pier.

Leotis sang as he approached. "On the day I was born the nurses all gathered 'round. And they gazed in wide wonder at the joy they had found...B-b-bad to the bone."

"Leotis, I almost got you a singing gig!"

"I don't think I could sing in front of strangers."

"How'd you like to record an album? We can do it right here."

"Who will provide musical accompaniment?"

"Floyd plays trombone. That's all you need."

"What would I sing?"

"The George Thorogood Songbook."

"Let me think about it."

"Leotis, I need your advice."

"That's why I'm here."

"Should I buy a burial plot or just have myself cremated?"

"Gary, I'm concerned. You're in the prime of life. Why would you ask such a thing?"

"Well yesterday we were attacked by a python and it nearly killed us. It just reminded me of life's fleeting nature and that any of us could be struck down at any time for any reason."

"Gary, that's terrible! I'm so relieved that you're all right! And I feel a deep sense of shame in that these pythons come from my corner of the world. They have no business here."

"Yeah, well, I also think I need to educate the next generation about my accomplishments. That's why I'm leaning toward the burial plot. I want the marker to say Gary Duba apprehended Plastic Surgeon to the Stars Dr. Vanderlay Mukerjee, caught the biggest python in state history, and was responsible for the death of Hogzilla, although Pincus pulled the trigger."

"Gary, history will remember you whether you get the marker or not. Did you know you have your own Wikipedia page?"

"No shit! How do you know that?"

"People drop their phones." A bubble broke the surface.

Gary pulled out his phone and Googled himself. It was iffy because he was at the very limit of the trailer's wireless transmitter. Sure enough, there he was, along with a photo of him receiving the key to the city, and him posing with dot com billionaire Oren Houtkooper and his prize-winning python, with the head duct-taped to the body.

"Ho shit! Hey, do you know where I could get a giant skunk suit for Major Sutton?"

"What size?"

"Major's about five nine but he goes two fifty."

"I would try eBay."

41 | APOCALYPTO

Delilah sent queries regarding the dinosaur skull to the Seminole Tribal Council, the Florida Museum of Natural History, and the Miami Museum of Modern Art, which had been restored following the Tallywhacker apocalypse. Art offered to donate ten thousand dollars to the Council "to preserve prehistoric fossils and structures" in exchange for hosting the skull in a month-long show, "Beautiful Bones."

Two lumberjacks arrived at Delilah's house at three p.m. on Wednesday, while Krystal was showering from her four-hour workout. The two bearded men stood slack jawed staring until Delilah stormed from the house and yanked the plastic curtain shut. Krystal turned toward her surprised. Krystal was wearing earbuds and was bopping out to "Uptown Funk" and hadn't heard them arrive.

"We came for the dino skull," said the driver, a jumbo in baggy cargo trou and a wife beater that revealed enough body hair to knit a sweater."

"It's at the museum in Clewiston. Let's go."

They got in the lumberjacks' truck and drove to the Ah-Tah-Thi-Ki Museum on West Boundary Road. The skull was in the prep room. The lumberjacks walked around it, whistling.

"I'll take the front. You take the back."

Delilah watched as the two men hoisted the skull, carried it outside, and set it gently on a stack of moving blankets in the back of their van. They covered the skull with more moving blankets and bungeed it down tight. They drove back to Delilah's place. The driver handed Delilah four tickets.

"These are good for the duration of the show, which starts November 10 and will run for thirty days."

The men stood hoping for another glimpse of Krystal. Delilah put her hands on her hips. "Anything else?"

"No, ma'am. Thank you."

The other pointed. "Is that a bottle tree?"

"No, it's a begonia."

They got in the truck and left. Krystal put on a shirt and coveralls. "Who was that?"

"Museum of Modern Art. Beautiful Bones." She handed Krystal the tickets. "They'd better have food."

"What are you gonna do about your car? Was it insured?"

"Ain't no insurance will cover that. I'll just buy a new one. I got money. All of us livin' on the res got money. We get a guaranteed income of one hundred and thirty-eight thousand dollars a year."

"For what?"

"For bein' Seminole."

"Holy shit. That would save us so much trouble. Can you adopt us?"

Delilah looked her up and down. "Don't work that way."

"Well ain't we blood kin now? We took that oath."

"Don't work that way."

"What are we doing for dinner?"

Delilah ducked inside the dome and came out with a fishing pole, tacklebox and bait box. She thrust the pole at Krystal.

Krystal wrinkled her nose in disgust. "You're kidding."

Delilah thrust the pole more forcefully. Krystal took it.

"You don't have no problem eating fish. 'Bout time you catch your own fish. I can't believe you was raised in the swamp and never done any fishing."

"My brothers did all the fishing."

"You even know how to clean a fish?"

"Yuck!"

"Let's go." Delilah strode into the swamp. Krystal had no choice but to follow. Delilah wore black combat boots. Krystal wore Danner Waffle Stompers for Ladies. Mosquitoes dogged their every move. Krystal waved her hat like a bronc buster. They came to the edge of a deep pool surrounded by cat tails, sawgrass, and mangrove. Two duck asses stuck out of the water.

Delilah sat on a sawed-off log and spread her legs. She set the tackle box and bait bucket between her feet. "Gimme the hook."

Krystal extended the narrow end of the pole. Delilah

jammed an earthworm the size of her thumb on the hook, working it around so the hook pierced it twice. Krystal fanned her face.

Delilah pointed. "Now you cast that line right there in the deep spot."

Krystal drew the pole back like a buggy whip and flung. "OWW! Oh my God there's a worm in my hair!"

Delilah spat. She stood and worked the hooked worm out of Krystal's hair.

"Oh my God."

"Do you want me to slap you?"

Krystal straightened up. "All right. Show me what I got to do."

"You cast that line right there in the deep spot."

This time Krystal managed not to snag herself. The fat worm splatted ten feet from shore in the deep spot and sank.

"Ol' catfish'll see that worm wriggling in ten...nine... eight..."

Something yanked on the line. "I got it!" Krystal screamed. "I got it!"

"Well pull it in."

Krystal wound the reel. She needed both hands on the pole to haul the two-foot catfish.

"What's in the bait box?"

Delilah unlatched the bait box and opened it. "Primo Mich, Turkish tobacco, peyote, psilocybin, hash oil, hashpipe, papers. Aspirin."

"Not now. Maybe later."

"Well put that fish in the bait bucket and sit your ass down."

"With the worms?"

"Don't worry about it. Those worms are clean. What is the plan?"

"Javelina and I are meeting on the fourteenth to work out the moves. You gotta be there."

"What is the plan if she don't stick to the plan?"

"Javelina? She's sweet. We're friends!"

"You only think you're friends. She wants what you've got. You're ranked number seven flyweight. She's number ten. She beats you, you change places. You get paid less. You gotta go *lucha libre.* And believe me, honey, you don't want to wrassle in front of a hundred drunk Mexicans in a bar in Juarez. Next thing you know you're strippin', and then you're in a donkey show."

Delilah tamped tobacco into her corncob pipe, stroked a kitchen match on a rock, and puffed her bowl to a glow. "What is the plan?"

"Flying knee to the chin. I might throw up on her too."

"They'll be waiting for that."

"Should I do it?"

"Nah. Once was an accident. Twice it looks like it's a tactic. Let's go back. You get to clean this fish."

"Yuck!"

"Girl, this is your lucky day."

When they returned to the house, Delilah slapped the catfish down on the sawed-off cypress stump they used as a butcher's block. Krystal stared at it with curled lip.

"You can't tell Gary anything about this."

"Are you kidding? A wife who cleans fish?"

"We can't tell him it's a catfish."

"Why not?"

"He's got this fixation. Every night he thinks he talks to a giant catfish at the end of the pier. Leotis."

"What does the Leotis tell him?"

"It told him about the three harbingers. The bat, the rabbit, the turtle. We've got the bat and the rabbit. It's like we're waiting for the third shoe to drop."

"Watch out for that turtle."

Krystal cleaned the fish. Delilah stuffed the fish with herbs and mushrooms, wrapped it in palm fronds and grilled on the Weber. They ate at the picnic table.

"These mosquitoes are killing me."

Delilah cast a mosquito net over Krystal like a fisherman. She lifted the end and slid under. They sat opposite each other draped with netting and ate. Delilah sipped shine and smoked her pipe. Krystal smoked a joint. Dusk fell. The cat crawled under the netting and wrapped around Krystal's feet meowing.

"What does it want?"

"Catfish."

Krystal lowered her paper plate to the ground.

"Come on," Delilah said. "We'll watch *Apocalypto.*"

42 | THE ROYAL DUCATS REQUEST

Friday morning Major picked Gary up and took him to breakfast at the Waffle Hut in Turpentine. They sat in a booth looking out on the parking lot next to Walmart, sipping coffee.

"It's all set," Major said. "The Royal Ducats are arriving Palm Beach this afternoon, will spend the evening at the Breakers, and come out to your place tomorrow morning to begin filming their segment."

"What's the theme?"

"Gator hunting. You'll take them out on your swamp boat. I'll follow in a skiff with a camera crew. I've asked Pincus to join us to provide aerial footage."

"Maj, there's already a show about gator hunting. It's called *Swamp People.* Every show, same thing. Troy says, well there's some big bull gators up at Johnson's Hole, and we better go get 'um 'less Junior beats us to it. They go get the gator. They haul it in. Troy says, shoot it, Chase! Shoot it! They show the gator. They show Chase from a gator point of view sighting along the barrel. But they never show them actually shooting the gator!"

"Well, that's where we're gonna go one better. The Duke is going to shoot the gator, and we're going to show it getting plugged right in the skull, and if it splashes blood on the camera, so be it!"

"Has the Duke ever shot a gator?"

"No, but he's been quail hunting his whole life, and he shot a hippo in Africa."

"Well hell. I shot a hippo on the ninth hole at Shangri-La. Maybe we oughtta go hippo hunting."

"Not enough hippos. Didn't you tell me that swamp was thick with gators?"

"It's lousy with 'em. I can guaran-dog-tee you a gator."

"Well, all right then."

The waitress brought platters. "Here ya go, hon." Omelet for Major, waffles for Gary.

They ate.

"Major, what do you know about psychedelic toads?"

Major looked up; his mouth full of omelet. He chewed. He swallowed. "Huh?"

"I know this dude's doing a segment on 'em for his show on the History Channel. *Bizarre Bazaar*."

"What prompts this?"

"I was just thinking, I could get hold of one of them toads, lick it, and then you could follow me around filming my experience."

"Not a good idea."

"Why not?"

"Are the toads indigenous to Florida?"

"Hell no. They're invasive, just like every other critter that jumps out at me from a pond."

"No."

"How 'bout we trick the Duke into licking one?"

Major smiled. "Gary, I have to admit, that would make great television. But it's likely a felony and you would lose the good will of the American people, and probably the British too."

"Just a thought."

"What are you gonna do about your truck?"

"I'm going to Dealin' Doug."

"Do you trust Dealin' Doug?"

"He ain't gonna screw me over. We've known each other too long. Did you hear about that couple living in the Walmart attic?"

"Yeah. What a hoot. Love to interview them for the show."

"Yeah, I met 'em. Nice folks."

"How'd you meet them?"

"Florida Man Leads Police On Two Hour Chase Through Walmart Attic."

"That was you?"

Gary beamed. "I got in a fight with the self-checkout machine and it called the cops on me. I got away clean!"

Major's phone buzzed. He put a finger in his ear and talked.

"The Royal Ducats want to know if you'd like to join

them tonight at the Breakers."

"Sure, why not."

"You'll have to wear a jacket and tie."

Gary racked his brain. He had one jacket and one tie. "I can do that."

"Please arrive at six and phone their suite. They will come down and then you'll go to the Flagler Steak House."

"Why don't we just meet in the steak house?"

Major laced his fingers. "They're British royalty. They're used to having people wait on them."

"This here's America! We already kicked their asses once, and by God we'll do it again! Everybody talks about how the British are so nice. Nice my ass! They're a bunch of bloodthirsty savages! Look at this Duke. Flying down to Africa to shoot a hippo! We got hippos rightchere need shooting! We oughtta take him out on a golf course. He'll see hippos, gators, you name it. Hell, I'll even caddie."

"The Duke has a nine handicap. He plans to play the Shangri-La while he's here."

"I'd be happy to caddie for him. I'll bring the guns."

"You can discuss that at dinner. Don't bring your guns."

Gary clapped his hands together and rubbed. "Hot diggity! We gonna film this?"

"No, this will be a private meeting. Krystal is invited as well. I'm meeting elsewhere with their producer."

Major dropped Gary off at Dealin' Doug's, a used car emporium on the east side highway. Gary walked the rows of sparkling vehicles. They had twenty-two pickups. Gary had always been a Ford guy. He was looking over a clean '15 with 85,000 miles when Dealin' Doug zeroed in like a shark smelling blood. Dealin' Doug was in his fifties with a florid drinker's face, a shock of white hair, and a beige Banlon shirt that bulged over his wide leather belt with a dinner plate sized buckle.

"If it isn't Turpentine's famous son! How you doin', Gary?"

"Doin' great, Doug."

"You interested in this truck?"

"Gotta drive something. Sinkhole swallowed the last one."

"No kiddin'! Hope you weren't in it when it happened."

"I was, Doug. It was quite an adventure. I discovered a dinosaur skull. It's going on display right now at the Miami Museum of Modern Art."

"Why is a dinosaur skull on display at a modern art museum?"

"Hell if I know."

Doug ran his hand along the truck's fender. "This one's ultra-clean, was owned by a little old lady who only used it on weekends to drive to thrift stores. It's got the three and a half liter V6, which is really all you need, unless you're haulin' a tractor trailer. Sirius XM, cruise control."

Doug's seven-year-old son Howie marched up. "Nobody beats a Dealin' Doug deal! Nobody!"

"This one's a steal, Gary. Eighteen thou and you drive it off the lot. You want to finance, I can give you a great deal."

Gary pulled out his fat wallet. "I got cash."

Doug's eyes popped. "That's a lot of money to be walkin' around with."

"Let me take it for a drive."

"Follow me back to the shop and we'll get you the keys."

Five minutes later, Gary exited the lot and headed west on Eighty. He turned south on Weldon Way. "All right, you sumbitches," he snarled. "Let's see how you handle a real truck!"

43 | SOLD

A blue Chevy Blazer sat in the yard when Gary arrived. He looked around for Venezuelans. But there were no Venezuelans. The front door opened, and Krystal came out wearing short shorts and a man's shirt tied at the midriff.

She motioned toward him. "Get your buns up here!"

Gary bounded up the steps, enveloped her like a squid and kissed her.

"Who's got the Blazer?"

"That's Delilah's. We just picked it up from Honest John's."

"Where'd she get the scratch?"

"Every res Indian gets a hundred and thirty-eight thousand smackers a year."

"Where do we sign up?"

"I already tried that, boss. We don't qualify."

Inside, Delilah sat Injun-style on the rainbow throw rug in the living room, wearing a brown wrapped headdress and an ankle-length dashiki, eyes shut, hands in the lotus position, chanting. "Witchi-tie-to, gimee rah, whoa rah neeko, whoa rah neeko, hey ney, hey ney, no way..."

"Izzat Seminole?"

Krystal pulled Gary into the bedroom.

"Leave her be. She's meditating."

"How's training?"

"Let's ball. Then I'll tell you."

Fifteen minutes later she sat up. "I'm good to go. I'm a mean motor scooter and a meat-eating mama. I'm a hemi-driven semi pulling four tons of hurt. My mother was a badger, and my other mother was a honey badger."

"Hey guess what. We're having dinner with the Ducats!"

"Who?"

"The royal couple! The Duke and Duchess of Ducats!"

"Well, what are we gonna feed 'em?"

"At the Breakers! As their guests!"

"No way."

"For reals."

"What'll I wear?"

"Wear that yellow shift with the Popeye characters."

"For the Breakers? I ain't never been to the Breakers! I never dreamed I would go to the Breakers! I'll wear my wedding dress."

"That's bad luck, baby. Why don't we stop by Target on the way and you can pick something up?"

"That's a good idea! Is that the new truck?"

"Yeah. Ain't it purty?"

They put on clothes and went to the living room. Delilah

was poking around in the kitchen rattling pans. "There's nothing to eat but frozen tacos and beer. Gary, go out and shoot something."

"You picky?"

"Don't shoot no panther."

"What about python?"

"Shoot a hog. What's the matter with you?"

"Nothing, I guess."

Gary went into the bedroom and pulled down the bolt action 308 Marlin his father had ordered from Montgomery Ward in 1969. He grabbed a box of ammo and stuck them in the mag. He doused himself with bug spray, pulled his NRA hat low over his eyes, filled a quart water bottle and put it in his backpack. He followed the game trail between the sawgrass and mangrove heading toward the pond. Gary lived on a peninsula surrounded on three sides by swamp and open water.

The buzzards and hogs had licked the road clean of python. Soon Gary was entirely surrounded by green. Ten feet and he could see the water, but in this dense little thicket he might as well be in Myanmar. He inhaled the sweet and rotten smell of the swamp. A whiff of decay.

The Sumatran corpse flower! Was it possible that fool Garrison was right? Could the giant Sumatran corpse flower invade Florida? If so, what a boon to tourism! Everyone wanted to be photographed with the giant corpse flower! It only bloomed once every eleven years! Was it possible to stagger their planting, so that one would bloom every year? Or were they synchronized like girls all getting their periods at the same time?

A faint breeze stirred the wind, and it was gone. Snorting. With any luck, Gary would find a nice, twenty-five-pound pig. He wasn't shooting anything bigger. Silent as a cat, Gary whispered toward the water, parting the grass with the rifle. He crouched in a three-foot stand of saw grass beyond which lay opaque water. He parted the grass and saw three feral pigs wallowing across the shallow inlet. Resting his left elbow on his left knee, he snugged the rifle butt to his shoulder and took aim.

KABLAMMO! A pig flopped. The others disappeared squealing. That pig was dead. Right through the heart. Leaning the rifle against a mangrove tree, Gary waded into the water. Two feet was enough for most crocs. Gary grabbed the pig before the scent of blood spread through the water. He swung the pig over his shoulders and waded back to shore, blood running down his neck, picked up his rifle and inserted himself sideways into the jungle. As he entered the little clearing, a dark oval the size of a serving platter confronted him.

The turtle! He set the pig on marshy ground.

"Tell me, turtle. What is my fate? What I gotta do to move up and out?"

The turtle disappeared in the weeds. Gary picked up the pig and carried it to the tree stump. It had been a mighty water oak until lightning struck. The pig hit with a thump. Krystal and Delilah were on the porch drinking.

"Gotcher pig, Delilah, but you'll have to butcher it yourself. Me and Krystal are outta here to dine with the royal couple."

"What royal couple?"

"The Duke and Duchess of Ducats."

"Nothing surprises me."

Gary went inside and got the big Bowie. "Here, use this. Put the slops in that bait bucket, won'tcha? Leotis likes 'em."

Delilah gave Krystal a look.

"See? I told you."

Gary showered, got his sports jacket and black tie with little green alligators, hung them in the back of the new truck. "We'll change when we get there. You think these shorts are okay?"

"Bring long pants, Gary."

Gary changed into his only pair of Dockers and they headed into town. The parking lot was busy. Gary parked his new truck across two spaces in the back near a light pole so he wouldn't get dinged by some brain-dead teen. Inside, Krystal beelined for a women's short sleeve knit dress. "Wild Fable." Eight dollars and forty cents. She checked the size. She grabbed the dress and headed for the checkout lane.

"Sold."

"Don't you want to try it on?"

"No. It'll fit. I got stuff here before. Let's go."

When they came outside, a man was on his knees drawing "ASSHOLE PARKING" in big white letters all the way around Gary's truck.

44 | ELEGANCE

"Hey asshole!" Gary said.

The man looked up. "Is this your truck?"

"Yeah. What the fuck do you think you're doing?"

The man stood. He was six six. He looked like an Easter Island statue. "You're the asshole, man. Look at the way you park. Can't you see the lines?"

"What the fuck do you care? The nearest car is twenty feet away!"

"Y'know, man, the trouble with this world is that most people just don't give a shit. They see a wrong or an injustice and they just tell themselves it's none of my business and keep walking. But not the Main Man. You're lucky I didn't smash the windshield or snap off your rearview mirrors."

"Do I know you?"

"Not likely."

"How'd you like a fat lip?"

The man towered and glowered. "Why is it people like

you always resort to violence and threats of violence?"

"I'm not the one calling names!"

The man bristled and whistled. "Youuuu..." He turned and stalked off.

"That's right, asshole! Run! Run like the cowardly dog you are!"

Krystal put her hand on Gary's arm. "Enough. Let's go. We'll be late."

They drove to the Breakers. Gary tipped the valet ten bucks. "Careful with my baby."

The doorman looked askance as they entered clutching their finery, hers in a Target bag, his folded under his arm. When they came out of the restrooms in their evening wear, Major was sitting in the lobby, reading the *Palm Beach Post Gazette.* He looked up.

"Well don't you two look swell. Look at this." He held up the front page.

FLORIDA MAN LEADS POLICE ON THREE AND A HALF HOUR CHASE THROUGH WALMART ATTIC.

"Well damn!" Gary said. "That blows my record all to hell!"

"I didn't know you led police on a chase through a Walmart attic."

"I try not to brag."

"The royal couple are waiting to hear from you."

Gary went to a house phone. Regan answered.

"The Royal Ducats."

"Hey, Regan! Krystal and I are in the lobby."

"We'll be right down."

They joined Major in the lobby.

"We're shooting tomorrow. Muriel Martinez will film. I've asked Pincus to operate the drones."

"We're getting the old gang back together!"

"The Royal Couple have a list of requirements." Major handed Gary a stapled document.

1. You will address the royal couple as Duke and Duchess, or your highness or highnesses.

2. No vulgarities.

3. When the Duke and Duchess speak, you must listen attentively. Please watch this short video of the Queen's corgis.

4. All technical persons such as camera persons, director, et al must refrain from looking the Duke and Duchess in the eye.

5. Gary and Krystal may look the Royal Couple in the eye only when speaking directly to them.

The list went on for five pages.

"Are you kidding?" Gary said. "Have they ever seen my show?"

"Gary, this will be ratings gold. Your viewership is certain to at least double. I have a list of advertisers who will jump on board the day after this airs. It goes without saying you must not put the Royal Couple in any danger. Toward that end, we have arranged to release several drugged alligators in the pond, where you will wrangle the gator next to the boat so the Duke can shoot it."

"It's a set-up!"

The elevator disgorged the Royal Couple, he in an Abitto

Blinder Blue Estate Herringbone Tweed Three Piece, she in a Prada wool blend Lurex ribbed turtleneck, pearls the size of marbles around her neck.

"Get up!" Major hissed.

Krystal and Gary rose to greet the Royal Couple.

"Jolly good!" the prince declared. "Let's walk down the veranda to the restaurant."

The Steak House was an elegant three-story building in the Southern style.

"Flagler Steakhouse is a refreshing interpretation of the traditional, masculine spirit with a twist of Palm Beach prep, putting a contemporary, lighthearted spin on the island's clubby legacy," the Duke recited with aplomb. "A celebration of a time-honored tradition, its air of exclusivity cleverly plays on its location, yet the restaurant remains open to the public with convenient access right off South County Road. The members-only feeling is evident upon arrival, as guests driving up are warmly greeted by the valet on-site and know they're in the right place."

Regan patted the Duke on the arm. "Larry considered a career in the theater, but the Queen Mother crushed his hopes and dreams as one might step on an ant."

The manager, a tall, bald man in an impeccable ecru suit, met them at the door.

"Your highnesses, we are thrilled beyond measure that you grace us with our presence. And who are your delightful companions?"

Regan put her hand on Gary's arm. "Gary Duba is the

man who apprehended Plastic Surgeon to the Stars and serial killer Dr. Vanderlay Mukerjee, caught the biggest python in state history, and is the inventor of House Suspenders. His delightful wife Krystal is ranked number ten women's flyweight among the Stunning Ladies of Wrestling."

"I'm fighting Javelina next week at the Roxy," Krystal said. "Y'all come."

"Delighted. This way please."

The *maitre d'* led them up winding colonial stairs to the second floor, through a broad dining room humming with conversation and the clink of crystal, onto the veranda, overlooking the golf course. A table at the end was set off from the other diners by velvet ropes. The *maitre d'* unlatched the rope and gestured for them to enter. Two white liveried waiters pulled back chairs for the ladies, and then the men.

A slim metrosexual with patent leather hair displayed his chiclets. "Good evening. The Flagler is honored by your presence. I am Yoel and I will be your waiter tonight. Can I get you something to drink?"

"Are you Cuban?"

"I was born in Havana, Your Highness."

"Oh, I just adore Cubans. I'm part Cuban myself."

"I'll have a glass of Glenmorangie on the rocks," said Prince Larry. "And the lady will have a dry Boodles martini. Gary?"

"I'll have whatever beer you have on draft and a Buffalo Trace chaser."

"Sir, I'm not sure we have Buffalo Trace."

"Whatever bourbon you got."

Yoel turned to Krystal. "And for the lady?"

"I'll take your finest rosé. Bring the bottle."

"Perfect."

"Gary," the prince said, "I've been following your exploits. I wasn't aware you caught a serial killer."

"Well, all credit goes to the monitor lizard, Prince. He's the one that bit him."

"Oh? Pray tell."

"Yeah, I had a restaurant that specialized in iguana. The Lizard Lounge. The cook caught a monitor lizard only we couldn't cook it, on account they're poison. We was riding around with the lizard in a cage and when Mukerjee stole my truck, it bit him."

"How did it get out of the cage?"

"That's my fault," Krystal said. "I took pity on the poor creature and unlatched the gate."

"But I did catch the biggest python in state history. I cut its head off with a samurai sword and had to tape it back on to claim the prize."

45 | SHAZAM!

"What did you do before your sudden rise to fame?" the prince asked.

"I was a roofer and I'd help Floyd kill palmetto bugs. Floyd's my best friend. We known each other since high school. You?"

Regan grabbed the prince's arm. "Larry went to Eton and Sandhurst. Then he enlisted in the Blues and Royals cavalry regiment and served five months in Afghanistan."

"But you're a prince," Krystal said. "You didn't have to go!"

"What kind of a man would I be if I didn't go with my mates? Let's look at the menu, shall we?"

The menus weighed a pound.

"Oh, I could go for those crab dumplings," Regan said. "Will you split them with me?"

Prince Larry put his hand on hers. "Assuredly."

"Look at this!" Gary said. "A-foot-long hot dog for sixteen

bucks! You know how many foot longs I can get in Turpentine for sixteen bucks?"

Yoel returned with their drinks. "Have you had an opportunity to look at the menu?"

"Give us a minute," Regan said.

"Would you like me to tell you about the specials?"

"In a minute."

"Excellent."

"Larry will have the all-natural roasted chicken."

"Must I? I would really prefer the surf and turf."

"Yes, you must. You must watch your cholesterol."

Krystal ordered the Yellowfin Tuna Au Poivre.

"Gimme that foot long!" Gary said.

"Perfect," Yoel declared and backed away bowing.

Prince Larry raised his glass. "Cheers!"

Gary raised his beer. "Ashes to ashes, dust to dust, if the liquor don't getcha, the women must! Down the hatch!"

The prince rubbed his hands together. "Very excited about tomorrow's alligator hunt. I brought my Harrison. That should do the trick, eh wot?"

Gary polished off his bourbon and signaled for another. "What's a Harrison?"

"Custom shotgun, old chap. Twenty-eight-inch S&S chopper-lump barrels with smooth concave rib choked cylinder and modified thirteen and five eights pull. Perished old Silvers pad. Fully figured European walnut stock with Anson push button release splinter forend, straight English grip with semi-diamond had, teardrops, classic point pattern checkering with mullered borders and gold oval. Case-hardened, small frame, sidelock action stocked to the fences with gold-line cocking indicators, intercepting sears, automatic ejectors, and automatic top tang safety with SAFE inlaid in gold. I'll let you fire it. It will spoil you on all other shotguns."

"We hunt gators with a pistol. Don't worry, Lar. I gotcha covered. I got a neat little Taurus .38 you can use. Cost two hundred bucks."

"A pistol?"

"Fuck yeah. We're only shooting from two feet away. We snug that gator up close to the boat and drill it through the skull. It's the only way to hunt."

Regan wrapped her hands around the prince's arm. "Larry, that sounds positively revolting. I forbid you from participating in this insanity."

Gary polished off his second bourbon and signaled for another. "Prince don't come, we ain't got no show."

The prince patted her hand. "It will be lovely, my darling, I assure you. I'll be perfectly safe in Gary's hands. This isn't his first shooting match! This is the chap who bagged the largest feral hog in state history."

"That was Pincus. He'll be there to run the drones."

Regan's lip curled. "Pincus?"

"One smart little Jew boy. You'll love him."

"What time should we get there?" Regan said.

"Well, there's no rush. Those gators ain't going nowhere. Why don'tcha come over around noon. We'll catch that gator and rustle up some ribs. You'll love Delilah's BBQ sauce."

"Who is Delilah?"

"Witchee woman who trains Krystal. Her recipe is a closely guarded secret, but I know it involves chili peppers and two mouthfuls of vinegar."

"Fights?"

"Oh yeah! Krystal's fighting Javelina in two weeks! We gotcha ringside seats, right next to the governor."

Yoel returned with a young woman wheeling a tinkling silver serving cart. He served the ladies first, whisking off the sterling silver covers with a flourish.

"Will there be anything else?"

Gary pointed to his foot long. "I'd like some ketchup. And another bourbon."

Regan's lip flew up like a window blind. "Ketchup?"

"Some people don't like ketchup on their dogs. Me 'n Floyd had a fight over it. You want to put mustard on your dog, you go right ahead. It's a free country. Me, I'll take ketchup any day of the week and twice on Sundays."

"Oh brother," Regan muttered.

Krystal held her fork like an ice pick. "Can't wait for you to meet Delilah. You two are gonna hit it off."

"Tell me more about this fascinating creature."

"She's a Seminole witchee woman. The Seminole are the original settlers. They own all the Hard Rock cafes and casinos. She don't have to work, but she can't just sit around. She's been wrassling since she was a papoose, and now she's my trainer."

"How do you train?"

"Well, I run to build up my endurance, and I wrassle a black bear named Samson. Only Samson's a girl."

"Samson and Delilah?"

"Yeah, ain't that a stitch? Delilah's not religious, 'less you count all those debbil dolls she's got sitting around her place, and when she goes into a trance and starts calling on the old gods."

Krystal tucked her chin down and looked grim. "Witchi-tie-to, gimee rah, whoa rah neeko, whoa rah neeko, hey ney, hey ney, no way..." she said in a guttural voice.

Regan laughed and clapped her hands. "You must teach me those words! I can use them in my role as Captain Megastar!"

"Who's Captain Megastar?"

Gary poked the remainder of the foot long into his mouth and chewed furiously. "Captain Megastar is the new Marvel superhero! And this here little lady's playin' her in the movie! Ain't that right, Reg?"

"You are correct, sir."

"And Sean Sheen's co-starring!"

"That hasn't been set yet. They're also talking to Astin Preen and Broderick Lawford."

"You a comic fan?"

"Not really. In fact, I'd never heard of Marvel comics until my agent brought me the offer."

"Well, I know a little bit about show biz myself," Gary said. "I had over three million YouTube subscribers."

"What happened?"

"You do one lousy episode about goat sex and people go nuts. Here's hoping this'll bring 'em back. I also know a few magic tricks."

"Oh really?" Regan said. "Would you show us one?"

Gary pushed back from the table, took off his jacket and showed his hands. "Nothing up my sleeve."

"Don't," Krystal said.

Gary turned around and pulled out his shirt. "Nothing behind my back."

Krystal stood, crossed her arms, and looked out at the golf course.

Gary gripped the white tablecloth in both hands. "Shazam!"

Gary yanked the tablecloth sending glasses, dishes, and silverware to the floor.

46 | THE THIRD HARBINGER

Major, Muriel Martinez, and Pincus arrived at Gary's place at nine Saturday morning in a Rustix van towing a Boston Whaler with a ninety horse Johnson. Pincus wore a life vest.

"Y'all come up," Gary said. "I got coffee and doughnuts."

Gary waited until they carbed up. "Okay, listen. The Royal Ducats are coming over so we'd better go over the rules. You gotta call 'em your highnesses, okay? You can't call 'em Larry and Regan cuz they ain't like you and me. Also try not to look 'em in the eye."

Major belched. "We fought a war, so we didn't have to put up with this bullshit!"

"Did you fight in the war? No? 'Cuz your ancestors didn't arrive until later!"

"And then we fought a war, so we didn't have to put up with your bullshit!"

Muriel Martinez, a small woman with a tight cap of black hair and horn-rimmed glasses, said, "You call them duke or duchess. Let's not refight the Civil War. Now as Maj explains it, you're taking the duke croc hunting."

"That's right."

"Well let's not have a repeat of what happened last time."

Gary drew his magnum. "Nobody's eating the duke. I'll make sure of that."

"Don't shoot him either."

"Nobody's shooting the duke. He'll have his own gun."

"Let's not refight the Revolutionary War."

"What about the Korean War?" Gary asked. "Can we refight that? I'm not crazy about how it ended."

Krystal came out wearing Daisy Dukes, a men's shirt tied over her taut midriff, cat's eye sunglasses, and an Explorers Club cap, carrying two hand axes. "I thought I'd teach the duchess how to throw an ax."

"She'll enjoy that!" Gary said.

A black Escalade pulled into the yard followed by a History Channel van. A man in a chauffeur's uniform hopped out of the Caddy, ran around the front and opened the rear door. Out stepped the duke and duchess. Karen Sullivan and a tech guy with ear buds got out of the van. Everybody but Major went down the steps to greet the royal couple.

"We fought a war, so we didn't have to do this shit," Major mumbled.

The chauffeur opened the rear gate and took out two bottles of Moet & Chandon.

Prince Larry took a bottle. "I thought we would take this occasion to offer a toast. Martin, bring out the glasses."

The chauffeur poked around in the back. "I'm sorry, your Lordship. The glasses were left behind."

Prince Larry frowned. "I say. Do you have any flutes?"

"Come on up, Prince!" Gary said, leading the way. "I got just the thing."

Gary went in the house and returned with a stack of Red Solo Cups. He went back in, got the boombox, and plugged it in. Toby Keith's "Red Solo Cup" boomed as Krystal took charge of the champagne bottles, filling cups and handing them out. Gary brought out a plastic tray covered with Ding Dongs, Twinkies, and Li'l Debbie Snack Cakes. The duke picked one up and examined it.

"Take a bite outta that, Duke! You won't regret it."

The duke tentatively nibbled. "I say! This is a tasty little treat!" He pushed the Twinkie into his mouth. A half hour later, Major waved his arms.

"Let's get these boats in the water! Gary, you gonna use your swamp buggy?"

"Yeah, will you be able to keep up?"

Karen Sullivan gave the thumb's up. Pincus unpacked his drones and handed Gary a wrist band.

"The drone will focus on you as long as you wear this transmitter."

"You got one for the duke?"

"No. I only have one."

Gary handed the wrist band to the duke. "You wear it, Duke. You're the star attraction."

The duke fastened it around his wrist. While Muriel

backed the Boston Whaler into the water, Gary led the duke to the end of the pier and stepped down into the swamp buggy. He reached in his pocket and pulled out a plastic container of Flent's Ear Stopples.

"Jam these in your ears while we're rolling. It gets pretty loud."

The duke examined the used wax ear plugs with distaste. "I don't think these are necessary."

"Suit yourself." Gary grabbed a pair and screwed them in. "I set some pig haunches over in Piss Poor Pond last night, and with any luck, we'll have gators waiting."

The duke pointed at a turtle the size of a dinner plate swimming away from the shore.

"I say! It's a monster!"

"That's a snapper. Stay away from those. Here's what's gonna happen. Ahmina pull the gator right up to the boat, you're gonna take this here magnum and plug it straight through the top of the skull between the eyes. Think you can do that?"

"I jolly well think so."

Muriel tied the Boston Whaler to the end of the pier. "Major, you and Pincus are with me."

"I'm staying here," Pincus said. "I'll be able to track you and communicate in real time. The drone is waterproof, but my monitor isn't."

Gary held his hand out to the duke. "Let's go!"

The duke stepped into the swamp buggy. Gary took his seat in front of the big fan and pushed the starter button. The small block Ford V8 roared into life. The duke shouted, "I say, may I see those ear plugs again?"

Major used a pole to push the air boat away from the dock, turning slowly until it pointed away from shore. Gary engaged the propeller and with a roar they skimmed into the swamp, followed moments later by Major and Muriel in the Whaler. The duke sat on an aluminum bench in front of Gary, grinning like a dog.

"I say! This is quite exhilarating!"

Gary steered the air boat around a shaggy peninsula toward a deeper section surrounded by mangrove and cypress. A taut line extended from a cypress branch into the water.

"See that line?" Gary yelled. "This is gonna be easier than I thought! You got the gun?"

The duke held his pistol up. "Tally ho!"

The Whaler followed them into the inlet, staying well back. Gary brought the air boat up to the line, killed the engine, and pulled on a pair of leather gloves.

"Omma pull that gator up to the boat. All you got to do is plug it!"

"Who is filming?"

Gary pointed at the four-rotor drone hovering at twenty feet. "Ready?"

The duke gave him the thumb's up. Gary pulled the line in hand over hand. Judging by the resistance, he was dealing with a five-hundred-pounder. The gator surfaced, thrashing and gnashing. Gary braced his feet against the gunwale and hauled until the gator was up against the boat, dunking and dodging.

"Shoot it!" Gary said.

The duke hunkered at the rim holding the pistol in both hands. He drilled the gator through the top of its head, the shot reverberating in the sudden silence. Gary took out his earplugs.

"Hot damn! You get that, Pincus?"

"Clear as a bell."

"Help me get this puppy in the boat!"

Together, he and the duke rolled the eight-foot gator into the swamp buggy while the drone hovered. The duke took out his earplugs.

"I say, old chap. I have to drain my lizard. Could you put me ashore for a minute?"

Gary picked up a fiberglass pole. "No prob." He poled the boat ten feet to where the duke could jump onto solid ground. The duke walked a few feet into the forest until only his red hair was visible. The drone followed.

The duke's scream erupted from the jungle. The duke exploded from the green clutching his trousers, a snapping turtle dangling from his manhood.

47 | THE ROYAL SHLONG

Gary leaped from the boat, grabbed the duke by the back of his collar and his belt, and rushed him into the water. The duke bent over, eyes screwed shut, tears streaming.

"Hang on. It'll let go in a sec."

The turtle let go and swam away. The duke sank to a sitting position, water up to his armpits. "My God. I've never felt such pain."

"You just sit there a minute. Leotis, is this the third harbinger?"

"To whom are you speaking?"

"Leotis. He's my counselor."

The duke looked around. "I don't see anyone."

Gary pointed at the opaque water. "He could be right there, and you wouldn't know. He's a catfish."

The prince was in too much pain to pursue the conversation. The Whaler putted over. "What's wrong?" Muriel said. "Is he all right?"

"Nothing serious. A snapping turtle grabbed his Johnson, is all."

"Holy fuck," Major declared.

Muriel phoned Pincus. "Did you get it?"

"I got it. But I don't think you can use it."

Gradually, the duke relaxed. Cautiously, he felt around. "Everything is still attached, but the royal wang is temporarily out of service."

Gary helped him to his feet. They sat on the tufted grass. The duke's penis was black and blue, but there was no blood.

"Corngrats! You got yourself a gator!"

The duke laughed, then cried. "I will never forget this day."

"Yeah, and hey, if her highness wants some tonight, I'm available." Gary slapped the duke on the back. "Just joshing, hoss!"

The duke fastened his royal belt. His clothes were soaked. They got back in the swamp buggy where the duke carefully got down on one knee to pose with the gator while Gary snapped pictures. Ear plugs in place, Gary started the engine and they returned to the dock. Pincus gave them the okay sign. The duchess, Karen Sullivan and Krystal ran toward the dock. The duchess was shocked, Sullivan alarmed, Krystal trying not to laugh. Behind them came the chauffeur.

"Oh my God!" the duchess declared. "Are you all right?"

Grabbing hold of her hand, the duke stepped up on the pier. "I'll be all right, but it will take time. How do you know what happened?"

"We were watching on Zoom!"

"That video must be expunged," Sullivan declared. "It must be immediately expunged."

"That's up to the duke, don'tcha think?" Gary said. "If that footage was to air, it would show the duke can laugh at his own expense. That makes him likable."

Sullivan bristled. "Are you suggesting he's not likable?"

The duchess shot out her arm like Mussolini. "Absolutely not. We will not have the royal appendage paraded in front of the masses."

The duchess pointed at the drone hovering overhead. "Get that thing out of here!"

Sullivan addressed Pincus sitting in a folding chair absorbed in his laptop. "You. Put away your drone or so help me I'll shoot it out of the sky myself!"

"Can you even shoot, sis?" Krystal said.

Sullivan hopped up and down swinging her feedbag purse trying to knock the drone out of the sky. Pincus never looked up, but the drone rose and fell with her swings, just out of reach.

"Now look here, Karen," Gary said. "This here's America! We fought a war so we wouldn't have to turn in our footage, besides which, you think those won't get publicity? I guaran-dog-tee you, if we put up that clip of that turtle snapping up the Duke's Johnson, you'll have five million hits in the morning!"

Major loomed. "We fought a war so we wouldn't have to give up our video clips."

Sullivan was apoplectic. "The royal couple have not

agreed to showing that footage. You wouldn't dare. We'll sue you for everything you're worth."

"Not much," Gary said. "That's why we keep going through these contortions. Howzis? When I come on your show, I'll light my farts."

Sullivan turned away in disgust.

"Of course, we're not going to show it," Major said. "Pincus, erase the turtle."

Pincus looked up. "I will, Major, but I may have been hacked."

"Say what?"

"Yeah. I got a reading here says there's a third party feeding off my stream."

The duchess snapped her fingers at the chauffeur. "Martin! Search the premises."

"Hold on thar," Gary said. "Just the other day, dude got et by a python."

Martin had movie star good looks. "Pythons are peaceful by nature and will not attack a human unless threatened."

"We got water moccasins."

Martin raised his leg modeling a cavalry boot.

"Well, all right. If you see a feral hog, you can shoot those, and I'll cook it up. That'd be a great ending for today's show."

Pincus held up his hand. "They're not on the property. They could be anywhere."

"Can you trace it?" Sullivan asked.

"Yes, but it will take time."

Sullivan shook her head. "We don't have time. If they put

that up on YouTube, we're doomed."

"Not so fast," the duchess said. "Gary has a point here. We've been accused of being aloof and condescending. Footage of this turtle biting Larry could be just what we need to appear warm and more human."

The duke sputtered. "Any fool can dangle his manhood before a snapping turtle!"

"My point exactly, my love. It occurs to me that you might need medical help. I believe we should go to the hospital. Where's the nearest hospital?"

"That would be St. John's in Turpentine," Gary said. "Happy to take you there in my new Ram."

"I think we'll be more comfortable in the Cadillac," Regan said. "We have to get this looked at. Martin, take us to the hospital."

"Right away, mum."

Gary put his hand on the duke's shoulder. "Oh hey, before I forget, y'all are invited to Krystal's match next week. She's fighting Javelina."

"We'll consult our schedule and let you know," Regan said. *Shed-jewel.*

With the duke leaning on her shoulder, the duchess led him to the car. The doors slammed shut and the car went back the way it came.

"Oh my God," Sullivan wailed.

"It'll be fine," Major assured her.

"Just the sight of the duke plugging that gator's gonna make him a hero," Gary said. "Maj, how soon can you get it up?"

"Couple days. Gotta record your commentary and add the soundtrack and do a little editing."

Sullivan glowered, hands on hips. "Everything must have our approval. You're not posting anything until we've signed off."

"No, of course not," Major said. "We're planning a relaunch. This won't air for several weeks yet."

"Well hell," Gary said. "Let's go back to the house and smoke a bowl."

Sullivan clopped up the pier. "I really should have gone with them. Major, can you give me a ride to the hospital?"

"Me too," Muriel said.

"Sure. Sorry, Gar. Too early for me. I'll talk to you later. Let's go. What about you, Pincus?"

Pincus held up his hand. "I'll stay here. Gary can give me a ride home later."

"Sure."

Pincus carried his equipment up on the deck, sat and opened the laptop. The screen showed the Escalade pulling up outside the emergency entrance.

"If I can't film through a window, I'll hack into their surveillance system."

"Smooth move, Pincus. Our viewers have a right to view the royal shlong."

"We fought a war over it," Pincus said.

48 | HERETOFORE UNDISCOVERED

Friday, Gary and Krystal drove to Miami for the opening of the "Beautiful Bones" exhibit, held in the Miami Museum of Modern Art, an Art Deco monolith in North Miami. Gary wore the same outfit in which he'd dined with the Ducats, while Krystal wore a new dress she'd bought at Target for fifteen dollars. They parked in the 125th Street Ramp and walked the two blocks to the museum at 591 NW 27th St, where couples wearing tuxedos and evening dresses lined up on the red carpet waiting for the doors to open.

A liveried employee opened the double glass doors. Music from a string quartet drifted into the street. The soaring atrium was restored to its former glory following Tallywhacker's rampage. Bartenders in white shirts mixed cocktails opposite a buffet laden with finger food.

Krystal grabbed Gary by the elbow. "I'm famished."

They loaded their paper plates, decorated with dinosaur skeletons, with marinated artichoke hearts, bacon-wrapped scallops, and stuffed mushrooms, placing them on plinths displaying free form sculpture.

Gary pointed at a clay blob with his plastic fork. "What do you think that is?"

"Dinosaur turd."

Gary found the label on the side. "Armadillo Dreams by Luther Dross."

They swilled champagne. Dropping their dishes in a plastic bin, they presented their tickets at the door to the Voinovitch Gallery, previously home to the Glory of Glass. The hall had been transformed to make room for a complete brontosaurus skeleton. The skeleton was seventy feet long, mounted on a black platform six inches off the floor, the neck and head extending eleven feet beyond the frame, hanging from the ceiling by invisible wires.

Gary and Krystal craned their necks. "I wonder what kind of gun I could use," Gary said.

"Gary! Krystal!"

They turned. Their former neighbors, Boris and Marie Bongo Box, strode toward them in a tux and black dress, carrying flutes of champagne.

"Boris and Marie!" Gary boomed. "How the hell are ya?"

"The neighborhood's not the same with you," Boris said. "It's just not the same. We were hoping you'd rebuild."

"Yeah, well, Kensington Gardens really ain't our thing. We feel more at home in the swamp. I got some sad news for you, Boris."

Boris' brow furrowed. "What is it?"

"Tallywhacker is gone."

"What do you mean?"

"A flying saucer came and scooped him up. I saw it myself. I guess those aliens think he's one of them now. He didn't want to go. He kept calling out your name."

Boris, a middle-aged man with a paunch, visibly relaxed. "You're certain?"

"I saw it with my own eyes."

"To tell you the truth, Gary, I'm not sorry to see him go. The CIA, FBI, and National Security have been hounding me ever since he took off. Do they know about this?"

"No. Should I tell 'em?"

"I wish you would."

"I'll do it!"

Marie gave Krystal an approving glance. "You look marvelous, Krystal!"

"Thanks, Marie. I'm fighting Javelina tomorrow night. The Royal Ducats will be there, and the governor and his wife. I can set aside tickets for you if you like. It's at the Roxy."

"Oh dear," Marie said. "I'm afraid we have another engagement."

"Maybe you can get out of it."

"We'll let you know. Do we have your phone number?"

Gary pulled out his phone. "Got to check it myself. I've switched phones so many times, I don't know what all I got. Here it is." He held the phone out to Boris.

"Why don't you text it to me. You still have my number?"

"Give it to me."

Boris pulled out his ostrich skin wallet and handed Gary his card. Boris Bongo Box, Chief Engineer Skoal Robotix, along with his contact info. "May I have one of yours?"

"Dang! I been meaning to have cards made up, I just don't know what they should say."

More people gathered in the great hall, surrounding the skeletons and snapping pictures.

"Where'dja get the hooch?"

"We brought it in from the lobby."

By now, a sizable crowd surrounded the bar.

"Come on. Let's find that Dubasaurus."

"Yes!" Marie sang. "We read in the program that you have discovered a heretofore unknown dinosaur. Gary, we are simply amazed at your accomplishments. How do you do it?"

"I don't know, Marie. I guess I'm just in the right place at the right time."

Gary sensed a disturbance in the force, a hint of sandalwood, and turned to see Delilah enter on the arm of her brother Bob, wearing a beaded deerskin dress, black hair in a 'fro, and moccasins. Bob wore a dark blue suit. People spoke softly to one another and took surreptitious pictures, as if they were the Royal Ducats. Delilah had that air of exoticism and she looked like a million bucks, putting all the designer threads to shame.

Gary introduced Delilah and Bob to the Bongo Boxes. "Delilah's on the Seminole Arts Council. She talked 'em into showing the Dubasaurus! And Boris here is the man behind Tallywhacker."

The Bongo Boxes fawned.

"I regret I never got to meet Tallywhacker," Delilah said.

A man in a tux and a bad rug clapped his hands. "Ladies and gentlemen, we are honored to have with us tonight the man who discovered this heretofore unknown discovery, the man who apprehended Plastic Surgeon to the Stars and serial killer Dr. Vanderlay Mukerjee, bagged the biggest python in state history, and the inventor of house suspenders, Mr. Gary Duba, and his lovely wife Krystal!"

A spotlight shone. Dozens applauded. Gary cupped his hands.

"Ya'll come down to the Roxy tomorrow night where Krystal's fighting the Javelina! We still got tickets."

"And now, sir," the tux said, "would you please cut the ribbon to the Hearst Gallery, where the dinosaur skull, which we have dubbed 'Gary', is displayed."

The announcer extended his arm.

"Who you?" Krystal said.

"Levander K. Collindale, curator of the museum. I should have introduced myself."

"Gotta card?" Gary said.

Collindale forked over a card. Gary stuck it in his pocket. "I'm working on one, I just don't know what to say. I don't want to come off like I'm bragging."

"I think, Mr. Duba, with your accomplishments all you need is your name and your contact information."

The string quartet had relocated to the Voinovitch Gallery and were sawing up a storm. Gary followed the red carpet past the brontosaurus, the stegosaurus, and beneath the hanging ichthyosaur to another gallery, twin glass doors open. The crowd broke into spontaneous applause as he cut the ribbon and entered the darkened gallery, spotlights gleaming off the polished skull. It looked like it had been hand-waxed. Only hard sediment remained along the base of the skull.

The string quartet broke into the Flintstones theme.

Collindale motioned Gary and Krystal over, beaming like a lighthouse, holding a wireless mic.

"Welcome! Welcome paleontologists, dinosaur enthusiasts, and kids of all ages! The Museum of Modern Art is thrilled to present to you, for the first time anywhere, a heretofore unknown dinosaur from prehistoric times. And here is the man who found this skull, the man who apprehended Plastic Surgeon to the Stars and serial killer Dr. Vanderlay Mukerjee, caught the biggest python in state history, and the inventor of house suspenders, Gary Duba."

Thunderous applause. Krystal beamed. Delilah sipped from a silver flask.

"Gary, will you say a few words?"

"Well folks, it's an honor and a privilege, and don't forget, Krystal, or Steely Danielle as she's known on the circuit, is fighting Javelina at the Roxy tomorrow night! Y'all come."

As Gary spoke, an old man with long, scraggly hair wearing a tuxedo crept up on the skull from the other side with a putty knife and began scraping the residue. A docent informed Collindale who stormed around the base, followed by Gary, Krystal, half the crowd, and the media.

“Stop!” Collindale barked. “What do you think you’re doing?”

The man wiped the base of the skull with a handkerchief uncovering a signature etched deep into the bone.

“What does that say?” he said in a wheezy voice.

Gary squinted at the signature. “Claude Balls?”

49 | THE ESCHATON

Collindale snapped his fingers. "Call security."

"Wait a minute," Gary said. "Are you Claude Balls?"

The wizened homunculus crossed his arms. "I am."

Gary turned to Collindale. "Don't you know who this is? It's Claude Balls, the inventor of performance art! Claude Balls, the dadaist and contemporary of Hemingway, Lord Buckley, and Jack Kerouac! Claude Balls, man!"

An older woman with a towering gray beehive put her hand to her mouth. "Claude Balls? Oh my God...we have your painting of the Pristine Sistine Christine hanging in our dining room! I met you at the Furman Gallery in the Village when I was a little girl! You were signing golf balls!"

"I stole those golf balls while posing as a caddie at the U.S. Open in 1965. Gary Player won, miserable prick."

"Claude!" Gary said. "I'm a caddie too! I shot a hippo on the Shangri La fairway!"

The old man put his hand on Gary's shoulder. "A brilliant

piece of performance art."

Collindale poked at his phone while visitors whispered. A young man clutching a program approached.

"Mr. Balls, may I have your autograph?"

Balls held the program against the skull and signed.

A young man in a navy sports jacket and white shirt holding a recording device sidled in. "Mr. Balls, I'm Terry Gold for the *Miami Herald.* Can you tell me why and how you created this skull?"

A hush fell over the crowd.

"To immanentize the eschaton ex post haste de facto."

"Would you explain please sir?"

"First, the how. I began collecting bones from slaughterhouses in 1959. I baked them in a kiln. I ground them into a powder which I mixed with toad secretions and wolf spider webbing. I heated this mixture to four hundred and eighty-two degrees and poured it into a bronze cast made for me by the great Erroll Swansea of Loveland, Colorado. I designed this cast to combine elements of birds, ferrets, dinosaurs, and the lowly armadillo. Voila!" The old man pointed at his creation, running his other hand through his long, lank hair. "The skull was born!"

"You mean it's fake?" asked a thin woman toward the back.

Ball whirled. He looked like Beethoven. "Fake? Nothing I do is fake! It is real! It is vital! It has been my life's mission to usher in enlightenment, an age of reason, where each individual is free to fulfill his full potential, be it a barber, or president of the United States!"

"Are you running for something?" the woman asked.

"I am running toward enlightenment."

Krystal caught it all on camera. The string quartet played the *Flintstones.*

"There's a man in the funny papers we all know," Ball said. "He lived 'way back a long time ago. He don't eat nothing but a bear cat stew. WHAT'S HIS NAME?"

The crowd stared befuddled.

"Alley Oop!" Gary said.

"But Mr. Balls," Gold said. "Why would you want to bring about the end of the world?"

"Why would I welcome the afterlife? In the immortal words Ronaldus Magnus, let's have the blood bath now and get it over with!"

"I think what Mr. Ball is saying," Gary said, "is that we're worm food anyway. Why not just go ahead and have a cosmic event?"

"Like Jim Jones?" Gold said. "Or Heaven's Gate?"

"Not at all. I do not advocate mass suicide. Quite the contrary! I wish to pull humanity back from the brink. I am calling for a new enlightenment to free man from the shackles of conventional morality and hook his fortune to the stars!"

"Why is it always men?" a woman with blue hair demanded.

Balls posed, amazingly supple for a man his age. "This is a man's world. This is a man's world. But it wouldn't be nothing without a woman or a girl..."

"How is this fake dinosaur head supposed to do that?" Gold demanded.

"I want to know how you got it down there," Gary said. "Weren't for that sinkhole, it would have stayed there forever."

"The land was very different in 1967."

"You mean it's fake?" the woman at the back said.

"Fake, madame? Fake? It has my signature! It is real! It is so real, that if I could pick it up, and drop it on your head, you would die!"

An older man in a tux drew Collindale aside and whispered in his ear. The gallery filled to capacity. A string of supplicants lined up to have their programs signed.

"Claude!" Gary said. "Krystal's fighting tomorrow night at the Roxy. How'd you like to be our guest?"

"A brilliant piece of performance art. I'd like to bring a friend."

"Sure, no prob. The Duke and Duchess of Ducats will also be there. They're big fans of yours."

"What time?"

"Doors open at four, first bout is at five, but Krystal and Javelina don't come on until nine."

"I would be happy to recite a poem between bouts."

"Well, we already got a rabbit and a skunk in a rap battle, but I'll look into that."

Krystal tapped Gary on the shoulder. "Did you secure the rabbit and the skunk?"

Gary smacked his forehead. "Holy shit! I'll call 'em right now."

Leaving Balls at the center of an admiring crowd, Gary returned to the cavernous lobby and phoned Grosz. “Got a gig for ya! You and a skunk are gonna have a rap battle between bouts at the Roxy Theater tomorrow night.”

“What’s it pay?”

“It’s for exposure.”

“Piss off!”

“Waidaminit! Two fifty.”

“Can I wear my roller blades?”

“Dubious.”

“Who’s the skunk?”

“Major Sutton. He’s an old friend of mine. Come on. It’s a big crowd. My gal Krystal’s fighting Javelina. You may know her as the Black Dildo.”

“The Black Dildo? Hell yeah! I’m in!”

Next, he called Major. “Got a gig for ya! You and a rabbit are gonna have a rap battle between bouts at the Roxy Theater tomorrow night.”

“What’s it pay?”

“It’s for exposure.”

“Really, Gary? Really?”

“Two fifty.”

“Who’s the rabbit?”

“Rodell Grosz. He used to be Rapid Rabbit at Wacky World until he got drunk and started insulting customers. You know Krystal’s fighting Javelina.”

“What time?”

“Be there at five. Come on back to our dressing room. I’ll

have a skunk costume for ya."

"Do you already have the costume?"

"Nah. I'll pick it up tomorrow from Funky Costume in Palm Beach."

"'Cuz I got a Santa Claus outfit and it's the season. You could give me whatever you were gonna pay for the skunk outfit."

"Sounds good to me."

50 | THE MURDEROUS BISON

Gary and Krystal got home at nine. Gary phoned Karen Sullivan. “Tell the royal couple that Claude Balls will be at the fight tomorrow night. We are holding two ringside seats for them. The governor and his wife will also be there.”

“This is exciting news! I’ll let them know.”

Gary phoned Anthony Viola. “Tell the governor that the Duke and Duchess of Ducats will be at the fight tomorrow night. We are holding two ringside seats for the governor and first lady.”

“I will make sure that they attend. Thank you very much.”

Gary heard Krystal rummaging around in the bedroom. She came out.

“Where’d you put that blow?”

“Are you nuts? You’ve got a fight tomorrow night.”

“Come on. One little line won’t kill me.”

“Forget it! Ten minutes and you’ll want another.”

“It makes me horny.”

"Horace Horse Collar makes you horny."

"I'm an adult. I can handle my drugs."

"Fuggedaboudit."

"You can forget getting any pussy tonight!"

"I'll live. Go to bed. This is the most important fight of your career!"

Krystal flipped him the bird, stormed into the bedroom and slammed the door. Gary thought about visiting *Wet Hot American Pussy* on his laptop. Instead, he filled a Mason jar with shine and went to talk to Leotis.

As Gary approached the end of the pier, Leotis sang, "We've been waiting for so long...to sing and play for you some of our songs..."

"Leotis, Krystal's got a hair up her ass because I won't let her have any cocaine."

"Cocaine is bad for you. I saw what it did to Leo."

"Tomorrow's the biggest fight of her career. Javelina is heavily favored. If Krystal can pull off the upset, there's no telling where it will lead."

"I wish I could be there."

"Well it's being broadcast live on goontv, if you have cable."

"I don't," Leotis said morosely.

Gary felt bad for Leotis. "You ain't missing out."

"I've been thinking of branching out," the catfish said.

"Branching out how?"

"Marketing catfish-scented candles. I got the idea from Gwyneth Paltrow."

"Who's your audience?"

"Single ladies."

"It's not a bad idea, I just don't how you'd market such a thing."

"I would purchase advertising on your YouTube channel."

"With what?"

"Sunken treasure. I'm also thinking of cutting an alt country album. I'm a big fan of Charlie Pride and Hank Williams Junior. I've been writing songs."

"You have the voice."

"I was a huge fan of *Sons of Anarchy.* If I were to be reborn, it would be as a human so I could ride motorcycles. I call this one 'Live Wire'."

Leotis sang in a soulful baritone. "The Live Wire bites the blue bizuti. It fails to garner any booty. Do bikers dream of bikes electric? I'd rather spend time in ditches septic. They should call that thing the Apoplectic. If it doesn't smell like gas, you can stick it up your ass. It has to go potato, or I give it hard pass. Potato, potato, and potato, creep these tubers in lieu of Ubers..."

"And here's the bridge. Potato, potato, potato. That's what makes it gnarly. The ebike ain't been born that can call itself a Harley."

"Catchy."

"Oh it was thunder, thunder, over thunder road," Leotis sang. "Thunder was his engine and white lightning was his load."

"Now that's country."

"If only I could reach out to my old friend Leo. I know he

would support me."

"I can help you there, Leotis. I'm seeing the Royal Ducats tomorrow. All those celebrities know each other. It would help if I had a copy of your song."

"I need recording equipment. I can survive for up to an hour on land."

"No shit? That doesn't give us much time, unless we bring the studio to you."

"That's a great idea, Gary. Do you know anybody who does live recording?"

"Well, you can't just sing it all yourself. You need a band. Bass, drums, guitar, keyboards. Maybe some horns. I've always been a sucker for a band with horns."

"That appeals to me too, Gary. Big Tower of Power fan."

"I'll ask around. Floyd plays trombone. Major might know somebody. He knows everybody."

"I was sorry to hear about Tallywhacker."

"Did you know him?"

"We talked. I admired what he did. Well, he's in a better place now. You ought to get some sleep, Gary. You've got a big day ahead of you."

"Yeah, I'll be sleeping on the sofa. I wouldn't give Krystal blow and now she's locked me out of the bedroom."

"I wouldn't stand for that treatment."

"You're a catfish."

"You know, Gary, when I hear the terrible things people do to each other, I'm glad I'm a catfish."

"Leotis," Gary said with a hitch in his voice, "I'm glad

you're a catfish too."

Too wired to sleep, Gary tuned into Mr. Mephisto, a late-night horror host. *Barfalo* was playing. It had been Tallywhacker's favorite movie. A bulimic buffalo terrorizes settlers in eighteen eighties Nebraska. It was the *Jaws* scene, where the settlers first come across one of Barfalo's victims, a German lad, almost unrecognizable due to the acidity of Barfalo's vomit.

"Ya can't hardly recognize it as human," said Sheriff Avery, holding a bandanna to his nose.

"Jayzus, Sheriff," said his deputy Dolph. "That stinks worse than the tannery over in Lewisville."

Cut to Habib Rodriguez in a yoked jacket, aviator shades and ten-gallon hat. "Have you been attacked by a buffalo, and the insurance company wouldn't give you the money you deserve? Call me, Habib Rodriguez, the Long Arm. I've been dealing with insurance companies all my life and they don't scare me."

Gary tipped his Mason jar to the screen. "Habib!"

"Gary, you should go to bed. You've got a long day tomorrow."

"You can see me?"

Mr. Mephisto, a demonic figure in his newsboy hat and fright makeup, gazed out from his red desk, beneath Dollar Store letters strung behind him party style spelling MR. MEPHISTO. "Exciting news, fear hounds! Acidic Pictures has just announced *Barfalo 2: Welcome to the Vomitorium*! And now, back to the murderous bison!"

Gary shook his head. "I shouldn't have licked that toad."

51 | UNFRIEND ME NOW

Friday morning before the big event, Krystal and Javelina met at Ferd Ludlow's gym to choreograph their fight. Delilah brought her notes. So did Javelina's trainer, Topher Santana, the Mexican Ernest Borgnine. Santana did indeed resemble the famous actor, save for the hairline mustache on his upper lip.

Krystal, Delilah, Javelina and Santana stood by the ring to toss a coin determining the winner. Delilah wore a turban, and fawn slacks. Krystal wore a gray cotton jumpsuit with red stripes. Two young men, who looked Cuban, worked heavy bags in a corner. Delilah asked Ferd to toss the coin. The conspiracy theorist and radio show host, a thin man with thin hair and a pronounced Adam's apple, dressed in carpenter's pants and a blue work shirt, stood between the two parties balancing a fifty cent piece on his thumb.

"Ready?"

"Not so fast," Santana said. "First we toss the coin to determine who calls it."

Delilah put her hands on her hips. “Well then we have to toss the coin to determine who gets to call who gets to call.”

“Hey, Teofilo!” Ferd called to one of the young fighters. “Would you come here a minute?”

The young welterweight bopped over wearing gym shoes, red sweatpants and a wife beater. “What’s up, Mr. Ludlow?”

“I’m going to toss the coin. You call either Krystal or Javelina. This will determine who gets to call the coin toss choosing the winner. Krystal here will be heads, Javelina will be tails.”

“Not so fast,” Santana said. “Why should Krystal go first? Because she’s a white woman? Why not advance a woman of color to address historic inequities?”

“Fine,” Krystal said. “Javelina can be heads.”

Ferd looked at the young fighter. “Ready?”

Teofilo nodded. Ferd tossed the coin. “Heads!” Teofilo called.

The coin hit the wooden floor and rolled. The parties gathered around.

“It’s tails,” Ferd announced. “Javelina will call the coin toss determining who wins the fight. Ready?”

“Not so fast,” Santana said. “Would you have any objection to Teofilo tossing the coin?”

Delilah crossed her arms. “Fine.”

Teofilo tossed the coin.

“Heads!” Javelina sang.

The coin hit the wooden floor and rolled. The parties gathered around.

"It's tails," Ferd said. "Krystal will be the victor."

Javelina sneered.

"How about two out of three?" Santana said.

Ferd crossed his arms like an umpire. "Get to work. At this rate, you'll be at it all day."

"Hey, Ferd," Krystal said. "You coming to the fight?"

"I wouldn't miss it. My show doesn't come on until midnight."

"Will aliens be watching the fight?" Javelina said.

"Yes. They watch everything we do. You all remember last year when they threatened to blow Earth up if we didn't stop broadcasting *The Curse of Oak Island*."

"Yet it's still on and we're still here," Delilah said.

"The nearest aliens are on Alpha Centauri. It would take them years to get here, even traveling through black holes, so we have a little time."

"But couldn't aliens seize control of some human, like they did Tallywhacker?" Krystal said.

"Well, Tallywhacker was a unique individual combining advanced cyberware with human DNA. I have no doubt they're trying. In fact, I've had several callers claim that aliens have abducted them."

"But if the nearest aliens are years away, how do the flying saucers keep showing up?"

Ferd shrugged. "The flying saucers that show up probably represent a more primitive type of alien, not sophisticated enough to demonically possess a human."

Teofilo crossed himself and muttered in Spanish.

Krystal, Delilah, Javelina and Santana sat at a folding card table next to the ring and went over the notes. The fight was intricately choreographed. Javelina would attack with her patented Klein Bottle maneuver. Krystal would counter with Paddling Blowfish. There would be a back-and-forth exchange combining boxing, ju jitsu, wrestling, the sharp-shooter, chokeslam, pile driver, powerbomb, enzuigiri, atomic drop, doomsday device, Boston crab, facebuster and Alabama. They agreed to fight for forty-five minutes. At a signal from the referee, Javelina would lunge for a takedown, Krystal would leapfrog over her back, roll and go for the leg lock.

Krystal and Javelina posed for pictures with their fists up. They shook hands.

Delilah grabbed her backpack. "Let's get breakfast."

They walked down the street to Fernando's, a Cuban diner featuring cafe con leche, tortillas, Cuba homelettes filled with ham and onions, potatoes, and plantains. They took a booth looking out on SW 8th Avenue and ordered homelettes. A Spanish language TV on one wall showed soccer players racing around like frenzied ants. Krystal ordered a ham and onion homelette, Delilah cafe con leche and a Cubano. Delilah looked at the TV screen.

"You can run, but you can't hide."

Krystal turned in her seat to see Habib speaking silently while a Spanish language scroll ran along the bottom. "¿Ha sido lesionado en un accidente automovilístico?"

She turned back and dug into her homelette. "Habib's

coming. He's bringing Auburn."

"What about the Duke and Duchess."

Krystal stared at Delilah chewing with determination. She swallowed. Glunk. "Not only are the Royal Ducats coming, so are Claude Balls and the governor."

"Claude Balls? The guy that faked the dino skull?"

"Yeah. The Royal Ducats are big fans. They came over to our house to retrieve their Claude Balls painting. That's when we cut the deal to be on each other's shows."

"Those Royal Ducats make my flesh crawl. The way she leads him around by the nose, it's embarrassing. All she's done with her life are some brassiere ads and being spokesperson for Your Pillow. You'll sleep like a baby blah blah blah as if the pillow is the most important factor on whether you get a good night's sleep. You know what the most important factor is? State of mind. I can sleep anywhere. Japanese use a wood block as a pillow. And now they're branching out into mattresses, bed covers, doggie dishes, and bed truck linings. America does not want to make pillows. America wants to make weapons and vehicles."

"You know what rankles my ass?" Krystal said.

Delilah steepled her fingers and placed them below her chin. "I'm all ears."

"People who post some shit about Patrick Stewart or cute Chihuahuas on Facebook and write, 'you're welcome', like they're doing us a favor."

"I don't even have a computer."

"How do you live?"

"I think I'm a lot happier without a computer. All I hear are strife and threats."

"You ain't wrong. Hardly a day goes by somebody don't post if you do this and that, then thus and so, UNFRIEND ME NOW!"

"Sounds like a bunch of iguanas fighting."

Krystal stared at Delilah chewing with determination. Delilah swallowed. Glunk.

"Well said," Krystal said.

52 | PRESTIDIGITATION

Gary, Claude Balls, and the Royal Ducats met for cocktails at five pm at the Beanery, an upscale restaurant two blocks from the Roxy. Gary reserved a private dining room on the second floor overlooking Northwest Seventh Street, the room decorated tiki style with bamboo wainscoting, a dozen potted ferns, tiki masks on the wall, and a parrot on a brass stand.

Claude Balls was waiting for Gary when he arrived, seated at the table with a sketchpad in his lap, a glass of rum before him. He had signed the white tablecloth, "Claude Balls," along with a smiley face.

"Claude! How they hanging?"

"Low and slow. Take a look at this." Balls held up a drawing of an athletic looking man in baggy trousers juggling four weasels.

"Great! What do you call it?"

"Four weasels."

Gary wore fresh blue jeans with the cuffs turned up, gator

boots made from a gator he shot, silver belt buckle inlaid with a pink flamingo, a STEELY DANIELLE Tee-shirt, and his Gators cap, which he set on the floor.

The Ducats arrived in their black Escalade, Martin guarding their flank. No one recognized them. The *maître d'*, a Cuban man in a white jacket, black pants and goatee entered. "This way, your royal highnesses."

The duke and duchess entered, he in a blue blazer with gold buttons and a Royal Fusiliers tie, she in black evening dress and mink stole, followed by Martin in chauffeur's livery. Martin sat by the door. Claude Balls and Gary stood. The duke took Balls' hand in both of his.

"This is such an honor. I have admired you ever since I was a child and I read your book, *Immanentizing the Eschaton.*"

"A work of towering genius."

"I dabble in the arts myself. I'm a bit of a photographer."

Gary grabbed a chair. "Let's sit, you guys. I'm so hungry I could eat a baby's butt through a park bench."

They sat. A cute Cuban waitress swished in. "Can I get you some drinks?"

Gary ordered a Cuba Libre. The duke ordered Glenmorangie. The duchess ordered a Boodles martini. Claude Balls ordered a bottle of champagne.

The duke sat between Balls and Gary. "How old are you, Mr. Balls?"

The duchess swatted him on the arm.

"I am ninety-three years young."

"How do you account for your amazing vitality?"

"Art, sir. It is art to which I awaken, and toward which I stumble. There is no greater calling than interpreting the world for lesser mortals through the medium of art. The steel-worker at the end of the day. The exhausted secretary. What do they have to look forward to but the delight and escapism of music? Paintings? Movies? We can argue *ad infinitum* which Star Wars is better, but at the end of the day, it is *Star Wars* itself which confers life."

"What is your favorite movie, sir?"

"*Nothing but Trouble.* A work of towering genius. Dan Aykroyd is greatly underrated."

"And what are you working on now, sir?"

"I am casting famous vaginas and penises in bronze. Have you heard of the Plaster Casters? They got the idea from me. Frank Zappa was a dear friend. I told him to lay off the fags. In fact, Duke, I've been meaning to talk to you."

The duke turned beet red.

The waitress returned with their drinks. "Would you like to hear the specials?"

"By all means," Balls said.

"Curried iguana en brochette with pineapple and mush-rooms, nutria chili, giant African land snails in garlic butter, and lionfish on a bed of wild rice with pepper sauce."

The duchess picked up the two-pound menu. "Give us a minute please."

"The hell's a lionfish?" Gary said.

Balls set down his flute. "Stripped of its venomous spines

and filleted like any other fish, the lionfish is a rare delicacy. I will have the lionfish."

The waitress returned. Gary ordered a hamburger. The duke ordered the iguana. The duchess ordered the nutria.

"May I see the lionfish?" Balls said. "I'd like to choose my own."

"The lionfish are fresh today. They are not in an aquarium."

"That's no way to serve lionfish. Like its mighty namesake, the lionfish is highly territorial and ferocious. You can judge the lionfish by its aggression. It's a simple test. You merely deposit a goldfish or some other small tidbit in the tank and see which lionfish emerges the victor. The only problem, of course, is that the quality of the meal deteriorates the more fish you select. I will have the *ropa vieja.* Its Cuba's national dish. Fidel Castro introduced me to it."

The duchess sipped her martini. "We have always had the greatest admiration for him. A true revolutionary."

"Claude," the duke said, "what have you been working on lately?"

"A series of paintings about invasive species. I would like to paint Gary shooting the hippo, if that's all right."

Gary raised his glass. "Hell, yeah!"

"I'm also working on a unified field theory of everything. The move from a structuralist account in which capital is understood to structure social relations in relatively homologous ways to a view of hegemony in which power relations are subject to repetition, convergence, and rearticulation brings the question of temporality into the thinking of structure, and marks a shift from a form of Althusserian theory that takes structural tonalities as theoretical objects to one in which the insights into the contingent possibility of structure inaugurate a renewed conception of hegemony as bound up with the contingent sites and strategies of the rearticulation of power."

The duchess put her elegant fingers to her mouth. "Mr. Balls. I've never heard it stated so eloquently. When will it be done?"

"Next year, I hope. I've also been reviving performance art. It warms my heart to see someone like Gary, a common man, a kulak, transcending class limitations to create brilliant sequences such as the hippo. You know, I'm a bit of a prestidigitator."

Balls extended his hand, palm down, and suddenly he was holding five cards. He reached behind the duchess' ear and plucked a fifty-cent piece.

"Oh, that's marvelous! You must be great with kids! Do you have children, Mr. Balls?"

"I have eight grandchildren. They come see me from time to time. I've got a place down on Plantation Key."

The duchess settled her perfect chin on top of her cross fingers. "Show us more, please."

"Certainly." Balls stood, cleared his chair out of the way. "Gary, would you slide over a little please?"

Balls surveyed the elegant table set with dishes, china, silverware and candles. He took the white tablecloth in both hands and yanked, sending glasses, dishes, and silverware to the floor.

53 | PRELIMS

The prelims were under way when the rappers arrived. Gary excused himself to meet with Rodell Grosz and Major Sutton, waiting backstage with their costumes under their arms. Gary motioned them into an empty dressing room. Rodell carried two heads, a rabbit and a panda.

"What's with the panda?" Gary said.

"I gotta scout the room. I can't be caught in the rabbit head. Wacky World will hang me out to dry. Something feels off, I'm going with the panda."

"But people want the rabbit."

"We'll see."

"So, it's just a precaution."

"Exactly."

"The panda head really doesn't go with the rabbit suit."

"Nevertheless."

"Maybe Santa should wear the panda head."

"Fuck that. People want to see a black Santa."

"I would actually prefer to wear the panda head," Major said.

"You're going on at six. Aldo will announce a rap-off between Rappin' Rabbit and St. Nick. We can't say Rapid Rabbit for obvious reasons..."

"What if somebody turns me into Wacky World?"

Gary shrugged. "Put on the panda head."

Major raised a finger. "I'd like to wear the panda head."

"Where am I gonna get another animal suit? This was your idea!"

"Chill, Rodell. It's not as if the audience is filled with members of the Fourth Estate!"

"But there's gonna be video and shit."

"Rodell, if you don't want to do it, just say so."

"What, and let this clown get the best of me?"

Major bristled. He outweighed Rodell by fifty pounds. "Excuse me?"

Gary pointed to Rodell's roller blades. "Why'd you bring those?"

"Just in case."

"Aldo says he can provide a beat track."

Major held up a thumb drive. "I brought my own."

Gary held out his hand. "I'll give it a listen. Nothing gross or disgusting. The Royal Ducats and the governor will be here. You boys okay back here?"

Major gave him the thumb's up.

"I'll survive," Rodell said.

Gary entered Krystal's dressing room. Delilah sat on

a chair facing Krystal while Airwrecka weaved her hair into corn rows. He asked Airwrecka to step aside while he rubbed Krystal's shoulders. She wore a black onesie with STEELY DANIELLE written on the front in script, and HABIB RODRIGUEZ—THE LONG ARM with his phone number, on her butt.

"You ready?"

"I'm ready!"

"Did you have dinner?"

"I ate at four. Clam chowder and corn bread."

"All right! Listen, I got to go out front and make sure the governor knows where to go, check on the Royals, all that good shit."

"What about Claude Balls?"

"He's covering the event for the New Yorker. This is a big night, little lady. Networks, newspapers, Tik Tok influencers, two Elvis impersonators and a Tom Petty."

They hugged. "Love you," she said into his ear.

Delilah pointed to the door. "Outta here. This is girls only."

Gary went back to the lobby, bought a jumbo dog and an orange soda, and made his way through the crowd to his ringside seat. A group of Saudis in white robes filled a row halfway back. Chinese in dark blue suits and sunglasses. Boys from the hood in dashikis and gold chains. A group of Hasidim in black robes and hats. A united nations of wrestling.

Lena the Hyena had the Mongoose in a headlock. Mongoose lifted Lena's leg and swept her back into a takedown. Mongoose got on top and tried a can opener. Lena swept her to the side and reversed. Lena was a stocky woman. The match went on and on, first one woman on top, then the other. It ended when Lena slid up over Mongoose's head and released a fart that could be heard in the back rows. Mongoose tapped out. The referee, a statuesque Brazilian in hot pants and striped shirt named Giselle, held Lena's hand aloft. The auditorium was still filling up, extended families filling clusters of seats, often in two rows.

Three kids sat behind Gary, their parents behind them. Gary stretched and turned around. Two boys, nine and twelve wearing torn jeans. The older boy wore a Rappin' Rabbit T-shirt. The youngest, a girl of around seven, wore blue denim coveralls and pink shoes. The dad, fortyish, greasy black DA, Dukes of Hazard Tee, Confederate flag cap, with knobby wrists and rough hands. The woman looked like the Mona Lisa after some nutso tourist got done redesigning her with Magic Markers and Silly Putty.

The boys buried their snouts in their Fonebones. The ring was set in the center of the big hall with seats radiating on all sides. Portable tables were set up next to the ring for the sportscasters. The match had attracted unusual attention due to the Royal Ducats and the Guv, who would not arrive until after the intermission.

Aldo Maldonado in a metallic lavender suit took the center of the ring. "Hey, what a terrific fight, am I right? Let's give it up for both those ferocious warriors!"

Cheers, whistling, vuvuzelas.

"Our next bout is the featured fight of the undercard,

two tough broads you know well—Sweet Charlotte takes on Baby Jane!"

Sweet Charlotte weighed one eighty-five with arms the size of anacondas. She'd dyed her hair purple. Baby Jane wore a black and white county jail deal and looked like Nurse Ratched. They grappled Greco style before breaking and circling, stances low, arms outspread, making kissey poo to each other.

"Jane, you ignorant slut," Sweet Charlotte cooed. "You couldn't crush an egg if your life depended on it."

"Oh yeah, fat ass? What happened to your boyfriend, Mr. Wonderful? Wasn't he sockin' it to Libretta last time I looked? Oh yes he was."

Charlotte went for a takedown. Jane grabbed her by her cornrows, rolled onto her back, and threw her judo style. Charlotte rolled and popped to her feet. They circled. Someone threw a teddy bear into the ring. The public address system blasted "Disco Inferno" for ten seconds and went silent.

Charlotte finally won with a rare earth spring roll.

Moldanado took the stage. "How about that Baby Jane! Does she know how to hit or what? I'm giving both these ladies a performance of the night bonus. I might even cast 'em in a movie, you never know. We're going to have a short intermission. Then, we have a very special treat for you! Rappin' Rabbit versus Santa Claus, in a rap battle of the ages!"

Holy shit!

Gary sprang out of his chair and raced backstage, where Grosz and Major stood on opposite sides of the aisle, Grosz in his rabbit suit clutching the rabbit head, Maj dressed like Santa holding the panda head.

54 | THE HELICOPTER

Gary took the center of the ring holding a wireless mic. "Hey, ya'll! I'm Gary Duba, the man who apprehended Plastic Surgeon..."

"...to the Stars and serial killer Dr. Vanderlay Mukerjee!" the audience shot back.

"That's right! Y'all watch my YouTube channel and follow me on twitter @localyokel. Now before we get to the main event, we got a very special treat for you. Come on up, boys!"

Grosz crawled through the robes in costume. Major crawled in opposite wearing the Santa outfit with the panda head.

"What the hell is that?" someone shouted. "Saint Panda?"

"It's Panda Santa," Gary said. "He knows what you've been doing. Now this here is Rappin' Rabbit, all the way from Fort Meyers!"

"That's Rapid Rabbit!" bellowed the boy in the Rapid Rabbit shirt, standing on his chair. His brother popped up like a prairie dog.

Gary fake laughed. "It's Rappin' Rabbit. Ain't no Rapid Rabbit. Dude can barely walk in that suit. And his opponent, who usually introduces me, is Panda Santa! Let 'er rip!"

As Gary slid out between the ropes, the funk beat vibrated and Grosz danced forward.

"I'm Rappin' Rabbit, the people's choice! People say that my Johnson's noice! I got long ears and a cotton tail!" He spun around ass out. He slapped his butt and straightened up. "I've been in and out of jail! I purchase cocaine cheap in Mexico and sell it by the heap in Texico!" Grosz boogied R. Crumb style around the ring.

Panda Santa leaped high in the air and landed in a Maori stance, fists clenched, head vibrating as crazy buzzing blasted. "They call me Santa Panda cuz with the girls I'm handa. They love to search my goodie bag, no tellin' what you'll find. The keychain for a Jag, or a lady with a hind..."

Gary's phone buzzed. The Royals had arrived. In the lobby, police had set up velvet ropes to cordon off the governor, wife Greta, Royal Ducats and Claude Balls while photographers snapped pictures. The Ducat's man Martin headed off a line of autograph seekers. When Gary tried to enter, a policeman held out his hand.

"Where do you think you're going?"

The duke came up. "It's all right, Officer. That's Gary Duba, the man who apprehended Plastic Surgeon to the Stars and serial killer Dr. Vanderlay Mukerjee."

"The man who captured the largest python in state

history," the governor added.

"The man married to tonight's odds-on favorite, Steely Danielle," Aldo Moldanado said.

The cop let him through. Gary posed for pictures.

"You're not going to vomit on me, are you?" the governor said out of the side of his mouth.

"No way, Guv! That was a once in a lifetime experience! Hope you enjoy the show."

Aldo Moldanado posed for a picture. "I would be delighted to show our company to their box seats."

"I'll be up, folks!" Gary promised. "First, I got to take care of business."

"Tell your lovely wife I've bet on her," the duke said.

"Not too much I hope."

"Ten thousand pounds."

"Okay! No pressure."

Inside, Maje had Grosz down in the center of the ring and was flailing away with his great, cloth covered paws.

"BOOO!"

"EAT SHIT YOU ASSHOLES!"

"GET OUT!"

"RAPID RABBIT!" an adolescent yodel.

Gary ran down the aisle, fairly leaped into the ring and started kicking both men savagely.

"Knock it off, you assholes!"

Rapid Rabbit got on one elbow and gasped. "Where are the fucking tips?"

The ring was filled with cigarette butts, empty cups, a

used condom, and a Rubik's Cube.

"I'll pay you out of the gate. Just get the fuck out of here."

"How much?" the panda demanded.

"I told you, two fifty! Come on, Maje! Get out of here before they kill us!"

The trio beat a hasty retreat down the back aisle. Not until they ducked into the backstage area did rabbit and panda rip off their heads with a velcro buzz. They staggered into folding card chairs and collapsed, gasping, heads rolling at their feet.

"You both get two fifty, okay?"

Grosz looked like he was strangling. "Two fifty?!"

Major leaned forward, arms on knees. "You don't need to pay me, Gary. It was worth it just to pound on this asshole."

"Gimme his two fifty too," Grosz gasped.

"We'll talk about it. There are showers in your dressing rooms."

"Ho ho ho," Major gasped.

A roar penetrated backstage, followed by the chant. "Black Dildo! Black Dildo! Black Dildo!"

Gary headed out. "Gotta go. Krystal's on."

He raced to her dressing room and they began the long walk to the ring.

As they entered the theater, every Mexican and half the Latinos were on their feet chanting, "Javelina! Javelina! Javelina!"

Aldo preened in the spotlight. "And now, mi gente, the moment you've been waiting for! El momento del destino!

At the catch weight of one hundred and thirty, two of the toughest ladies in the biz...in this corner, hailing from Jaurez, twenty-five and four as a professional, the daughter of legendary Lucha Libre fighter El Matador, Marcela "Javelina" Aguilar!

Standing, roaring, whistles, vuvuzelas, firecrackers as Javelina bounced out of the D corridor, head poking up through a hole in a white towel, chin down, hands on her trainer's shoulders in front of her, corn-rowed black hair, wearing a metallic crimson onesie with the black silhouette of the javelina on the breast, Modelo Especial on the butt.

"JAVELINA, JAVELINA, JAVELINA!"

"And in this corner, hailing from Turpentine..."

"BLACK DILDO! BLACK DILDO! BLACK DILDO!"

"STEELY DANIELLLLLLLE..." Aldo drew it out.

Fonebones jockeyed. People stood. Gary led Krystal out of the back followed by Delilah, Airwrecka, and Ferd Ludlow. Habib, Auburn, Floyd, Patrice, and some kid Patrice picked up stood and slapped palms as they went by. They stepped into the ring. The contingents tried to drown each other out. The governor, wife, Royal Ducats and Claude Balls sat front row, ninety degrees from Gary's seat. Claude Balls was on his feet. The duke poked the governor in the ribs with his elbow.

Gary lip read, "Jolly good, wot?"

Giselle stood in the center. "Seconds out of the ring!" Krystal faced Javelina in the opposite corner. Giselle chopped down. "Wrestle!"

Javelina rushed low for a takedown. Krystal cartwheeled

out of the way. They circled. They clashed. Krystal turned Javelina's thrust kick into a Bruce Lee three sixty. The Mexican fighter stuck the landing in a superhero pose. Cheers, laughter, cursing, money exchanged. The Arabs had leaned over the near empty row separating them from the Chinese and were passing money back and forth.

The sharpshooter. The chokeslam. The pile driver. The atomic drop. The Boston Crab. Something happened to the choreography. They'd stopped exchanging blows, but the grappling was for real, each struggling to control the other. Leg locks. Kimuras. Choke holds, until unexpectedly, Javelina squatted as Krystal attacked, got her in a fireman's carry, held Krystal overhead by the back of her neck and trunks, and gave her the helicopter. Javelina moved to the edge of the stage and released. Krystal flew into the governor, slid down in his lap, and gacked up a warm stew of partially digested clam chowder.

55 | THE CUCARACHA

Grosz staggered to his dressing room, a head under each arm. His roller blades lay on the floor. He had hoped to show what he could do to a producer, but there wasn't a producer to be found. Peeling off his rabbit suit, he stripped naked and took a shower in the tiny bathroom. He could always go back to selling used cars for Dealin' Doug.

Grosz felt sorry for himself. He hadn't been laid in three months and getting shit-faced and canned from his job at Wacky World was the cherry on the sundae. But he had skills. Mad skills. Grosz could make up rhymes on the spot. He would challenge Eminem, Yellow Wolf, and Macklemore to a contest. First, they would ignore him, but after he built up his YouTube channel with his mad skills, they would not be able to ignore him. Millions of fans would bury those pretenders under mountains of abuse until they either agreed to meet him or did the right thing and committed ritual suicide. Grosz only had two hundred and nineteen followers. The problem was, he wasn't on enough. He needed to stir controversy. That's how you built an online audience, by claiming Star Wars sucks, Will Ferrell isn't funny and Billy Eilish can't sing.

"Oh, how I wish Billy Eilish would slip on some soap and piss up a rope. Eminem? Don't make me laugh. He ain't nothin' but a white flour muffin. You call for Macklemore, I call for Mackle Less! When he raps, he leaves a mess! Beastie Boys may make some noise, but when they're finished, ain't no joys!"

If only he could remember the lyrics when he dried off. He had a couple stock phrases he used all the time, but so did everybody. He shut off the shower and heard the faint roar of the crowd through the curtains and the walls. That Black Dildo bitch was hot. He wouldn't mind banging her, but her old man was straight out of *Deliverance.* Fucker better pay or Grosz might have to cut him. He still had time to get on over to the El Tigre and pick up one of those bored Latina secretaries. Grosz toweled off. The bathroom smelled like Pinesol.

He stepped out of the bathroom and looked around. All his clothes were gone. Everything. The rabbit suit, his pants, his wallet, car keys, the works. Only his roller blades and the panda head remained.

"SHIT!"

He opened the door. The corridor was empty, with a window at the far end looking out on 7th Ave. Grosz ran to the window and looked out just in time to see a punk on a skateboard stroking up the avenue in a hoodie with a stuffed backpack, one rabbit ear dangling. Grosz ran back to his dressing room. A woman wrestler stepped out in front of him and her instincts took over. Grabbing Grosz by his sweaty black hair, she executed a perfect *hane goshi*, throwing him to the hardwood floor with a smack.

"Fuck outta here, you perv!" she screamed, sinking into a karate stance. She looked about one forty and none of it was fat.

Grosz slid back on his ass, hands up. "Someone stole my clothes! I have to catch them!"

"I'm calling security." The woman stepped inside and slammed her door.

Grosz grabbed his roller blades and the panda head and pounded down the stairwell at the end of the hall. Just inside the alley exit, he sat on the cold stoop, strapped on his roller blades, pulled the Panda head on and exited into the sour-smelling alley. Wheels crunching on broken glass, he exploded from the alley, startling pedestrians including several Japanese tourists who whipped out their phones and took pictures. He veered into traffic, causing a green Prius to swerve.

"WHAT THE FUCK!" echoed through the Prius' open window. As he approached Highway Nine, an oscillating '67 Chevy low rider pulled up next to him, windows open. Two cholos wearing bandannas slapped their arms against the car doors whooping and hollering.

"YOU GO PANDA! GO, GO, GO!"

"LOOK AT THAT WHITE BOY SCOOT!"

Grosz shot through the red light at North Twenty-eighth, his honor brigade forced to stop. The traffic camera blinked. As he slalomed east, he caught a glimpse of the skateboard, a block ahead, cruising along without a care in the world. That motherfucker was in for a rude awakening.

An open convertible with three college girls heading west laughed, pointed, took pictures. More low riders joined the parade. The Chevy caught up blasting "*Latin Boogaloo.*" A '67 Riviera low rider pulled in front. Now he had an honor guard. The Chevy pulled up on his left.

"Whatchoo runnin' from?" asked the cholo in the shotgun seat.

"I ain't runnin' from nothin'! I'm chasing the motherfucker who stole my clothes!"

The cholo hooted. The cars blasted tunes. Two bike riders in spandex and teardrop helmets, their asses in the air, joined the pursuit.

"Who is it?" the cholo yelled.

"It's that motherfucker in the gray hoodie on the skateboard!"

The Chevy peeled out, racing down the left lane blasting "*The Cucaracha*".

It was all flat. Grosz could see all the way to Wagner Creek. The Chevy zigged, zagged, and cut off the skateboarder who slammed into the front fender and went airborne, spiraling over the hood. Grosz gasped like a fat man on a treadmill as he pressed on. As he pulled up at the shakedown, the cholos had the hoodie backed against the brick wall of a taqueria and were going through his backpack.

One held up the rabbit suit. Another held the head.

"Looks like we got a real superhero!" crowed the one with the head. He wore a plaid shirt over a blinding white wife beater, red bandanna wrapped around his head. He had a goatee.

Grosz bent over gasping. "Thanks," he croaked.

"You gonna show us your secret identity?"

"Let me put my pants on first."

A cholo handed him his pants. He pulled them on and tore off the panda head. "Where's my wallet, motherfucker?" he snarled at the skateboarder, a pierced and pimpled white boy with half his head shaved, the other half purple.

"I don't know man! It was in the bag!"

Grosz searched the bag. He looked around. "Oh come on! I haven't had enough shit you're gonna rob me too?"

A police vehicle whooped. The cholos bundled in their rides and peeled out. Grosz was too exhausted to flee. He sat on the curb with the panda head in his lap. The police cruiser pulled up. Two Latino cops got out, a man and a woman. The woman came up to him.

"May I see some identification?"

"Those cholos stole my wallet."

"We have reports of a man skating naked wearing a panda head. Was that you?"

Grosz looked up, all innocence. "Me?"

FLORIDA MAN SKATES NAKED WEARING ONLY PANDA HEAD

56 | PERFORMANCE ART

"This contest has been declared a draw!" Aldo Moldanado said. Cups, crumpled programs, old socks, popcorn and peanuts sailed through the air. Fights erupted. Vuvuzelas brayed. The Royal Ducats and the governor skedaddled. Claude Balls found Gary and Delilah in the dressing room while Krystal showered. He hefted a bottle of champagne.

"What are we celebrating?" Gary said. "It was a draw!"

The cork ricocheted off the ceiling. "Is it true this is the third time you've vomited on the governor?"

"Yeah, but most of the credit goes to Krystal."

"She is the queen of everything. It is the most significant piece of performance art since Hugh Grant got in a brawl with a transvestite at the intersection of Hollywood and Vine. I'm inspired. I will write a play about it. Perhaps you and Krystal would consent to playing yourselves. As for the governor, I have my eye on Leonardo DiCaprio."

"I may have a connection."

"Perhaps you'll introduce us."

"What are you gonna call it?"

"*Three Rainbows.* It says so much about our times right now, about how the interior becomes the exterior, and how long festering resentments inevitably lead to mass revolution."

Delilah made a face. "I think those clams were bad."

"*Bad Clams*! I shall call it *Bad Clams.* I might be able to get financing from Liechtenstein. Prince Albert is a great supporter of the arts. Several years ago, the Royal Shakespeare Society performed my play, *Crumbling Infrastructure.* I am a Royal Knight of the Arts."

Balls reached into his shirt and took out a heavy medallion which he showed around and stuffed back in his shirt.

"'Scuse me," Delilah said. "'Scuse me. Ain't what you call performance art just field variety bullshit? Lemme see that medal."

"I will not have my honor questioned."

Delilah duck faced, grabbed the chain around Balls' neck and ripped it out. She studied the medallion. "Uh-huh." She held it in front of Gary. A bas relief of Regis Gator, Wacky World, 1999. "Regis Gator Challenge Coin."

Balls smiled. "I congratulate you on recognizing performance art when you see it. I am going to write a play, and you're going to be in it."

"Hells no."

"You'll play Marie Laveau, the witch queen of New Orleans."

Delilah's eyes narrowed. "Whatchoo know about Marie

Laveau?"

"In 1982, the punk band Misfits broke into her tomb. The police arrested fifteen, wearing dramatic theatrical makeup. It was a brilliant piece of performance art."

"Is taking a shit performance art?"

"Everything is on the table."

Krystal came out of the bathroom in a terrycloth robe. "Did I win?"

"Draw," Delilah said. "We're looking at a rematch in March."

"I shoulda grabbed her hair when I had the chance."

"All right," Gary said, "Pack up. I'm taking y'all to dinner. You too, Claude."

Krystal put her hand on Gary's shoulder. "You're not gonna dump any rats, are ya?"

"I got cash. Let's go. There's a nice Cuban place right down the street."

The Havana Grill on NW 7th featured reproductions of famous Cuban and Mexican artists on the walls including Frida Kahlo, Wilfredo Lam, and Robert Fabelo. Photographs showed Havana in the fifties and sixties, black and white pictures of the beaches, boulevards filled with Packards and Fords, palm trees in front of the Grand Hotel. A rapier thin waiter seated them at a round table covered with white linen in a corner, next to a Mitch O'Connell painting of a matador and a bull.

Balls held the chair for Krystal, then Delilah.

"Whoops!" Gary said.

Krystal fingered the white linen. “No herky jerky stuff, okay?”

Balls seated himself. “I never repeat myself before the same audience.”

A raven-haired waitress took their orders. Gary ordered a Cuba Libre, Balls ordered Don Papa, Krystal ordered Bacardi, and Delilah ordered Jack Daniels. A Cuban family with five small children took a big round table. The kids swooped around giggling and shrieking, bumping into the back of a chair occupied by a tall man wearing a turtleneck. The tall man turned, displaying a profile like an Easter Island statue.

“It’s the Main Man,” Gary said.

The Main Man glared at the children. He glared at the parents. He jerked his chair back and stalked to the foyer, confronting the manager and gesticulating. His voice rose.

“Others may cower in the face of this uncivilized disruption, but the Main Man will not tolerate it! This is a restaurant, not a preschool!”

The manager offered to seat the Main Man elsewhere. The Main Man would have none of it. His eyes found Gary. “Youuuu!” he hissed.

Gary pointed at himself. “Me!”

The Main Man left, leaving his partly consumed meal on the table. One of the waiters made as if to give chase, but the manager held him back.

Delilah shook her head clucking.

“What was that?” Krystal said.

“The Main Man!”

The waitress took their orders. Krystal had the clam chowder. Gary had the *bistec de palomilla.* Delilah had the *fillete de puerco.* Balls had the *iguana linguini.* Balls inhaled individual *linguini* with a moist sucking sound.

"Where's the Main Man when you need him," Delilah muttered. The waitress cleared their plates. Delilah reached for Balls' hand.

"You have an interesting palm."

"Tell me."

Delilah traced a line with her forefinger. "You have royal blood. You are the heir to the Kingdom of Pottawotamie, an indigenous people found in Oklahoma."

"I was born in Casablanca of a French father and a Greek mother."

"You have a beautiful voice."

"I was thrown out of boys' choir."

"Someday you will win the Iditarod."

"What is it?"

"A dogsled race."

"Would you like a bouquet?" Balls said.

"Sure."

Balls plucked five nose hairs and held them out.

"No thank you."

The waitress returned. "Would you like to see the dessert menu?"

Gary patted his tummy and belched. "No thanks, hon. Just the check."

She returned a minute later. Two hundred and seventy-five

dollars.

Balls held up his hand. “You must allow me to pay.”

“Hell, Claude! It was our fight.”

“Nevertheless.”

Claude pulled a wad of cash from his pocket. It looked like Gary’s wad of cash. He opened his wallet. He turned to Balls, who smiled self-deprecatingly.

Grunts and scuffling. The Main Man was back, clutching something to his chest. The manager and waiter trued to restrain him. Shaking them off, he wound up like Barry Bonds and let fly. A rat landed in the center of Gary’s table and sprang up squeaking.

Everyone leaped to their feet.

“Run!” Gary said.

“Wait!” Balls cried, gripping the white linen tablecloth.

57 | A FEW GOOD DUCATS

Just before sunrise, pounding woke Gary. The pounding in his head. The pounding at the door. He remembered getting home at one in the morning. The rest was a blur. He pulled on his pants and padded through the trailer, noting the overturned Dixie cups and smeared mirror in the living room, Krystal's bra on the dining room table, a vuvuzela.

Gary opened the door. Red-faced Pincus, with a handbag and a stuffed backpack.

"You've got to hide me, Mr. Duba."

"Hide you from what?"

"Someone hacked my computer and posted the turtle."

"What turtle?"

Pincus pointed to his crotch and made a snapping gesture with his hand.

"Oh fuck. Do they know who you are?"

"Not yet, but anybody good enough to do this already knows. It's only a matter of time before they come for me.

The Ducats could sue me. I could go to debtors' prison."

"Ain't no debtors' prison."

"They'll be after you too."

Gary's phone beeped. Karen Sullivan. Gary canceled the call.

"Come inside. I gotta drink something."

They went in the kitchen. Gary drained three red solo cups of water. "You want something?"

"You got coffee?"

Gary made coffee in the percolator, found some stale Li'l Debbies in the cupboard. Pincus opened his laptop, turned it toward Gary. "TMZ: WARNING—GRAPHIC CONTENT—please read and sign the waiver along with all appropriate information. What are your parents' maiden names? What is your social security number? Where do you currently live? In what banks do you hold accounts?"

Pincus pressed buttons. The turtle dangled while the prince hopped in agony holding it by the shell like some primitive tribal dance. Gary's phone rang. He turned it off. He turned off Krystal's too. Major slid to a stop at nine. Gary opened the door for him, and he stormed into the kitchen and poured himself a cup.

"The shit has hit the fan."

"I heard."

"How could you let this happen? Why didn't that fool erase the video?"

Pincus looked down in shame.

"Hey, it ain't like anybody put that turtle up to it. I

tried to warn his high and mighty dukeness that this here was swamp country. Weren't my idea to go gator hunting. That was his idea!"

Krystal stood in the entry wearing pedal pushers and a halter top. "Fuck's the matter with you? This is a ratings bonanza! Who owns that video? We do! We hired Pincus to shoot the show! Pincus, you right on this. We need to control that video."

"Too late, Mrs. Duba. By now it's been copied a million times. It's playing in New Guinea. It's playing in the Rub al Khali."

Major slurped and inserted a Li'l Debbie like a log in a woodchipper. "Krystal could have a point. No one set out to make the duke look foolish. This will humanize him. This can only increase his popularity. People can relate."

Krystal poured herself a cup. "It could start a trend."

A van marked KMST CHANNEL 27 pulled up in the yard. Out popped a glamour babe and her cameraman. Gary went out on the porch and put his hands up.

"Woah. That's far enough."

The woman stood at the bottom of the steps, holding a mic. She had a big pouf of copper colored hair and had a tiny mic clipped to her sundress. The cameraman aimed. "Mr. Duba, I'm Brenda Babe of KMST Miami. What can you tell us about the snapping turtle?"

"It's just your average, everyday snapping turtle. The duke was just in the wrong place at the wrong time."

"Wasn't the duke participating in your show? *The Gary*

Duba Show?"

"The duke and I are old friends and have agreed to appear in each other's shows. He was filming his first segment."

"Do you feel any responsibility for his injuries?"

"It could have happened to anybody. This is Florida!"

Habib pulled into the lot in his GS, got out and waved his arms. "Not another word. If you have any questions for my client Gary Duba, you can ask me."

The media swiveled. "Who are you, sir?"

"I'm Habib Rodriguez. Have you been in an auto accident and the insurance company didn't give you what you deserved? Call me, the Long Arm." He handed Brenda his card.

"Why are you here if Mr. Duba did nothing wrong?"

"Why are *you* here?"

"It's news. A scion of the royal family has his unit snatched by a turtle, people want to know."

"Why don't you ask the duke?"

"We've reached out to the Royal Ducats for a response."

Gary cupped his hands. "Habib! This is private property! I can't have these bums swarming around!"

"You heard the man."

Brenda Babe put her hands on her hips. "Do you realize to whom you're speaking? I have 285,000 twitter followers."

"Tweet away. Just don't do it from here."

"The people have a right to know."

"I will hit you with a writ of *ad coelum*. I will smack you with an *ad hominem ad infintum*. I will bring a suit of *animus nocendi*. I will bring a writ of *condicio sine qua non consensus ad idem crimen faisi*, and *ex aequo et bono*."

Habib gestured toward Krystal on the deck, holding her Fonebone. He pointed skyward, at Pincus' drone. "We have the proof on camera."

It was a Mexican stand-off.

Brenda Babe whirled and headed for the van. "Let's go."

At the last minute she whirled. "FLORIDA MAN REPEATEDLY VOMITS IN GOVERNOR'S LAP!"

"Come on up here, Habib! Wet your whistle!"

Habib went up on the porch. "I can't drink. I've got to be in court at eleven. You need to get the duke to sign this form absolving you of all liability in case something else latches on to him."

"Ain't this a bit late?"

"You have a special relationship with the Royal Ducats. Maybe Krystal can get him to do it."

"I'll have fun trying."

"Regan'll spit you out like a chicken bone."

"Maybe that girl'd like to meet me in the ring."

"Now you're talking! You think a match between the Black Dildo and Duchess of Ducats might sell tickets?"

Habib shook his head. "Dream on."

The black Escalade pulled into the yard. Karen Sullivan got out wearing a pleated beige skirt, matching jacket and toreador blouse and advanced, her face a clenched fist. "If you think you can get away with humiliating the royal heir, you're mistaken!"

Habib stood on the steps, arms crossed. "Are you accusing

my client of biting the duke's cock?"

Gary tamped it down. "Hang on there, Karen. Look at the upside. This is gonna make Larry a lot more relatable to a lot more gals and guys. You know he has a PR problem. This'll make him seem like just a regular guy."

"Because a turtle snapped on to him?"

"Because it could happen to anybody! Say, how'd you feel about your gal the duchess meeting my gal the Black Dildo in the wrestling ring? Think that might attract a few Ducats?"

58 | THE JUNGLE BEARS FRUIT

A three wheeled Morgan banged into the yard, duke at the wheel, the duchess' eyes screwed shut, hanging on for dear life. Prince Larry shut off the engine and boosted himself out of the doorless tin can.

"I say, Karen. What are you doing here?"

Sullivan stomped. "What are you doing here? After what they did to you? Should you even be out of bed? Why aren't you in the hospital?"

"Pish tosh, old girl. We Ducats are made of sterner stuff. Doctor says I'll be good to go in a few days." The prince thrust his pelvis in and out. The duchess looked away. "What are you doing here?"

"Looking out for your interests, Your Highness. You must be aware that the video is out. It has over five million views. Pornhub called."

The duke waved it away. Pish tosh. What did they see but my manhood, ten inches long at rest?"

"That's with the turtle pulling," Gary said. "That turtle went twenty pounds, easy."

The duchess boosted herself out. She had a way of cocking her hip that commanded attention. "We should let people know. The Duke of Ducats can lift more with his manhood than most men can lift with a wheelbarrow."

Krystal leaped to the ground without spilling her Mason jar and went to the duchess. "Girl, we have got a fantastic idea that'll increase our popularity and make us both a fortune."

"Do tell."

"You know I wrestle."

"You vomited in the governor's lap."

"What if you and I was to have a match? Nobody'll get hurt. We'll map it out beforehand. You could call yourself the Duchess of Destruction."

Regan morphed through four seasons and ended up with a smile. "Her Royal Heinie versus the Black Dildo."

Gary snapped his fingers. "Now that's class!"

Habib beckoned from the porch. "Duchess, come on up. Lemme getcha something to drink. What are you having?"

"Do you have a nice Cabernet?" Regan asked.

"I got Boone's Farm," Krystal said.

"By all means. Boone's Farm it is."

The Royal Ducats sat in Adirondacks on the deck. Gary hauled out a couple folding chairs. He opened the door and yelled, "PINCUS, YOU CAN COME OUT NOW."

Pincus came out looking down. He sidled over to the duke. "I'm very sorry what happened, Your Highness. I never intended for that video to go anywhere."

The duke slapped Pincus on the back. "Think nothing of it, old chap. It's all good, as you Yanks are wont to say."

Habib put his elbows on the rail. "Duke, Gary's prepared to show you things no Englishman has ever seen. You may be required to take a blood oath. In return, he only asks that you sign this release absolving him of any liability in the event of an accident. Not that we anticipate anything. I mean, what else could possibly happen, right?"

"What did you have in mind?"

"Did you see Krystal's trainer the other night at the Roxy? The woman in the brown turban?"

"I did indeed. She looked very exotic. Who is she? Where is she from?"

"Delilah's a Seminole oracle. She's the seventh daughter of a seventh son. She can foresee the future."

"Pish tosh."

"No, really. She cleaned up on last year's Superbowl. She lives in the middle of the reservation. Few white men have ever been that far. In fact, I can name them on one hand. Gary."

"And Garrison Gland."

"Who?"

"The dude socking it to your client's wife. Got a show on History. *Bizarre Bazaar.* Might do a segment on me."

The duchess wrinkled her nose. "What is that stench?"

Gary smelled it too. "Now that you mention it, it does stink a little around here. Maybe we should go take a look."

The duchess threw up her hands. "I hope you're not including us in your adventure."

"Hey, only if you wanna. Whatddaya say, Duke? Up for a little hike in the woods?"

"Why not! Jolly good, eh?"

"Hey lemme getcha some swamp boots."

Gary went in the house and returned with big rubber boots that rose to just below the knee and two caps. The duke pulled them on. Gary wore a Select Sires hat, a machete on one side and a pistol on the other.

The duke put on his KFC hat. "I say. Should I be armed?"

"Yeah, hang on a sec." Gary returned with an AR 15.

The duke checked the action and the magazine. "I say! I've always wanted to shoot one of these!"

"Well, no shooting unless we're attacked by a python or something."

The duke bounded down the steps. "Tally ho!"

Gary led him down a game trail that snaked through the overgrowth to the swamp. They passed the place where the Venezuelan pancaked. The duke crouched, examining the flattened grass and bent twigs.

"From my studies of the American Indian, I would say something fell out of the trees."

"Fell out of an airplane. We gave him a proper burial."

"You mean a man?"

"A Venezuelan. They keep coming out here for some reason. I asked 'em to stop."

Through the trees they glimpsed water. The duke crouched again. He stood. He raised his head and sniffed.

"I think the smell is getting stronger." He pointed away from the water. "This way."

"Yeah, it's getting riper. Hold on there, Your Highness. Better let me take the lead. I know these woods."

Gary drew his machete and lopped off a branch. Gary thrust out his arm as a python slithered across the path.

"I say!"

"You got any snakes in England?"

"Just your garden variety. Nothing venomous. How did you kill that python?"

"I cut its head off with a samurai sword. Then I had to duct tape it back on to claim the reward."

The woods crackled around them. Monkeys screeched. Birds hooted. Something plopped in the water. Gary stopped, putting his hand up behind him. "Wait a minute. I think we found it."

"What is it? It smells like a rotting corpse!"

Gary parted the foliage and stepped into a clearing. In the center of the clearing, a huge, cabbage like base displayed a green, tongue-like blossom. The clearing reeked of rotting meat. The duke pulled a bandanna from his pocket and tied it around his face. He staggered. He walked a little ways into the jungle and gagged. He returned, wiping his mouth on his sleeve.

"What is it?"

"Feck if I know."

Garrison Gland approached wearing a safari jacket, pith helmet, and jodhpurs. "I knew it! The giant Sumatran corpse flower!"

His cameraman gagged in the bushes.

59 | THE QUEEN MOTHER

To: Lawrence Atterbury Newman Windsor-Smith and Regan Euphonia Sparkle Windsor-Smith

From: The Queen of England

Heretofore: In as much as the person formally known as Prince Larry and the Duke of Ducats has besmirched and disgraced his royal lineage by taking up with a commoner, wherefore and therefore, as he has abdicated his royal duties and decamped to the former colonies in search of fame and a quick buck, herefore and unto as he has dragged the royal name through mud and besmirched the honorable tradition, going back seven centuries, of maintaining the royal bloodline, be it therefore known that the Queen Mother, pursuant to her sworn duties to protect the crown and the kingdom from clownery and humiliation does hereby strip the Windsor-Smiths of their royal titles. They are henceforth forbidden from using the term royal in any context, save that of their chosen liquor. They may no longer refer to themselves as the

Royal Ducats, prince, or princess.

Although the Queen wishes them every happiness, she cannot permit the continued degradation of the royal lineage through their entertainment business shenanigans, talk show appearances, or base appeals for fame.

The letter had been waiting for Larry when he returned from the expedition. It had been delivered by special courier and stamped with the royal seal. They sat in Gary's living room beneath the spot formerly occupied by Claude Balls' painting, now by Big Mouth Billy Bass. Every time the entity formerly known as Prince Larry shook his head, Billy Bass turned toward the room and sang, "Take Me to the River".

Regan was on her third gin and tonic. In a show of solidarity, Krystal matched her drink for drink. Regan turned toward her beloved with a sneer.

"What's that stink?"

"We discovered a giant Sumatran corpse flower. I was so excited. Now this."

"What does it mean?" Gary asked.

"It's a devastating blow to our marketability," Regan said. "This jeopardizes everything! Our show, Captain Megastar, my line of bath products..."

"You should wrestle," Krystal slurred. "You've got the name recognition. You'll have 'em lined up around the block. In fact, we should wrestle each other. Queen of the Swamp versus the Entity Formerly Known as the Duchess of Ducats."

"Royal Heinie versus Black Dildo," Regan asserted.

"Yeah, but can you call yourself the Royal Heinie?"

"It's wrestling," Gary said. "She can call herself whatever she wants! She can call herself the Queen of Sheba!"

"Where is Sheba, exactly?" Habib said.

Pincus looked up from his laptop. "The region of Sheba has been identified as the Kingdom of Saba in southern Arabia. But it may be in Ethiopia. In the Bible, the queen brings Solomon lavish gifts and praises his wisdom and kingdom before returning to her country."

Habib poked his Fonebone. "For ninety-five dollars, you can purchase a square meter of land in Scotland and claim royal lineage."

Karen Sullivan set her coffee on the kitchen table. "I am not opposed to the idea."

"What idea?" Regan said. "Wrestling or Scottish royalty?"

"Why not both? We'll purchase the land, you become Princess Regan of Scotland and wrestle under that name. You were a gymnast, correct?"

"In college."

Regan glared daggers at Larry. "You stink! Take a shower or get out!"

"Go ahead, Larry," Gary said. "I'll hang outside until you're done."

"But who will train Her Royal Heinie?" Habib said.

Gary was halfway out the door. "What about Ferd Ludlow?"

Regan's mouth looked like a saber jet. "The conspiracy guy?"

"He's not just conspiracies. He's got a gym. He trained Whip 'er Forth Wippurfurth for the world heavyweight title."

Regan held her glass out for a refill. "Never heard of him."

"You've never heard of Whip 'er Forth Wippurfurth?! One of the greatest matches in history! He fought Gadzilla Harambe on the Fourth of July in Qualcomm Stadium."

Karen stared at her Fonebone. "Let's float the idea on our YouTube channel. The good news is, your recognition quotient has exploded, thanks to that snapping turtle. The Royal Ducats are now more widely recognized than Sean Sheen."

"But we're not the Royal Ducats anymore, are we?"

Gary spoke through the screened window. "How 'bout we brainstorm a new catchphrase for these guys? We'll debut it on my show!"

Krystal slammed the window shut.

Gary came back in bringing with him the stench of the grave. "I have another great idea! We can cut the corpse flower up and sell chunks!"

"Are you out of your mind?" Krystal said.

Pincus poked his laptop. "The giant corpse flower weighs about one hundred and seventy pounds. If you were to cut it into quarter-pounders, that would yield six hundred and eighty pieces. Suppose you were to sell them at one hundred dollars the chunk? That would gross six hundred and eighty thousand dollars. Of course, you would have to factor in shipping. The shipping must be air-tight, perhaps frozen with dry ice, because if the smell leaks out, they won't get anywhere."

"Are you out of your mind?" Krystal said.

Pincus poked. “The giant corpse flower is an enormous attraction wherever it grows in the United States. The last time it bloomed at the Florida Botanical Gardens, they had over twenty thousand people willing to pony up fifteen dollars per ticket. *Star Trek: The Floundering’s* ratings shot through the roof during the corpse flower segment. Wackheim is planning an animated musical.”

“If we cut it up, won’t that kill it?” Karen said.

“Pincus, find everything we need to know. We’ll feature it on an upcoming segment.”

Larry appeared at the end of the hall, wearing baggy trousers that fell almost to his ankles and a Scurrilous Lies Tee-shirt. “It’s too bad we can’t broadcast the smell.”

“We can suggest things people can do at home to approximate the smell. I’m taking a shower. Let’s talk to Major.”

Pincus folded his laptop. “I’ve got to go. I have to take Elisha for a walk, and I have a date with Helen.”

Gary pointed a finger. “I told ya I’d get you laid!”

Pincus turned pink. “Oh, Mr. Duba, we’re just getting to know each other.”

“She’s a novitiate, for Christ’s sake!” Sullivan snapped.

Regan rose, stumbled, caught herself. “I think we must be going. I need a shower. Larry, we should discuss this wrestling idea.”

“You cawn’t be serious.”

“Larry, we have to raise some money! The Queen has cut us off!”

60 | LOW RENT

The svelte creature in the form-hugging dress stood in Dealin' Doug's lot, used vehicles gleaming in the sun, her hand on the hood of a bright yellow Porsche 944. "Hi! I'm Regan Sparkle, formerly the Duchess of Ducats! Have you dreamed of owning a Porsche but can't afford one? Come on down to Dealin' Doug's Used Cars in Turpentine! This little beauty has only eighty-two thousand miles and was driven by a grandmother to and from the bingo parlor!"

Doug's seven-year-old son Howie marched up. "Nobody beats a Dealin' Doug deal! Nobody!"

Habib Rodriguez appeared. Regan muted the sound and twirled. "What do you think?"

Gary, Krystal, and Major sat in the Presidential Suite at the Breakers, with an expansive view of the beach and ocean.

"Hot damn!" Gary said. "You nailed it. If that don't move some cars, nothing will."

Larry sipped his Boodles on the rocks. "We got the

bad news yesterday. Wackenheim has cast Gretel Vichysoisse-Mankiller as Captain Megastar."

Gary fell to his knees, hands clutching the sky. "Why?"

"They said the publicity attending Regan's announcement that she intends to join the Stunning Ladies of Wrestling was not the image they wished to project."

Gary got up. "I've half a mind to go to Wacky World and bust some heads!"

"Pro wrestling is bad publicity for a comic book superhero?" Krystal said.

Larry went to the bar. "They only cast her for her royal connections. She was going to be the first royal to star in a motion picture."

"Well hail," Gary said. "We'll make our own damn movie! Major can direct."

"What's it about?" Major said.

"It's about two bad-ass babes who find themselves stranded in the jungle and have to fight through pythons, hippo, and alligators and take down a terrorist nation."

"What terrorist nation?"

"Venezuela."

Major waved it away. "Let's not get ahead of ourselves. A wrestling match featuring the former Duchess of Ducats has international appeal. We can sell the rights in Europe, Australia, China, and Russia. It will be a pay-per-view event, too big for the Roxy. We can charge thousands of dollars for box seats. We will secure Veeblefetzer Stadium in Miami. The networks will bid for the rights. It will be the biggest event since the 2008 Summer Olympics. Bigger than *We Are the World.* Hundreds of millions of viewers. We'll charge millions for a thirty second spot. Every major corporation will spend millions to produce the cleverest, most memorable advertisements.

"After this event, we can all retire." He crossed his arms and sat back, thrusting his jaw.

Krystal couldn't stop grinning and nodding her head. "Hell yeah, baby! We should open with some musical act, like the Superbowl halftime show!"

Larry leaped to his feet and smacked his fist against the table. "Smashing! I say! Gary, you old tosser, we should put on an exhibition match as well!"

Major shook his finger. "Krystal needs Gary in her corner, and Regan needs you. Let's stick to ladies' wrestling. Yokohama Mama. Devil Girl. The Pink Mink. These are some of the names that could fill out the undercard. I'll contact Aldo and see if he can put me in touch."

Gary stooped at the servery bar and grabbed a half-dozen minis. Scotch, bourbon, vodka, good stuff. "Dealin' Doug will want in."

Major snorted. "Dealin' Doug can't even afford a ticket. We're looking at General Motors, Farmers Insurance, whole nations. We'll need international representation. Got anybody?"

Larry smacked his fist into his palm. "Right-o! Let's get Karen in here!"

Regan picked up her Fonebone. Seconds later, she said,

"Hello, Karen! Have I got news for you!"

Holding up a finger, she went out on the balcony to talk in private. Krystal grabbed the swank notepad and pen and sat down at the desk. "We got to figure this out! We got to give the folks a show!"

Megan returned.

"Look here, girl. You ever wrestle?"

"Only with my brothers when I was growing up."

"Good enough. That's how 'Lilah learned. My signature moves are the paddling blowfish and foaming pipesnake. What are yours?"

Regan blushed. "I don't actually have any signature moves yet."

"Don'tchoo worry. Me an' 'Lilah will work some up for you. We can clear out this furniture and go over the basics right now."

"I think we'd better wait on that. Let's wait for Delilah."

"You're right, but here's what I'm thinking. We gotta put on a show. That means the match has to last for a minimum of twenty-five minutes. Joo ever do acrobatics?"

"As a matter of fact, I was on the Wellesley cheerleading squad. The boys tossed me fifteen feet in the air where I somersaulted and landed in Randy Connelly's arms."

Larry grimaced. "Randy Connelly?"

"Don't be absurd. I haven't seen him since college."

"I could have him removed with one phone call."

"Oh, don't start flexing your mob muscles. You're not exactly Sammy the Bull. You're not exactly Conor McGregor."

Larry stiffened. "I fought in the regimental boxing competition I'll have you know! I was a finalist at fourteen stones! You saw me hold my own against this hillbilly!"

Gary bristled. "You see any hills around here?"

Larry's mouth opened. "Well! I mean you're sort of a rustic, aren't you? You live in a trailer in the swamp and drink what, moonshine? I'm not disparaging you, old chap! I rather admire you! You make the most of what you have. It's all very admirable. I couldn't live that way."

Gary thrust out his chest. "What are you saying? That we're trailer trash? And you're lording it over us 'cuz you got a mansion in Hollywood?"

"It's Brentwood, eckshually."

"I may not wait for fight night. Maybe you and me'll have another go rightchere, right now!"

Larry stuck out his chin. "Why you impertinent bumpkin! I should give you a sound thrashing! Perhaps then you'll learn to appreciate your betters!"

"My betters!" Gary hauled back and socked Larry in the jaw, sending the former prince crashing into a sideboard knocking over a modernist glass sculpture that Tallywhacker had missed. Larry put up his dukes and advanced firing off his jab. Gary went low and took him to the ground, cracking the glass coffee table, destroying an art nouveau lamp. Krystal and Major whipped out their Fonebones. Gary and Larry rolled into a teak desk, removing one leg. They rolled away and the desk came down with the phone, pens, and six bottles from the servery bar.

"Stop it!" Regan snapped from the patio entrance. She looked stricken. "You idiots! You fools!"

"What's wrong, love?" Larry asked from the floor, combing shards of glass from his beard.

"Karen just called. The agency dropped us! They said we were too low rent."

61 | THE NUCLEAR OPTION

The Queen had decamped to Windsor Castle. She slept better without the constant chanting and car horns. Windsor was "the most expensive secular building project of the entire Middle Ages in England". It was Henry VIII's favorite abode. He had expanded it to include a second chapel, and the majestic arch that bore his name. Herman's Hermits memorialized his accomplishments in song. Edward VIII modernized the castle "with enthusiasm and zest", adding saunas, hot tubs, and a bowling alley, and commissioning a series of whoopie cushions featuring all the Henrys and all the Edwards. King George VI brought his own traditions, including the Garter Service, in which every female staff member lined up to have their garters snapped.

During World War II, the entire castle was blacked out by an enormous tarp, variously attributed to Christo and Claude Balls. Balls has denied this, claiming he was only three at the time. Balls' painting of the Queen's corgis in St. George's chapel has been much duplicated. Fire swept through the castle in 1992 requiring expansive repairs. Royal carpenters took this opportunity to install an indoor swimming pool, a home theater, a casino, and a heliport. The cost of renovating the castle led to a national debate on who should pay. Parliament settled on a national lottery dubbed POTRI, paying off the royal invoice. The Royal Family also sold the rights to certain venues and ballrooms.

After a traditional English breakfast of bangers and mash, the Queen Mother awaited the prime minister in the Jaguar Land Rover room, formerly the Sir Walter Scott room. She sat the royal throne with Benedict, her favorite corgi, in her lap as the PM, a mild man with a bad comb over, was ushered into her presence. He carried an electronic notepad. Due to her age, the Queen did not arise, but took the PM's hand.

"Welcome, John."

"Your Majesty. It is with the utmost regret I must report to you the most appalling events."

"Please sit. Will you have tea?"

"By all means."

A liveried servant placed a Queen Ann chair beneath the PM's bum, and they waited while a servant brought in a jangling tea service on a cart, pouring the tea into gold-rimmed china cups that had once belonged to King Ferdinand III. They sipped. The PM waited for the Queen Mother to speak.

The fat corgi rolled on its back, mouth open, tongue lolling. The Queen Mother stroked its belly, cooing, "How is HARM HMRP? Hmmm? Is HRM HMRP happy?"

The dog purred.

"It's good to see HRM HMRP enjoying himself, Mum. How many cabinets has he witnessed?"

"Her Royal Majesty's Holy Moly Roly Poly has lived through six administrations. HRM HMRP is the oldest living corgi."

"May he live through six more."

"John, I have heard the reports. My grandson's wife has forfeited whatever dignity she once had by joining the women's pro-wrestling circuit. I have instructed the royal scriveners to remove both Lawrence and Regan's names from all official correspondence. They will no longer collect the Royal Stipend and I am considering revoking their citizenship. If they want to be Yanks so badly, let them be Yanks."

"Mum, I couldn't agree more. Fabled Albion has suffered many blows over the centuries. The Roman invasion. The Saxon invasion. The Sex Pistols. The Loss of Empire. The Asian invasion. But to have the royal bloodline dragged through the mud, it's simply too much, and I can tell you that the overwhelming majority of Britons revile them. I wished to see you because this latest embarrassment may do irreparable harm not only to the Royal Family, but to our standing around the world. Already, China has made overtures to have Regan fight, if that's the proper term, in China. She plays to bill herself as the Royal Heinie."

"What does that mean?"

"The Royal Bum, your majesty."

"Dear God."

"I have asked the royal barristers to look into that. I have forbidden them from calling themselves royal, but I gather that in the world of professional wrestling, anything goes, and that the name Royal Heinie is greeted with irreverence and hilarity."

"I can imagine."

"Do you know about her opponent?"

"I'm afraid not. I don't follow professional wrestling, although my great grandson Eustace thinks I should."

"Well, ah, at the chance of sounding indelicate, she is known to her fans as the Black Dildo."

The Queen's nose wrinkled, as if HRM HMRP had farted. HARM HMRP farted. A servant rushed over, lit several matches, and waved them around.

"Thank you, Poldark," the Queen Mother said. "Dare I ask how she acquired this moniker?"

"Mum, you have proven your resilience through a world war and many dark days. But I must warn you, what I am about to show you is vulgar, and has been viewed twenty million times. It is especially popular throughout the former colonies and Asia."

"Does it involve anything gruesome?"

"No, Mum. But it is shocking."

The Queen Mother sighed. "Fire away."

The PM opened his laptop and held it before the Queen. On the screen, Krystal flew off the stoop of their former home, dildo upraised like Excalibur, and whacked several coppers before being tased and led away in handcuffs. The

PM closed the laptop.

Silence reigned. HRM HMRP farted audibly. Poldark rushed in with matches.

Finally, the Queen Mother spoke. "I can't imagine the circumstances that led to this event."

"It occurred as the constabulary were trying to evict these bumpkins from their house, which they'd purchased some months previously with their lottery winnings. The man you see being led away in handcuffs is Gary Duba. His wife Krystal is the Black Dildo. But even in America that moniker is too crude for the mass media, so she campaigns under the name of Steely Danielle."

"Steely Danielle?"

"Yes. Apparently, it's a play on words after the American pop band Steely Dan, which was named after a dildo, as per William Burroughs."

"This is all very confusing."

"If Mum will hear me out, I have a rather elegant solution which will spare the Royal Family misery in the years to come."

"Speak freely, John."

"Mum, I believe this calls for a clandestine operation from MI6."

The Queen Mother put a hand to her mouth. "Oh dear."

"I know it seems severe, but this is the greatest crisis in public confidence the crown has ever faced. We must send a message that these kinds of shenanigans will simply not be tolerated. It will look like an accident. Nobody will suspect a thing."

"Are you suggesting we deal with both Larry and Regan in this manner?"

"Well, that's up to you, of course. I know he's your grandson."

"I think perhaps it would be prudent to just remove Regan from the picture. Larry's a handsome young man with many good qualities. I curse the day he met that succubus."

"Yes, Mum. Double oh seven is waiting outside. Would you like to meet him?"

"It must look like an accident. Like Diana."

"Of course, mum."

"Bring him in."

The PM spoke into his phone. A short man with a big nose and thick glasses entered, approached the Queen Mother and knelt.

"Your highness."

"Oh please, do rise. What is your name?"

"Bruce, mum. Dave Bruce."

62 | THUDPUCKER'S

STUNNING LADIES OF WRESTLING PRESENTS
STEELY DANIELLE VS ROYAL HEINIE
JANUARY 4, VEEBLEFETZER STADIUM
A PAY-PER-VIEW EVENT
SEATING IS LIMITED

LENA THE HYENA VS STICK BUG
HOWLER MONKEY VS MAUDE MACAQUE
JAVELINA VS CHUPACABRA
BANDICOOT VS SWEET CHARLOTTE
BABY JANE VS THE SHE BITCH OF BALTIMORE

Gary was sitting on the porch Monday morning with a cup of coffee when Garrison Gland arrived in his RAV4 to go over their segment.

Garrison's hands flew. "We will approach gradually, through the jungle, and suddenly..." His hands framed the scene. "We see the corpse flower for the first time, as Lord Carnarvon stumbled upon the Tomb of Tutankhamun. As Hiram Bingham rounding a corner and seeing Machu Picchu. I want a sense of wonder. If only there were some way to convey smell."

"My old man told me about smellovision. It was popular in the sixties."

"If only it were possible to transmit smell through your personal device."

"That'd be the greatest thing since sliced bread."

"The only thing I can do, is to try and convey the scent visually, with pictures of rotting corpses, piles of feces, and perhaps a jackal vomiting."

"Hey, I can vomit for ya."

"Would you? I can't tell you how much that would mean to me."

"One thing I know how to do, it's toss my cookies. I only wish you could have been at the State Fair and see me toss those beetles."

"What's your method, if you don't mind sharing."

"I train. Day by day, I build up my tolerance. I use hot sauce."

"Marvelous."

Gary looked around. He spoke in a low voice. "We combine two episodes. A reenactment of my palmetto eating triumph and the giant corpse flower. You can film me eating those bugs."

"Are you serious?"

"I'm dead serious. My friend Floyd can provide all the bugs we need. I might microwave 'em first to make 'em crispy. We can start out with a segment how to survive in the wilderness. Floyd'll glue the bugs to branches and leaves along the way, so it'll seem as if I'm just pulling 'em in from wherever. Meanwhile, you're following me with the camera and maybe some kind of jungle boogie."

"What do you mean?"

Gary put his hands to his mouth and chuffed beat box like Rodell Grosz, with guttural plosives. *BOOM shaka-lak-ka-lakka, BOOM shakka-lakka-lakka.*

"Here in the wilds of Turpentine," Garrison said in a plummy voice, "Gary Duba forages for food as his ancestors have done for centuries, wandering aimlessly through the jungle plucking palmetto bugs from roots and logs."

Gary mimed popping them into his mouth. "We reach the corpse flower. Then what?"

Garrison spread his arms. "After forcing our way at a snail's pace through this impenetrable jungle, a clearing appears, and in the center of that clearing, a majestic bloom, a monstrous bloom, a penis-shaped flower six feet tall, and the smell hits us. This is the Sumatran giant corpse flower, one of the world's rarest orchids, blooming once every eleven years. Because the flower is considered a delicacy by certain sects of the Uggabugga, it has been hunted to extinction. How rare, then, to find this beauty blazing beneath Florida skies!

"While most invasive species have proven deleterious to Florida's ecosystem, here, at least, is one invasive species we can all welcome. The giant Sumatran corpse flower! But wait, what's this? Our intrepid guide, Gary Duba, the man who apprehended Plastic Surgeon to the Stars and serial killer Dr. Vanderlay Mukerjee, caught the largest python in state history, the inventor of house suspenders, and the killer of Hogzilla, is looking a little green around the gills! What say you, Gary?" He swung his hands toward Gary.

Gary puffed out his cheeks and made a vomiting noise, bending over in his chair and pointing a finger at his mouth.

"How was that?"

"You're a natural. Of course, you'll have to sign a waiver absolving the History Channel of any liability."

"You're gonna have to sign a waiver absolving Gary Duba of any liability."

"What liability?"

"In case you get bit by a gator, strangled by a python, or kilt by feral hogs."

Garrison laughed. "No problem! Did you know there is a cult that worships the giant Sumatran corpse flower as a god? They call themselves the Aroma and they're based in California. In 1999, four members of the Aroma broke into the University of Wisconsin botanical gardens while the corpse flower was in bloom, cut it up and ate it. A cleaning crew found them in the morning, belly up like palmetto bugs."

"Why would they eat it?"

"To them it was a holy sacrament, like the eucharist. They had hoped to gain divine knowledge and immortality."

"They still around?"

"Well not that lot, obviously, but the cult lives on. I hear there's a branch in Surinam. Can you get me seats for the battle royal?"

"I guess you heard about that."

"Everybody has heard about it. It's historic. A former member of the British royal family to wrestle professionally."

"What about the Duke of Destruction, Prince Reinhold, Lord Whiplash and Princess Suplex?"

"I wasn't aware. This event may boost professional wrestling from a sideshow attraction to universal appeal. Villages in Africa have installed satellite dishes just so they can watch. Can you get me seats?"

"Worse comes to worst, you can always share our skybox. You ain't bringin' Rose, are ya?"

"No, Rose and I are kaput."

"Aw now I feel bad."

"It was for the best. She had the most irritating laugh. She made a nasal sucking sound, like a pig. 'Hahaha, *snuckkkkk*. Hahaha *snuckkkkk*.' Let's schedule the corpse flower for one week from today. Is that doable?"

Gary dug out his Fonebone. "Sure. Be here at nine."

"It would be wonderful if Krystal could make a cameo."

"I don't think she digs the corpse flower like we do. She's in training."

"Of course. I would be fascinated by her routine."

"Mostly drinking and watching kung fu movies. She's got some blow stashed somewhere. It ain't like Regan's a threat."

"Of course. Next Monday then."

As Garrison drove away, Rodell Grosz called.

"I want in on the royal rumble."

"I don't think so, dude. This is a high-class affair."

"I used to work at Wacky World! You can't get any classier!"

"Dude, the last time I saw you, you were rollerblading naked wearing a panda head."

"People loved it!"

"Sorry, Rodell. You'll have to watch it on pay-per-view like everybody else."

"Fuck that! I'll go to Thudpucker's and watch it for free!"

63 | VEEBLEFETZER

Veeblefetzer Stadium was 20,000-seat multipurpose entertainment arena located on Biscayne Bay, one of the nation's premier sports and entertainment facilities and home to the 2006, 2012 and 2013 NBA champion Miami Heat, concerts, family shows and special events. One thousand tickets had been reserved for a lottery and people began lining up the night before. The ultra-modern facility looked like a hat box. Four garages served the arena, ranging in price from twenty-five dollars to forty dollars, the latter with valet parking.

The main event was scheduled for nine p.m., but Gary and Krystal left home at one to beat the crowds, arriving two hours later. Traffic ground to a halt a mile from the stadium. Gary turned the engine off and got out, standing in the truck bed trying to see what caused the delay. A man wearing a rabbit suit and a panda head stood in the middle of the boulevard vamping to a boom-box beat. A police car made its way down the shoulder, lights flashing.

The police car pulled up. The officer was young, wore aviator shades and had a brush mustache.

"Officer," Gary said, "I'm Gary Duba. My wife Krystal is the headliner, and we need to get to the stadium."

"Follow me."

Gary got back in the truck and pulled in behind the Dade County cruiser as it crawled up the shoulder. The cruiser stopped next to Grosz, who'd set up a beat box and a portable amplifier.

"I'm Panda Rabbit, the people's choice! A harmless herbivore, to give the people voice! When titans clash, I break out in a rash! If I were a car, I'd be a Rolls Royce!"

A boy of ten cupped his hands. "Pandas are highly endangered! They should not be made fun of!"

Grosz dipped and shuffled. "How do you know, you spineless twerp? Can you beat box boy, or only chirp?"

The officer approached Grosz. "Sir, pick up your beat box and leave or I'll arrest you."

"Arrest me for what? Rappin' to the beat? Get out of the kitchen if you can't stand the heat!"

The cop spun Grosz around, snapped on cuffs, and put him in the back seat.

"What about my gear?" Grosz howled.

Gary got out of the truck. "I'll get your gear, Rodell. You can pick it up later."

He put the amp and beat box in the back of his truck and followed the cruiser. Fifteen minutes later, they came to a traffic cop directing traffic toward one of the four garages.

The Oscar Mayer Wienermobile and the Planters Peanutmobile were on the apron, waiting for permission to drive around back. When they reached the garage, Gary showed his VIP tag and a valet handed him a chit. Their backstage suite consisted of four rooms and two baths, with a built-in kitchenette. Inside was a gift basket stuffed with fresh fruit, macadamia nuts, chocolate truffles and a bottle of champagne. Krystal opened the card.

"It's from Kensington Gardens HOA."

She plucked the champagne and reached for a towel. Gary wrenched it away.

"Are you nuts? You've got a fight today!"

"Oh, come on! Her Royal Heinie? She's probably never been hit in the face! She'll curl up like a carpet worm!"

"You gotta be professional. We'll save this for later."

"I suppose you're gonna bitch if I do a little line."

Gary wrenched her backpack away and emptied it on the table, grabbing the bindle in a tiny Ziplock bag. "Everything is on the line tonight!"

"Oh, come on! We've already made more money than we can ever spend!"

"Don't count your chickens before they hatch. Anything can happen. A meteor. Murder hornets."

Krystal stuck out her lower lip. "Oh pooh!"

Knocking at the door. Delilah and Airwrecka entered, each carrying a gym bag. Airwrecka pointed at a straight-backed chair. "Sit."

Gary napped. When he woke, it was five and the prelims

were about to begin. They watched as Major Sutton, wearing a red tux, took the center of the ring in front of twenty thousand screaming people.

"Good evening fight fans and WELCOME TO THE ROYAL RUMBLE!"

They could hear the crowd in the soundproof suite, like a 747 ramping up. Krystal was in her onesie with Steely Danielle on the breasts, and Habib Rodriguez on her rump, stretching in front of the big screen TV. Her hair was done in cornrows. Patrice, Floyd and Ginger had wormed their way into the dressing room. High fives all around.

"Noble mon," Patrice said.

"Gary, honey," Krystal said, "would you be a dear and get me one of those hot dogs from the concession stand?"

Gary pointed to the fruit basket. "Can't you find anything you like in here? Did you check the servie bar?"

"Please, hon. I just want one of those hot dogs."

"You're not gonna puke, are ya?"

"Of course not! I'm staying away from clams from now on."

"Floyd, you wanna come?"

Floyd was decked out in a Wacky World shirt featuring Regis Gator, Rapid Rabbit, Funky Monkey, Goth Sloth and Punk Skunk. "What else I got to do?"

They wound their way out of the guest suites down a utility corridor that led to the enormous arched hallway that circled the arena, restrooms and concession stands evenly spaced. There was a line at every concession stand as people lined up for soda, popcorn, candy, hot dogs, empanadas, tacos, nachos, and Cubanos. Major announced Baby Jane versus the She Bitch of Baltimore. Gary looked at the big menu made of white plastic letters on a black velvet background. Five bucks for a hot dog. Three bucks for a soda. Three bucks for a bag of popcorn, or you could get the family tub, for nine. Peanuts in the shell. Pretzels.

A warning bell went off in Gary's skull.

"Floyd, you want a hot dog?"

"Yeah. Ginger wants one too."

"Hell. I might as well get everyone a hot dog."

They headed back toward the suite with seven hot dogs and seven sodas. Sound burst through the tunnel openings like a locomotive. By the time they reached the suite, the She Bitch of Baltimore had defeated Baby Jane via horse collar and Major was announcing the next match.

"TWO MULES VS SISTER SARA!"

Back at the suite, Gary and Floyd handed out hot dogs. Five minutes later, the dogs were gone. Three hours remained before the main event. Because the bouts were mostly staged, it was easy to stick to a schedule. A bramble of unease lurked in Gary's gut.

Patrice sat next to Delilah. "Delilah, you kind woman, would you read my palm?"

Delilah took Patrice's right hand, palm side up, in her own. "Hmmm. This line is usually unbroken but here it's disrupted, indicating a possible cataclysmic event."

"What cataclysmic event?"

The lights went out, then flashed red as a klaxon sounded.

The noise was magnified by the klaxons in the corridor and in every other suite.

"ATTENTION," a voice boomed over the PA system. "PLEASE LEAVE THE STADIUM BY THE NEAREST EXIT. DO NOT PANIC. PLEASE LEAVE THE STADIUM AS SOON AS POSSIBLE IN A CALM AND ORDERLY MANNER."

64 | THE PLAN

The day before the fight, Bruce, Dave Bruce stood in the main terminal at Miami International waiting for a passenger who had flown in from Seattle. And here he came, unmistakably Waldo in his thick glasses, striped shirt and beret, carrying a beat-up suitcase. Bruce fell in beside the man as they walked toward the exit.

"Edgar Panny?"

"Yup."

"Let's go to the smoking area."

Exiting the terminal, they stood with a handful of nicotine addicts in a trash-strewn area marked by concrete barriers. Panny handed Bruce the suitcase. Bruce handed Panny an envelope.

"How does one get in this line of work?" Bruce asked.

"We Pannys have been smuggling exotic animals for fifty years. I learned from my father."

"Is he still in the business?"

"My father disappeared last year. My sister and I have no clue what happened to him."

"I'm very sorry to hear that."

"He was trying out a new courier, but I never found out who. I have dedicated my life to learning the details of my father's death. When I find those responsible, I will act."

"Bit of the old hugger mugger, eh?"

"The suitcase is insulated. They should be fine."

Bruce retrieved his rented Chevy and drove to the Lamplighter Motel in Opa Locka. Once inside, he drew the drapes, put on heavy leather gloves and a clear plastic shield to cover his face, and carefully opened the suitcase. Inside a shoe box stuffed with shredded paper, three *Vespa mandarinia, or "murder hornets" as they were more popularly known, slept, anesthetized by diethyl-ether. MI6 had identified Regan's vehicle as a black Cadillac Escalade, license number PW 145.*

The next morning, wearing facial recognition fooling glasses and prosthetics, a backpack, a blue Paragon Valet Service uniform with Vern stitched on the breast and a laminated ID around his neck, Bruce approached the Veeblefetzer loading docks where the Weinermobile and the Peanutmobile were parked. Two men stood between them, one wearing a Green Bay Packers shirt and hat, the other dressed as a giant peanut with top hat and monocle.

Packer: "That baby's got a turbo-charged Dodge hemi. It would suck your hubcaps off, if you even have hubcaps, bro."

Peanut: "Not in a million years, bro. The Peanutmobile packs a supercharged 454 big block. It does the quarter in twelve flat. It would blow the mustard off your dog."

Packer: "Not in a million years, bro. The Wienermobile's been clocked at 125 in the quarter mile. It would crack your nut wide open."

Peanut: "Do you even drag, bro?"

As Bruce approached, Packer said, "Dude. Who's faster? The Wienermobile or the Peanuttiest?"

"Why don't you boys race and find out?"

The drivers ruminated.

"Say, guys, where do they keep the celebrity rides? Her Royal Heinie wants me to retrieve a make-up kit."

Mr. Peanut pointed across Biscayne Boulevard to a parking structure. "Bottom floor."

"Thanks." Bruce turned around and headed toward the front. Traffic was chock-a-block with four policemen standing in the road, blowing whistles and signaling. Bruce waited with several dozen until a cop blew his whistle, put his hand out, and stopped traffic so they could cross the street. Bruce entered the cavernous parking garage and noted a series of black SU Vs lined up on the ground floor behind a sawhorse barrier. Several liveried chauffeurs stood around smoking, staring at their Fonebones and shooting the shit. No one paid him any attention as he walked purposefully down the concrete floor passing four black Escalades until he came to the one he wanted. It was backed against the concrete abutment with barely enough room for him to stand. Crouching between vehicles, he removed a 1206i Multi-Frequency RF Bug Detector, scanned for the vehicle's car alarm, set the frequency, and pushed the button, shutting off the car alarm. Lying on his back, he stuck a magnetic transmitter to the chassis.

Using a lockout kit with an air wedge to unlock the front door, reached back and unlocked the left rear passenger door. Discreetly opening the door, he slipped inside, crouching low, and shut the door behind him. He felt beneath the seats. Not much room. The cargo area was filled with suitcases. Removing the shoe box of murder hornets, he placed them discreetly near the tailgate. Sunlight caused hornets to become active, but Her Royal Heinie wouldn't leave the auditorium until well after dark. Bruce peeled the backing off a glue-on therapy light. He would wait until the royal party was en route before triggering the light by remote control.

Mission accomplished, he walked several blocks to the Li'l Greenhouse Grill at Overtown Park, sat outside, and ordered a cheeseburger. Now all he had to do was wait. His car was parked nearby. He would follow at a discreet distance and trigger the hornets once the vehicle was up to speed on the Interstate. Her Royal Heinie would die in a pile-up on the Interstate caused by murder hornets.

His waitress, a young Latina, wore a green skirt and blouse with "Debbie" stitched on the breast. "Would you like something to drink?"

"A Vesper martini, shaken, not stirred." He looked around. "Not very busy tonight."

"No. Everybody's at the wrestling match. You'd think the Heat was playing the Knicks or something."

"You're not a wrestling fan?"

Debbie rolled her eyes. "As if. But I would like to see Her Royal Heinie make a fool of herself. Oh well. I guess I'll just have to wait until they show it for free. What brings you to Miami?"

"Oh, you guessed I'm not local."

"Not with that accent!"

Bruce grinned. "I'm on holiday! Plan to visit the Everglades, see some alligators, do a little windsurfing, that sort of thing."

"You know, I've been here five years and I have yet to visit the Everglades."

"Where are you from?"

"Guatemala."

"Your English is excellent."

"Thank you."

"Bruce, Dave Bruce."

"Pleased to meet you, Mr. Bruce. I'd offer to show you around, but all I do is work."

Bruce thought about asking her out, but there was no time. He'd be on a plane back to Old Blighty in the morning. A stir rippled through the diners. Voices rose. Police sirens sounded in the distance.

Debbie looked around. "What's going on?"

Bruce took out his Fonebone. "They're evacuating the stadium. There's been a bomb threat."

65 | DRAG RACE

An hour and a half later, Gary, Krystal and Delilah reached the truck on the top level of the parking garage. It took another hour to get out of the garage. Traffic was gridlocked on Biscayne Boulevard as far as the eye could see. Krystal turned on the radio.

"Veeblefetzer Stadium was evacuated this afternoon due to a bomb threat. Dade County sheriff's deputies are working with Metro Miami SWAT squad and bomb-sniffing dogs. It may take up to three days to clear the venue, which was to host the first appearance of the former Duchess of Ducats, Regan Sparkle, in her debut match against local hero Steely Danielle.

"Authorities are working to determine the source of the bomb threat."

Gary pounded the wheel. "Fuck, fuck, fuck!"

"Best not cash no checks," Delilah said from the back seat.

"Now we have to run the snapping turtle."

Krystal swigged from the champagne bottle. "Every-body's sheen it."

"But they haven't seen it with the duke providing color commentary!"

"Girl," Delilah said, "pass me that bottle."

Delilah glugged. "Has anyone spoken with the Ducats? Did they get out of the arena all right?"

Krystal pulled out her Fonebone and turned off the radio. "I'll call 'em."

"Hi, girl! It's Steely Danielle!"

A rift of concern creased Krystal's forehead. "Oh no. Oh no. Are you all right?"

"What?" Gary demanded.

"Omma put you on speaker phone, izzat okay?"

"We're trapped in traffic!" Regan wailed. "We're on our way to Sunset Island but the traffic here is appalling. I mean, we are basically stuck at a standstill. And there's some awful man dressed in a rabbit suit and panda head going from car to car, begging. I shan't be responsible for Larry."

Gary wrinkled his nose. "Is she talking with a Brit accent?"

"Well thank God you're out of there!" Krystal said. "They say it was a bomb threat! I'm just glad you're all right. We're going back to the trailer. We were kinda counting on that money too."

Traffic started to move. Gary pointed. "There's the one ninety-five up ahead. Hang on, gurls! We're almost outta here!"

"Turn on the radio," Delilah said.

Krystal turned it on.

"Police have arrested Ronald Baitch for making terrorist threats and attempted murder. The police found a truck bomb in the utility garage beneath the arena, filled with a mixture of nitrogen, liquid oxygen, and fertilizer. Police say it had the potential to kill thousands of people. Police located Baitch watching from the Museum Park Baywalk across the inlet. Baitch has refused to speak. He handed the arresting officer the following statement:

"*I have warned Veeblefetzer repeatedly, and the Miami Heat in particular, that peanuts are deadly to people of allergy. I have tried to raise awareness about this situation for years. I have spoken. I have posted. I have tried to contact them over and over. But they will not listen. I have also warned them about the pretzels. They will not listen until it's too late. Well now it's too late.*"

"Ain't that the guy..." Krystal slurred.

"That's the dude planted the bomb on the airplane when I was bringing in those tarantulas! I hope he eats a peanut and chokes!"

"Have you been in an auto accident and the insurance company failed to give you what you deserve? The law offices of Habib Rodriguez specialize in insurance claims. You don't pay a dime unless we collect for you. Call the law offices of Habib Rodriguez today."

Important fanfare. "In further developments, we have learned that two years ago, Ronald Baitch was responsible for the bombing of United #298 which made an emergency landing in Miami minutes before the bomb was set to go off. Fortunately, all one hundred and twelve passengers and the crew were evacuated in time. Many who had been aboard the flight reported that minutes before the forced landing, the cabin filled with tarantulas. It sounds like something out of a horror movie, folks.

"And now Mr. Baitch has retained famous criminal defense attorney Habib Rodriguez to represent him."

Gary pounded the wheel. "My ass!"

Krystal turned off the radio.

They got on the Ninety-Five and headed north, sun lowering on the left. Traffic was ferocious. The Oscar Mayer Wienermobile passed them at ninety, followed seconds later by the Planters Peanutmobile. Gary floored it.

"Fuck you doing, Gary?"

"See that Peanutmobile? Omma drive it down Baitch's throat."

"Stop it! You'll get us all arrested!"

Delilah put her hand on Gary's shoulder. "Slow down. Don't make me put a curse on you."

Krystal put her hand on Gary's thigh. "You want me to give you a hand job? Maybe that'll calm you down."

"Not on my watch," Delilah said.

The Oscar Mayer Wiener song floated in through open windows. Gary saw flashing red and blue lights in his rearview.

"Here come de popo."

Four squad cars squealed around on the left, tires on the

median, racing after the dueling behemoths. Traffic stopped. People got out of their cars and stood on the roofs. Cops had corralled the corporate vehicles. Two men leaned against the Wienermobile as police went through their pockets. Mr. Peanut leaned against the Peanutmobile, wearing his top hat and monocle.

It was dark when they finally inched past, Krystal hanging out the window with her Fonebone. She turned on the radio.

"We have just learned that Interstate Ninety-Five is at a standstill, due to a high-speed chase involving the Oscar Mayer Wienermobile and the Planters Peanutmobile. Eyewitnesses claim to have seen the drivers drinking this afternoon and arguing over whose rig was fastest. Travelers are advised to use alternative routes."

Krystal twisted the knob.

"Welcome to the Ferd Ludlow Show. Folks, I've been telling you for years and today we have definitive proof that America is under siege from alien forces. Do you really think a loser like Ronald Baitch is capable of planting a truck bomb beneath Veeblefetzer Stadium? Isn't it all a little too perfect? Two years ago, they arrest him for blowing up an airplane, and today he was walking around free. How did he get out? He had to have alien help. No other explanation is possible.

"We have a very special guest tonight, someone who knows a thing or two about alien invasion. He has led the Church of Necroeconomics and he ran for governor. Please give a big Ferd Ludlow welcome to Tallywhacker, the alien bull."

66 | THE BOB'S ASS AWARDS

As soon as the warning sounded, Martin popped in. "We're leaving through the loading zone. Regan, please put on this trench coat, sunglasses, and hat. Lawrence, please don this jacket, sunglasses, and hat." He handed Larry a Miami Heat jacket and cap. "Her highness, follow me with your hands on my shoulders. Sir Larry, you follow Regan with your hands on her shoulders. Ready? Let's go."

The corridor was jammed with wrestlers, stadium employees, publicists, and hangers-on. Martin placed his palms together in front of him to form a wedge and within minutes, there were standing in the loading zone, in brilliant sunshine. Twenty minutes later, they reached the vehicle. The parking garage was jammed with vehicles all trying to exit at once. Two MPD officers stood at the Biscayne Boulevard exit trying to direct traffic. Larry got in the front seat with Martin, Regan in back.

"Must we wait for all these commoners?" Regan said.

"Now, now, dear, we're in the colonies. The classless society and all that."

"What a lot of rubbish! These Yanks are worse than our own bloody peasants!"

It was hard to believe Regan had been born in Cleveland.

They reached the exit. Larry rolled down his window and gestured to the nearest cop. "I say, officer! Hate to trouble you, old chap, but we really must be going."

The cop's snarl morphed into open-mouthed surprise. He blew his whistle, held out his palm, and motioned the Royal Carriage forward. Soon they were inching their way north on Biscayne Boulevard.

"Classless society, my arse!" her Royal Heinie griped.

"I say! You're turning into a right toff! Do come off it, darling."

"What? What did you say to me?"

"Just joking, my dear."

"Well, this is hardly a joking matter. A madman has threatened to blow up the stadium!"

"*Black Sunday*," Martin said.

"I beg your pardon?"

"It's a movie about terrorists planning to blow up a football stadium."

"I forgot your love of movies."

"Also, *Sudden Death*, and *Sudden Death 2*."

"Of course."

"Have you seen those, sir?"

"I have not."

“What movies would you recommend?” Regan said.

“I recommend *Alien Vs. Predator.* It’s about two hideous monsters fighting to the death. You’ll love it.”

Regan handed two bottled waters to Larry. She drained hers and opened another. Her Fonebone chimed the theme to *Dallas.*

“It’s Boobsie!” she said excitedly. Boobsie Suefield was her agent.

“Boobsie! We’re fine, thank you. We managed to escape that madhouse. I’m only sorry to disappoint my millions of fans.”

Regan put a finger in her ear and listened. “What?”

The Escalade joined the river of metal flowing west on 195 to get to 95. The sun slanted in from the west. Martin turned the AC to the max.

“Who?”

The Oscar Mayer Wienermobile screamed past followed seconds later by the Peanutmobile.

Regan squealed. “Marvelous! Boobsie, you’re a genius! Wait until I tell Larry! Listen, dearest. Let me call you when we get to the hotel. Oh! I’m so excited!”

She put the phone away and sat smugly, hands in lap, smiling like Meg Ryan.

“What?”

“I’ve been offered the part of Sabra in *Barfalo 2: the Sickening.*”

“Congratulations, my love! This is a great triumph! Tell me more.”

"I'm excited to be working with Mickey Orc."

"Marvelous."

Martin turned on the radio. "I just need a situation update."

"...the stadium has been evacuated. A SWAT squad is about to enter with a bomb dog. Police have arrested Ronald Baitch, responsible for the bombing of United Flight #298 two years ago. You may recall, that was the flight on which many passengers claim to have seen spiders. We'll be right back."

"Have you been in an auto accident..."

Martin turned it off.

"I haven't even seen *Barfalo 1*," Larry said.

"I would rate it right up there with *Saw IV*."

"What's it about?"

"A bulimic buffalo terrorizes settlers in eighteen eighties Nebraska. I can find it for you, if you like."

"Thank you, no. What's this about, then?"

"*Barfalo 2* takes place in the present. A group of engineers digging foundations for windmills inadvertently disturb the bones of the cursed buffalo, which rises as the undead..."

"Wait a minute," Larry said. "You mean as a vampire?"

"Precisely."

"But if it's bulimic, how does it get close enough to people to bite them? And wouldn't the, uh, bile sterilize or purify any vampire bite? Wouldn't this buffalo be its own worst enemy?"

"We'll know more when we get the script," Regan said.

"The writer won the Bob's Ass Award at last year's Abraxis Film Festival for *Never Say Nebudchadnezzar Again.*"

"And what, pray tell, is the Bob's Ass Award?"

"Orin Houtkooper is one of the sponsors. An impression of his dog's rectum, modeled in bronze and mounted on a handsome walnut plaque."

"Blimey! Is this a thing?"

"Never miss 'em. They're on Ruxtix. Last year, *Drunk Octopus Wants To Fight* won for Best Picture."

Regan pointed. "Turn the radio back on."

"...have just been contacted by the alien bull Tallywhacker. You may remember Tallywhacker for destroying the Miami Museum of Modern Art last year, taking over the Church of Necroeconomics, and running for governor. Tallywhacker said, and I quote, "'People of Miami. Aliens had nothing to do with this. Multiple alien sources have assured me that they are following developments but wouldn't dream of interfering. In fact, at least a dozen aliens were caught flat-footed on the arena floor when the announcement broke. Alien money has changed hands. Aliens were keenly interested in the outcome.' End quote. We'll be right back."

"Have you been injured..."

Martin flicked it off.

In the back of the vehicle, the sun beat down. The air conditioning didn't penetrate well beyond the second passenger row, and the murder hornets were warming up.

Four car lengths back, Bruce followed in his plain Jane Malibu, listening to the radio.

"Baitch handed the arresting officer a manifesto, which we have obtained."

I have warned Veeblefetzer repeatedly, and the Miami Heat in particular, that peanuts are deadly to people of allergy. I have tried to raise awareness about this situation for years. I have spoken. I have posted. I have tried to contact them over and over. But they will not listen. I have also warned them about the pretzels. They will not listen until it's too late. Well now it's too late...

Several car lengths ahead, someone leaned on their horn. The clash of metal. The black Escalade shot onto the right shoulder, striking the concrete barrier and doing a barrel roll.

67 | IF AT FIRST YOU DON'T SUCCEED

Gary rolled north on Twenty-Seven, passing tire stores, Walmart, the Miramar exit, and miles upon miles of swamp. "Keep your eyes peeled for hippos."

Krystal put her Fonebone away. "Either she ain't answering or I can't reach 'em."

"Don't worry. If that bomb went off, we woulda heard it."

"Maybe this time they'll lock that shithead up for good."

Gary reached for the radio. Krystal knocked his hand away.

"What's your problem?"

"I don't want to hear any shit about aliens, and I've had enough Habib to last a lifetime!"

Delilah laughed and swatted her knee.

"How 'bout I put on some music?"

"All right."

"Doris, play some Tammy Wynette."

"Your Good Girl's Gonna Go Bad" burst upon them.

It was dusk by the time they reached State Highway Eighty.

"Grab that shotgun, Delilah."

"What for?"

"Hogs, hippos, I don't know what all's gonna pop up. We seen every kind of critter back there 'cept a polar bear."

"Just drive. This is suburban Palm Beach."

They turned onto Weldon Way. They heard loud music and laughter as they passed the Wokenoki Trailer Park. They turned a corner and the headlights picked up a large python crossing the road.

"Hot damn," Gary said, clutching the wheel.

Krystal elbowed him in the ribs. "Don't you dare."

"Aw shit! Can't I have any fun?"

"How many cars do you intend to sacrifice to the python god?"

Gary waited for the python to cross the road. A quarter mile from the trailer, they saw lights flickering through the mangrove. Gary stopped the truck and reached for his magnum in the glove compartment.

"Fuck you doing?" Krystal said.

"May be more Venezuelans," Gary whispered. "They tried to kill me last time."

Krystal turned around. "Hand me that shotgun, wouldja, Di?"

Delilah forked over the twelve gauge, dug around in her purse for her works and rolled a cigarette. Gary pulled onto the shoulder and parked, shutting the door quietly behind him. Krystal got out and sprayed herself with Off! She handed the can to Gary. Even with the repellent, the mosquitoes were voracious. They made their way through the swamp by bright moonlight, stepping on hummocks and roots. As they got closer, they heard chanting.

“Do the titan rock, lead with swingin’ cock. Follow the giant corpse flower, it leads to personal power. Dance beneath the stink, it puts you in the pink.”

They saw a half dozen men and women dancing around the giant corpse flower, holding torches, naked, bodies smeared with paint. Garrison Gland, face painted blue, led them. Krystal pulled out her Fonebone. “Okay,” she said. “I think I got the whole chant.”

“The History Channel will love this,” Gary said. He stepped into the clearing.

“HEY!”

Men gasped and women eeped. They clustered together like meerkats, covering their private parts.

“Garrison! What the hell are you doing?”

Garrison hustled into the bushes and emerged looking like a tourist in a Hawaiian shirt and parachute pants. He cleared his throat. “Very sorry if we disturbed you, it was my understanding you would be gone all evening. I should have asked permission.”

“Permission for what?”

The others retrieved their clothes and headed for the road their faces averted. Krystal ratcheted a shell into the chamber.

“Hold it right there.”

A woman screamed. The rest stampeded. Gary put his hand out. “Let ‘em go. Garrison, you ain’t going nowhere 'til you 'splain yourself. First, you turn me in for innocently shooting a Florida panther, next, you diddle the wife of a client of a friend of mine, and now here you are on private property threatening my giant corpse flower."

"*Your* giant corpse flower? It belongs to the world! The giant corpse flower is too important to be left to obscurity in the swamp!"

"How'd you like a punch in the mouth?"

Garrison's eyes grew wide. "You threaten me? After what we've been through?"

Gary pointed to the road. "Get your ass out of here and don't come back. And if I see one word about my giant corpse flower on your show, I'm gonna send the History Channel the video we just made of you and your followers prancing around butt naked."

Garrison put his hands up. "Don't do that. We meant no harm. We're leaving now. I guess this means I won't be doing a segment on you either."

"Kiss my ass."

They got back in the truck and drove up to the trailer.

"Oh no!" Krystal wailed.

"What?"

"The Ducats were in a car accident. Their vehicle flipped on the interstate!"

"Jeez, are they all right?"

"Doesn't say. Says they were all taken to the hospital."

"Well shit. That ain't good. Does it say what hospital?"

"University."

"Well, you girls go on in the house. Omma do a search for any Venezuelans may have pancaked while we were away."

Delilah got out of the truck. "Venezuelans?"

Krystal rolled her eyes. "We should ask Claude Balls. Maybe it's just performance art."

Gary grabbed his magnum and a flashlight and walked the perimeter. He smelled the giant corpse flower. He sent a feral hog squealing. His route led him to the end of the dock.

"Leotis, you there?"

"I'm always here for you, Gary."

"You seen any Venezuelans?"

"Not today. Of course, they could have approached on land and I would never know."

"Now you got me thinking. One if by land, two if by sea, right?"

"That's right, Gary. Paul Revere is one of my heroes."

"So if you see 'em coming through the swamp, you'll let me know?"

"I don't see how I can do that, Gary, unless you come down here."

"Hmmm. I got to tell ya, Leotis, I been through your three harbingers and I ain't got much to show for it."

"Can you describe the circumstances?"

"Well, the Venezuelan who crash landed in the woods had the first Batman comic. I sold it, but before I got the goods, the IRS confiscated every motherfucking dime. The rabbit turned out to be a whack job. Last I saw, he was dancing next to the freeway, wearing a panda head begging for change.

The turtle glommed on to Prince Larry's wang, which increased his profile and marketability about two thousand per cent. Me, I'm still trying to make a living. We're gonna air the wang episode, which should increase our ratings and bring in some ad dollars, but the IRS is hip to that shit. All I got is my prize winnings from eating the most palmetto bugs, and what's left from the sale of *Zap #0.*"

"Gary, I'm not sure I gave you the right harbingers. Let me try again."

68 | TROLLING

In the morning, Gary and Krystal drove to University Hospital in Palm Beach. Larry and Regan were not badly dinged. The hospital had kept them overnight for observation just in case. Gary and Krystal ran into them in the lobby as they were checking out.

"Hey, where ya going? I was gonna get you flowers in the gift shop."

A flesh-colored bandage covered Regan's forehead. "Not necessary, although we appreciate the thought. The air bags deployed, and no one was seriously hurt."

"Why'dja crash?"

"Hornets," Larry said. "Someone planted hornets in the vehicle, and when they got in the sun, they woke up. They stung me on the neck." Larry peeled back his collar to show a white bandage. "They stung Martin on his hand. It was sabotage. It was a deliberate attempt on our lives."

"This is her majesty's doing," Regan said through gritted

teeth. "No doubt about it. She simply cannot tolerate any of her brood going off reservation."

"Jeez. Did you tell the cops?"

"Yes. The police caught one of the hornets. It was enormous. I've never seen anything like it."

They walked out front where Martin, his hand bandaged, pulled up in a new white Escalade. He popped out and held the door.

"Mr. Duba. Good to see you again."

"Hold on a minute," Gary said. "I talked to Major and he's looking at a rematch on the twenty-seventh. Do you think that's doable?"

Regan's forehead rippled. "I don't know, Gary. This might be a sign."

"Oh, come on! You were looking at a ten-million-dollar payday!"

"Barfalo 2 starts shooting at the end of the month. What if I injure myself?"

"Oh, come on! What's that job pay?"

"It's not the money, it's the direction I'm heading. Captain Megstar dropped me over the turtle thing. Amber Alert has the part now."

"Well listen. At least let's have dinner before you take off. Why'ntcha come out to the trailer Thursday night? I'll grill."

"I don't know."

"Claude Balls will be there."

Larry took Regan's hand. "Oh, mummy! May we?"

Regan sighed. "Oh, very well. Is there anything I can

bring?"

"Bring some Chardonnay."

Gary and Larry hugged in a manly manner. Krystal and Regan embraced. Gary and Krystal headed back to the swamp. They had just passed the Wokenoki Trailer Park when Gary spotted a python slithering across the road. Krystal punched him in the shoulder.

"OW! Whadja do that for?"

"Don't even think about it."

Gary waited for the python to pass. The trailer was as they had left it. The yard smelled of giant corpse flower. They went inside and cranked up the AC.

"Well hell," Gary said. "I might as well put the show together."

Krystal plopped herself in the living room with a bottle of Deep Eddy, a half gram, and What's Your Problem On Demand. Gary closed the door to his office and went to work. It took all day. He went on at nine.

"Welcome to the Gary Duba Show! We're back, and we have the Royal Ducats with us. I took the prince hunting the other day and this is what we caught." He showed all the footage. Comments poured in.

"Now that's a man, baby!"

"I feel better about Lawrence after seeing that."

"Hello, my name is Sudafed. I saw your profile on Facebook and would like to talk to you."

"Brilliant performance art."

Gary highlighted that. "Claude Balls, are you watching?

I'll send you a link."

Claude Balls appeared on a split screen. "I regret I was unable to attend."

"We're having a little get together Thursday night. Why don't you come? The Ducats will be there."

"I saw footage of their vehicle doing the barrel roll. Brilliant performance art."

Gary showed footage of the corpse flower dance, faces blurred. "Let's give a hearty Florida welcome to our newest invasive species, the giant Sumatran corpse flower! Unlike some critters, the corpse flower stays in one place and only blooms every ten years. Upkeep is minimal, and the aroma is something else! We're planning to sell corpse flower candles! Gwyneth Paltrow gave me the idea."

Claude popped up. "Shouldn't the whooping crane be considered an invasive species?"

"Good point!"

"I'll bring my bag of magician's tricks."

Krystal appeared in the office door, wearing a filmy black negligee, pupils dilated.

"Gotta go! See you next week!"

Gary woke to his phone buzzing. He had sixteen messages. Krystal lay on her back snoring. TMZ, the alphabets, Scuzz Daily, the Late Night Show all wanted permission to show the turtle. Overnight, he'd picked up sixteen major advertisers. He called Pincus.

"Pincus, I want to sign contracts with these advertisers, but I don't want the IRS to get it."

"Mr. Duba, surely with all these new advertisers you can work out an arrangement with the IRS. They don't want to put you in jail. They want money."

A woman said, "Can I make coffee?"

"Whozat?"

"Helen," Pincus whispered.

"Congrats! I knew you had it in you! Hey, we're having a little get together Thursday night. Why don't you bring Helen? I'll be grilling hog. I don't know what all I'll be grilling. Bring a salad."

"Hang on."

Gary heard Pincus whispering to Helen.

"Sure. What time?"

"Come by around five. Say. People love the turtle."

"Really?"

"Oh yeah! I picked up a half million new viewers overnight! I'm thinking if one is good, more is better. I want to do a series of snapping turtles pulling on celebrity wangs. Think of all the has-beens who will sign on just to get their face before the public. Randy Quaid, Caitlyn Jenner, Joaquin Closet, that kid from Home Alone... Omma audition some turtles."

"Be careful, Mr. Duba."

"I can't very well ask them to do something I wouldn't do. In fact, omma go out there right now and look for a snapper."

"I wouldn't do that..."

Gary ended the call, put on his boots and searched his toolbox. Wait a minute! He had the perfect lure. Bounding up the steps, he went through the bedroom closet and found the two-foot black dildo Barb had given Krystal as a wedding present. It was the source of her fame! Outside, he went to the giant corpse flower and rubbed the dildo back and forth until it smelled like rotting meat. Gripping the dildo firmly with his right hand, he stuck it through the open zipper and walked the swamp.

"Here, turtle! Here turtle!"

He circled the trailer squishing through the marsh until he came to the pier. Leotis burbled up.

"What are you doing, Gary?"

"I'm trolling for snapping turtles."

"'Cuz of you, ya big fish! I can't make sense of the turtle! Rodell Grosz is batshit crazy!"

"It's not my job to explain these things to you, Gary. I am but a conduit."

"Garrrrrry!" Krystal called from the deck. "Where's my dildo?"

Gary jogged to the trailer, dildo leading the way. He stopped at the steps. "Whaddaya need the dildo for? You got me."

"I'm mixing batter."

"Let me wash it off first."

69 | RIBS

Gary shot a hog. Krystal went to Cane Toad Liquor and came home with two boxes. They set the boom box up on the deck and played Porter Wagonner. Floyd and Ginger arrived with an ounce of primo Winter Lights a friend had sent from Colorado. Habib and Auburn arrived with a case of Cutty Sark.

Habib and Gary leaned on the rail, passing the joint.

"What's that smell?" Habib said.

"Giant corpse flower."

"Can't you do something about it?"

"Well, I don't know what to do, Habib. It's just out there growing. Not bothering anyone."

"It's bothering' the ladies. It's bothering the men. What's it doing there?"

"Just showed up. Some folks are real excited. I'll show you the footage we shot later. I ain't got enough Febreze for the whole swamp."

"We could burn it."

"No sirree bob. I tried that with that gator. Didn't work out so good. Sides which, it's an endangered species."

"It's invasive. There are no corpse flowers in Florida."

"Want to bet?"

"How much?"

"A hunnert."

Habib thought about it. "Nahhh. I'll pass."

Delilah arrived, ejected Porter Waggoner and put in Smoky Robinson.

Claude Balls arrived via Uber, .45 at his waist, wearing combat boots and an old-fashioned fedora. "Where's the corpse flower?"

"Follow your nose."

"Do you want me to bring you some?"

"No thanks, Claude. You can have it. Just don't bring it here."

Balls stalked toward the jungle.

Gary turned to Krystal. "Maybe I should go with him."

"You're the host. Claude's fine. He's a survivor."

Barb and Jen pulled up in Jen's Solara, did lines, swigged wine, and danced. Pincus and Helen arrived in Pincus' Versus. Gary started the grill.

"Mr. Duba," Pincus said, "Helen wants to know if the Royal Couple are gonna be here."

"Doubtful. They were in a car accident and their chauffeur got stung by a hornet sting."

"Oh no!" Helen said, looking seventeen years old in black slacks and pink shirt. "That sounds serious."

Pincus took Helen's hand. "The Department of Natural Resources is concerned. These are the first murder hornets found on the east coast. Florida doesn't need another destructive invasive species."

"Y'know what we need?" Gary said. "Ocelots."

Delilah tapped him on the shoulder. "What's this I hear about a giant catfish?"

Gary felt ashamed. "I was gonna tell you. It ain't like he's my spirit animal or anything."

"Krystal tells me he's giving you advice. Gary, I'm worried about you. Are you tripping?"

Gary formed a beak with his fingers, put it to his nose and flung it away, watching for tracers. "I don't think so."

"Show me the catfish."

"Well, he's shy. I tried to introduce him, but he only shows up when I'm by myself."

"Go to the end of the pier and try and talk to it. I'm going to sneak up on it."

"Watch out for snakes and leeches."

"They won't touch me."

Gary waved Krystal over. "Watch the grill, willya? Delilah wants to talk to Leotis."

Krystal shook her head. "I don't know what you're on, but you need an intervention."

Gary walked to the end of the pier and sat. "You out there, Leotis?"

The swamp thrummed. Loons called, macaques chattered, mosquitoes buzzed. Gary smoked an American Spirit.

"Leotis, are you out there? Someone wants to meet you."

"No one can see me but you, Gary."

"Well how you gonna record that album then? Can't they hear you?"

"Gary, are you trying to crush my hopes and dreams?"

"It's just Delilah, my witchee woman. Listen. She doesn't have to see you. Why don't you sing something? She's a soul woman."

"What would you suggest?"

"She likes Smoky Robinson and the Miracles."

"Her name's Delilah?"

"That's right."

"Is she listening now?"

"Prob'ly."

"I saw the light on the night that I passed by her window..." Leotis sang. "I saw the flickering shadows of love on her blind. She was my woman as she deceived me, I watched and went out of my mind..."

Delilah popped up like a prairie dog in the weeds.

"My, my, my, Delilah...Why, why, why, Delilah..."

Delilah whooped and ran to the end of the pier. "Where is he?"

Gary stared deep into the water. "He's gone."

"Hold still while I search you."

"For what?"

"A hidden transmitter."

"RIBS ARE READY!" Krystal sang.

Gary and Delilah returned to the deck. As Gary sat on the

top step with a paper platter of ribs in his pocket, two black SUVs and a panel van pulled into the yard. Gary spat ribs.

"Shit! It's the Venezuelans! Get the guns!"

Floyd raced to his Viper and pulled out a K-Tel with a fifty round mag. Habib put his hand on Gary's shoulder. "As your attorney I advise you to hold your fire."

Someone shut off the boom box. An eerie silence descended on the clearing. Gary and Floyd crouched on the deck holding guns. The front passenger window on the lead SUV lowered and a man waved a white handkerchief.

"We come in peace," he shouted. "This is a diplomatic mission. Did you not get our letter?"

Gary crouched. "Sorry! Ain't got the mail in two days! We pick it up in town. They don't deliver out here."

"Are you Gary Duba?"

"Maybe."

"President Elfuncio Quetzacoatl would like to speak with you."

"Bring him on!"

"Yes, if you would only be so kind as to lower your weapons. El Presidente comes in peace and with the greatest admiration. He has come to apologize for abusing your hospitality."

"Just so's you know, I got snipers in the trees!"

The man with the handkerchief got out wearing a dark green military dress uniform, a billed cap wrapped in gold wreaths, gold epaulets on the shoulders and a full plate of fruit salad. He strode to the bottom of the steps, came to attention, and saluted. "I am Major Rohero Sala of the National Bolivarians. Con su permisio, I would like to introduce you to his excellency, El Presidente."

"Bring him on, but no funny stuff! We're all on drugs and we're heavily armed."

A man popped out of the second vehicle and held the rear door. The president had a thick head and a thick mustache. He wore a black suit with a yellow, blue, and red sash from left shoulder to right hip. The Venezuelan Medal of Honor hung from his neck. He opened his arms.

"Senor Duba! It is an honor to meet you!"

Gary put his gun away. "Come on up, El Presidente!"

They embraced at the head of the stairs. Everybody took pictures.

"I was unaware of your accomplishments, Senor Duba. I have decided to honor you with the Order of the Bolivar. I have brought you a gift, Senor Duba."

"Well shit. You didn't have to do that. Just your presence is enough."

El Presidente clapped his hands. Four men in combat fatigues unloaded two wheeled cages from the panel van and pushed them toward the front of the house. The wheels squeaked. They stopped at the bottom of the stairs and stepped back. One animal in each cage, sleek and sinewy.

"Whatcha got there, El Presidente?"

"Ocelots. In your honor, we release them."

El Presidente clapped his hands. The men stepped forward and opened the hatches. The ocelots raced into the swamp.

A LOOK AT BIKER—BIKER 1 BY MIKE BARON

MASTER OF THE ACTION ADVENTURE GENRE, MIKE BARON DELIVERS THE FIRST BOOK IN THE INTOXICATING BIKER SERIES.

Josh Pratt is an ex-con turned private investigator. Ginger Munz, a woman dying of cancer hires him to find the son she lost as a baby. The child's father is a sadistic sociopath named Moon who has vowed to kill her and Josh's girlfriend Cass, for ratting him out. The trail leads to the Sturgis Motorcycle Rally and west into no-man's land where Josh learns the monstrous fate of the stolen child.

Josh is the BIKER, caught up in a race for survival against a human monster on the road between heaven and hell at the end of which lies either salvation or damnation.

Baron spins a tale of unrelenting suspense and horror that moves across his narrative landscape like the roar of a chopper's engine.

AVAILABLE NOW ON AMAZON

ABOUT THE AUTHOR

Mike Baron is the creator of Nexus (with artist Steve Rude) and Badger two of the longest lasting independent superhero comics. Nexus is about a cosmic avenger 500 years in the future. Badger, about a multiple personality one of whom is a costumed crime fighter. First/Devils Due is publishing all new Badger stories. Baron has won two Eisners and an Inkpot award and written The Punisher, Flash, Deadman and Star Wars among many other titles.

Baron has published ten novels that span a variety of topics. They have satanic rock bands, biker zombies, spontaneous human combustion, ghosts, and overall hard-boiled crimes.

Mike Baron has written for The Boston Phoenix, Boston Globe, Oui, Fusion, Creem, Isthmus, Front Page Mag, and Ellery Queen's Mystery Magazine.

CPSIA information can be obtained
at www.ICGtesting.com
Printed in the USA
LVHW041606120421
684240LV00012B/1974